Praise For
Operation Arctic Sting

Operation Arctic Sting is the third in Robert G. Williscroft's exciting *Mac McDowell Mission Series,* which began with *Operation Ivy Bells. Operation Arctic Sting* follows Mac's exploits as he leads a team to recover the Soviet *Alfa* submarine abandoned in the previous *Operation Ice Breaker.* Naturally, the Soviets aren't too happy about this, and the chase is on to sneak the crippled sub back across the Arctic ice pack to a US naval base while eluding the Russian pursuers. Further, Mac's romantic interest, Kate Perry (also from *Ice Breaker*), is under threat by Russian agents. The tale is told with Williscroft's usual attention to technical detail, while providing side encounters with everything from polar bears to killer whales to enemy divers. This Cold War adventure is a definite page-turner.

–Alastair Mayer Author of the T-Space Series

Operation Arctic Sting is another great sea story, a worthy sequel to *Operation Ice Breaker.* Once again, we experience the adventures of Mac McDowell, a most resourceful Navy officer. In Operation Arctic Sting, American forces take over an abandoned Soviet *Alfa* submarine, and Mac maneuvers it through and under the Arctic ice pack all the way to the East Coast while eluding Soviet subs that want to recapture or sink it. It's cat and mouse, chase and hide, with separated lovers adding to the tension. I especially love Borysko, the warrior Orca who comes to the rescue when hungry polar bears and hostile Spetsnaz divers attack Mac's team. If you want to know what it's like to fight for your life and country on a submarine and as a diver under the ice, then this is the novel for you. It's as realistic as it gets, written by someone who lived it.

–Professor John B. Rosenman, Norfolk State University
Former Chairman of the Board, Horror Writers Association
Author of The Inspector of the Cross Series

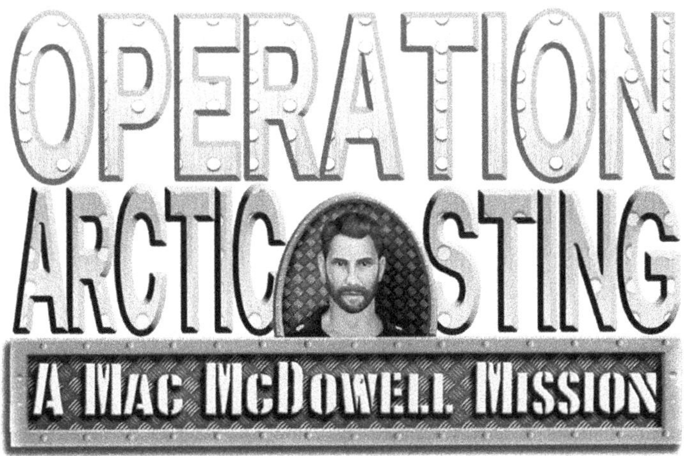
OPERATION ARCTIC STING
A MAC McDOWELL MISSION

USS Teuthis Tracks through the Arctic

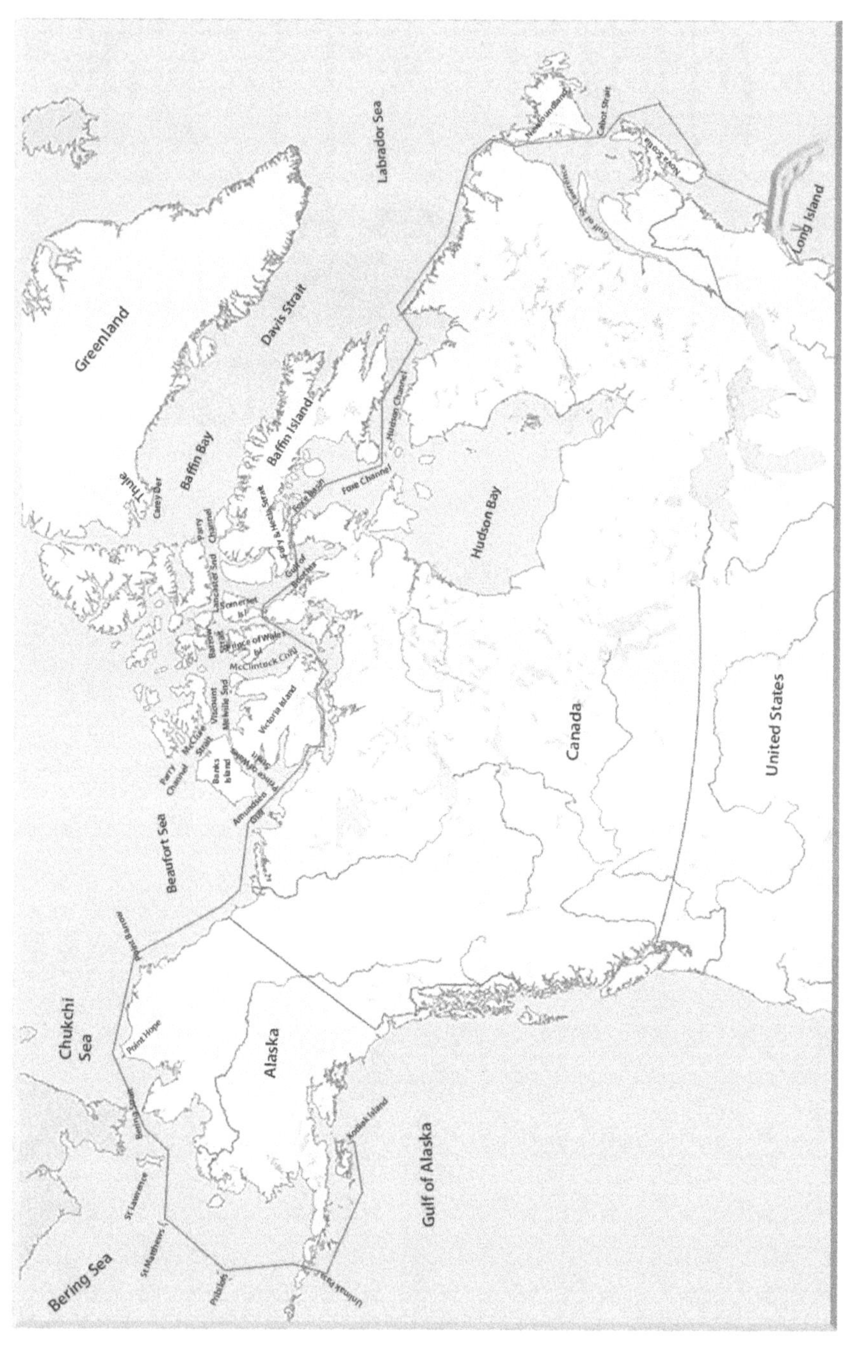

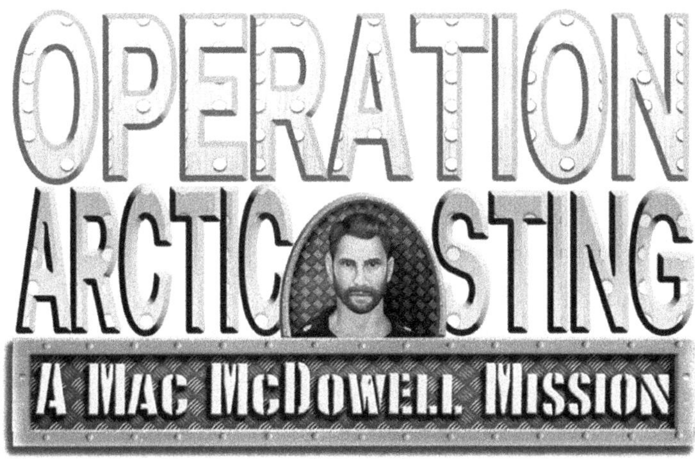

Robert G. Williscroft

Centennial, Colorado

**Operation Arctic Sting:
A Mac McDowell Mission**

Copyright © 2021 through 2025
by Robert G. Williscroft
All rights reserved

Starman Press

Email: rgw@RobertWilliscroft.com
Website: RobertWilliscroft.com

Edition 1.0 2021
Edition 2.0 2025

Cover art by Anik
Cover by Stephen Geez
Book design by Robert G. Williscroft

Except as permitted under the U.S. Copyright Act of 1976 and except for brief quotations in critical reviews or articles, no portion of this book's content may be stored in any medium, transmitted in any form, used in whole or part, or sourced for derivative works such as videos, television, and motion pictures, without prior written permission from the publisher.

All characters appearing in this work are fictitious.
Any resemblance to real persons, living or dead, is purely coincidental.

BISAC Subject Headings:
FIC032000 FICTION / War & Military
FIC031050 FICTION / Thrillers / Military
FIC036000 FICTION / Thrillers / Technological

Library of Congress Control Number: 2021908224

ISBN-13: 978-1-968367-25-1 Papercover
ISBN-13: 978-1-968367-24-4 Hardcover
ISBN-13: 978-1-968367-03-9 Ebooks
ISBN-13: 978-1-968367-26-8 Audio

Dedication

To "Kate," who still inspires me.

Table of Contents

Foreword

by
Captain George W. Jackson USN
(Ret.) Aka G. William Weatherly

WOW! Dr. Robert G. Williscroft has done it again in this latest sequel. Mac McDowell and his intrepid group of saturation divers embark on the *USS Teuthis* to take on an impossible mission. They will attempt to retrieve the Soviet Alpha submarine lost in *Operation Ice Breaker* for an intelligence coup of incalculable value to the United States. Soviet sleeper agents bent on revenge for the disastrous loss of their prized automated nuclear submarine—the fastest and most capable in the world—attempt to assassinate the man responsible and his loved ones. The Soviet submarine force musters its most capable nuclear attack submarines to retrieve or destroy the crippled Alpha at all costs.

Williscroft creates a believable scenario for *Teuthis* and additional fast-attack subs to escort the crippled nuclear Alpha from Point Barrow, Alaska, to New London, Connecticut, under the Arctic ice. Mac's saturation divers must overcome Soviet Spetsnaz, polar bears, and the difficulty of recharging the Alpha's batteries daily underwater since her liquid metal cooled reactor is now just a solid piece of junk. An unlikely ally in an Orca intervenes at critical junctures preventing Mac's team from becoming just the latest meal for hungry bears.

Dr. Williscroft is uniquely qualified to write thrillers about saturation divers and their secret submarine adventures in service to the United States. He has lived the life, first as a saturation diver on some of the Navy's most secretive submarines and then as a student of the Arctic to become a well-regarded expert in a region of increasing strategic importance. He accurately describes the cat and mouse game under the polar ice cap that has been going on for decades since *USS Nautilus* transited to the North Pole in July and August of 1958. Few men are as well versed in the continuing effort to ensure our national security.

The Cold War of the twentieth century and the role of submarines carrying submarine-launched ballistic missiles became the ultimate deterrent providing impetus for both the Soviets and Americans to devote massive resources to developing anti-submarine warfare (ASW). NATO prevailed in that competition with the Sound Surveillance or SOSUS systems (read *Operation Icebreaker*) and airborne platforms to quickly locate and isolate detected submarines. The Soviets could easily track hydrophone-array-laying ships, and often were able to rip up SOSUS arrays. To maintain a credible deterrent, the Soviets developed ever longer-range missiles to allow Soviet missile subs to move farther away.

Eventually, they moved into the Soviet home waters in the Arctic and under the ice, safe from any airborne attack.

The only NATO assets able to operate in the marginal ice zone and under pack ice to search for Soviet missile subs were American fast-attack submarines. This resulted in a decades-long cat and mouse game under the Arctic ice. Sturgeon and *Los Angeles class* submarines—like *USS Drum* and *USS San Francisco* respectively in this tale—were NATO's premier assets during the cold war and were built in large numbers. The earlier *Los Angeles class* subs were somewhat limited in their under-ice capabilities until the development of a fully under-ice-capable subclass fixed that, but *Sturgeon class* subs roamed freely under the ice, as did the older *Skate class* subs—like *USS Swordfish* in this tale. Publicized polar expeditions and surfacing's through the ice were not-so-subtle reminders that there was no place on Earth that American ASW assets could not operate and that Soviet missile subs everywhere were at risk.

With the reemergence of Russia as a strategic threat, under-ice operations have continued to this date. Publicized Mk48 advanced capability torpedoes, ADCAP for short, have demonstrated that we will still place Russian missile subs at risk anywhere on Earth, even under the Arctic ice pack.

The game will continue, as will the intrepid saturation divers who have been part of the greatest espionage gains of the twentieth century. The subs they rode are now gone, but modern saturation divers are embarked on the *USS Jimmy Carter* (SSN 22), an updated version of the *USS Teuthis* in this tale. Dr. Williscroft will continue to illuminate this shadowy world. I look forward to his next novel with great anticipation.

G. William Weatherly is the pen name Captain Jackson uses to write his alternative history novels of WWII naval thrillers.

Acknowledgments

Several people contributed to the creation of this book.

Most significantly, my wonderful wife, Jill, pored over each chapter with her discerning engineer's eye. She kept my timeline honest and made sure that regular readers could understand fully the arcane details of nuclear submarine and saturation diving operations.

Prof. John B. Rosenman, bestselling science fiction and horror author who taught science fiction writing at Norfolk State University, reviewed the manuscript with his discerning professor's eye, helping me fine-tune the story. Hard science fiction author Alastair Mayer reviewed the manuscript and offered his scientific, engineering, and editorial insight, and military writer and former submarine commander George Jackson supplied his unique insight.

Others have contributed with their comments and observations, and I thank them. You know who you are.

A tip of the hat to John L. "Dugan" Shipway, who actually commanded the USS Los Angeles during the timeframe of this story. I did not want the actions of my character to be mistaken for those of the actual captain. Cmdr. Shipway advanced to Rear Admiral before retiring to become CEO of Bath Iron Works in Main.

It goes without saying that any remaining omissions, errors, and mistakes fall directly on my shoulders.

Robert G. Williscroft, PhD
Centennial, Colorado
June 2021

USS Teuthis Organizational Chart

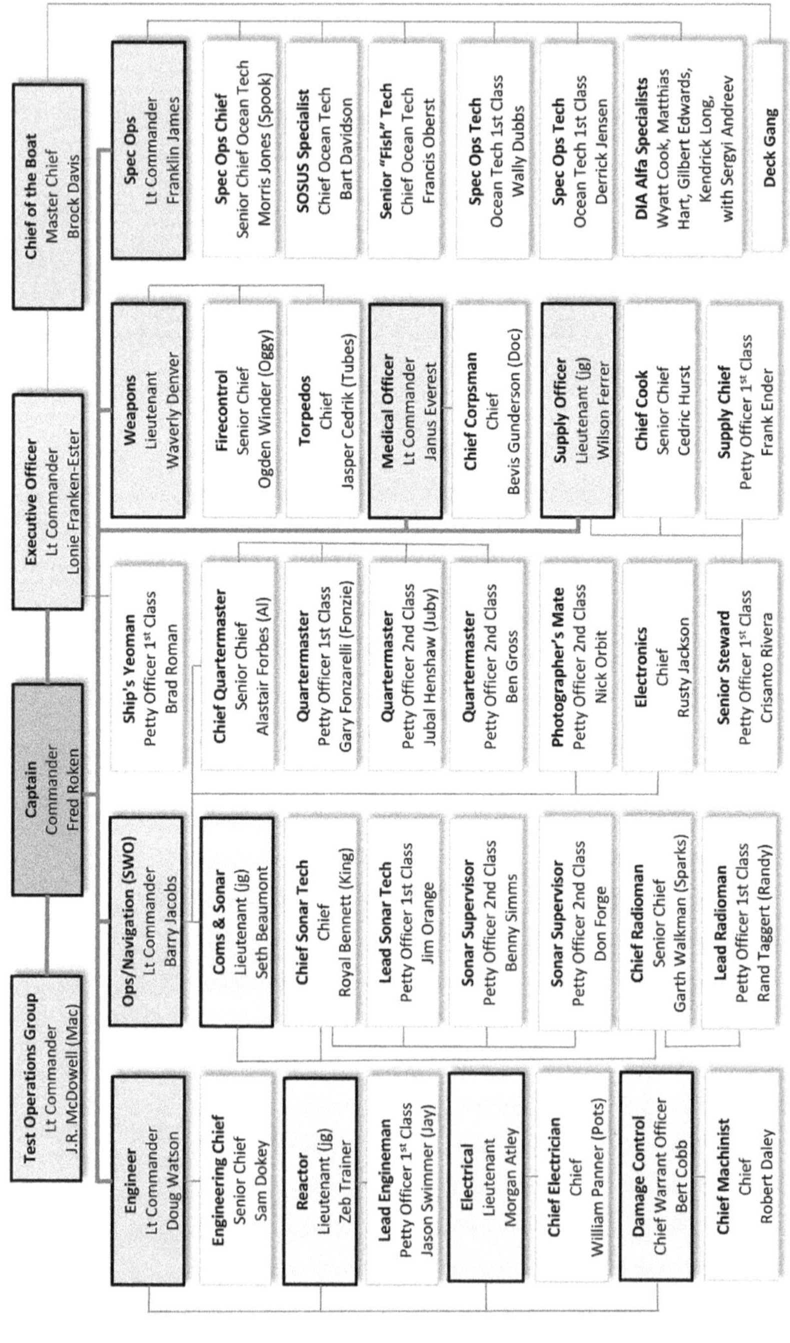

Cast of Characters

Test Operations Group (TOG)

Lt. Cmdr. J.R. McDowell (Mac)—*Officer in Charge TOG (Narrator)*.

Master Chief Hamilton Comstock (Ham)—Master Saturation Diver—Came from Experimental Diving Unit and Man-in-the-Sea Program—Ivy Bells.

Chief William Fisher (Bill)—*Master Saturation Diver—Sonar Tech—Ivy Bells*.

Petty Officer 1st Class Harry Blackwell—*Saturation Diver; qualified Dive Console operator—Electronics Tech— Ivy Bells*.

Petty Officer 1st Class James Tanner (Jimmy)—*Saturation Diver; qualified Dive Console operator—Battlefield medic turned saturation diver—Ivy Bells*.

Petty Officer 2nd Class Melvin Ford (Whitey)—*Saturation Diver; qualified Dive Console operator—Quartermaster— Ivy Bells*.

Petty Officer 2nd Class Wlodek Cslauski (Ski)—*Saturation Diver; qualified Dive Console operator—Submariner (Engineman) turned saturation diver—Ivy Bells*.

Petty Officer 2nd Class Jeremy Romain (Jer)—*Saturation Diver; qualified Dive Console operator—Submariner (Auxiliaryman) turned saturation diver—Ivy Bells*.

Petty Officer 2nd Class Jacob Palmer (Jake)—*Saturation Diver; qualified Dive Console Operator*—Submariner (Electronics Tech) turned saturation diver; Recent graduate of saturation dive class.

USS Teuthis

(See Organizational Chart on previous page)

USS Teuthis Deck Gang

Seaman Joe Spanker (Spanky)—Topside Watch, Lookout / Helmsman / Planesman.

Seaman Fred Jackson (Jack)—Topside Watch, Lookout / Helmsman / Planesman.

Seaman Jake Boller—Topside Watch, Lookout / Helmsman / Planesman.

Seaman Jeremiah Walker (Jerry)—Topside Watch, Lookout /
Helmsman / Planesman.
Seaman Todd Bennett—Topside Watch, Lookout /
Helmsman / Planesman.
Seaman Steve Decker—Topside Watch, Lookout /
Helmsman / Planesman.
Seaman Josh Raker—Topside Watch, Lookout /
Helmsman / Planesman.
Seaman Julius Hoppenstein (Hoppy)—Topside Watch,
Lookout / Helmsman / Planesman.
Seaman Fritz Able—Topside Watch, Lookout / Planesman
Seaman Greg Patterson—Topside Watch, Lookout / Planesman.
Seaman Billy-Bob Yokum—Topside Watch, Lookout /
Planesman.
Seaman Randolph Zimmerman (Zimm)—Topside Watch,
Lookout / Planesman.

Mystic (DSRV 2)

Lt. Robert Taggert—*Chief Pilot.*
Lt. James Deckhart—Second Pilot.
Senior Chief Sonar Tech Gaspard Abelé—*Mystic* technician
Electronics Tech 1st Class Parker Flanger—*Mystic* technician.

Submarine Development Group One

(SubDevGruOne)

Captain Dan Richardson—Commands Submarine Development
Group One.

Submarine Fleet Pacific

(SubPac)

Rear Adm. Austin B. Scott, Jr.—*Commander Submarine Fleet Pacific*

(ComSubPac).

U.S. Pacific Fleet

(PacFlt)

Adm. James A. Lyons, Jr.—Commander in Chief
U.S. Pacific Fleet (CinCPacFlt).

Defense Intelligence Agency (DIA)

Lt. Gen. Eugene Tighe—*Commander DIA.*

DIA Alfa Specialist Team

Gilbert Edwards—*DIA Soviet submarine reactor specialist.*

Kendrick Long—*DIA Soviet submarine hull specialist.*

Matthias Hart—*DIA Soviet sonar specialist.*

Sergyi Andreev—*Soviet defector; saturation diver; on loan from NSA to DIA.*

Wyatt Cook—*Senior DIA Alfa specialist—In charge of DIA team.*

DIA Security Team

Arturo Rodriguez (Arty)—*Special Agent.*

Darrell Capland (Cappy)—*Special Supervisory Agent.*

Jennifer Coolerage—*Special Agent.*

USS Los Angeles

Cmdr. Archibald Desmond—*Commanding Officer.*
Lt. Cmdr. Lew Brockhurst—*Executive Officer.*

Kodiak, Alaska

Master Pilot Sven Jakobsen—*Woman's Bay channel pilot.*
Master Mariner Jack Petrikoff— *Skipper of the Kodiak fishing boat* St. Kate.
Katherine Perry (Kate)—*Widow of Coast Guard Lt. j.g. Josh Perry killed in rescue of Petrikoff (Mac's new love).*

Mascot

Borysko—(Ukrainian name means *fighter/warrior*) *the 30-foot-long, 12,000-pound Orca that saved Ski from a Polar Bear.*

Incidental Characters

Aleksandr Alexeyev—*captured Soviet Spetsnaz diver.*
Boris Kuznetsov—*captured Soviet Spetsnaz diver.*
Jeremy Foggybottom—*Soviet agent.*
John Peel—*Wreck diver at St. Paul Island.*
Marchand Baptiste—*Wreck diver at St. Paul Island.*

Teuthis Watch Sections

Section One—0600 to 1200

    Deck—Lt. Cmdr. J.R. McDowell (Mac)

    JOOD— Lt. j.g. Seth Beaumont

    Dive—Chief Torpedoman Jasper Cedrik (Tubes)

    COW—Senior Chief Engineman Sam Dokey

    Nav—Senior Chief Quartermaster Alastair Forbes (Al)

    Fairwater/Helm—Seaman Joe Spanker (Spanky) Stern/Lookout—
        Seaman Fred Jackson (Jack)

    Stern/Lookout—Seaman Fritz Abele

    Sonar—Chief Sonar Tech Royal Bennett (King)

    EOOW—Lt. j.g. Zeb Trainer

Section Two—1200 to 1800

    Deck—Lt. Waverly Denver (Weaps)

    JOOD—Assigned as needed

    Dive—Chief Ocean Tech Bart Davidson

    COW—Senior Chief Firecontrol Tech Ogden Winder (Oggy)

    Nav—Quartermaster 1st Class Gary Fonzarelli (Fonzie)

    Fairwater/Helm—Seaman Jake Boller

    Stern/Lookout—Seaman Jeremiah Walker (Jerry)

    Stern/Lookout—Seaman Greg Patterson

    Sonar—Sonar Tech 1st Class Jim Orange

    EOW—Chief Warrant Officer Bert Cobb

Section Three—1800-2400

    Deck—Lt. Cmdr. Barry Jacobs (Nav)

    JOOD— Assigned as needed

    Dive—Chief Ocean Tech Francis Oberst

    COW—Chief Electrician William Panner (Pots)

    Nav—Quartermaster 2nd Class Ben Gross

    Fairwater/Helm—Seaman Todd Bennett

    Stern/Lookout—Seaman Steve Decker

    Stern/Lookout—Seaman Billy-Bob Yokum

    Sonar—Sonar Tech 2nd Class Benny Simms

    EOOW— Lt. Cmdr. Doug Watson (Eng)

Section Four—2400-0600

Deck—Lt. Cmdr. Franklin James

JOOD— Assigned as needed

Dive—Chief Electronics Tech Rusty Jackson

COW—Senior Chief Radioman Garth Walkman (Sparks)

Nav—Quartermaster 2nd Class Jubal Henshaw (Juby)

Fairwater/Helm –Seaman Josh Raker

Stern/Lookout—Seaman Julius Hoppenstein (Hoppy)

Stern/Lookout—Seaman Randolph Zimmerman (Zimm)

Sonar—Sonar Tech 2nd Class Don Forg

EOOW—Lt. Morgan Atley

Ships and Submarines

Admiral Isachenkov—A Project 1134A Soviet *Berkut A-class* Large Antisubmarine Cruiser.

Carp—Advanced Soviet *Sierra III class* nuclear fast-attack submarine.

Lyre—A Project-705 Lira advanced Soviet *Alfa class* nuclear fast-attack submarine.

Shchuka—Advanced Soviet *Victor III class* nuclear fast-attack submarine.

St. Kate—Jack Petrikoff's fishing vessel named after Kate Perry.

Unknown—Advanced Soviet *Victor III class* nuclear fast-attack submarine.

USS Drum (SSN 677)—A *Sturgeon class* nuclear fast-attack submarine.

USS San Francisco (SSN 711)—A *Los Angeles class* nuclear fast-attack submarine.

USS Swordfish (SSN 579)—A *Skate class* nuclear fast-attack submarine.

USS Teuthis (SSNR-2)—A specially modified nuclear submarine outfitted for special operations.

Vega—A project B-419 Soviet fishing trawler outfitted as a spy ship.

Volgograd—Advanced Soviet *Victor III class* nuclear fast-attack submarine.

Zadornyy (959)—A Project 1135 Soviet *Burevestnik-class* Frigate.

USS Teuthis—Cross Section

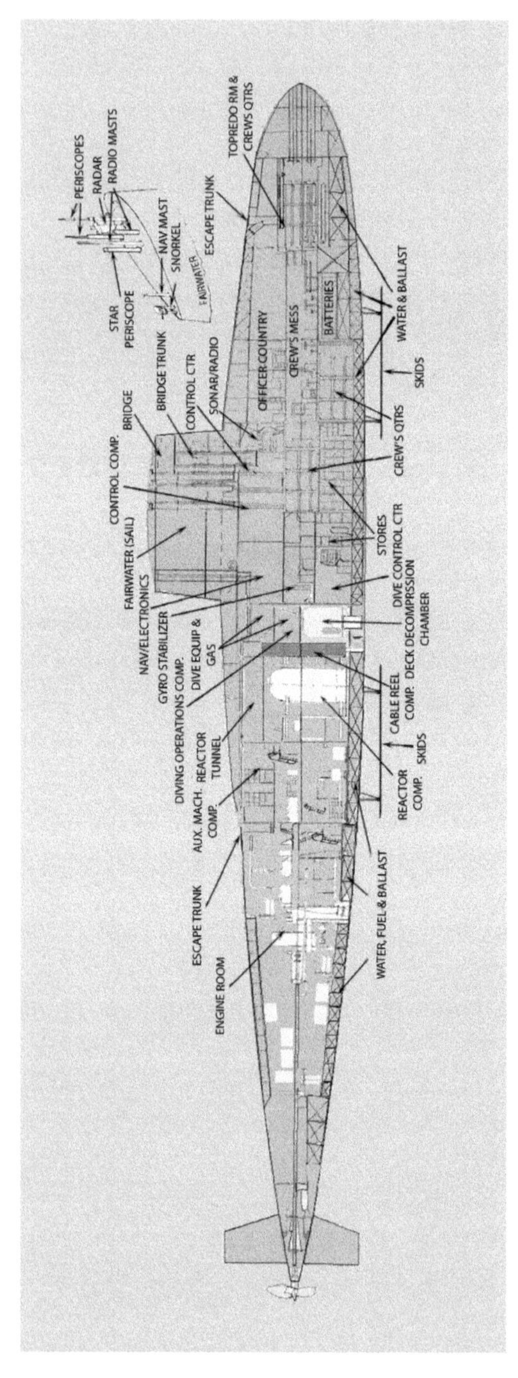

USS Teuthis—Cutaway

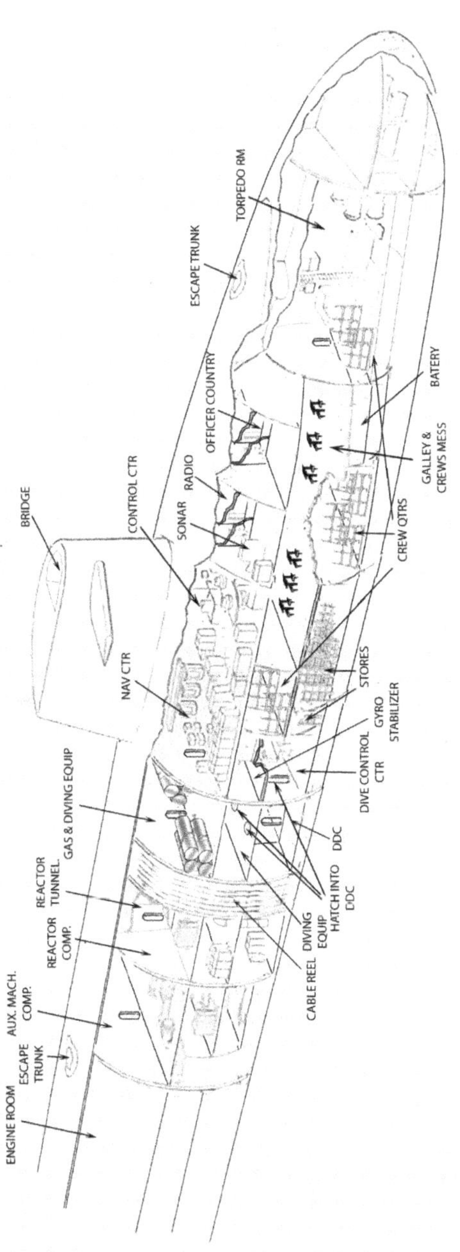

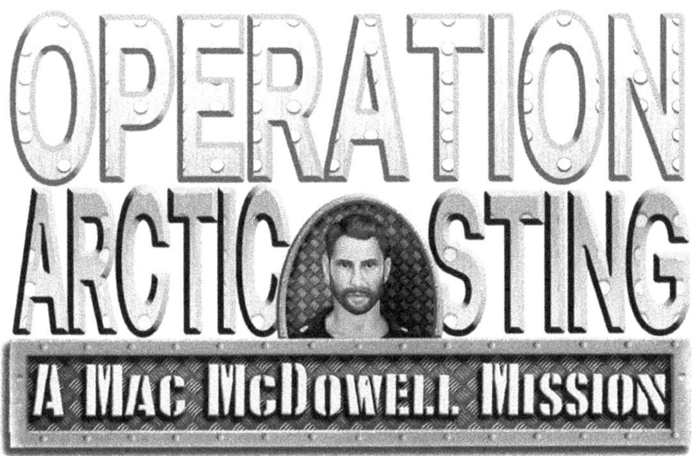

OPERATION
ARCTIC STING
A MAC McDOWELL MISSION

PART ONE

The Snatch

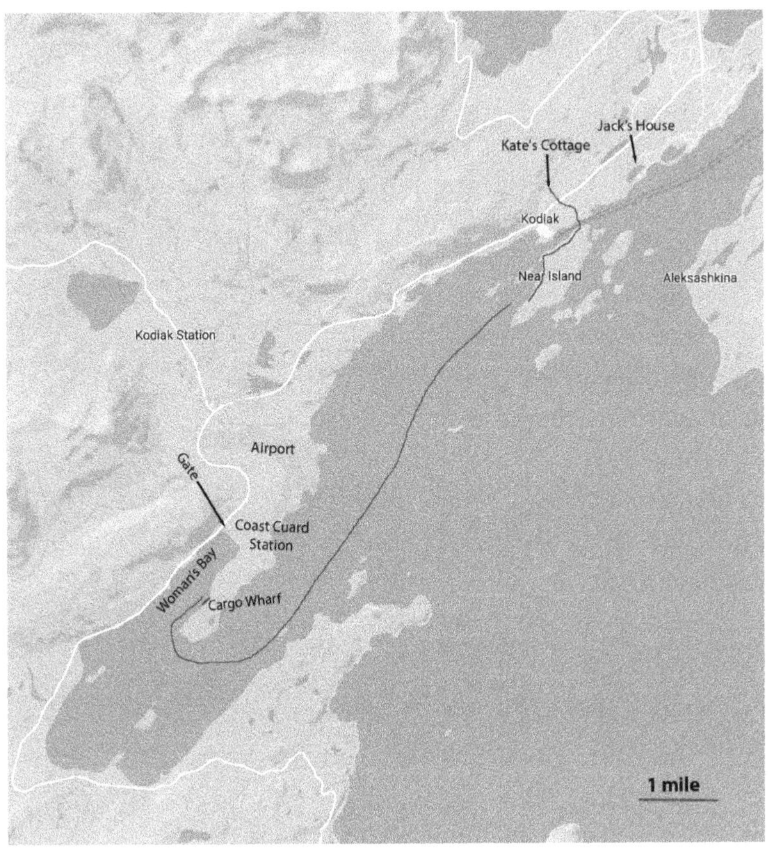

*Kate's cottage & Jack's house. Route from Kate's cottage to
St. Kate, and then to Woman's Bay.*

CHAPTER ONE—Kodiak, Alaska

KATE PERRY'S COTTAGE—KODIAK, ALASKA

I opened my eyes just enough to see Kate's golden hair spread across
the pillow, her head resting on my chest, a sweet, contented smile on
her lips. I felt overwhelmed by her presence. My heartbeat quickened.

This cannot be happening, I told myself.

Kate brushed her left arm across my stomach and pulled herself
closer to my body. *But it is…* The phone rang. I started at the sound, but
Kate just snuggled closer and moaned softly. I picked up the Princess

handset and brought it to my right ear, wincing a bit at the pain in my left shoulder. That was a wound I received from a Soviet dart underwater off Pt. Barrow shortly before we transited to Kodiak, and I still had my left arm in a sling. The bedroom window across the room was dark, but this was Kodiak in the winter. It would remain dark for several hours still. Outside was bitter cold; even the room air was more than chilly.

"Yeah, it's Mac."

"Mac, it's Jack…Petrikoff. Jack Petrikoff," his Russian accent heavy. "Wake up, Buddy!"

Kate stirred and sat up, rubbing her eyes, the sheet slipping from her pert nipples. "Wha…?" she started to ask, but I put a finger to her lips and shook my head.

"No time explain, Mac. You and Kate get out of there right now…I mean RIGHT NOW!"

"Jack…"

"RIGHT NOW, Buddy…house gonna blow…you and Kate gonna die!"

That got my attention.

Kate looked at me through sleepy eyes, her tongue moistening her lips. She reached under the covers, a coy smile creeping over her face.

"Mac, you hear me? RIGHT NOW!"

I grabbed Kate's wrist, interrupting her ministrations.

"Kate, we got a problem. Don't know what it is, but Jack says we need to get out of here now!"

Kate looked at me in shock.

"He means it…says we're in mortal danger."

Kate pulled the sheet up around her chin, her eyes like saucers. I grabbed her arms and pulled her to her feet.

"Get dressed warm, Girl…now!" I said sharply. "We're leaving ASAP!"

"We'll be out of here in a minute, Jack. We'll take Kate's Datsun. Shit…where do we go?"

"Don't take her car. It's gonna blow too!"

I heard some yelling from his end and then, "Jesus, Fuck!" apparently not directed at me.

"One of my guys will meet you out back on Poplar. He take you to my boat. Grab what you can to stay warm."

I heard a shot.

"Go, go, GO!" Jack yelled, and the phone connection went dead.

SOVIET SLEEPER CELL—KODIAK, ALASKA

We rushed out Kate's back door to Poplar, I in hastily donned uniform with my peacoat tossed over my sling, and Kate in a long skirt, sweater, and fur-lined topcoat. We both wore unlaced mukluks on our feet. The bitter cold stung my nostrils.

One of Jack's crew was at the back gate in a beat-up pickup with the passenger door open.

"Get in quick!" the driver said. "We gotta get the hell outa here!" Kate clambered into the cab, and I followed. The driver peeled away before I could shut the door. As we reached the curve where Poplar turned to end at Maple, a loud explosion ripped through the nighttime air, the low overcast reflecting a bright flash. I looked over my right shoulder in time to see pieces of Kate's cottage tumbling through the air, reflecting flickering flames from the twisted mess below.

As we turned right to approach Maple, a second explosion shattered the night air. In the reflected flames from what was left of Kate's cottage, I saw her Datsun roadster flip on its side, gasoline-fed fire engulfing it. Our driver knew Kodiak well. We ripped down side streets, through alleys, across a couple of empty parking lots, and finally down East Rezanof Drive toward Alimaq and the bridge across the bay. At the end of the bridge, he turned hard right, and after about a minute, pulled into a parking lot overlooking St. Herman's Harbor.

"Hurry," he urged as we tumbled out of his rig and ran across a road to the outermost floating dock

We ran down the walkway to an illuminated floating causeway that linked two brightly lit floating docks stretching into the harbor. The right one was filled with boat slips for smaller commercial boats. The left one, our destination, had six slips berthing larger vessels. Jack's boat, the *St. Kate*, was moored to the outer dockside away from the slips, starboard side to. A crew member stood on the brow, urging us forward. A shot rang out behind us. We ran faster. I could see that the lines were already cast off. Another shot ricocheted off *St. Kate's* steel side. The crew member pulled us across and then retrieved the brow.

Up in the pilothouse, Jack revved the engines and pulled away from the dock, pushing chunks of ice aside. As quickly as possible, he maneuvered past the breakwater and out to ice-pad-filled open water. Three more shots followed, one shattering a pilothouse window.

Our driver took us to the pilothouse where we met Jack standing at the helm—all five feet, eight inches of him. He gripped the large mahogany ten-spoked wheel with practiced ease. A Russian-style ushanka without a red star covered his salt and pepper hair, and his full beard was trimmed short. He reached out an arm to wrap around Kate's shoulders and kissed her cheeks. He shook my hand warmly and gave me a quick hug.

"That close call," he said. "I explain. My parents recruited in 1935 as members of Soviet sleeper cell in Kodiak. They die in 1950s. I never part of cell, but Soviets not agree. Last night, Soviets activate all ten members of cell with orders to kill Kate, blow up home and business, kill you, and destroy *Teuthis*. I call Coast Guard—they barricade front gate and notify *Teuthis*. I say I bring you and Kate by boat to Woman's Bay. Later, we talk more, but first, you call *Teuthis*. Say you and Kate safe. Say we be there in thirty minutes. Tie up behind *Teuthis*." He handed me a mike and set the hailing frequency on his overhead unit. That was a lot to digest, but Jack was right. First, I had to call *Teuthis*.

"*USS Teuthis*, this is fishing vessel *Saint Kate*, over."

"*Saint Kate*, this is *Teuthis*. Switch to channel forty-three, over." Jack changed the channel.

"*Teuthis*, this is *Saint Kate*…"

I asked to speak directly with the captain. When he came on, I briefly told him that Kate and I were okay and that we would arrive in Woman's Bay shortly. I asked him to set up a meeting in his cabin for the four of us.

I glanced at my watch. It was 0530.

✳

Forty minutes later, Kate and I were sitting on the red Naugahyde couch in the skipper's cabin, and Jack was in the easy chair. Commander (Cmdr.) Roken sat in his desk chair with his back to a fold-down desk. Jack had just finished explaining the background to his involvement.

"So, when I get activation order, I send my guy to Kate. I quickly call Kate, and Mac answers. I tell them to get out. A cell member tries to shoot me. I nail him, but cell blows up Kate's home, car, and shop. Mac and Kate escape to my boat, and we come to here." Jack's face was filled with worry. "Now, what to do?"

"Why do you think they are after Mac and Kate?" the skipper asked. "After Kate, no reason," Jack said, "except she's with Mac." He sighed. "Sometimes the Soviets seek revenge for a serious wrong. Revenge often kill entire family, close friends, even pets. Must be something Mac did." He stopped talking and shut his eyes. "I introduce Mac and Kate when I take Mac to *Kate's This & That?*" The skipper lifted his eyebrows.

"That the shop Kate set up after Josh killed. It was a beautiful little shop, but all gone now." He put his head in his hands, "My fault, all my fault."

Kate stood and put her arm around him. "Jack, I'm a big girl. I chose to be with Mac. You made that possible, and I love you for it." The skipper's phone rang. He answered, and his face dropped. He looked at Kate. "I don't have time to explain, Kate. Please stay in my cabin, no matter what you hear or feel." Then he addressed Jack and me. "The Coast Guard Station has been attacked, and the front gate breached. The combatants are on their way here." He looked at Jack. "Jack, get your vessel out into Woman's Bay. Arm your crew to hold off boarders from small craft." Then he turned to me. "Mac, get us underway from the wharf in the shortest time possible—two to three minutes. I'll be in Radio."

Jack sprinted topside to take care of *St. Kate*. I ran to Control and grabbed the 1MC mike.

"This is Lieutenant Commander McDowell. We have an all-hands emergency. We're getting underway and moving away from the wharf as rapidly as possible. Chief of the Boat, take men topside and cast off all lines by the quickest means possible."

I turned to the Chief of the Watch. "Sound the general alarm. Prepare to repel boarders. Get someone on the helm or take it yourself."

I still wore my peacoat, so I headed for the Bridge.

"Send two lookouts with rifles to the Bridge ASAP, and send up a sidearm for me," I told the Chief of the Watch.

When I got to the Bridge, the COB had just cast off the final line, letting the lines fall into the frigid water. I grabbed the squawk box mike. "Port full on both thrusters," I ordered. *St. Kate* had already pulled away from the wharf and was standing by in the south end of Woman's Bay.

"Stop the rear thruster. Ahead slow, right full rudder."

We developed a good angle to the wharf and moved slowly toward the middle of Woman's Bay, cracking the thin ice layer. I brought the sub to a standstill about a hundred yards from the wharf, with the wharf broad on the port bow.

Just then, an old pickup screeched to a halt on the wharf, several men jumping out, waving rifles. One climbed onto the hood, rifle pointed toward us.

"Billy-Bob," I said to Seaman Yokum, who was with me on the Bridge, "how's your aim?"

"Never better, Sir."

"Okay, take out the guy standing on the pickup hood."

"Yes, Sir!" His rifle cracked, and the man pitched forward, a hole between his eyes.

A second vehicle drove up—an older model, dark-green something-or-other, driven by one guy. One of the three remaining men did something to the pickup load, and then all three sprinted to the waiting vehicle.

"Can you take out the driver, Billy-Bob?"

"Yes, Sir." His rifle cracked, and the driver slumped over.

The three runners pushed his body out of the car and drove away in a hurry.

About five seconds later, the entire wharf erupted in flames as the pickup load exploded. The percussion hit the sub's sail and rocked the boat slightly but otherwise caused no harm. I examined the concrete wharf through my binocs. I saw a large, blackened area and pickup pieces scattered across the wharf but no significant damage otherwise. "Radio," I called on the squawk box, "immediately inform the Coast Guard that an older model dark-green sedan with three occupants just exploded a pickup on the cargo wharf. They are headed toward the front gate. Stop them at all costs!"

✳

The Coasties killed the driver and captured the other two.

✳

I eased *Teuthis* back against the wharf, port side to, and the COB with his Deck Gang moored us securely to the bollards.

USS TEUTHIS—WOMAN'S BAY, KODIAK, ALASKA

"Officers' call! Officers' call!" the Chief of the Watch announced on the 1MC.

The Executive Officer, the XO, Lt. Cmdr. Lonie Franken-Ester, went aft to relieve the Engineering Officer of the Watch, the EOW. Ten minutes later, all the officers except the XO had assembled in the Wardroom of *USS Teuthis* (SSNR 2)—the Nuclear Research Submarine-2. It was a bit crowded, but we all knew each other and didn't mind the close quarters.

"You may have heard by now," the skipper said quietly, "but the Soviets activated a sleeper cell in Kodiak several hours ago. They nearly killed Mac and his girlfriend, Kate. They attacked the Coast Guard Station, and—as you all know—they detonated an explosives-laden pickup on the wharf." He looked at each officer. "I'm going to the Coast Guard comm center where they have sophisticated secure communications. I need to brief SubPac[1] and arrange for Kate's safety and that of your families and those of your men."

He stood up. "Brief your people. I'll have more information when I return. Stay alert and be ready to move away from the wharf into Woman's Bay again on a moment's notice."

✳

"Commander McDowell to Radio," the 1MC announced about a half-hour later. I was sitting with Kate in the Captain's Cabin, so I stepped down the hall and to the right into the Radio Shack. Senior Chief Radioman Garth Walkman handed me a phone handset. I took it with my right hand, still favoring my left arm a bit.

"It's the captain," he said.

---

1 Submarine Fleet Pacific, in this case the SubPac Commander, Rear Admiral (Rear Adm.) Austin B. Scott, Jr.

"Thanks, Sparks," I responded, and then into the phone, "Yes, Sir, it's Mac."

"Tell me what you know about Kate's family."

"She has no family, Skipper. Her folks and older brother perished September 1965 in New Orleans during hurricane Betsy. Authorities found their bodies almost three weeks later. You know about Josh. She's got no one…'cept me now."

"Okay, Mac. Thank you." The skipper hung up.

I stood quietly in Radio after passing the handset back to Sparks. The skipper's question had put Kate's situation into sharp focus. She was attending Westover School for girls in Connecticut on that terrible September day when hurricane Betsy took her family. Somehow, although only a teen, she got through that tragedy to graduate as valedictorian. Kate attended Connecticut College on a full history scholarship, graduating *magna cum laude*. She met Coast Guard Cadet Josh Perry in his junior year at the Coast Guard Academy homecoming ball. They married the day he received his butter bars. Following his promotion to Lieutenant junior grade a year later, they moved to Kodiak, where he was assigned as Executive Officer on a Coast Guard Cutter out of Woman's Bay.

Kate lost Josh when he was swept overboard during the rescue of Jack Petrikoff two years ago. And now, we were an item—something I had never anticipated.

✳

The XO had posted the Duty Officer, Lt. j.g. Seth Beaumont, to the Bridge with sidearm along with a lookout armed with a sniper rifle. About a half-hour after Cmdr. Roken called me, Seth announced over the 1MC, "*Teuthis* returning… *Teuthis* returning," indicating that the captain had returned to the sub.

I was sitting in the skipper's cabin with Kate when he returned to the sub. Normally, I would not have been there in his absence, but this was a special circumstance. About ten minutes after the 1MC announcement, I got to my feet as Cmdr. Roken entered his stateroom. He waved me back to the couch beside Kate and sat in his chair, back to his fold-down desk. He smiled at Kate.

"How are you holding up, Kate?"

"Okay, I guess. Things are happening so fast I haven't had time to digest them." She smiled tentatively.

"Mac told me about your family. I'm terribly sorry. Life has not been very kind to you."

"I've coped," Kate said, "and now I have Mac." She took my hand in hers, and her face brightened.

"Kate, your life is in danger through no fault of yours. To keep you safe, you will ship out with us tomorrow and will transfer at sea to the *USS Los Angeles*, a fast-attack submarine that will take you to Mare Island, north of San Francisco. There, you will be met by agents from the Defense Intelligence Agency who will escort you to Washington. The DIA will arrange for secure housing and, if you wish, because of your history major, employment as a security analyst with the agency."

"I…I…don't know what to say," Kate stammered.

"You don't have to say anything," the skipper said with a warm smile. "We got you into this mess, and we'll get you out of it."

He picked up his phone, dialed a number, and spoke quietly into the handset. A few minutes later, the Senior Steward, Petty Officer First Class Crisanto Rivera, knocked on the door. He was a Filipino, a couple of inches shorter than Kate, with slightly longish, neatly trimmed black hair. With a professional smile, he presented Kate with a wrapped package.

"This should take care of you until you until you reach Mare Island, Miss Perry," he said in flawless, unaccented English.

Kate opened the package on the couch. It contained two folded sets of blue submarine coveralls emblazoned with the name *PERRY, K* over the right pocket and *USS Teuthis SSNR 2* at the left shoulder seam, a coiled up khaki belt with gold buckle, several pair of men's white boxer shorts and tee-shirts, several pair of blue socks, hairbrush, toothpaste and brush, soap and towel, and a pair of steel-toed black deck shoes.

"If the shoes don't fit, let me know, and I'll find a pair that will," Rivera said with a grin and turned to leave.

"You can change in my head," the skipper told Kate. She looked at him quizzically.

He chuckled and said, "On a ship, we call a bathroom a head. Please use mine. While onboard, you have the range of the sub except for the Radio Shack, but please only enter the engineering spaces with an escort. Mac will be pretty busy getting ready for underway. I think you'll find Sonar and the Control Room the most interesting places to be. Just stay out of the way as things happen."

The skipper got to his feet, and both Kate and I stood up. "Welcome aboard *Teuthis*," he told her.

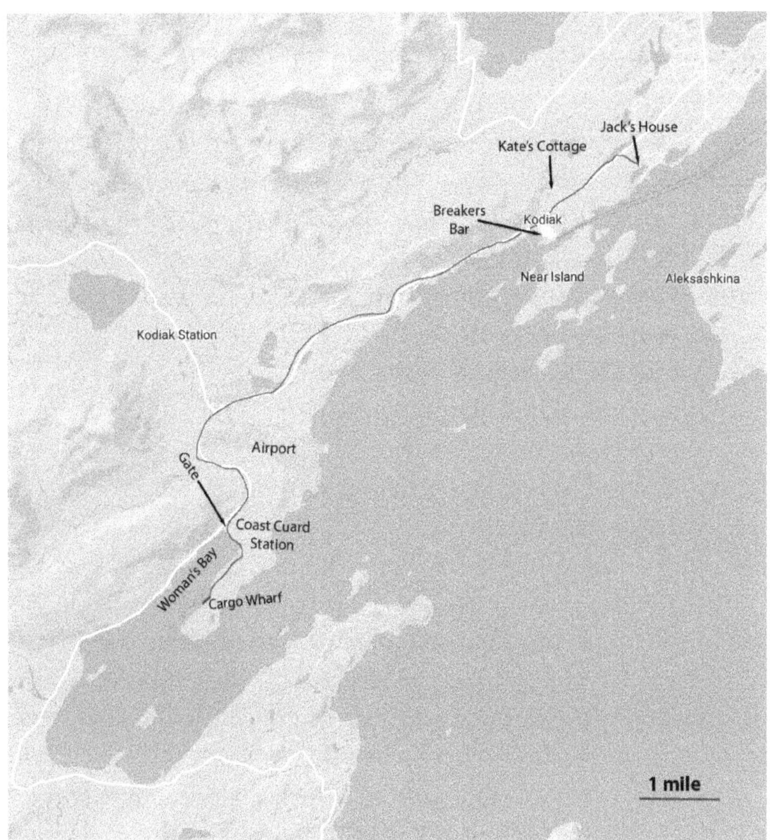

Breaker's Bar. Route from Jack's house to the cargo wharf on Woman's Bay

CHAPTER TWO—Kodiak, Alaska

USS TEUTHIS—WOMAN'S BAY, KODIAK, ALASKA

We had just completed an incredible operation. Although it seemed like ages ago, just a bit over two months earlier, *USS Teuthis* had departed Electric Boat (EB)[2] at the mouth of the Thames River in Connecticut for a top-secret assignment to lay two SOSUS arrays under the Arctic ice pack.[3]

---

2 General Dynamics Electric Boat Division, Groton, Connecticut, where *Teuthis* was overhauled

3 See *Operation Ice Breaker*, the second book in the *Mac McDowell Mission Series*.

USS Teuthis was a modified *Lafayette class* boomer.[4] Electric Boat had removed the Missile Compartment and replaced it with a ten-foot Diving Operations Compartment (DOC) and a seven-foot Cable Reel Compartment (CRC)—together, giving the boat a true Special Operations capability.

I was the Officer in Charge (OIC) of the Test Operations Group (TOG), a team of saturation divers originally assembled to tap into Soviet underwater communications cables on the floor of the Sea of Okhotsk—Operation Ivy Bells.[5] My team and I had joined *Teuthis* shortly before she set sail.

We successfully laid the first array west of Thule, Greenland, and then crossed the Arctic under the ice to lay the second array north of Bering Strait. During this whole operation, we were dogged by a Soviet *Alfa class* submarine.

In the Prince of Wales Strait, we were forced to use divers to work our way through a passage blocked by ice down to the seafloor. While trying to follow us, the *Alfa* sustained serious damage transiting the same passage. In its damaged condition, as it neared our position off Pt. Barrow, the *Alfa's* reactor scrammed due to the damage, and the crew was unable to start it up.

The small crew was forced to abandon the sub in an escape pod that failed to break through the solid ice cover. Although they were unaware of our presence, we contacted Dev Group,[6] who arranged to rescue the *Alfa* crew.

We couldn't pass up this unique opportunity to gather intel on a new, high-tech, highly automated Soviet sub, but we needed special equipment to access her interior.

We transited to Kodiak, where we onloaded the *Mystic*, one of the Navy's two Deep Submergence Rescue Vehicles (DSRV), and her crew of four. The *Mystic* also was accompanied by four DIA *Alfa* submarine specialists and someone out of the past, Sergyi Andreev. Sergyi was a Ukrainian saturation diver we had captured on the bottom of the

---

4 Fleet Ballistic Missile Submarine.
5 See *Operation Ivy Bells*, the first book in the *Mac McDowell Mission Series*.
6 Submarine Development Group One in San Diego, California, the group originally

Sea of Okhotsk during Operation Ivy Bells.[7] I had personally saved his life, and later in the operation, he saved mine. Since then, we had become fast friends. When we returned from Operation Ivy Bells, the National Security Agency (NSA) snatched him up, and then later loaned Sergyi to the DIA for this project.

Then we returned to the bottomed *Alfa* with the *Mystic* and the DIA *Alfa* specialists. While the specialists were inside the *Alfa* collecting intel, a much larger Soviet Sierra *class* sub showed up. The sub's divers emerged to investigate the *Alfa*, and my divers and I managed to overpower them and scram the Sierra reactor, forcing it to the surface. Because we had killed or captured all their divers, the Sierra had no way of knowing what had happened, except that somehow they had lost their dive team.

❋

Now we were back in Kodiak, preparing to pull off the inconceivable—return to the *Alfa*, still bottomed in a 500-foot-deep hole about eight nautical miles northwest of Pt. Barrow, and actually drive her back to a secure U.S. port while avoiding Soviet detection and retaliation. The *Alfa* had a distinctive silhouette. If we were going to bring her to Electric Boat on the East Coast, we would have to disguise her for the last leg on the surface —well, at least her sail.

The DIA working with NSA obviously had done a lot of scrambling. I'm sure they contacted the Dev Group in San Diego, who probably reached out to the Experimental Diving Unit (EDU) in Panama City, Florida. I'm also fairly certain they brought EB to the problem as well. In any case, they came up with a slick, lightweight erector-set-like titanium frame with longer pieces that pivoted like a carpenter's rule so the entire thing could be deployed through one of the DDC[8] hatches on *Teuthis*. The frame simulated fairwater planes and fitted around the *Alfa* sail. It was covered with a Kevlar sleeve held in place with appropriately placed Velcro strips, Velcro fasteners along the undersides of the fairwater planes, and two belly straps. The *Alfa* would normally be limited to seven-and-a-half knots underwater with the false sail in place,

---

7 See Operation Ivy Bells, the first book in the Mac McDowell Mission Series.

8 Deck Decompression Chamber.

but it would be installed by divers underwater at the closest possible location to the designated East Coast port. Furthermore, according to the DIA team, it could endure ten-knot sprints for thirty minutes or so. Both sides of the sleeve displayed the hull number 592—the *Sculpin's* number. *USS Sculpin* was scheduled for decommissioning in late 1986, so this was a fitting number.

My dive team loaded all the false sail components onto *Teuthis* and down into the DDC in about two hours. Sergyi, who obviously felt like he was a member of the saturation diving team, worked alongside his friends.

Following loading of the false sail components, large bottles of compressed oxygen and helium arrived on a truck with an extendable crane. During an earlier onload of paraffin drums, my guys had come up with a simple way to load them into the DOC. They broke up the ice near the wharf and lowered the drums into the water. Then they weighted them as necessary and swam them under the sub into the DDC hatches.

The divers onloaded the compressed gas bottles in the same way. They pressurized the DDC to keel depth, opened the bottom hatches, and moved the large bottles into the DDC with the help of a small hoist in the DDC. Then they sealed the hatches, decompressed the chamber to atmospheric pressure, opened the upper hatches, and lifted the bottles into place with another small hoist.

Master Chief Fire Control Tech Hamilton Comstock, everyone called him *Ham*, was my Master Saturation Diver and second in command of TOG. Chief Sonar Tech William Fisher was his understudy.

Ham had let Bill run most of the saturation dives during our just completed array-laying operation. Bill was about ready to test for Master Saturation Diver; by the time we delivered the *Alfa* to EB, he certainly would be. Working with the rest of the divers, Ham and Bill took a careful inventory of our consumables. On our transit to Kodiak, we had wired ahead for what we needed.

While the divers secured the gas bottles in their racks, Ham and Bill ensured we had received everything we ordered, including an extra supply of CO_2 cartridges for our gas-powered dart guns.

Those of you familiar with our just completed Operation Ice Breaker already know my dive team. For the record, in addition to

Ham and Bill, the team consisted of First Class Electronics Tech Harry Blackwell, First Class Corpsman James Tanner (we called him Jimmy), Second Class Quartermaster Melvin Ford (we called him Whitey), Second Class Engineman Wlodek Cslauski (Ski), Second Class Auxiliaryman Jeremy Romain (we called him Jer), and Second Class Electronics Tech Jacob Palmer (we called him Jake). Except for Ham and Jimmy, they all arrived on *Teuthis* wearing silver dolphins, and everyone qualified or requalified on *Teuthis* during Operation Ice Breaker, even Jimmy.

✳

The *Alfa* reactor was a solid piece of useless metal. The high-tech sub had a Soviet-designed liquid-lead-bismuth-cooled reactor. After the *Alfa's* drive train sustained damage from the ice, the misalignment eventually caused its reactor to scram, after which the liquid lead bismuth solidified, permanently disabling the reactor.

With her reactor not working, the *Alfa* had no power except for her bank of 112 zinc-silver batteries. On our way under the Arctic ice to the East Coast, we would have to stop every day or so to recharge the battery bank by connecting an underwater shorepower cable from *Teuthis*. This meant there was no spare power to create oxygen from seawater for our atmosphere. The Dev Group had figured this out already. It flew in 100 oxygen candles that were waiting when we arrived. These are canisters containing a mixture of sodium chlorate and iron pellets. When they are ignited, they produce about 150 man-hours of oxygen each. Ten of us would need about thirty-one days of oxygen for the journey. Do the math. Add a hundred percent safety factor, and you arrive at 100 canisters—weighing thirty pounds each.

While my guys were onloading the false sail components, the Deck Gang loaded the hundred oxygen candles and stowed them into *Mystic* under the close supervision of Senior Chief Sonar Tech Gaspard Abelé, *Mystic's* chief technician. Following that, the deck gang replenished the *Teuthis* fresh food stores, spare parts, consumables, and loaded 930 Long Range Patrol (LRP) rations that the ten-man crew on the *Alfa* would require for the estimated thirty-one days of the transit.

While the crew loaded stores, the *Mystic* crew opened *Mystic's* sound-transparent nosecone and installed a Secure Gertrude transducer. They installed the telephone box in the Control Sphere. The Secure Gertrude was a highly classified code division multiple access (CDMA) underwater telephone that had recently found its way onto some U.S. submarines. *Teuthis* was outfitted with one which would allow undetectable underwater communications between *Teuthis* and *Mystic*.

※

During the hours it took to get everything aboard *Teuthis*, Kate—wearing coveralls, steel-toed shoes, and an official ball cap someone had given her—remained below decks and out of the way. She spent most of the morning in Sonar with Chief Sonar Tech Royal Bennett, much to his delight. King, as we called him, explained to her how sonar worked and let her sit at a listening station with a headset connected to a tape recording of actual underway footage. Kate was fascinated, especially so when King informed her that I used to be a Sonar Tech before I got my commission.

After lunch in the Wardroom—pea soup with ham and swiss sandwiches, I took Kate down to Dive Control, where I delivered her into Ski's care. Ski was short, stocky, and tough, with dark hair as long as regs allowed. He was still on light duty because of a knife wound to his right shoulder that a Soviet diver gave him on his last dive near the bottomed *Alfa*. My left arm was still in a sling from the Soviet dart I had taken at the same time, but I was ready to cast it off and return to full duty myself.

Ski, ever the lady's man, took good care of Kate during the afternoon. He even pressurized the DDC so she could experience opening the bottom hatch and touching the water from inside the chamber. He regaled her with tales of derring-do and the part I played in them—probably exaggerating my role.

※

It was long since dark by the end of our workday. I assembled my guys and told them they could go ashore, but they had to return by 2200. I told Ham to take them to Breakers.

"No more than two drinks each, and stay alert," I told him. I issued Ham a sidearm with a concealed shoulder holster just to be sure. I called Jack, asking that he pick Kate and me up in a half-hour. He promised us a salmon dinner washed down with homegrown applejack.

I briefed the skipper on our status and my plans for the divers for the evening. I said that Kate and I would be at Jack's and would return by 0730. I told him I had issued Ham a sidearm and was taking one myself. I finished with the traditional request, "Request permission to go ashore, Sir."

"Granted," the skipper said. "Take care of him, Kate!"

BREAKER'S BAR—KODIAK, ALASKA

On our first visit to Kodiak, my guys and I had met most of the local commercial fishermen at Breaker's Bar. These locals, many of Russian extraction, were as tough as they came, but I softened that encounter when I bought the bar for the evening.

I met Captain Jack Petrikoff at Breaker's Bar. He was the man whose rescue at sea had caused the death of Kate's husband, Josh. Jack renamed his fishing boat to *St. Kate* immediately after that and assumed the role of Kate's guardian protector—like an older brother or close uncle. He introduced me to Kate. My resolve to remain a bachelor crumbled the moment we met, something Jack recognized as it happened.

Kate had changed back into her skirt, sweater, and fur-lined topcoat for the evening—the only personal clothing she still possessed. I wore jeans and turtleneck, western boots, and a brown leather flight jacket worn by most sub officers. I carried the holstered .45 under my left arm, adjusting it to accommodate my still sore shoulder, although I had discarded the sling. Because the temperature was expected to hit forty below, I topped my outfit with a hooded, down parka.

Jack was waiting on the wharf in his pickup when we climbed out the forward hatch and crossed the brow. From inside, he pushed the passenger door open, and Kate and I squeezed inside, glad to be out of the frigid cold.

"We go to Breaker's Bar for drink and say 'Hello' to guys before dinner," Jack said gruffly. "All love Kate." He turned and smiled at her. "Sad to see go." He turned to me. "Sad see you go too," he said. "You local hero!"

Kate dug me in the ribs with her elbow.

✳

The three of us walked into Breaker's Bar. The concrete floor, with its permanently attached tables, had not changed. At the back of the room, the concrete horseshoe-shaped bar was as uninviting as always. The place was filled with smoke and a half-dozen accents as tough local commercial fishermen, many with Russian heritage, filled the tables and crowded the bar.

Shouts of, "Yo, Jack! Yo, Kate! Yo, Diver Boy!" greeted us as we entered.

Unlike my first visit to Breaker's Bar, my money was no good this time. Kate and I both sipped scotch-on-the-rocks as the tough fishermen crowded around.

"Yo, Diver Boy…you one tough sonofabitch!"

"Those motherfuckers need a teaching! We gonna teach!"

"We gonna miss you, Kate, girl. You the best thing what happened to Kodiak in long time."

"You got friends here, Kate…always!" "You too, Diver Boy!"

"What the fuck is your name, anyway?"

"Mac," I said. "Mac McDowell." I signaled Kate and rose to leave. "My guys'll be here in a bit. Save some beer for 'em."

"Yo, Kate! Yo, Diver Boy! Yo, Mac!" echoed in our ears as we exited through the double doors.

JACK PETRIKOFF'S PLACE—KODIAK, ALASKA

Jack Petrikoff was a successful commercial fisherman, but success had not gone to his head. His house was a well-maintained two-story Craftsman occupying, Jack told me, about a half-acre of lawn on the corner of Spruce Cape Road and Anderson Way. He pulled into the driveway. In the light from his headlights, all I could see was a foot or so of snow surrounding the house on all sides. Pointing at a pickup parked at the curb, Jack said, "Ling, the *Saint Kate's* cook. He fixin' salmon."

We exited the warm cab into the stinging cold and hurried to the front door. The porch was clear of snow, and a fancy light by the door welcomed us.

We stepped through the door onto a tiled foyer where Kate left her mukluks. Jack indicated to me to keep wearing my boots. We doffed our outer clothing, and Jack hung them on large hooks. When I removed my leather jacket, he saw my .45.

"You wanna keep wearing or leave here?" he asked, pointing to a cabinet top. "Makes me no difference."

I grinned and removed the shoulder holster and .45. "Don't think I'll need it here," I said.

"I show room. Then have drink and dinner," Jack said, moving toward a staircase.

The room was large, with a big bed and its own bathroom that Kate promptly occupied. I flopped into an easy chair beside a rustic end table with a shaded lamp and leaned back, thinking about the last eighteen hours. It seemed like something out of a dream…or a deadly nightmare. Kate came out of the bathroom, tripped over to my chair, and plunked herself into my lap. She kissed me solidly for about a minute, arms wrapped around my neck. When we came up for air, I said with a grin, "We gotta go down for drinks and dinner, you know."

She grabbed my face between her hands and looked deep into my eyes. "I'm gonna say it, Diver Boy. I love you!"

I wasn't shocked or surprised. I opened my mouth to respond and heard myself say, "I love you too, Kate, with everything I am!" as tears filled my eyes.

✳

Dinner was a rousing success. Plank broiled salmon, accompanied by baker potatoes topped with butter and sour cream, washed down with applejack is a hard combination to beat. It was the best meal I had consumed in ages, and I had to restrain myself not to get outrageously drunk on the Jack. Kate ate less than I but obviously enjoyed it just as much.

When we were done, Jack said, "You guys need be alone, so hustle topside. I get you up and feed you breakfast plenty time for go to Teuthis by 0730."

✳

It was a night to be remembered, filled with passion, tears, sweet coupling, hard sex, even recriminations about my heading to the Arctic in the morning, but totally loving and goddammed fulfilling.

Ling awakened us with two steaming cups of black coffee, discreetly averting his eyes from Kate's nakedness. My watch said 0530.

At 0600, we sat down at a breakfast table heaped with fried eggs, bacon, pancakes and maple syrup, more coffee, and what tasted like fresh orange juice.

"You eat like this all the time, Jack?" I asked.

He grinned. "Hell no! But this be special occasion. Kate like my own kid. I love her. She love you. You love her…"

I looked at him sharply.

"You can no hide fact!" he said with a chuckle. "I bring you together. Now, you stuck with each other!"

✳

At that moment, a shot rang out, and a bullet pierced the double glazed dining room window.

"Under table!" Jack ordered.

While Kate and Jack dove under the table, I sprinted to the foyer and grabbed my .45. A second shot rang out.

"You okay?" I yelled. "Yeah…Kate too!"

As I drew my weapon and cleared the safety, the front door smashed inward, admitting a rush of frigid air. I whipped around in the bitter cold blast and snapped off two shots at a figure silhouetted against the porch light. As he crumpled, I dropped prone to the floor. A flash from the darkness beyond the porch, and a bullet whizzed past my right ear. I shifted position and squeezed off a round at the flash and heard a grunt followed by a thud. Another flash from farther left as I rolled to my right and got off two more rounds. I heard one bullet ricochet off the side of Jack's pickup, but apparently, my second shot found its target. I heard a yell and a thud.

"You guys okay?" I hollered back into the house.

"We okay," Jack said. "There were only three left…me think you got all."

USS TEUTHIS—WOMAN'S BAY

Jack got us to the wharf a few minutes before 0730. Kate had been silent during the entire drive. As we sat on the wharf, engine running to maintain the cab warmth, Kate put her arms around me and buried her head on my chest.

"I love you, Mac," she said quietly. "I haven't forgotten Josh, but you are my knight in shining armor, my soulmate, my eternal love!"

Jack winked at me as I opened the passenger door of his pickup. "Kate, darlin'," he said. "You be careful. Let Jack know you be well. I can no take care of you when you gone. Be sharp. Be smart. Call Jack time-to-time."

Kate hugged him and kissed his cheeks, tears flowing down hers. Then she grabbed my hand, jumped out of the cab, and ran with me to the brow. As soon as we were below decks, we went to see Cmdr. Roken. I told him what had happened and that I believed I had shot the remaining three cell members. He took a couple of notes, made sure Kate was okay, and then left for Radio to brief the Coast Guard before Teuthis departed.

"Use my head to change," he told Kate as he left.

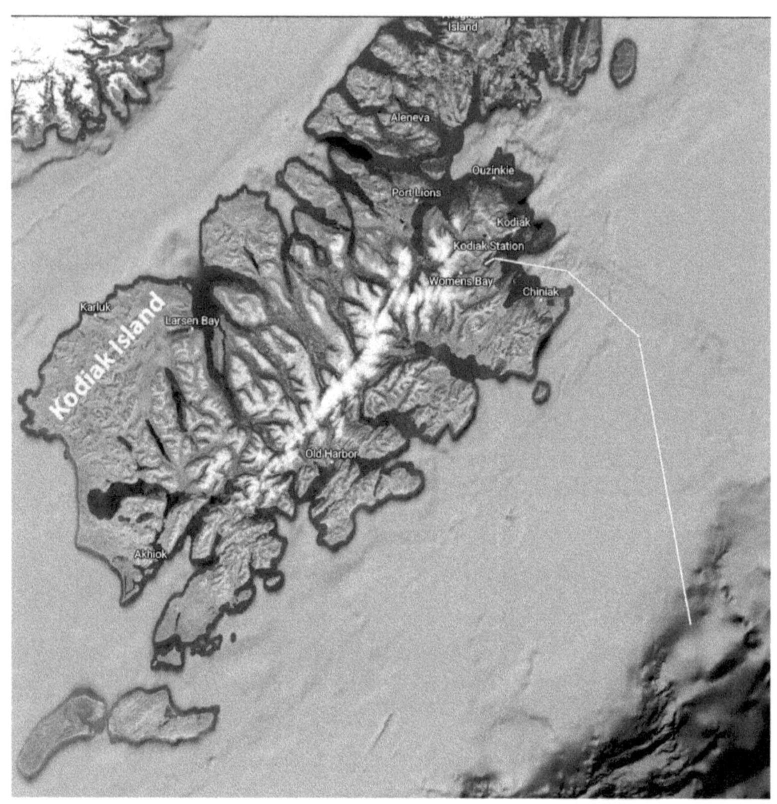

USS Teuthis & Mystic underway from Woman's Bay to a 1,000-foot-deep ledge on the Aleutian Trench wall.

CHAPTER THREE—Underway

USS TEUTHIS—UNDERWAY FROM WOMAN'S BAY

As I headed to the Bridge, I told the Chief of the Watch to set the Maneuvering Watch.

"Station the Maneuvering Watch! Station the Maneuvering Watch!" the Chief of the Watch announced over the 1MC. Throughout the submarine, sailors hurried to their designated slots. The COB and his topside deck crew raised the fore and after capstans, even though they probably would not be used. Master Pilot Sven Jakobsen crossed the brow and clambered up the sail to the Bridge.

"Commander McDowell," he said with a ready smile, shaking my hand. We had met twice before, when we first arrived at Woman's Bay and when we left. The skipper had arranged for him to spend two hours with us, participating in underwater operations. It probably was the highlight of his career.

Jakobsen was short, dressed in cold-weather gear, wearing a woolen watch cap. His weathered face made guessing his age difficult, but I made him for sixty-plus. His close-cropped full blond beard was peppered with grey, and his crinkled eyes showed permanent smile lines.

"Where's Commander Roken?" he asked.

"On his way," I answered as two men hauled in the brow and stowed it, and Coasties placed themselves at both bollards on the wharf, ready to handle lines from dockside.

"Captain's on the Bridge," one of the lookouts announced as the skipper poked his head through the hatch.

"Mr. Jakobsen," the skipper said, shaking the pilot's hand. "Commander Roken," the pilot said. Turning to me, he asked. "Is your draft still about twenty-seven feet?" "Close enough," I responded.

In the dim morning twilight, Jakobsen looked at his waterproof stainless chronometer. "High tide is at eight forty-three, Captain—seven feet." He checked his watch again. "That's in eleven minutes. We'll want to ride it out through the channel."

"Maneuvering Watch set," the squawk box announced. I looked at the skipper, and he nodded.

"Single up all lines," I ordered.

The Coasties tossed off the extra turn of line around the bollards, and the deck crew hauled the slack line aboard.

"Lower the outboards," I told the Chief of the Watch. "Cast off the bow line," I signaled to the COB.

"Forward thruster, starboard full; after thruster starboard easy." "Cast off all lines," I told the COB.

When Teuthis' bow angled away from the dock, and the stern was about ten yards from the dock, I ordered, "Ahead slow, right full rudder. Stop and stow the thrusters."

I kept an eye on the stern as Teuthis angled out into Woman's Bay, pushing thin sheets of ice aside as she moved. When we were twenty yards from the dock, I turned to the pilot.

"You ready to take it, Mr. Jakobsen?"

"Aye that," he answered.

"Master Pilot Jakobsen has the Conn," I announced through the squawk box.

I glanced up at the two periscopes protruding from the top of the sail—rotating and stopping, rotating and stopping. The navigation team under Ship's Navigator Lt. Cmdr. Barry Jacobs was taking bearings to prominent objects. The radar mast turned slowly while his team captured range and bearing to radar points as they traced our track out of Woman's Bay and into the channel. As we turned left into the channel, Jakobsen said, "Let's take her to ten knots."

"Ahead two-thirds," I ordered over the squawk box, and then called Maneuvering. "Make turns for ten knots."

Our wake stood out against the thin ice cover, showing some phosphorescence in the still dim morning twilight. The wake was practically ice-free except for a few small ice-pads that floated back into the wake farther behind us. We were headed into the wind, so our extra speed dramatically lowered the chill factor on the Bridge. I called the lookouts from the fairwater planes into the bridge well and ordered hot coffee for everyone.

After fifteen minutes, we turned right at the end of the channel and threaded our way between a couple of islands toward the Pilot Buoy about three nautical miles out. The ocean was throwing ten foot waves at our bow, mostly from the southeast out of the Alaska Gulf. Wave intensity began to lessen as we crossed the fifty-fathom curve. Ahead of us, the pilot boat was standing by at the Pilot Buoy, awaiting our arrival.

As we neared the Pilot Boat, to my total surprise, Jack Petrikoff stepped onto the bridge wing and waved to us. The skipper picked up the squawk box mike and announced over the 1MC, "Kate Perry to the Bridge! Kate Perry to the Bridge!"

About a minute later, Kate's ball-cap-covered head poked through the Bridge hatch. She was wearing her fur-lined topcoat to protect her from the sub-zero cold. I reached down and took her hand, helping her up. As I did so, it seemed like electric shocks coursed through my body. My love for this girl nearly overwhelmed me. The skipper pretended not to notice and pointed to the Pilot Boat and Jack.

Kate squealed with delight, waving both arms. Jack cupped his mouth and shouted, "Bon Voyage! Stay safe, Kate, darlin'!"

Jakobsen held out his hand to the skipper. "It's been a great pleasure, Captain."

I announced to Control, "Commander McDowell has the deck and the conn."

Two minutes later, the pilot was gone, and his boat had pulled away. Jack waved again as the Pilot Boat turned and headed back to the safety of Woman's Bay.

"Bridge, Radar, contact bearing zero-eight-five, designate Romeo-one." I acknowledged. That was fifteen degrees off the port bow. The skipper, both lookouts, and I all lifted our binoculars and scanned in that direction.

"Bridge, Nav, I have the contact visually at zero-eight-five, range four nautical miles. Redesignate Mike-one. It's a trawler, angle-on-the bow starboard-eight-zero. He's bristling with antennas. I think he's a Soviet spy trawler. Mike-one is doing six knots on an intercept course." We were just beyond the territorial limit of three nautical miles.

Soviet trawlers like this one frequently loitered just beyond the territorial limits of important ports, not only of the U.S. but also other nations, especially where there was military traffic. Since Kodiak rarely hosted military traffic, except for Coast Guard traffic, finding this trawler here was significant.

"It looks like they are keeping track of us," the skipper said. "Take us to decks awash to give him a smaller profile, increase speed to ten knots, and set a course of one-zero-five. Dive as soon as you can." He turned to Kate. "Come below with me, Kate. We'll let Mac do his job.

It will be more interesting in Control anyway." He gestured toward the hatch.

As they dropped below, I called the Chief of the Watch on the squawk box handset and had him flood us down so the decks were awash. "What's the status of rig-for-dive?" I asked, knowing that the process had been ongoing since we left Woman's Bay.

"We're ready to dive except for the Bridge hatches, Sir." "Very well, Chief. Who's the officer in Control?"

"Lieutenant junior grade Beaumont," he said, indicating gangly, blond Seth Beaumont, the Communications and Sonar Officer who was my Junior-Officer of the Deck (JOOD) in our normal watch cycle.

"Let me speak with him," I said. "Lieutenant junior grade Beaumont, Sir."

"Seth, we're going to dive shortly, more quickly than we normally dive. You take the Conn while I secure the Bridge. Keep a close eye on Mike-one, the trawler. Tell Sonar to be on the lookout for a Soviet sub nearby. I think they have our number and are keeping close track on us."

USS TEUTHIS— SUBMERGED OFF KODIAK ISLAND

Over the Squawk box, I said to Control, "Lieutenant Beaumont has the Conn." I handed the box to one of the lookouts and ordered, "Clear the bridge!"

The lookouts had already removed the safety stanchions from the fairwater planes. They dropped below while I set the Bridge fairing and dropped through the hatch, swinging the hatch down after me. Someone pulled the lanyard tight while I cranked the handle, locking the hatch tight. Then I dropped through the next hatch and repeated the process.

"Status?" I asked the Chief of the Watch.

"Green board," he answered, indicating that the sub was fully ready to dive.

I quickly glanced around Control. The skipper was on the nav scope, Seth on the attack scope. Kate stood out of the way behind the nav table against the fire control computer. Barry stood next to her, quietly explaining the activities.

"I have the Deck and the Conn," I announced. "Bearing and range to Mike-one?"

"Zero-eight-five," the radar operator answered, "range three-point five nautical miles."

"Depth beneath the keel?" I asked.

"Two-eight-zero feet," the Nav Watch told me. "Dive the ship!" I ordered.

The 1MC blared, "Dive! Dive!" followed by two long Aoogahs! on the klaxon.

"Helmsman, ahead two-thirds, come right to one-zero-five. Diving Officer, ten-degree down bubble. Make your depth one-two-zero feet smartly." Then I called Maneuvering on the sound-powered phone. "Make turns for ten knots," I ordered.

The skipper looked at me. "Set the underway watch, Mac. I'll be in my cabin."

✳

When we got underway, we shifted to East Coast Time since that was our ultimate destination. We had two hours remaining on the first watch. The Chief of the Watch announced, "Set the underway watch, section one."

Seth and I remained in Control. The other watchstanders shifted as the regular watch personnel assumed their normal watch stations. We were headed for the fifty-fathom curve where we would angle farther south until we crossed the Aleutian Trench edge, where we anticipated meeting up with the Los Angeles. We had a bit under six hours on this leg.

"Lieutenant Beaumont has the Conn," I announced. Seth had been running the show on our watch for most of the past month. I wanted him to gain as much experience as possible before I transferred to the *Alfa*. "Conn, Sonar," King, the lead Sonar Tech for section one, said over the sonar circuit, "contact Mike-one bears zero-eight-three, falling off to port. I have a new contact bearing one-zero-zero, designate Sierra-one. Sierra-one has suppressed cavitation. It's a submerged sub, Sir. I'll give you more info as soon as possible."

King was telling me that he heard the characteristic squeaking sound of a rotating propeller that is well submerged. This can only come from a deep-draft tanker or a submerged submarine.

A few minutes later, King called me. "Sierra-one is a *Victor III*," he told me, "the *Shchuka*. Can you step into Sonar and listen to her screws?"

I stepped off the periscope stand and walked a few feet forward to the Sonar Shack on the right. What I heard was a sound new to me. I clearly heard four blades, but I also heard a strange, syncopation-like pattern. I looked at King with the question in my eyes.

"She's got tandem, twin four-bladed screws," King said. "Put her on our beam for a few minutes, and I can tell you more."

I stepped back to Control and told Seth to come to course 185 and slow to five knots for ten minutes. Seth did, and we watched and waited while King and his guys did their magic. About eight minutes later, King called me to Sonar again.

"Sierra-one is sixty-two nautical miles distant, bearing zero-nine-four, on a course of one-eight-zero at five knots. *Shchuka's* the lead ship of the class. Because she's going five knots, I think she's towing an array looking for us." "Come back to base course," I told Seth, "but remain at five knots."

I turned to the Chief of the Watch, Senior Chief Engineman Sam Dokey. "Rig ship for ultra-quiet quickly but quietly."

Then I called the skipper and briefed him on the situation. He left his cabin and stepped into Sonar to see for himself.

Senior Chief Dokey passed the word throughout the sub by sound powered phone. Within moments, the engineers powered down the reactor to minimum power, secured the turbines, shifted propulsion to electric motors, and shut down ventilation fans throughout the sub. Everyone who was not doing something immediately critical either sat where he was or went to his bunk. In less than a minute, you could not have detected Teuthis from fifty yards away.

I looked at Kate, put my finger to my lips, and pointed to Sonar. She smiled and went there. A moment later, my sound-powered handset chirped. I picked it up. It was King.

"I have a new submerged contact bearing zero-eight-zero, drifting right, designate Sierra-two. I think it's the *Los Angeles*, Sir."

"Can you estimate her range?"

"She's a lot quieter than the *Shchuka*. I estimate thirty nautical miles or so. I'll need her on the beam to be more accurate."

I told Seth to bring us back to course 185. About ten minutes later, King reported, "Sierra-two *is* the *Los Angeles*. She bears zero-eight-five, range two-eight nautical miles, on course two-three-seven at fourteen knots. I think she was tracking us before we went to ultra-quiet."

Senior Chief Quartermaster Alastair Forbes, the section navigator, spoke up. "That puts her on a course to intercept us at the one thousand fathom curve."

"No way she can track us now," King added.

"King," I asked, "does *Los Angeles* know about *Shchuka*?"

"Most likely," King said. "She's half as far from *Shchuka* as we are." The skipper stepped to the periscope stand. "What's on your mind, Mac?"

"If I were the *Los Angeles*," I said, "needing to rendezvous with us and finding *Shchuka* out there, I would do my best to sever her towed array, and then establish contact with us."

USS TEUTHIS— SUBMERGED OFF KODIAK ISLAND

It was as if the *Los Angeles* skipper had read my thoughts. During the watch change, while Lieutenant Waverly Denver, the Weapons Officer (Weaps), assumed the watch, Los Angeles made a radical course change for an intercept course with Shchuka.

Shchuka almost certainly had not been aware of Los Angeles before that maneuver, even though the Los Angeles was half our distance. The new watch navigator, Quartermaster First Class Gary Fonzarelli (Fonzie), spoke up shortly after.

"*Los Angeles* is doing fourteen knots now. She's about two hours away from *Shchuka*, depending on what the Soviet sub does."

I chimed in. "If *Shchuka* figures out what's up, she will retract her towed array since she's dramatically limited in speed and maneuverability with that wire out." Then I stepped into Sonar to see how Kate was doing.

To my delight, King had put her at the spare sonar console. With the limited number of contacts at our current location, manning two consoles was not required. Kate looked up at me with a grin and moved her wheel to three different bearings.

"This," she said, "is Mike-one, the trawler. This is Sierra-one, the *Shchuka*, and this is Sierra-two, the *Los Angeles*. How about that," she said, obviously pleased with her performance. "What's weird is that I can barely hear *Los Angeles*, but *Shchuka* is loud and clear even though it's twice as far away. Why is that?"

"There are many things that affect the sound you hear from a contact. The bottom line is that the Soviet sub is much noisier than *Los Angeles*. I think Los Angeles is trying to sneak up on *Shchuka* and then cut her towed array. We don't know if she has sufficient additional array cable in that pod on her fin to float a second array. I don't think she does, so cutting her array significantly reduces her sonar capability. This makes life much easier for us." I squeezed her shoulders. "Come out to Control, and I'll show you the big picture."

✳

Thereafter, we went to the Wardroom for a cup of coffee. I brought a chart with me and laid out the relative positions of the three subs. Kate had never been exposed to vessels moving in three dimensions relative to each other. Nevertheless, she picked it up quickly.

When we returned to Control, *Los Angeles* was close by *Shchuka*, hiding in her baffles—the angle behind her propellers where their noise made it impossible for *Shchuka* to hear anything.

"At their distance," I said to Kate, "we do not have any meaningful vertical definition. Let's just watch."

On Fonzie's chart, both subs seemed to be at the same location. "Won't they bump into each other?" Kate asked.

"*Los Angeles* knows the precise position and depth of *Shchuka*," I said. "She'll maneuver so that she can cut the towed array with her screw. Once it's cut, *Shchuka* is no longer restricted in its movements. If I were running *Los Angeles*," I said, "I would get below *Shchuka* and then drift back into her baffles. Then I would assume a steep down angle and move up until my screw cut the cable. *Shchuka* would remain on course and speed for a few minutes to assess the situation. In the meantime, I would drop *Los Angeles* as deep as possible and head in our direction."

"What will *Shchuka* do without her array?" Kate asked.

"She couldn't hear us with her array, so it's most unlikely she will do better without it. But, she'll be more maneuverable without the array, and she'll be fairly certain she did not lose the array by accident. She'll suspect a U.S. sub nearby and will start looking for it in earnest. "She was out here looking for us. The trawler may have given her some info, but she probably thinks we cut her array."

The skipper joined us at the nav table. "We'll rendezvous with *Los Angeles* in about six hours. In the meantime, we'll find a nice quiet spot along the continental slope to hang out."

PEARL HARBOR— COMSUBPAC HQ

Rear Admiral Austin B. Scott, Jr., Commander of Submarine Fleet Pacific, sat in his expansive office on the third floor of the Morton Street complex overlooking the Magazine Lock at Pearl Harbor, contemplating the events in Kodiak during the past several days. Outside was warm and humid as always, but a fresh breeze off the water passed through the louvered glass slats of his windows, keeping his office comfortable without air-conditioning.

A file on his desk carried the prominent label:

TOP SECRET
J.R. "Mac" McDowell, Lt. Cmdr., USN

He opened it and read quietly for a few minutes. Then he looked up and stared through his window across the water to Ford Island. "Ivy Bells, Ice Breaker, and now this. Single-handedly wiping out a Soviet sleeper cell…you're a remarkable officer, Mac," he said quietly, "and one tough sonofabitch! I wish I had several dozen like you."

He checked a chart on the wall to his right. Small magnetic icons marked the current deployment of his submarines. The *Los Angeles* was transiting to Mare Island carrying Katherine Perry—Kate, Coast Guard Lt. j.g. Josh Perry's widow and now Lt. Cmdr. McDowell's love.

The Admiral punched his intercom. "Master Chief," he addressed his Command Master Chief Petty Officer, "please arrange for me to meet the *Los Angeles* in Mare Island."

San Francisco, a *Los Angeles class* sub, and *Drum*, a *Sturgeon class* sub, were in the North Pacific, and the *Skate class* sub *Swordfish* had just departed from Pearl for the North Pacific.

Not ideal, Adm. Scott thought. *San Francisco has limited under-ice capability*. Drum *and* Swordfish *are old hands at under-ice ops. That's good.*

He checked the distance of each to Pt. Barrow. *There's sufficient time,* he thought, nodding to himself with a smile. He punched his intercom again. "Master Chief, have Comms report to my office," referring to his Sub Fleet Communications Officer.

While he waited, Adm. Scott picked up the secure phone handset on his desk and dialed the Commander-in-Chief, Pacific Fleet, whose offices were third-of-a-mile to the north past a tank farm and over Kamehameha Highway on Makalapa Drive.

"Jim, it's Austin," he said over the secure circuit to Adm. James A. Lyons, Jr. "Remember that incident off Point Barrow involving the Soviet *Alfa*?"

Adm. Lyons acknowledged.

"Looks like we can board the *Alfa* and drive her to New London through the Arctic. I'm assigning that remarkable young officer, Lt. Cmdr. Mac McDowell to take command. The *Alfa* and *Teuthis* will transit together, with *Teuthis* recharging the *Alfa's* batteries daily using Mac's divers."

"You've assigned an escort, right?" Adm. Lyons asked.

"I'm sending my three available subs, *San Francisco*, *Drum*, and *Swordfish*. *Drum* and *Swordfish* are fully ice-capable, but *San Francisco* is limited in that she cannot break through thick ice in the event of an emergency. To get our hands on an operating *Alfa*, it's a risk worth taking. I'm generating a formal exception to protocol to handle this, and I'll issue pertinent precautionary instructions."

"I trust your judgment, Austin. Copy me on your comms." "Aye, Sir."

❋

"Master Chief," Adm. Scott said, "set up a secure conference call with Subrons one, seven, and eleven."

"Aye, Sir."

When all three commanders were online, Adm. Scott addressed them. "Gentlemen, this briefing is Top Secret with the strictest need-to-know dissemination, and it is being recorded. Will you each state your name, rank, command, and acknowledge what I have just said."

The three Navy submarine squadron commanders, senior Captains all, so acknowledged. Adm. Scott then briefed them on *Teuthis* and the *Alfa* and his requirement for the services of *Swordfish* from Subron 1, *San Francisco* from Subron 7, and *Drum* from Subron 11.

"I am originating a ComSubPac message following this call diverting all three subs to this mission. I will require them for a minimum of forty-five days."

"What about *San Francisco's* under-ice worthiness?" Subron 7 wanted to know.

"I will cover that in my forthcoming message, but remember, capturing an intact Soviet *Alfa* is worth a reasonable risk to *San Francisco* and her crew. I'll keep each of you in the loop on any developments. Are there any further questions?"

✴

The message was drafted and transmitted within the hour.

TOP SECRET...TOP SECRET

FM: COMSUBPAC

TO: USS SWORDFISH SSN-579
       USS SAN FRANCISCO SSN-711
       USS DRUM SSN-677
       USS TEUTHIS SSNR-02

COPY: CINCPACFLT
       SUBRON ONE
       SUBRON SEVEN
       SUBRON ELEVEN
       COMSUBDEVGRUONE

1. USS SAN FRANCISCO, USS DRUM, AND USS SWORD-
    FISH PROCEED SUBMERGED TO POINT TEN NM
    SOUTH OF UNIMAK PASS TO RENDEZVOUS FOUR
    DAYS FROM DATE OF THIS MSG.
2. PROCEED TOGETHER UNDER ICE CANOPY TO BER-
    ING STRAIT AND FROM THENCE TO A POINT 25 NM
    DUE NORTH OF PT BARROW.
3. LOCATE USS TEUTHIS AND UNDESIGNATED SOVI-
    ET ALFA SUB UNDER US COMMAND. THEIR INITIAL
    PRESUMED LOCATION 8 NM NW OF PT BARROW.
4. BE ALERT FOR SOVIET VICTOR AND SIERRA SUBS IN
    VICINITY. THEIR PRESUMED INTENT IS TO RECAP-
    TURE OR SINK ALFA.
5. FORM PROTECTIVE SCREEN AROUND
    TEUTHIS AND ALFA, AND ACCOMPANY THEM

THROUGH ARCTIC TO GENERAL DYNAMICS ELECTRIC BOAT, GROTON, CT.

6. TEUTHIS AND ALFA WILL STOP APPROX EVERY 24 HOURS TO CHARGE ALFA BATTERIES USING TEUTH- IS DIVER PERSONNEL.
7. TEUTHIS AND ALFA MAY DEVIATE FROM PRO- JECTED TRACK AS NECESSARY AS DETERMINED BY CO TEUTHIS.
8. TEUTHIS AND ALFA EXPECTED TO STOP NEAR SEAL ISLAND TO INSTALL A FALSE SAIL ON THE ALFA FOR ITS SURFACED TRANSIT INTO THE THAMES RIVER.
9. TEUTHIS AND ALFA EXPECTED TRACK: PT. BARROW TO DEMARCATION POINT, AMUNDSEN GULF, DOLPHIN AND UNION STRAIT, CORONA- TION GULF, DEASE STRAIT, QUEEN MAUD GULF, ICEBREAKER CHANNEL, VICTORIA STRAIT, LARS- EN SOUND, BELLOT STRAIT, PT. KENDALL, FURY AND HECLA STRAIT, LABRADOR NARROWS, FOXE BASIN, FOXE CHANNEL, HUDSON STRAIT, GALVAND ISLANDS, NAIN BASIN, HAMILTON INLET, GULF OF ST. LAWRENCE, SEAL ISLAND (ATTACH FALSE SAIL TO *Alfa*), GENERAL DYNAMICS EB.
10. RULES OF ENGAGEMENT:
    1. DO NOT INITIATE HOSTILE CONTACT.
    2. IF FIRED UPON, RETURN FIRE AUTHORIZED.
    3. UNDERWATER DIVER-TO-DIVER DEADLY FORCE AUTHORIZED.
    4. FOR SAN FRANCISCO: THIS MSG IS AN EXCEP- TION TO THE GENERAL UNDER ICE PROTO- COL FOR 688 CLASS SUBS.
    5. STAY WITHIN COMMUNICATION DISTANCE OF SWORDFISH OR DRUM AT ALL TIMES.
    6. IN EVENT OF EMERGENCY REQUIRING SNOR- KELING OR SURFACING, COMMUNICATE WITH SWORDFISH OR DRUM BY WHATEVER MEANS AVAILABLE.

7. THE MOST OPPORTUNE OF EITHER SWORDFISH OR DRUM WILL APPROACH SAN FRANCISCO AND BREAK UP THE LOCAL ICE CANOPY.

11. GOOD LUCK AND GOD'S SPEED!

TOP SECRET...TOP SECRET

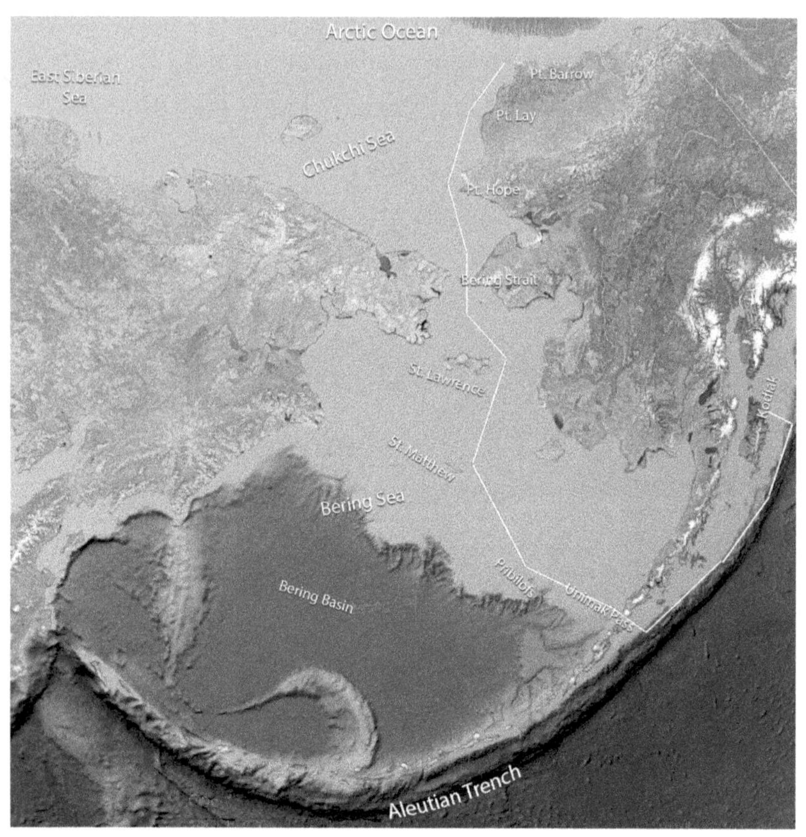

USS Teuthis transits from Kodiak Island to Pt. Barrow

CHAPTER FOUR—Transit to Pt. Barrow

USS TEUTHIS—A THOUSAND FOOT LEDGE ABOVE ALEUTIAN TRENCH

The continental slope dropped over several miles from 300 feet to over 20,000 feet at the bottom of the Aleutian Trench. It was not exactly a cliff, but the trench's shoreward side was cut with canyon that made Arizona's Grand Canyon seem puny by comparison.

We conducted a slow, careful search with our secure depth-sounder, a device that used spread-spectrum sound to give us an image of the bottom beneath our keel. We located a nice, steep slope facing east with a nearly flat, thirty-yard ledge at 1,000 feet.

Although we still were at ultra-quiet, the skipper had Waverly hover the sub 100 feet above the ledge and told him to prepare for fish-ops.

I took Kate down to Dive Control so she could observe the operation. We headed aft on the starboard side to the back of the Operations Compartment, dropped down a ladder well through the gyrostabilizer room to the Dive Control Center (DCC). Senior Chief Ocean Tech Morris Jones, everyone called him Spook, was there with his team preparing to launch the Fish.

I took Kate to the nest in the outer bulkhead that held the sidescan sonar tethered array. "We call this the Fish," I told her quietly, pointing to the three-foot-long torpedo-shaped device. We launch it here and feed it power through this cable. We guide it in a pattern over the bottom, and it transmits the image it receives from its sidescan array back to us. It prints out here." I showed her the thermal printer.

Because we still were at ultra-quiet, there was no announcement from the Control to commence Fish ops. Instead, the order was transmitted over sound-powered phones to First Class Ocean Tech Derrick Jensen, the team's junior guy. Chief Ocean Tech Francis Oberst, our Fish specialist, and First Class Ocean Tech Wally Dubbs set up the Fish and launched it, doing their level best to make no noise at all.

"We're doing a quick bottom survey," Spook told us, "to make sure the floor of the ledge is clear for bottoming the sub."

The whole process took about forty minutes. Kate watched the thermal printer output with total fascination. "You can actually see every little pebble on the bottom," she exclaimed. "It's absolutely amazing!" Chief Oberst taped the printouts together while Wally and Derrick retrieved and stowed the Fish and took them to Control for the skipper. Kate and I followed.

The skipper examined the sidescan printout closely and chose a position about ten yards from the wall about equally spaced from the ends of the ledge.

"Bottom us here facing south," he told Waverly.

"Lower the skids to full extension," Waverly ordered his Chief of the Watch, Senior Chief Firecontrol Tech Ogden Winder (Oggy). Over the sound-powered phones, he ordered Spook to launch the Basketball.

"You want to go down to DCC to watch the Basketball launch or stay here with the big picture?" I asked Kate.

"Can we watch the launch and then come back here?" she asked. "Sure," I said, and we returned to DCC, where Wally was just getting ready to launch the Basketball. "Give Kate a minute to look at it," I told him.

"The Basketball has a TV camera, a bright light, and ducted thrusters," I showed her. "Wally or one of the other guys drives it from this console. The image can be placed on any monitor in the sub."

Kate watched Wally drive the Basketball up over *Teuthis* so he could look down over the starboard side that would be close to the rock wall.

"Okay," Waverly said over the sound-powered phone from Control, "keep that orientation while I bring us up to the wall."

Kate and I went back up to Control, where she watched Waverly lower the outboards, bring *Teuthis* down to within a few feet of the ledge surface, and then walk the sub sideways to starboard. The view from the Basketball was perfectly clear, as if we were looking through air. The light beam was invisible in the water column, appearing as a circle on the ledge's sandy surface.

Waverly took it slow, the skipper watching his every move. He's a pro. I had only admiration for how he handled the sub. He set us down gently, just ten yards from the wall.

"Flood five thousand pounds, so we're firmly pressed to the ledge," he told Oggy. "Secure Basketball ops," he told Spook. Then he turned to the skipper. "On the bottom, at one thousand twelve feet, thirty feet from the wall in the middle of the ledge, port side out, Captain."

"Very well," the skipper said. "Well done! Have everyone stand easy but alert. Tell Sonar to keep a careful watch for whatever is out there."

✳

With our port side facing the ocean, getting range information on a contact was straightforward, especially so because we were at ultra quiet. I stepped into Sonar with Kate and asked King to show us the BQQ-2 waterfall printout.

"These dark lines," I said, pointing to the waterfall display, "represent sound frequencies coming from *Los Angeles*. We receive these sounds along the length of *Teuthis*." I pointed to two identical lines that were separated by a small amount. "This represents the difference in arrival times of the sounds, or stated differently, their phase difference. From the width of this gap, King can calculate the range of *Los Angeles*."

King jumped in. "Since it takes special training to interpret these charts, I give the information to the Nav team, and they chart the position of whatever we are tracking."

"When *Los Angeles* is close enough," I added, "we'll hail her on the secure underwater telephone—the Secure Gertrude." Because of its classification, I could not tell Kate any more. Fortunately, she didn't ask.

We had about two hours before *Los Angeles* was sufficiently close to hail. Kate and I hung out in the Wardroom, drinking coffee and snacking, and sharing details about each other's backgrounds. Kate was a pragmatist. As a teen, she had learned to accept what life threw at her—if possible, to make the most of it. My landing in her life was an unexpected bombshell. And now she was here, her life completely disrupted. Jack, her one stable element, was gone from her life, possibly forever. And me? I entered her life like a whirlwind and blew it to pieces. Now I was headed back into the high Arctic while Kate was headed in the opposite direction. As the crow flies, we would be 3,500 miles apart, but if you followed the sea route from Pt. Barrow to Vallejo and thence by air to Washington, D.C., the distance was more like 6,000 miles. I concluded that I had not done her any favors, but I was careful not to tell her that.

Kate was filled with a child-like fascination toward everything around her. Me, *Teuthis*, the divers, the crew, the machines and equipment, playing cat and mouse with a Soviet sub and trawler, sitting on a ledge a thousand feet below the surface, her forthcoming transfer by DSRV to *Los Angeles*—Kate was having the time of her life.

MYSTIC—A THOUSAND FEET DEEP OVER THE ALEUTIAN TRENCH

Cmdr. Roken entered the Wardroom, waving at me to remain seated. He looked at Kate.

"It's time, Kate," he said. "*Los Angeles* is hovering out over the trench, about a quarter mile from us. Lieutenant Taggert and his crew are preparing *Mystic* to transport you to *Los Angeles*. I'm sending Mac with you to introduce you to Commander Desmond. He won't remain very long—just sufficient time to get you introduced and settled." The skipper smiled warmly. "I have really enjoyed having you aboard my submarine. I'm putting you in good hands, and Commander Desmond will make sure you are safely transferred into the care of the DIA.

"Be sure to take the clothing and toiletries that you received from Petty Officer Rivera with you."

"Thank you for your hospitality, and especially for keeping me safe," Kate said, stepping close to the skipper, wrapping her arms around his neck, and kissing him on his cheek.

The skipper blushed and smiled. "It was my honor."

✳

On our way to the Engine Room escape hatch that led to the *Mystic*, Kate stuck her head into Sonar. King was there. She hugged him warmly.

"Thank you for taking me under your wing. It was so exciting to learn a bit about sonar and what my Mac used to do."

King's black face crinkled and his eyes twinkled. "It was my pleasure."

We continued aft through the Ops Compartment, across the top of the Diving Operations Compartment, over the Cable Reel Compartment, and through the Auxiliary Machinery Compartment to the Engine Room. First Class Electronics Tech Parker Flanger was waiting for us at the escape trunk. He worked directly under Senior Chief Sonar Tech Gaspard Abelé, *Mystic's* senior technician. Flanger took Kate's bag that contained everything she owned and passed it through the hatch to Senior Chief Abelé.

Kate mounted the ladder through the escape trunk into *Mystic*. I followed directly behind her. I thought I detected her faint spicy odor, the same smell that lingered in the ivory cylinder she gave me the last time I left—the one containing her silk panties. Parting this time would be bitter-sweet—she would be safe, but we would be a world apart.

Teuthis had done enough DSRV ops by this time for the launch to be routine, except that Kate wanted to see everything. Bob Taggert was busy piloting, but Lt. Jim Deckhart, the second pilot, took the time to explain what was happening. He pointed to the display from the skirt seal cameras.

"The sub shut its hatches, and so did we. Now we have to flood the skirt so we can equalize and launch. Bob just released the latches on the frame." He pointed to another display that shifted from latch to latch. "Okay, we're equalized." He pointed to a gauge. *Mystic* rocked slightly, and Jim said, "We're underway."

Mystic lifted about fifteen feet above the deck and then turned to point in the general direction of *Los Angeles.*

"*Los Angeles* is transmitting a faint, spread spectrum signal in our direction," Jim told her.

A screen directly in front of Taggert flashed and then displayed a series of distorted lines that looked like a funnel constructed of wire. "*Los Angeles* is at the narrow end of that funnel," Jim said. "Bob will maneuver us until we are looking straight down the funnel. Then he will power forward to bring us to *Los Angeles.*" He checked a reading. "It looks like she's about a quarter mile distant."

When the display indicated that *Mystic* was 200 yards from *Los Angeles*, Taggert turned on its powerful lights. The water was crystal clear so that the beams were not visible. Jim pointed at the forward-looking camera screen. Out of the darkness, a shadowy shape began to emerge. Then the two beams of light hit the sail and the deck after the sail—moving circles of light without any apparent source.

"*Los Angeles*, *Mystic*, you're in my sights," Taggert sent over the secure circuit.

"Roger that, *Mystic*. We're at All Stop, hovering at one-zero-ze-ro-zero feet. You are go to attach to the collar."

Taggert brought the DSRV in at an angle until we were hovering exactly over the collar around the *Los Angeles* after escape hatch. Then he rotated *Mystic* until we were pointed essentially northwest, directly at *Teuthis.* We settled down, made a soft seal, pumped out the water in the skirt to establish a hard seal, and then equalized the pressure between the skirt and DSRV. Flanger opened the hatch to the skirt and then reached down through the skirt and pounded on the submarine hatch with a hammer.

With a slight hiss, the submarine hatch opened outward, pushing a bit of the sub's air into *Mystic*, because our internal pressure was a smidgen lower than the sub's. Kate wrinkled her nose. The smell would have been familiar to every B-girl in any joint frequented by submarine sailors—a mixture of exhaust fumes, diesel oil, stale tobacco, cooking smells, and sewer. A smell that meant *that* sailor had more jingle in his jeans.

Kate looked at me. "Let me go first," I told her and dropped through the skirt, down through the escape hatch gripping the polished, stainless rails, into the *Los Angeles* Engine Room. Kate followed more slowly, step by step. Then Flanger dropped her duffle bag through the hatch. I looked up at him.

"Shut the hatches, but maintain your seal," I told him. "I might be a half-hour or more."

✳

As I picked up Kate's bag, Cmdr. Desmond stepped through the hatch from the Auxiliary Room. He held out his hand.

"Commander Archibald Desmond." We shook. Then he addressed Kate. "So you are the young woman who has been placed under my protection." His eyes twinkled as Kate shook his hand firmly. "Please join me in my cabin," he told us.

The captain led the way with Kate in tow. I followed with her bag. As we passed through the boat, sailors stopped what they were doing and stared until I glowered at them, and they returned their eyes to their work.

"*Los Angeles* is a very much modernized version of *Teuthis*," the captain said to Kate, "without her special equipment. *Teuthis* is a special operations sub. We are a kick-ass fighting boat—perhaps the best in the world."

We passed through the reactor tunnel into the Ops Compartment. "We'll let you experience some of what goes on in here before our trip is done," the captain told Kate.

We continued forward past Sonar and Radio to the Captain's Cabin.

"Where's the Wardroom?" Kate asked.

"It's one deck down," the Captain told her, "directly below the Control Center."

The captain's quarters were arranged much like on *Teuthis*, except the couch was green Naugahyde instead of red. He indicated the couch, so

Kate and I took our places while the captain turned his desk chair around and backed it against the fold-up desk. He looked at me quizzically.

"I've heard things about you, Commander. Not sure what to believe."

"If it sounds too good to be true, then it probably is, Cap'n," I told him with a grin. "My team and I have had some lucky breaks."

"The way I hear it, you guys make your own breaks." He turned to Kate. "Tell me a bit about yourself, Miss Perry—or Mrs., which do you prefer?"

"Kate will do just fine, Captain."

Kate summarized what had happened in her life since meeting me on that fateful morning when Jack Petrikoff introduced us. She made no bones about our relationship. To my mild discomfort, she told him I was the best thing ever to have happened to her.

"I mean no disrespect to Josh," she said as she finished her tale, "but Mac," she reached over and squeezed my hand, "has healed my hurt and made me a whole woman."

Cmdr. Desmond lifted an eyebrow as he cocked his head toward me. "That's an awesome responsibility, especially with you headed in the opposite direction into the ice." He smiled warmly at Kate.

Turning to me, he said, "You've got some details for me." It was a statement, not a question.

"Yes, Sir," I said, handing him a brown envelope. "Here are the classified details."

I then gave him a rundown of what had happened, leaving out any details that Kate was not cleared to know.

Cmdr. Desmond looked warmly at Kate. "You've experienced more in the last year than most people do in a lifetime. You're safe here, and I will make sure you stay safe!"

I believed him.

✻

The captain's sound-powered phone chirped. He put it to his ear, listened carefully, and then said to me, "We need to get you and the *Mystic* out of here right now. *Shchuka* is getting closer. I want *Mystic* off my stern so I can maneuver to draw that bastard away from *Teuthis*."

Cmdr. Desmond stood, and we joined him. "I'll leave you two alone for a minute, but then, Mac, you need to hustle aft and get the hell off my boat!" He winked as he shut the door behind himself.

Kate threw her arms around my neck, pressed her body against me, kissing me passionately. "You're my whole world!" she said through tears. "You do what you have to, but you come back to me… do you hear me?"

USS TEUTHIS—BERING SEA

Mystic lifted off *Los Angeles'* stern, and Taggert reported the DSRV clear. Immediately, *Los Angeles* dropped to 1,200 feet and accelerated to the northeast at flank speed.

Soviet sonar was not able to identify individual ships from their sound patterns as we could. The range at which they could acquire a sub was about half ours, even at two-thirds or full speed. Flank, however, was a different matter. When *Los Angeles* went to flank, the sonar guys on *Shchuka* heard her immediately. Their problem was that if *Shchuka* went to flank to match speed, she would lose the use of her sonar.

By the time *Mystic* returned to *Teuthis* and locked down, the Nav watch had figured out what probably had transpired. Instead of giving chase, *Shchuka* had waited until she could develop distance, course, and speed for *Los Angeles*—from her point of view, the probable American sub. Once *Shchuka* had a good sense of where the American sub was headed, she kicked her own speed to flank in pursuit.

I suspect that Cmdr. Desmond ran at flank for several hours and then set ultra-quiet at about ten knots. When *Shchuka* slowed to check the American sub position, *Los Angeles* would have vanished. In the meantime, we would be well on our way to Unimak Pass.

✳

This winter, the ice canopy stretched south to the Aleutian chain. Consequently, the normal tanker and container ship traffic through Unimak Pass had stopped.

On a globe, the Bering Sea looks like a giant rocking horse with the Aleutians forming an oversized rocker and the water near Bering

Strait forming the head. The head and body of the rocking horse are relatively shallow, never more than a few hundred feet at most. The open space between the legs is called the Bering Basin. It drops down to over 12,000 feet. The Pribilof Islands, St. George and St Paul, sit near the southeastern drop-off into the basin.

In the summer, the Bering Sea is mostly ice-free, at least to St. Mathew Island. In that condition, like any other ocean, beneath the surface it's mostly quiet except for sealife sounds, especially near the ice edge. It's noisier there anyway because the ice itself makes a lot of noise. Wind-driven waves break up the ice along the edge, causing ice chunks to grind against each other. This is just plain noisy.

You would think that an ice canopy would quiet the surrounding water. Compared to the ice edge, it is quieter, but it's a very noisy place compared to the open ocean. The Bering Sea ice canopy is not a static cover like the roof of a large building. Instead, it is a flexible, frangible surface in constant motion. It cracks with cannon-like explosive sounds, and the constant movement of the surface, driven by wind, current, and wave action, causes pieces of ice to form ridges that push both upward and down below the canopy.

Teuthis carried an under-ice sonar atop her sail, basically a high-frequency, upward-looking sonar for examining the undersurface and thickness of overhead ice. We depended on this anytime we were beneath the ice canopy relatively close to the underside of the ice.

With *Mystic* attached to our stern, we could not just push the sail through the canopy to get a sat fix as we might normally do. This could seriously damage *Mystic's* fiberglass hull. Instead, we had to take a significant up-angle, push our bow through the ice, and then carefully push the sail through without ever letting *Mystic* come into contact with the ice. If necessary, *Mystic* would have to dismount and stand by below the ice while we pushed through to get our fix.

With *Mystic* on our stern, we were limited to ten knots and had to be careful when approaching the ice canopy. To ensure that we were not being followed, we cleared baffles once every hour randomly. To do this, we slowed and turned radically right or left by a coin flip, so Sonar could check what was directly behind us. This maneuver added fifteen minutes to every hour of travel. Unimak Pass was 575 nautical miles from the ledge off Kodiak. With the extra fifteen minutes each hour, our total time at ten knots was three days. *Teuthis* had four watch sections standing six-hour watches, so each section stood the same six hours every twenty-four hours.

Consequently, the passage from the Kodiak ledge to Unimak Pass consumed three watch cycles with the fourth section on watch while transiting the pass. The Navigator (Nav), Lt. Cmdr. Barry Jacobs and his Watch Section Three got us underway from the ledge. I and my Watch Section One were on watch just before Unimak Pass. The Weapons Officer (Weaps), Lt. Waverly Denver and his Watch Section Two took us through the pass.

We were right on the edge of the continental shelf, where the bottom dropped to over 22,000 feet in the Aleutian Trench. I had just cleared baffles—Sonar heard nobody. Once we had departed the ledge, we remained on ultra-quiet for a complete six-hour watch. Sonar picked up nothing during that watch, so we went back to normal operation. I checked the under-ice sonar. There were occasional ice pads, some brash, and even a larger floe or two, but the surface was mostly open water and about as calm as it gets up here in the winter.

I called the skipper on the regular phone system. "It's the Officer of the Deck, Sir, Mac. We need to get a sat fix. In about fifteen minutes, we'll have two birds above the horizon." I briefed him on the surface conditions.

The skipper came out to Control, checked things personally, and then told me to get the fix, but to keep a ten-degree-up angle on the boat as insurance.

"Chief of the Watch," I ordered, "make your depth one-zero-zero feet." Once we were at one hundred feet, I said, "Helmsman, All Stop." And then, "Diving Officer, ten-degree up-bubble. We're going to hover with the ten-degree up-bubble." To the COW, I said, "Chief of the Watch, using ballast, make your depth six-five feet, and hover." After about five minutes, Chief Torpedoman Jasper Cedrik (we called him Tubes), my Diving Officer, announced, "At ten-degree up-bubble."

Senior Chief Engineman Sam Dokey, my COW, announced, "Hovering at six-five feet."

"Okay, now listen up!" I said. "Using ballast, ease us up until I can take a visual round with the attack scope."

"Al," I said to Senior Chief Forbes, "get your satnav antenna up and get your fix ASAP."

I raised the scope and pointed it aft. We broke the surface slowly. It was pitch dark, but we were surrounded by a faint phosphorescence that allowed me to see there were no ice floes or pads near us. The antenna cleared the water.

"Hold it there, Senior Chief," I said as the skipper raised the nav scope and swung it around twice before lowering it.

Ten minutes later, Al announced that he had his fix.

"Chief of the Watch," I said, "using ballast, make your depth one-ze-ro-zero feet. Diving Officer, zero bubble." I turned to Al. "What's your recommended course?"

"Two-eight-zero," he said.

"Helmsman," I ordered, "ahead two-thirds, make your course two-eight-zero." I called Maneuvering on the sound-powered phone. "Make turns for ten knots," I said.

✳

We worked our way through the shallow water at the pass and then turned toward the Pribilof Islands. Our route would take us to the north of the Pribilofs, 174 nautical miles distant. I had the watch when we arrived twenty-two hours later. Just before passing the watch to Waverly, I set course for St. Matthew Island, 245 nautical miles distant.

On my watch, thirty-one hours later, we turned toward St. Lawrence Island, that lay 200 nautical miles ahead, between us and Bering Strait. Fourteen hours later, on Lt. Cmdr. Franklin James' Section Four Watch, Sonar picked up two submerged contacts, *Shchuka* and *Carp*. We had tangled with *Carp* previously off Pt. Barrow. My divers forced a reactor scram by feeding liquid paraffin into *Carp's* coolant intakes, where it solidified. She surfaced and then headed for the barn at Petropavlovsk-Kamchatskiy.

Apparently, *Carp* was back and had hooked up with *Shchuka* in the deep water of the Bering Basin. They appeared to be headed toward Bering Strait at fifteen knots. They were blind as bats at this speed, but they would pass through the strait before us. So, it was likely they would be hanging around the *Alfa* when we arrived.

Waverly had just assumed the watch again eleven hours later when we arrived thirty-three nautical miles east of St. Lawrence Island in 116 feet of water with three feet of ice overhead. We needed to update the SIMS with a sat fix before we passed through Bering Strait. Because of the water depth, the skipper decided to detach *Mystic* before pushing through the canopy.

The process was simple enough. *Mystic* detached from her cradle while we hovered at eighty feet. Then she stood off 200 yards while we did a standard ice canopy penetration for three feet of ice—basically, with the fairwater planes turned vertical, we rose and bumped the ice with our sail. That cracked the ice sufficiently to allow us to extend the satnav antenna for a fix. Then we dropped back down to eighty feet, where *Mystic* returned to her cradle and latched in. The entire operation took two hours.

We arrived at the southern end of the Bering Strait transit channel at the start of my watch sixteen hours later, and in three more hours were carefully passing through the shallow waters of the strait.

USS TEUTHIS—BERING STRAIT TO PT. BARROW

Our transit's next leg took us past Point Hope, where we had laid the last SOSUS array forty-five nautical miles west of the point.

This was a twenty-hour trip through mostly shallow water, so we had to watch ourselves carefully. Franklin finished this leg and stopped for another satnav fix like the last one, with Mystic standing off 200 yards while he cracked through the canopy and got the fix. Then he commenced the next leg to Point Lay, fifteen hours ahead. I took over after the fix for the fifteen-hour-leg to Point Lay, and Barry started us on the final twenty-five-hour push to Pt. Barrow.

For the entire two days and sixteen hours from the strait, Sonar was on high alert for *Shchuka* and *Carp*. We knew they were up here, but noisy ice conditions made detecting them difficult. During the tenth hour of the final leg, I was relaxing in the skipper's chair on the periscope stand, watching over my crew while Seth actually managed the watch. We were cruising along at eighty feet, just forty feet over the bottom. Because we had already traveled this route several times, we were comfortable at ten knots, even this close to the bottom. I slowed for the hourly baffle clear and stood by for Sonar's report.

"Conn, Sonar," King announced over the circuit, "I've got *Carp* just off the port bow at zero-seven-five." "Roger, *Carp* off the port bow," Seth responded.

King continued. "If you can give me a beam aspect, he is sufficiently clear that I can get a range."

I nodded to Seth, and he turned west and slowed to bare steerageway.

I was just about to call Sonar when King announced, "Conn, Sonar, *Carp* bears zero-seven-eight at one-seven-eight nautical miles. He seems to be pretty much holding position."

My quartermaster, Al, said, "That puts him right over the drop into the Arctic Basin, on a bearing of zero-three-two, forty-nine miles from the *Alfa*."

I stepped over to look at his chart as the skipper joined me. Then he stepped into Sonar.

"Anything on *Shchuka*?" he asked King.

"Nothing, Sir, but she's quieter than *Carp*—a lot quieter." "Continue on track, Mac, but keep a close eye on *Carp*." He turned to King. "King, do your best to find *Shchuka*."

✳

At our next baffle clear, Sonar reported, "Conn, Sonar, I have a new submarine contact bearing due west with a right bearing drift, designate Sierra-three."

"Roger, Sonar. I'll slow to bare steerageway so you can get a range," Seth said since Sierra-3 was on our port beam.

Ten minutes later, Sonar told us, "Sierra-three bears two-seven-en-one at one-five-six nautical miles, on a course of zero-eight-zero." King paused and then said, "Lieutenant Beaumont, Sierra-three is the *USS San Francisco*!"

"Looks like he's heading for *Carp's* position," Al said.

I called the skipper, and a few moments later, he joined us on the periscope stand. "The Dev Group told me they would try to get us some help," he said. "It looks like the cavalry has arrived."

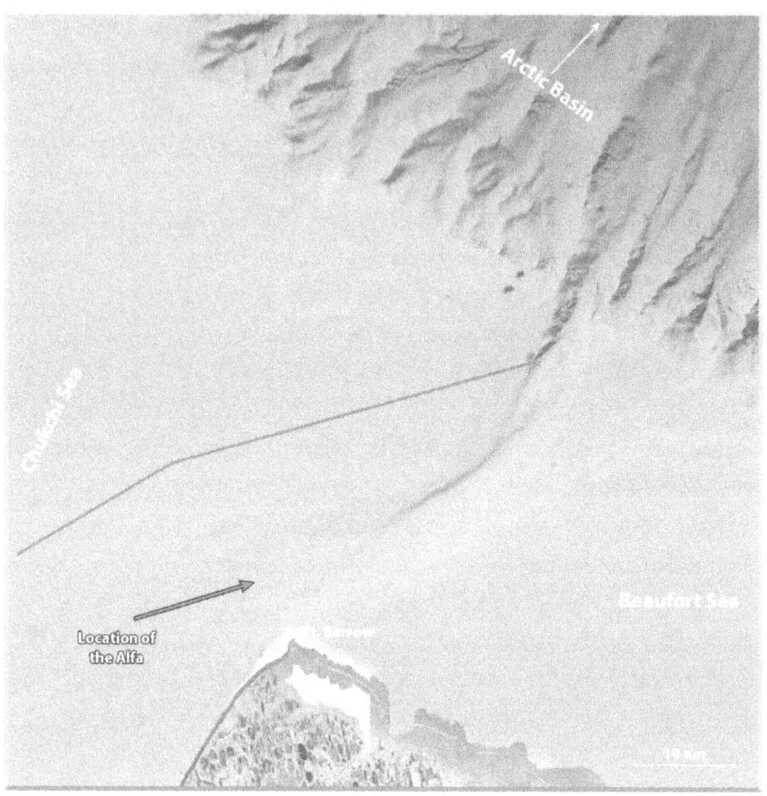

USS Teuthis transits from off Pt. Barrow to canyon on edge of Arctic Basin

CHAPTER FIVE—The Chase

USS TEUTHIS—PT. BARROW

We needed a couple of days on the bottom with the *Alfa* to ready her for the Arctic passage to Electric Boat. That would be difficult with *Carp* and potentially *Shchuka* looking over our shoulder. *San Francisco* would be a big help, diverting *Carp's* attention away from anything we might do. The skipper wanted another layer of protection, however. He called me to his cabin, where he had laid out a chart on the deck.

"Your divers did an excellent job of placing the transponder at the base of Hecla and Fury Island in the Gulf of Boothia," the skipper told me. "I want to do something similar here." He pointed to a spot northeast of Pt. Barrow, where the continental shelf dropped off steeply into the Arctic Basin. "When we completed sea trials in Hudson Canyon off New York City, we knew exactly where the canyon was, how long and how deep. Up here," he smiled ruefully, "our knowledge is pretty skimpy."

The skipper pointed to a penciled-in tongue-like shape extending for twenty miles from the shelf break toward Pt. Barrow. "We believe this canyon exists based on several soundings over the years. If it is there, we can slip into it, and your divers can place another transponder that will tend to keep *Carp* and *Shchuka* away from our activities."

"How deep is the canyon?" I asked.

"We know the Arctic Basin is deeper than twelve thousand feet," the skipper said. "The shelf break is fairly sharp, and the slope is steeper than most. This would imply a fairly deep canyon, estimating about five hundred feet here," he pointed to a spot halfway between the break and Pt. Barrow, "three thousand feet here," he pointed to where the canyon cut the break, "and six thousand feet here deepening to twelve," his pencil trailed along the chart in the general direction of the canyon into the Arctic Basin.

"It's doable, Sir. How deep do you wish to place the transponder?"
"I was thinking close to a thousand feet."

"That presents a problem, Skipper. My guys will press down to five hundred feet to service the *Alfa*. If we take them down to a thousand feet, it will be five days before they can dive at five hundred feet. We could split them into two groups, but the DDC has beds in only one lock, so that's not very practical."

We sat quietly while the skipper considered his options. I interrupted his thoughts. "We have another option, Sir. We can hover at five hundred feet in the canyon where my guys can attach the *Mystic's* manipulator. Then Lt. Taggert can find the best location for the transponder, even deeper than a thousand feet if you wish."

The skipper called Control and told Barry to have Bob Taggert report to the Captain's Cabin.

✳

"Yes, Sir," Bob Taggert said as he entered the door.

The skipper indicated that he sit on the couch next to me. The skipper briefly summarized our discussion, ending with, "Can we do this? Can *you* do this?"

"Mac's divers have never attached the manipulator, but the task is simple. If anyone can do it without prior training, it's these guys." He looked at me with a grin. "For what it's worth, Captain, I've never seen a group of guys pull off the kinds of stuff these guys do…and make it look so easy."

I grinned back. "Lots of training, and too dumb to know better."

"Seriously," the skipper interjected, "we all know what your guys can do. There's a reason for the accolades…and the reputation." He turned to Taggert. "So, you think this can work?"

"I do."

USS TEUTHIS—BEAUFORT SEA

Barry set course for the canyon—or at least where we thought it was. Six hours later, five hours into Franklin's watch, the bottom began to drop off significantly. Franklin slowed to five knots and ran the first of three reciprocal three-and-a-half-nautical-mile legs parallel to the shelf break while running the secure depth-sounder. I picked up the second leg. The legs were a nautical mile apart, stepping to the northeast toward the Arctic Basin. On leg three, the bottom dropped off to 2,000 feet over a nautical-mile-wide swath. We had our canyon. While Franklin and I ran the search, Ham pressed the divers, including Sergyi, down to 500 feet. They brought the articulated manipulator arm with them into the DDC.

✳

As Ham was settling into a watch routine with the divers under pressure, the skipper showed up in Dive Control with Franklin in tow and a rolled-up chart in his hand. The XO assumed my watch, so I could join them.

"We need to determine how best to place the transponder," the skipper said. "We know virtually nothing about this large gash in the continental slope." He rolled out the chart on the table and turned to Franklin.

"Commander James, we're going to hover at eight hundred feet near the center of the canyon, here." He pointed to the center of his penciled-in addition to the chart he had discussed with Taggert and me in his cabin. "Run your survey across the canyon, starting here and ending here." He indicated a point down the canyon. When we reach fifteen hundred feet of canyon depth, we'll terminate the survey."

"We'll run the fish at thirty feet doing ten knots, making thirty-five-foot swaths," Franklin said. "I'm anticipating runs of less than a mile, and I suspect the canyon drops rather quickly. Nevertheless, Captain, we better schedule at least eight hours for the survey."

USS TEUTHIS—BEAUFORT SEA CANYON

Six hours later, two hours into Waverly's watch, the bottom dropped off at 1,700 feet, and the skipper stopped the survey. My guys had reached 500 feet and were comfortably acclimatized, although not yet fully saturated. After examining the manipulator arm for several minutes, they spent the rest of their time working on their submarine quals.

The skipper and Franklin pored over the fish readouts looking for the ideal spot to put the transponder. They found it at 1,100 feet on the north canyon wall about a hundred feet from the bottom. The transponder would sit against a formation that would reflect its sounds in both directions along the canyon. And it would be virtually impossible to locate without either an appropriately outfitted deep submersible or saturated divers from a sub lockout system.

While Ham and my divers were prepping to commence their mid-water installation of *Mystic's* manipulator arm, Waverly brought us to a mid-canyon hover at 500 feet, a hundred feet below the canyon's edge. This masked most of our sound except that which was funneled in both directions along the canyon. Because we were at ultra-quiet, we were not producing much sound anyway.

I was not entirely certain why the DSRV arrived with the manipulator arm in the spare parts bin. Taggert told me that it had developed a problem several months ago, and our Ice Breaker[9] mission[9] interrupted his repairs. His guys had been working on it on and off since then. Chief Machinist Mate Robert Daley played an important role, manufacturing several precision parts that gave the manipulator arm its functionality. I learned this from Chief Warrant Officer Bert Cobb, Chief Daley's boss, during one of our late-night discussions over coffee in the Wardroom. Bert and I were mustangs—we both had come up through the ranks. This gave us a common bond lacking with a typical Ringknocker or ROTC officer.

✳

On the 1MC: "This the captain. We will shortly commence both dive ops and *Mystic* ops. We will not go to ultra-quiet, but I want each of you to go about your tasks as quietly as possible. We are especially vulnerable during these ops."

✳

To ensure that our operations at the *Alfa* site went as smoothly as possible, I decided to press down the entire dive team, including Sergyi, as I mentioned. As time passed, things would be a bit crowded in the DDC, but our efficiency at the *Alfa* site would get us out of there and away from the lurking Soviet subs more quickly.

Bill was in charge of the dive under Ham's eagle eye. During this underway, our in-water operations would be Bill's final test before we certified him as a Master Saturation Diver—one of a very elite club of specialists.

USS TEUTHIS—BEAUFORT SEA CANYON

Before *Mystic* launched or the divers exited the DDC, we deployed the Basketball. This tethered ROV with six-way thrusters and a TV camera, a bit larger than its namesake, allowed the Officer of the Deck in Control and the officer in charge of the operation (usually me) to follow visually what was happening in the water.

---

9 *See Operation Ice Breaker,* the second book in the *Mac McDowell Mission Series.*

Submarines normally operate without visual input. Without the Basketball, Ivy Bells could not have happened. Without the Basketball, our Ice Breaker array-laying operations would have been severely hampered, and we could not have made it through the Prince of Wales Strait. It would be physically possible to conduct our current *Mystic* and div ops without the Basketball, but being able to see in Control what is happening in the water makes the job much easier. Later, as we transit the Arctic with the *Alfa*, having the basketball will be critical.

Derrick Jensen was on tap to drive the Basketball. He eased it out of its berth and moved it up over the side to the deck just aft of the sail. In Dive Control, and two decks above us in Control, the Basketball view displayed on monitors. Additionally, Waverly sent the feed to other monitors scattered throughout the sub.

We watched Taggert detach *Mystic* and set her to hover thirty feet above *Teuthis'* after deck. Derrick moved the Basketball with *Mystic*, and focused on the skirt. I signaled Ham, and Bill deployed Harry, Jer, and Jake on umbilicals, and Sergyi on a rebreather. With my approval, Bill decided to keep Ski back to let him continue healing, and Whitey to give Jake more in-water time. We usually kept Jimmy in reserve in case something went wrong, so we would have medical expertise immediately available.

Derrick brought the Basketball back under the sub so we could observe the divers enter the water and wrestle the manipulator through the hatch. Because the arm was negatively buoyant, Jake attached a small float bag to its pivot point, and Sergyi carefully filled it from a high-pressure air hose Ski passed to him through the hatch. Retrieving a dropped manipulator arm from the bottom was possible where we were, but it would have set us back at least six days.

Derrick followed the divers closely as they swam the arm up to *Mystic* and tied it off to the forward shock absorber on the skirt. Taggert had extended the manipulator mechanism as far as possible. The divers needed to bolt the arm to the extended plate and then plug the waterproof power and signal plug into the socket. Derrick kept the work area brightly illuminated. As the senior diver, Harry floated a couple feet away to keep the whole task in view. Jer and Sergyi pivoted the arm so the pieces lined up, and Jake bolted it in place. Then he connected power and control. About a half-hour after they arrived at

Mystic, Harry told Dive Control they were finished, his squeaky voice distorted by helium and pressure.

Exercising due diligence, Bill had Derrick move in for a close-up look at the completed task while the four divers backed off.

"Hold it!" Bill ordered. Ham nudged him, and he repeated his order using proper protocol. "Stop!" Bill said clearly and distinctly over the circuit. Seldom used, this order caused everything to freeze—divers, tools, equipment, the console, everything.

Ham looked at me with a question in his eyes. Obviously, Bill had seen something.

"Harry," Bill said, "follow Jake's umbilical from his attachment point for several yards."

He did, and to everyone's surprise, it passed between the lead to the watertight connector and the manipulator arm. Stowing the arm would have pulled Jake's umbilical into the mechanism, probably tearing the lead, and possibly cutting the umbilical.

"Nice save," I said quietly to Bill. "Fix it," Bill told them.

While Harry and Jake hung a couple of feet away, Jer reached into the mechanism, untwisted the connector retaining ring, and pulled it loose. Sergyi handed him a tube of silicone grease. Jer squeezed the silicone into the socket until all the water that had flooded into it had been displaced. He pressed down on the silicone to force any remaining pockets of water out. Then he passed the plug under the umbilical and checked to ensure it was no longer tangled. Jake moved to the side, and Sergyi pulled his umbilical out of the way. Jer pressed the plug into the socket under Derrick's watchful eye and twisted the retaining ring with a grunt.

Bill backed off the divers, and Control took over. Waverly picked up the Secure Gertrude handset. "*Mystic*, this is *Teuthis*, over."

The response was immediate. "*Teuthis*, this is *Mystic*, over."

There was none of the echoing, warbling sound one associates with underwater telephone transmissions. The response was crisp, clear, and fully intelligible.

"*Mystic*, this is *Teuthis*. Installation of the manipulator arm is complete. Test at your discretion."

"Roger that. I've been observing on my skirt TV camera."

Taggert ran the arm through a series of programmed steps that tested its extension, arc, and articulation.

"Can you give me something to grasp?" Taggert asked.

Barry, who had just assumed the watch from Waverly, passed the request to me. I told Bill. He had Ski pass a large box-wrench to Harry, who had returned to the hatch at Bill's request.

"Tie it off with a piece of line in case Lt. Taggert drops it," Bill told him.

We watched on the monitor as Harry held out the wrench, and the manipulator gently took it from his hand. Taggert then put the arm through its paces again, this time holding the wrench. When he finished, the manipulator placed the wrench into Harry's hand. Harry grabbed it, and the manipulator tried to pull it away. When Harry resisted, the manipulator released the wrench.

"I wanted to make sure the diver had a tight grip before I let go," Taggert told Control.

❋

The divers had not taken the transponder with them when they pressed down because Franklin wanted to run a final test just before deployment. He ran the test with Spook while we tested the manipulator arm. As we finished the test, Spook handed the transponder to Ham. It had a bright white stripe running down its length.

"This baby will return pings with appropriate delay and doppler and will emit propeller and sub sounds when it picks up similar noise.

It can simulate an increasing or decreasing range and is powered by an RTG[10] with a lifespan of at least fifty years," Spook said.

While Bill called Harry back to the hatch once more, Ham passed the transponder into the DDC through the medical lock and called in some instructions. Ski passed the transponder to Harry and indicated that he should place it into the manipulator grip with the white stripe facing inward.

Harry headed back to the DSRV manipulator and waved the Basketball closer. Taggert opened the grip, and Harry placed the transponder into it with the white stripe facing the hinge, and Taggert closed the grip around the transponder. Before releasing the

---

10 Radioisotope Thermoelectric Generator. An electricity-generating device that uses an array of thermocouples to convert the heat released by the decay of suitable radioactive material into electricity. This generator has no moving parts.

transponder, Harry waved the Basketball even closer, pointing to the white stripe. Franklin examined the image on the monitor and gave his approval.

"Let *Mystic* have it," Bill said, and Harry released his grip and backed away.

✳

As the divers returned to the DDC, *Mystic* turned, moved a hundred feet away from *Teuthis*, tilted ten degrees down, and headed for the bottom, six hundred feet below.

Once the divers were back inside the DDC with the hatch closed, and once the Basketball was back in its cradle, I informed Barry in Control. He dropped *Teuthis* slowly until we hovered 200 feet above the canyon bottom, pointed toward the deep end of the canyon. Wally, who had taken over from Derrick, relaunched the Basketball.

As we watched, *Mystic* moved slowly and deliberately along the canyon wall off our port side until Taggert located the spot the skipper and Franklin had picked to deposit the transponder. Through the Basketball, we saw a small ledge jutting out from the wall no more than two feet. The wall behind the ledge was slightly V-shaped, with a vertical crack running up from the ledge. The crack was just a bit wider than the transponder. Slowly and carefully, Taggert slid the transponder along the ledge into the crack. He released the grip carefully and then used it to press the transponder into the crack about halfway. When he pulled the manipulator back, the white stripe ran from top to bottom along the transponder's exposed face.

"*Mystic*, this is *Teuthis*," Barry said over the Secure Gertrude, "excellent job. Now, return to *Teuthis*."

✳

"Conn, Sonar," Petty Officer Second Class Benny Simms, Watch Section Sonar Supervisor, announced from Sonar, "I have an intermittent submerged contact bearing two-eight-five, designate Sierra-four. It's the transponder, Sir. It sounds like a genuine sub at some distance, Sir, fading in and out."

Barry looked at the skipper and then responded, "Scrub the designation. Call it *Transponder-one* from now on." He looked at his Chief of the Watch, Chief Electrician William Panner. "Potts, set condition ultra-quiet…quietly."

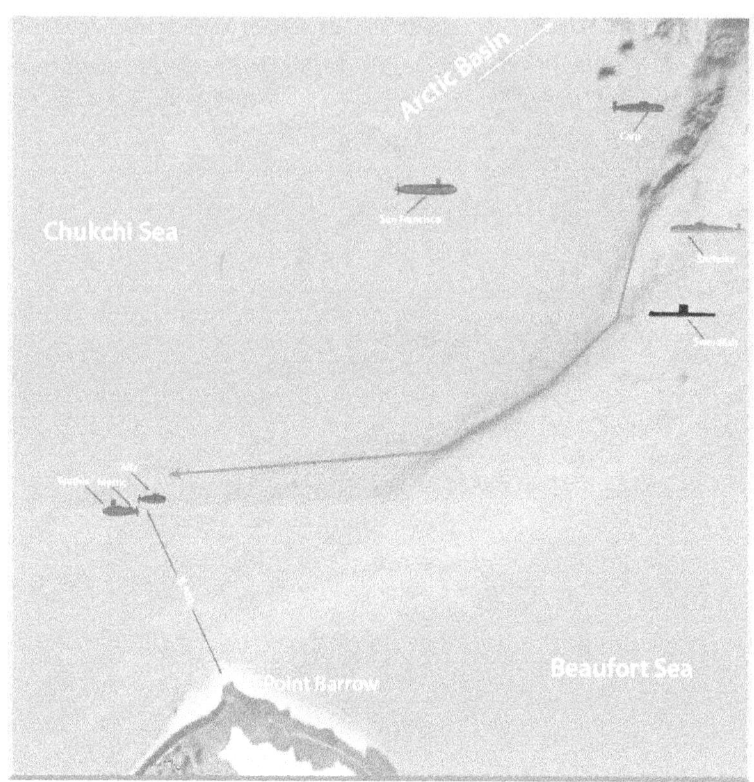

USS Teuthis transits from Arctic Basin canyon to the hole off Pt. Barrow

CHAPTER SIX—Alfa Preps

USS TEUTHIS—PT. BARROW

We were about forty-three nautical miles northeast of the *Alfa* and wanted to get there absolutely undetected. We were still below the canyon rim, but we knew that both *Carp* and *Shchuka* were somewhere nearby trying to ferret out our location. We also knew that *Frisco* was ready to draw both Soviet subs away from us. Barry eased *Teuthis* above the canyon rim so Sonar could get a good picture of what was out there.

"Conn, Sonar," Benny reported over the sound-powered phone, "I have four contacts. Sierra-three, the *Frisco*, is at two-seven-three. New contact bearing three-five-zero, designate Sierra-four. New contact bearing one-one-five, designate Sierra-five. New contact bearing one-six-three, designate Sierra-six. If you can remain here on this heading for ten minutes, I can give you more specific info."

Ten minutes later, Sonar reported, "*Frisco* bears two-seven-three at thirteen nautical miles, Sierra-four bears three-five-zero at seven nautical miles. Sierra-four is the *Carp*. At this distance, if we make any noise, she can hear us. Sierra-five bears one-one-five at five nautical miles. Sierra-five is the *Shchuka*. Ditto for *Shchuka*; she has better sonar than *Carp*. Sierra-six bears one-six-three at nine nautical miles. Sierra-six is the *USS Swordfish*."

"More cavalry," the skipper said with a satisfied smile. He was in Control closely monitoring the tactical situation, speaking quietly with Barry from time to time. I hung out in the open doorway to the Sonar Shack, where I could observe what was happening in both Control and Sonar. I figured every minute I could be near the skipper as he made tactical decisions was a minute well spent.

Barry, as Navigator, had laid out his best estimate of the canyon's position between us and the *Alfa*. The skipper wanted to remain below the canyon rim while following Barry's track. His thought was that the canyon would channel the transponder sounds both ways. *Frisco* and *Swordfish* would discourage the two Soviet subs from closing our position in the shallowing canyon while encouraging them to follow the sound toward the Arctic Basin. It seemed like a pretty good plan.

Barry dropped down below the canyon rim and put *Teuthis* on a course of 237 degrees at five knots. We were on the batteries at ultra-quiet. You could not have heard us a hundred yards away. The canyon curved generally to the right. Barry kept the secure depth-sounder running to make sure we didn't accidentally run into the canyon's northwestern wall, although as we progressed, the wall became more of a slope than a wall. Barry spent the entire remaining five hours of his watch creeping along the canyon's northwestern wall, staying below the rim. Early in the morning, two hours into Franklin's watch and just eight nautical miles from the *Alfa*, the skipper had him peek over the rim for a sonar survey.

"Conn, Sonar," Second Class Sonar Tech Don Forge, Section Four sonar supervisor, announced over the sound-powered phone, "*Frisco* bears zero-three-two at nineteen miles; Sierra-four, the *Carp*, bears zero-four-three at twenty-four miles; Sierra-five, the *Shchuka*, bears zero-four-five at twenty-six miles; and Sierra-six, the *Swordfish*, bears zero-six-two at twenty-two miles."

Franklin passed the contact information to Second Class Quartermaster Jubal Henshaw, the watch section navigator. Henshaw drew lines on his chart for a couple of minutes and then looked up.

"What do you have, Juby?" Franklin asked.

"It looks like *Frisco* and *Swordfish* are herding the Soviet boats down the canyon, Sir."

Both the skipper and Franklin stepped over to the chart table. "It sure looks that way," the skipper said.

I checked it out once they returned to the periscope stand. It was a pretty picture. *Carp* and *Shchuka* were following the transponder sound down the canyon, while *Frisco* and *Swordfish* guarded our back door.

USS TEUTHIS—BOTTOMED AT THE ALFA

Franklin brought us to the 500-foot hole off Pt. Barrow and crossed it northeast to southwest while Juby tracked the bottom on the secure depth-sounder. Halfway across the hole, Juby said, "I got it!"

He marked the position on his chart.

From his chair on the periscope stand, the skipper said, "Mr. James, take us down slowly and bottom us two hundred feet off the *Alfa*, starboard side to starboard side. Take your time. I want this to go as smoothly as possible."

As I turned to leave Control, the skipper gestured me over. "I've taken you off the Watchbill, Mac. We commence dive ops in about three hours. After that, you'll be getting ready to assume command of the *Alfa*."

ON THE SEAFLOOR—AT THE ALFA

I joined Ham in Dive Control to go over his dive plan. When we last left the *Alfa* what seemed like ages ago, the escape pod that normally formed part of the sail was still attached to the sail with a tether, but on its side next to the *Alfa*, flooded. A really close examination of the tether attachment inside the sail would have revealed that it had been detached and reattached, but we did not think it would have been that closely examined. In fact, the skipper doubted that anyone had visited the *Alfa* since we last left it.

Now, our job was to put the pieces back together so we could drive the *Alfa* out of the hole under its own power, and under the Arctic ice pack all the way to Electric Boat on the east shore of the Thames River in Connecticut.

Since the *Alfa's* reactor was useless, we would have to stop periodically to recharge her batteries using a shorepower cable brought from *Teuthis* with divers—something we would need to do every twenty-four hours. Once we were underway, we would want to surface our divers—a five-day task, and then try to do the battery charges at periscope depth to keep the divers from undergoing long decompressions.

Ham's plan was good, although I reminded him that plans tend to disintegrate once an operation commences. While we were discussing the plan, Control called on the sound-powered phone.

"This is the XO in Control. We're bottomed two hundred feet from the *Alfa*—starboard to starboard. You can deploy your divers when you are ready. As a reminder, we remain at ultra-quiet."

✳

Harry, Whitey, Jer, and Jake on umbilicals, and Sergyi on a rebreather, entered the water, trailing a high-pressure air hose and carrying four half-inch blended polypropylene lines. We did not know what size bubble would float the pod, so the divers intended to secure the pod to the *Alfa* sail before filling it with air. Wally illuminated their way with the Basketball.

The first order of business was to determine the orientation. By design, there were only two possible orientations. The pod lay on the bottom with its top pointed in the same direction as the *Alfa's* bow. When we flooded it and let it drop to the seafloor, it ended up with the port side facing up after a partial roll. This simplified our task. Harry and Sergyi attached lines to front and back anchor points on the exposed port side. Whitey and Jake attached the bitter ends of the lines to the sail so that when the pod lifted from the bottom, it would line up appropriately with its cradle in the sail. Harry and Sergyi attached the other two lines to starboard anchor points but left the bitter ends lying on the bottom. We would use those to stabilize the pod when it reached neutral buoyancy. Jer stood off several yards holding the HP air hose. In Dive Control, I activated my mike and said, "Harry, recheck each knot, not a cursory examination, but make sure all six knots will do their duty." Wally followed Harry, moving in for a close-up of each knot as Harry checked them.

"Okay, Jer," Bill told the divers, "commence adding air to the pod."

Making sure his umbilical was clear of the four lines, Jer swam to the pod base and commenced releasing air into the bottom hatch. Harry, backed up by Sergyi, grabbed the line attached to the starboard after anchor point. Whitey, backed up by Jake, grabbed the forward line. Then we waited.

The water pressure inside the pod, as on the outside, was about 237 psi. The HP air pressure was 4,000 psi. The pod was a slightly flattened sphere about eight feet in diameter with twenty-inch-wide trunks at top and bottom. Its internal volume was just under 300 cubic feet. I calculated the mass of the titanium in the pod at about 14,072 pounds. Based upon its volume, the pod's buoyant force was 18,720 pounds. When you run the numbers, it turns out that if the pod is one-quarter filled with water, it will be neutrally buoyant. The problem is that so long as the bottom hatch remains open, as you move the pod deeper, the air inside compresses, allowing more water to enter, making the pod heavier, forcing it deeper, compressing the air more...and so on.

Jer continuously filled the pod for more than a half-hour before we got any indication that the pod was nearing neutral buoyancy. Finally, it slowly tipped to vertical and then rose gently until it put a slight strain on the two attached lines. The divers holding onto the other two lines let them slip through their gloves until the pod floated just above the slot in the sail.

Harry and Sergyi retrieved two thick metal bars from their leg pockets and attached them to the port-side lines to shorten the lines by rolling them up on the bars. The strain caused by the pod was light enough that this was easily accomplished. As they slowly lowered the port side of the pod, Whitey and Jake pulled down on the starboard lines to keep the pod vertical. As they cranked the pod downward, increasing water pressure forced more water into the pod, making it less buoyant. They continued this process until the pod was floating two feet above the anchor points and was nearly at neutral buoyancy.

While they focused on the task, they did not notice the arrival of several narwhals and a couple of belugas. Their first awareness was when a particularly curious beluga rose off the bottom on the port side of the *Alfa* to examine closely what Sergyi was doing with his metal bar. The cetacean startled Sergyi so that he dropped his bar and then pulled down on it as he grabbed it again, cussing profusely in Ukrainian. His helium and pressure-modified stream of unintelligible words gave us no end of amusement in Dive Control. The sudden lowering of Sergyi's bar caused a sudden increase in water pressure at the hatch, and the pod suddenly became significantly heavier. Both Harry and Sergyi pushed away from the sail to avoid being trapped between the edges of the pod and sail. As the pod tilted to port, Whitey and Jake took a strain on their lines, digging their heels into the sandy bottom, forcing the pod back to vertical. Wally had backed the Basketball off to take in the larger picture. He focused first on Harry and Sergyi and then on Whitey and Jake.

As the events unfolded at the *Alfa*, we watched with bated breath in Dive Control, not saying anything that might distract the divers from regaining control of the situation.

As things seemed to be back under control, Bill asked, "Harry, what is your status?"

"Damn fool beluga knocked the bar out of Sergyi's hands," Harry squeaked. "He grabbed the bar and pulled it down…too far. We're okay now. We're going to close the hatch to keep this from happening again."

As he said this, Jer swam to the hatch with the HP hose still in his grip and secured it. The pod had a very small amount of positive buoyancy, keeping it out of the diver's way as they struggled to cinch the anchor lines.

I activated my mike. "Harry, is there an ingress access on the side of the sail?"

"I dunno," he squeaked, "Check it out, Jer."

"I found one, aft on the starboard side," Jer said. "My knife won't open it. Looks like it needs a T-shaped wrench."

"Harry," I said over the circuit, "send Sergyi to the DDC to pick up a T-wrench. I'm telling you over the umbilical, so I don't put any noise into the water with the water-born circuit."

Ski rummaged through the DDC toolbox and found a T-wrench. He handed it to Sergyi when he stuck his head up through the hatch. As he left, a curious narwhal approached the hatch and rolled over to look inside. Then it followed Sergyi back to the *Alfa*, rubbing his legs with its tusk. By this time, the divers had gotten used to narwhal antics. When one of the curious cetaceans rubbed his tusk against a part of their bodies, they knew he was just checking them out, like a dog sniffing or a cat rubbing.

Jer opened the access and worked himself inside. "The tie downs were secured with explosive bolts," he said. "Each tie down has an integrated U-bolt. We can attach the anchor cables with six-inch turnbuckles."

I looked at Ham. "Chief Daley should have a ready supply," Ham said, picking up the sound-powered phone. Five minutes later, he gave me a thumbs-up.

I called Harry. "Send Sergyi back to the DDC again for the turnbuckles."

※

The divers had been in the water for four hours as they tightened the turnbuckles and wrapped up the operation. The *Alfa* was whole again, although the pod could not be released because it was no longer held in place with explosive bolts. Otherwise, however, we were ready to move forward.

During much of the operation, narwhals and belugas came and went, apparently returning to a nearby polynya to replenish their air. The five divers were returning to *Teuthis*, swimming several feet over the bottom, four carrying the polypropylene line, and Jer holding onto the working end of the HP air hose while Ski retrieved it through the DDC hatch. A fifteen-foot-long beluga swam with them off to their left. Wally kept the Basketball over them, supplying light as they covered the 200 feet.

Wally saw it first. Out of the darkness to their left toward shore, a twenty-five-foot Orca slammed into the beluga's side, tearing out a massive lump of flesh. The divers were still fifty feet from the hatch.

"Drop everything!" I ordered. "Grab Sergyi's harness and push hard. In the DDC, haul the umbilicals with maximum effort. MOVE!" Then I turned to Wally. "Wally, place the Basketball between the Orca and the divers. Shine the light into his eyes. Do your best to distract him."

Instead of attacking the Basketball, however, the Orca brought his right eye right up to the Basketball and gave it a careful once over. Apparently, he decided the Basketball had no food value. During those seconds, the mortally wounded beluga struggled away toward our bow. Instead of going after the fleeing divers, the Orca dashed toward the smaller whale. Wally turned the Basketball to follow the larger whale with his light. As we watched, the Orca engulfed the fifteen-foot beluga's tail and removed it with one clean bite. The beluga ceased struggling, and the Orca spent several minutes feeding before he darted over *Teuthis* toward the surface and a polynya somewhere nearby to the south. With the five divers inside the DDC, I decided to leave the four polypropylene lines on the bottom. We could retrieve them on our next outside excursion.

As Wally was stowing the Basketball, the Orca returned. Wally pulled the Basketball up over *Teuthis* for a better look. First, the Orca took another bite from the slaughtered beluga—a large chunk from what remained of its lower back. Then it located one of the poly lines. To my surprise, using its lips, it picked up the bitter end of one line and shook it around like a shark shakes prey in its jaws. The line whipped around in the water, and the Orca seemed to be playing with it. Eventually, it swam off, trailing the line from its mouth like a dog or cat guarding a favorite toy.

USS TEUTHIS—BOTTOMED AT THE ALFA

The XO came off what would have been my watch just as we completed the in-water portion of the dive ops. He came down to Dive Control.

"Nice job, Petty Officer Dubbs," he said to Wally. "I suspect some of that footage will redefine Orca behavior." He turned to Ham and me. "I watched your guys handle the pod. I can't really offer enough praise." He smiled and looked directly at me. "You must be very proud of your team."

"I am, Sir, but the credit goes to Master Chief Comstock." I placed my hand on Ham's shoulder. "His hard work for the past two years made this team what it is."

The XO shook Ham's hand. "Well done, Master Chief!"

The sound-powered phone trilled. Ham picked it up. "Officer's call in ten minutes in the Wardroom," he said.

"That's my cue to reassume the watch in Control," the XO said with a grin as he departed Dive Control.

The sound-powered phone trilled again. Ham answered and then said, "The Captain wants Spook and me there as well."

✳

"We are about to do something that has never been done before," the skipper said to the assembled officers, including Ham, Senior Chief Jones, Senior Chief Dokey, and Chief Panner. In addition to the ship's crew members, the four DIA specialists and Sergyi Andreev were present. First Class Yeoman Brad Roman sat at the table, taking careful notes for the ship's log. What he wrote in his hardcovered green notebook would be the official record of this meeting.

"During the next two hours, you gentlemen will assemble everything you believe we will possibly need to make the *Alfa* underway ready, capable of transiting under the winter Arctic ice to Electric Boat. Commander McDowell will serve as Captain, Chief Warrant Officer Cobb will serve as Executive Officer. You will have to keep the *Alfa* running on the batteries, which is why I have chosen Chief Warrant Officer Cobb, Senior Chiefs Jones and Dokey, and Chief Panner to be part of the crew.

"The *Alfa* is more completely automated than any other Soviet sub. The five of you," he indicated the Navy guys, "should be able to drive the sub while getting sufficient sleep to retain your effectiveness—assuming, of course, that nothing serious goes wrong. You DIA people and you, Sergyi, will keep the *Alfa* and her equipment running. Under Commander McDowell's supervision, you can also participate in driving the sub. *Teuthis* will always be nearby, so we can assist with parts, personnel, or whatever else you may need. Should this become necessary, remember that it will take us at least a half-hour to launch *Mystic* and get her over to you.

"Since you will be on battery ops continuously, you will have to stop to charge the battery bank—probably every twenty-four hours or so. You'll be able to lock this down better after a couple of charge cycles. Each charge will require dive ops, so we want to charge as shallow as possible—even right up under the ice canopy, if we can do this.

"Master Chief Comstock, I am relying on you to step into Commander McDowell's shoes so he can focus entirely on his command responsibilities on the *Alfa*. What is Chief Fisher's qualification status?" "Except for his final test—something we need to do in port so we can throw every kind of problem at him—he is as ready as he will ever be, Captain."

I saw this coming, but I am not entirely sure Ham did.

"Very well. As of now, I am temporarily assigning Chief Petty Officer William Fisher as the Command Master Saturation Diver, and I am reassigning you, Master Chief Petty Officer Hamilton Comstock, as the Officer in Charge of TOG—the Test Operations Group. Your primary responsibility during our transit will be to have at least two divers available for each charging event, and when the time comes, have your divers install the false sail. Any questions, Master Chief?"

Ham glanced at me briefly, but I couldn't read his face. "No, Sir, but if I have any going forward, you will be the first to know."

Right answer, I thought, giving Ham a nod.

✳

The oxygen candles had been loaded into *Mystic* in Woman's Bay. We needed food and water on the *Alfa*, and two pieces of absolutely essential equipment, the Secure Gertrude unit and the secure depth-sounder. And we had to attach the transducer inside the *Alfa's* damaged nosecone and replace her fathometer transducer with our secure depth-sounder head.

We anticipated a thirty-one-day trip to Electric Boat and had loaded 930 LRP rations in Woman's Bay. Each meal required 1 ½ pints of water—that's about thirty five-gallon water bottles—just to reconstitute the freeze-dried main dishes. We loaded sixty bottles to be sure we had sufficient for drinking and washing.

By the time we were ready to go, *Mystic* was loaded to the gills with oxygen candles, LRPs, water bottles, and the tools and equipment my crew thought we needed.

I said my good-byes to Ham and the divers and the skipper, who came to the Engine Room to see us off. We settled into our places, such as they were, scattered among the cargo. Taggert released the clamps, and we were off.

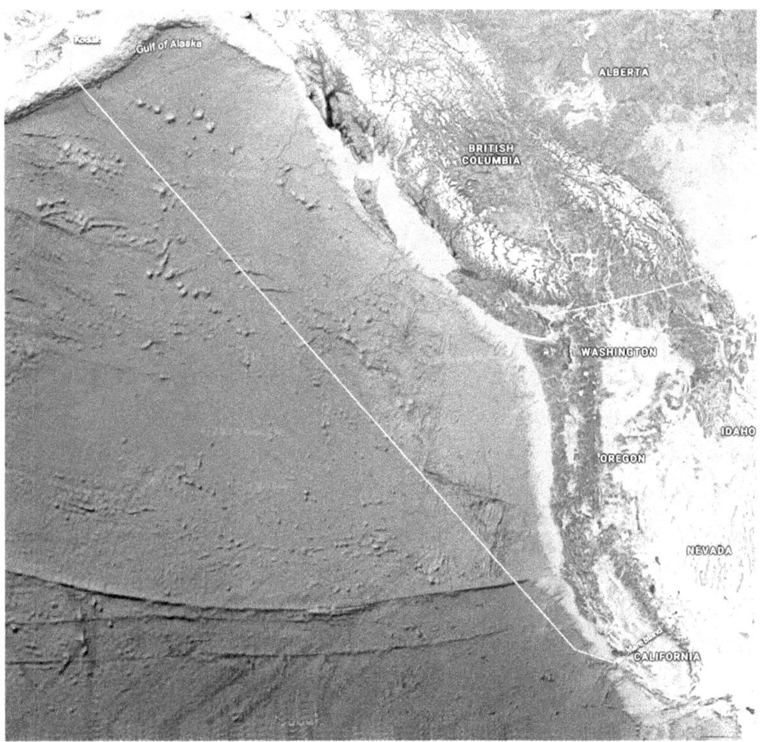

Kate's journey on USS Los Angeles *from Kodiak Island to Mare Island*

CHAPTER SEVEN—Kate's Journal 1

USS TEUTHIS—UNDERWAY FROM WOMAN'S BAY

I can't really begin to describe everything that's happened to me since I met Mac. From the moment we touched hands in the café next to my shop, I knew we had something special. Things got very personal after that, and I'm not going to discuss it any further here.

When Mac left the next day, I didn't think I could bear it. I was terrified that he wouldn't come back—but he did. I got to participate in the secret awards ceremony. My heart swelled with pride as I watched my guy receive personal accolades from the Secretary of the Navy, no less. As long as I live, I will never forget the following morning. In a flash, I lost everything—my home, my car, my shop. All I had left was Mac. His cool, his fearless response to the terror inflicted on us, gave me the strength and the courage to carry on. With Jack's help, we got through that awful day and night, and then everything changed.

It all started when Jack's telephone call woke Mac up in the middle of the night. Next thing I knew, Mac and I threw on some warm clothing and ran out of the house into a pickup driven by one of Jack's guys. Moments later, my house and car exploded! We raced to Jack's boat. While we boarded, somebody shot at us, and again as we departed! Thank God, they missed! Jack drove us over to Woman's Bay, and then suddenly Mac and I were on *Teuthis*, Mac's submarine. I had nothing except what was in my purse and the clothing I was wearing—absolutely nothing else. The Commanding Officer, Cmdr. (that's the Navy abbreviation for Commander) Roken, arranged for me to get suitable clothing and personal effects, and made me feel as at home as possible for a woman on a submarine in the midst of danger.

I stayed out of the way for the rest of the day while the crew prepared the sub to leave Kodiak. Mac had the evening off, so we went ashore, and Jack took us to Breaker's Bar, where I had a chance to say goodbye to friends, and then Jack invited us to stay at his place overnight. We had a wonderful Salmon dinner, and Mac and I had an unforgettable night together. I won't go into details about that. In the middle of a huge breakfast Jack prepared for us the next morning, guys started shooting at us again! Jack and I hid under the table as Mac sprang to action. I am SO grateful that Mac was there to defend us!

Then we were back onboard *Teuthis*, and I had to say goodbye to my dear friend, Jack. Cmdr. Roken must have pulled some strings with his superiors because we were soon safely on our way to sea, with ME aboard!

After we were underway, I got to drive the sub—my, how exciting that was. I so admire the men who do this every day. I met King, that's Chief Sonar Tech Royal Bennett, but everyone calls him King. Talk about an expert; this guy knows just about everything there is to know about sonar—that's a submarine's way of seeing underwater using sound. He even let me listen to and track a couple of contacts. I could be good at this, but women are not allowed to serve on submarines.

We were being stalked by a Soviet sub, *Shchuka*, one of the best they have, King told me. Then *USS Los Angeles* showed up to take the heat off us. Mac told me that would soon be my ride to safety in the U.S.

USS TEUTHIS—SUBMERGED OFF KODIAK ISLAND

While *Los Angeles* was distracting *Shchuka*, we dove down to a thousand feet and settled on a ledge overlooking the Aleutian Trench. Mac told me that the trench followed the Aleutian Island chain and dropped down to over 22,000 feet.

We remained on the ledge for quite some time. Mac and I were able to enjoy each other's company in the Wardroom, mostly undisturbed. Although we had no chance for genuine private time, the other officers respected our privacy and kept away from the Wardroom. Should I lose Mac on his forthcoming mission (Oh God, don't let that happen!), I will always have this time together to hold close.

Finally, but all too soon, Cmdr. Roken told us that *Los Angeles* was nearby and that it was time to transfer me.

Mac and I walked through the sub to the Engine Room, stopping to chat briefly with friends I had made during my short time aboard *Teuthis*. Then it was time to climb up the vertical ladder into the Deep Submergence Rescue Vehicle, *Mystic*. It seemed so tiny compared to the sub. Lt. Bob Taggert let me sit in the co-pilot's seat and even let me handle *Mystic* once we were underway.

There is no light at all at a thousand feet, but since *Mystic* had no windows, I couldn't see that. She did have several television cameras, including a color one that looked forward. Our beams of light disappeared in the clear water, but the light formed bright circles on the hull of *Los Angeles* as we approached. The *Los Angeles* was huge, much bigger than *Teuthis*, floating a thousand feet below the surface and 21,000 feet above the Aleutian Trench floor. This was, without a doubt, the most exciting thing I had done in my whole life.

Bob settled *Mystic* onto the deck, and then his people made the seal. The next thing I knew, I was stepping down into the fast-attack submarine *USS Los Angeles*. Commanding Officer, Cmdr. Archibald Desmond was there to greet me. He was a lovely man who became very much like a father to me.

✸

Mac and I went to Cmdr. Desmond's cabin where Mac briefed him on why I had become his high-priority passenger. He asked me about my story. I probably gushed, but I told him all about Mac and how he rescued me from my own personal isolation and from the very real threat of the Kodiak sleeper cell. Then the captain got a phone call. He said *Shchuka* was getting closer and that *Los Angeles* had to depart the area. He stood. "I'll leave you two alone for a minute," he said, "but then, Mac, you need to hustle aft and get the hell off my boat!" He winked as he shut the door.

I cried as I kissed Mac goodbye, but I'm a girl, and I'm allowed.

USS LOS ANGELES—NORTH PACIFIC

I remained in the Captain's Cabin for a while. Things were happening, but I didn't know what they were, and I knew that I should keep out of the way. We took a pretty steep down-angle, and then we leveled off, and things got quiet—not like ultra-quiet on *Teuthis*, but really quiet with a soft hissing and the subdued hums from the equipment in Control.

Finally, Cmdr. Desmond returned with another officer. "Kate, this is my Executive Officer, Lieutenant Commander Lew Brockhurst. He and I are the only officers on the sub with private staterooms. Lew is relinquishing his to you for the duration."

That floored me. "I can't do that, Commander."

"It's really our only option," the XO (that's short for Executive Officer) said. "The officer's staterooms all accommodate three officers, so we can't put you in one of those. The Goat Locker—the Chief's quarters—have no private accommodations. The crew bunk six to a curtained space, so that's out."

"It's either the XO or me," Cmdr. Desmond said, "and I pulled rank on Lew." He smiled warmly. "We're fine accommodating you. Lew will share my cabin so you can have the privacy you need as a woman."

✳

After I settled into Lew's stateroom, I took a hot shower and had a nap. Truthfully, I was near exhaustion from the events of the previous two days. A quiet knock on the stateroom door awakened me.

"Come in," I said.

A junior steward informed me that dinner would be served in the Wardroom in half an hour. I dressed in my *Teuthis* coveralls and made myself as presentable as possible, given that I had no makeup at all. Before I left the stateroom, a glance in the mirror told me that I was acceptable.

When I entered the Wardroom, everyone present, including Cmdr. Desmond, stood. I hurried to my chair, feeling a flush rush to my cheeks. Dinner was not formal, but it had an element of formality that I found quite pleasant. The steward staff served steaks to order, baked potatoes, canned vegetables, and a shredded-carrot-with-raisins salad. The officer sitting to my right explained to me that we were out of most things fresh. We washed the meal down with a beverage the officers called bug juice. It tasted like Kool-Aid. We finished the meal with coffee and fresh-baked apple pie with ice cream.

When we finished the meal, the officer to my right told me he had some free time and would be happy to show me around the sub.

When I looked at him, he smiled and said, "I know about Mac. I'm just trying to be a good host." I liked him.

※

My tour of *Los Angeles* was fascinating. Her sonar was hugely more sophisticated than on *Teuthis*. I suspect that King would have loved it, but I also knew that he felt very privileged to serve with Mac on *Teuthis*. Mac told me that King had served with him on the *Halibut*, and that Cmdr. Roken had specifically requested that King be assigned to his crew.

Los Angeles had more torpedoes, and their handling was way more sophisticated. This made sense to me because whereas *Teuthis* was set up as a research sub, *Los Angeles* was a fighting sub from bow to stern. (As you can tell, I have become more comfortable with naval terminology.) I could really see no major difference between the engineering spaces in *Los Angeles* and *Teuthis*. Of course, *Teuthis* had the Cable Reel Compartment and the Diving Operations Compartment that *Los Angeles* did not have.

While we were in the Control Center, I learned that we were at 900 feet running at flank—they told me that was about thirty-four knots, which I learned is incredibly fast for a large ship. Every hour, but not at exactly the same time, we slowed and ran a figure eight so Sonar could make sure we were not being followed close-in. They called it clearing the baffles. Cmdr. Desmond wanted *Shchuka* to follow us, although at a distance, as he pulled that Soviet sub away from *Teuthis* and my beloved. She followed us for several hours but falling more behind with each baffle clear. Finally, Sonar lost *Shchuka* completely, and Cmdr. Desmond presumed that she had turned back to find *Teuthis* since we seemed to be heading to the barn—another cool naval term I learned. We had about two and a half days still ahead of us. I spent my time hanging out in Sonar, where I got to play Sonar Tech, looking for contacts in the vast North Pacific, and in Control, where they let me steer the sub and conduct some depth changes. I cannot find the words to explain how I felt changing the direction or depth of this mighty 7,000-ton submarine by the slight turn of a wheel or the simple push or pull of the controller on which the wheel was mounted. It gave me goosebumps.

I can't say enough about the guys I met during my stay on *Los Angeles*. When I walked through the sub, I could feel their eyes on me, but not once did anyone say anything untoward to me. They all treated me with respect, answered my questions, even if they were dumb, and gave me the kind of courtesy a girl can only wish for. A couple even showed me photos of their girlfriends, and in one case, his kids.

✳

When we finally surfaced several miles outside the Golden Gate Bridge, the weather was unusually good. Cmdr. Desmond invited me to join him on the Bridge as we sailed under the Golden Gate and through San Francisco Bay to Vallejo and Mare Island at the bay's northeast end. The sun shined brightly in a sky filled with fleecy clouds. The wind was crisp so that I was glad to be wearing my fur-lined overcoat. San Francisco was fog-shrouded and only half visible off to my right, some of the taller buildings poking through the fog. Marin County, to my left, was golden brown under the winter sun.

I was beginning to feel a bit chilly as we finally pulled into our berth at Mare Island. Four men, two in uniform and two in civies, and a woman were waiting on the dock. While *Los Angeles* was being tied up, Cmdr. Desmond asked me to accompany him to the Wardroom, where we would meet the people waiting on the dock.

✳

I'm not entirely familiar with navy rank markings. Before he was killed, my Coast Guard husband Josh saved Jack Petrikoff's life. Josh was a Lt. j.g. We simply had no occasion to mix with senior officers, especially flag officers—admirals and such. When Cmdr. Desmond and I stepped into the Wardroom, he grinned and shook hands with a Navy Captain he introduced as his old friend Capt. Dan Richardson, Commander Submarine Development Group One. Then he turned to the other officer.

"Kate," he said to me, "please meet Rear Admiral Austin B. Scott, Jr., Commander of Submarine Fleet Pacific."

Adm. Scott smiled warmly and said, "So, you're the young lady who has caused such a ruckus." I suspect my face may have dropped at his words, so he added, "I mean that in the best possible way, Kate. It has been my personal pleasure to ensure your safety from the moment Commander Roken explained the problem to me."

To say the least, I was nonplussed. If I understood correctly, the man who told me this was in charge of the entire Pacific submarine fleet of the United States. In my mind, as a former Lt. j.g.'s wife, he was only slightly less powerful than God.

The Admiral turned to the three civilians. "These folks are with DIA Security—the Defense Intelligence Agency. You can think of them as highly trained security specialists whose job is to keep you safe on your cross-country trip." He turned to the three. "Agents…"

One man stepped forward—medium height, trim hard body, clean-shaven, short, brown crew cut, and warm brown eyes. "Special Supervisory Agent Darrell Capland," he said, showing me his badge and I.D., his voice a pleasant baritone. "Everyone calls me Cappy." We shook hands. He indicated a shorter, stockier, tough-looking guy with Hispanic features. "Special Agent Arturo Rodriguez—we call him Arty." I shook hands with Rodriguez after he displayed his credentials. His grip was firm but gentle. "And, Special Agent Jennifer Coolerage." Jennifer was somewhat shorter than me, tight trim body, shoulder-length brunette hair, with green eyes that twinkled as we shook hands. "The bosses figured you needed a woman as part of the team," Jennifer said, flipping her badge case open for my inspection.

Cmdr. Desmond signaled to the steward, and shortly we were sipping freshly brewed coffee while I told my story once more.

Adm. Scott asked me several pointed questions about my relationship with Jack and my knowledge about the sleeper cell. Then he stood up.

"That about wraps it up," he said. "I have a plane to catch. Can I give you all a lift?"

MARE ISLAND—VALLEJO, CA

I changed into the only civilian attire I had. To my delight, the steward staff had cleaned and ironed my skirt and blouse. Except for lack of make-up, I looked pretty decent.

This was my first helicopter ride. How exciting! It was noisier than I expected, but the ride was smooth. We flew down the bay and then east to Oakland, where we landed on the tarmac in an area reserved for helicopters—*choppers* they called them.

Adm. Scott shook my hand warmly and told me to relax and let his team take care of me. He assured me again that they would see to my safety. Capt. Richardson remained on the helicopter but also gave me a warm goodbye. Cmdr. Desmond made the trip with us, telling me that he would not let me out of his sight until he saw me safely aboard the transcontinental aircraft. If I could choose another father, it would be Archie Desmond.

Cmdr. Desmond, my three protectors, and I stood on the tarmac, with me waving, as the navy helicopter lifted into the air and headed west.

✳

As I stood waving, an odd ringing sound came from inside Capland's jacket. He reached inside and pulled out a strange-looking device a bit like a brick-sized phone, sort of. Capland pushed a button and put the device to his ear.

"Yeah…okay…will do!" he said into the device. Cmdr. Desmond and I stared at him.

"It's a DynaTAC 8000x—a portable telephone," Jennifer said. "They just came out a few months ago."

We all looked at Capland. "They caught a Soviet observer at Mare Island. Apparently, he reported Kate's departure by chopper."

The other two DIA agents took a defensive stance and looked about us sharply, weapons drawn. "We gotta get outa sight…right now!" Capland said. "Move it, people!"

That terrified me!

He hurried us into a hanger about 200 feet away.

"Arty," Capland said, "get us some transportation to the main terminal." He hustled us to a side door through which Rodriguez disappeared.

About ten minutes later, Rodriguez returned driving a golf cart with side curtains. We got in, and twenty minutes later, we pulled alongside a Continental Airlines 747.

"We got to get you aboard before any other passengers," Capland said urgently.

I knew what that meant. I started crying and threw my arms around Cmdr. Desmond's neck. He held me like the father I had lost so long ago.

"You'll be fine, Kid," he said quietly. "Cappy and his team will keep you safe, and I'll visit you when they get you settled." I looked at him, my eyes filled with tears. "I promise," he said.

A few minutes later, Jennifer hustled me onto the upper deck of the 747 while Capland and Rodriguez set up a perimeter. We had the entire lounge deck to ourselves.

✳

Once we were airborne, a flight attendant brought us four first class meals—absolutely excellent filleted salmon. While she was there, Capland asked her for the flight list. When she demurred, he presented his credentials, and she produced the list right away.

"Did any of these passengers book in the final few minutes?" he asked her.

The flight attendant pointed to a name, Jeremy Foggybottom. "Walk through the aircraft with me and point him out," Capland told her. "Don't let him know."

I was exhausted. The first-class seat converted into an excellent bed, so I took full advantage of this and tucked myself in for a full night's sleep. The last thing I remember is Jennifer leaning over me and whispering, "Sleep well, Hon. We got your back!"

My dreams were filled with terror. I was running in slow motion through a thick, clammy substance while men in Russian ushanka hats with big red stars shot at me. Sometime during the night, I felt gentle hands smooth my hair and stroke my face, and I finally fell into a sound sleep.

The next morning, when I awoke to the smell of fresh coffee handed to me by Jennifer, a man I didn't recognize occupied a seat on the other side of the deck. He was bound and gagged. Jennifer told me he was Soviet agent Foggybottom. They caught him last night, trying to gain entry to the upper deck. He was armed with a silenced small pistol that he had managed to fire through Rodriguez's left arm.

As Jennifer put it, "We had a quiet conversation with him after we subdued him. He was very happy to tell us what we needed to know." Apparently, after the sleeper cell's failed operation in Kodiak, the Soviets placed observers in every location on the west coast where they thought an incoming American sub might dock. The sum of events in Woman's Bay led them to believe that I had been transferred to an American sub. They blocked out my arrival window and waited for me to show up. Once they knew I was aboard Adm. Scott's chopper, they tracked it to Oakland. It was then only a matter of putting a man on every outgoing east coast flight for a couple of hours after the chopper landed.

Obviously, they had figured it out. I was lucky my security team knew what it was doing—and I was scared to death.

✳

The rest of my flight was uneventful. Shortly before we arrived at Washington National Airport, Capland placed a call on his mobile phone. After the other passengers departed, two DIA agents met us on the lounge deck and took charge of Foggybottom.

Once Foggybottom and his escort departed, Capland inspected the rest of the plane to make sure no one else was present. Then, on high alert, the team moved me to the tarmac, where we were met by a perfectly ordinary Chevy sedan with darkened windows on both sides. Jennifer told me that the car was more than it appeared to be. The doors and windows were bulletproof, she said and beckoned me to climb into the back seat.

I looked in all directions before getting into the car. I was worried and scared, and I'm pretty certain that my face showed it. As I sat down, Jennifer took my hand and squeezed.

"Try to relax, Kate," she said. "You're safe with us. You really are."

I know she meant well, and she was probably right, but I only felt really safe with Mac, and I had no idea where he was.

DIA—ANACOSTIA, DC

We drove a relatively short distance to a brand-new complex located in the southeast corner of the confluence of the Anacostia and Potomac Rivers.

"This is our new headquarters building," Jennifer told me. "We're going to stop here, so the director, Lt. Gen. Eugene Tighe, can meet you."

First, we were stopped at the outer gate, where guards examined our I.D.'s carefully. Then, we were stopped at the main doorway into the building. Construction was still ongoing, and the complex had not yet been officially dedicated, but the DIA was operating in full swing out of its new facility. We took an elevator to the sixth floor. The double door to the director's suite was prominently labeled. Rodriguez and Jennifer remained outside in the hall while Capland and I passed through the double doors. A senior enlisted man, I'm not sure of his rank, but he had a lot of stripes on his arm, announced our presence to the general, and opened the door to the director's inner office.

The office occupied the top southwest corner of the building with expansive windows on two sides. The window across from the general's desk overlooked the Potomac, and the one to his right overlooked the Anacostia. Three flags filled the corner where the windows met—the American flag, the DIA flag, and the Air Force flag, since Lt. Gen. Eugene Tighe was an Air Force general. A couch, a couple of chairs, and a coffee table filled the space between the main window and the general's desk.

Capland stepped back as I walked into the office. Gen. Tighe rose to his feet and walked around his desk, his hand extended.

"I have been looking forward to meeting you, Mrs. Perry." "Call me Kate, please," I said, shaking his hand.

He took my elbow and walked me to the couch, where he poured two cups of coffee. Then he waved Capland over.

"How was the trip?" the general asked.

"We had some tense moments," Capland said, "but Kate was a trooper. We got through them with only a bullet through Agent Rodriguez's left arm."

At the general's request, Capland detailed what had happened on the Continental Airline 747.

"Kate will stay at Agent Jennifer Coolerage's apartment as a roommate until we know she's safe," Capland added.

This was the first I had heard of that, but it was fine with me. I liked Jennifer, and the idea of having her around did a lot for my morale. As it was, I was jumping at every shadow.

We spent a few more minutes in small talk, and then the general welcomed me as one of his staff analysts.

"Your job is to discover everything you can about the sleeper cells in Kodiak, the attack, Jack Petrikoff—anything and everything. One of my supervisors will bring you up to speed when you show up for work in a couple of days."

He stood to his feet, again expressed his relief that I was okay, and then Capland and I left his office, joined Rodriguez and Jennifer, and took the elevator down to the front entrance. Ten minutes later, we crossed the 11th Street Bridge over the Anacostia to Interstate 695. We cut west past the National Mall and the Jefferson Memorial to Georgetown, where Jennifer owned a townhouse in the Papermill complex just east of the Key Bridge.

✳

The following morning, I awakened to the smell of fresh coffee and maple syrup. Jennifer stuck her head above the spiral staircase.

"Get up, Girl. Grab a robe from the closet and move your butt down here."

Jennifer's small townhouse was one of twenty-six units in shades of red brick clustered inside what used to be the old Georgetown Paper Mill. The brick smokestack had been retained as an eye-catching landmark jutting into the sky. The entryways faced an inner tiled court with several walkways bordered by bushes and small trees—and flowers when it wasn't winter, Jennifer told me. It was private and quiet. Jennifer's small two-story unit had a bedroom loft overlooking the living room. The loft had a queen bed that we shared. I think we spent half the night making girl talk, getting to know each other. She came from a working-class family. Her dad was a Philadelphia cop who was killed in the line of duty when she was twelve. This created a bond between us that was the closest thing to female friendship I had ever had.

Downstairs, over toaster waffles and maple syrup, we made plans for the day.

"We got to get you some clothes, Girl," Jennifer said. "You're too tall to wear most of my stuff except for a couple of skirts that should make you look sexy as hell."

When I hesitated, she said, "I know all about Mac, remember? Nothing says you can't play the game until you two are back together." That sort of made sense. "I don't have access to any of my accounts," I said. "I have no idea how long it will take to get my hands on some cash."

"Not long at all," Jennifer said. She got up, went to a closet, and returned with a duffle bag. She reached in and pulled out a wad of bills. "This is my go-bag stash for get-the-hell-out-of-dodge emergencies. Here's a thousand bucks. Don't worry! I'll replace it on Monday, and you can pay me back when you are able."

"You sure?" I asked, feeling stunned. "That's a lot of money." I hugged her. "Really a lot of money!"

"Washington's an expensive town," Jennifer said, her green eyes twinkling.

PART TWO

The Lyre

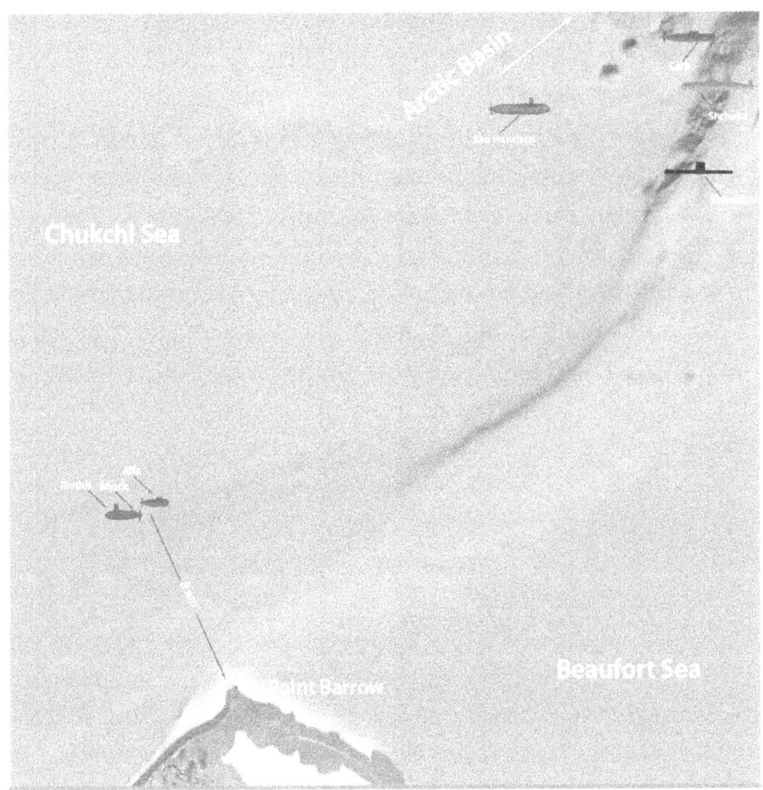

USS Teuthis & the Alfa *at the hole off Pt. Barrow, while* Shchuka *&* Carp *are being herded away by* USS San Francisco *&* USS Swordfish

CHAPTER EIGHT—THE HOLE

ON THE SEAFLOOR—*MYSTIC* OPS

This time around, we knew we would make a seal on the *Alfa* after-hatch. Since we had to cover only about 200 feet, getting there was trivial. We had barely gotten underway when Lt. Jim Deckhart announced our arrival. We settled to the ring around the hatch, and Petty Officer Parker Flanger pumped down the skirt.

After he relieved the pressure differential, he opened the *Alfa* hatch, and we entered.

Our first order of business, after turning on the lights, was unloading *Mystic* into the *Alfa*. We had a lot of oxygen candles, food, and water. It took us three full hours to get it all onboard and stowed. Pots and Spook grabbed the Secure Gertrude unit and the secure depth-sounder decoder. They went forward to install them in place of the *Alfa's* underwater communication rig and fathometer receiver, respectively. Bert and Dokey located the electrical system manuals and began tracing out the battery charging circuitry.

I grabbed Wyatt Cook, the DIA team leader, and we went to the Control Room to get a handle on the *Alfa's* operating controls. As we both were fluent in Russian, we were able to consult the operation manuals that we brought back with us. We spent an hour or so just looking at diagrams and reading descriptive paragraphs. The engineers who designed this integrated system obviously knew their stuff.

Turn the on/off switch on, set your current position, set your immediate destination, your desired depth below the surface or height above the bottom, your desired speed, and push the *Go* button. It wasn't quite that simple, but close.

We had some handicaps. There was no reliable sonar input, although Matt Hart, the DIA *Alfa* sonar specialist, was doing his best to get the damaged *Alfa* sonar system to give us some meaningful tactical input. Fortunately, we had live depth input because we had replaced the *Alfa's* fathometer with a secure depth-sounder. We could not get accurate radar or satellite readings for navigational input because we needed to remain beneath the ice canopy. On the other hand, we could use the Secure Gertrude to get accurate position info from *Teuthis* that we could input manually.

The biggest handicap, of course, was that we didn't have reactor power. We had made several assumptions about how long the batteries would last at different speeds. Our best guess was twenty-four hours at ten knots, but until we actually got underway and tried it out, it was just a *best guess.*

In the meantime, we had to make sure we could actually charge the battery bank. Two hours after we had completed unloading *Mystic,* Bert came forward.

"Mac, I think we have a handle on charging." He laid a schematic on the console in front of me. "Incoming power here," he pointed, "goes through this circuit, through this regulator," he pointed again, "to the battery bank terminal."

"How long does a battery charge take?" I asked.

"Depends on the remaining charge when you start charging, and your available current flow," Bert said. "In any case, we're ready to do a charge."

THE *ALFA*—BOTTOMED NEAR *TEUTHIS*

Until this moment, for every diving op we conducted, the buck stopped with me. Because the skipper had no specific diving training, especially saturation diving, the responsibility lay with me. This didn't change his absolute authority over *Teuthis* and her personnel nor his ultimate responsibility. On the other hand, if I and my divers screwed up royally, the skipper might have an out, unlike every other ship's operation where he would go down with the responsible officer. This time, things were different. Ham was on the hook. I was locked away on the *Alfa*, unable to do anything more than advise. Fortunately, Ham was probably the best master saturation diver in the fleet. If something were to go wrong, however, while Ham would take the rap, the skipper would go down for replacing me with Ham. I didn't see this as a problem because I trusted Ham implicitly. I was certain that he would do nothing that I would not do.

So, while I continued to familiarize myself with the *Alfa's* control systems, Ham got his divers ready to connect the shore-power cable. Normally, shorepower cables are connected between a submarine and power on the pier or dock. These connections are above water. While they can get wet from rain, they are not designed to be used underwater. The Engineer, Doug Watson, and his people fashioned a waterproof connector that could be hooked into *Teuthis'* shore socket.

They did the same for the *Alfa's* external connector. The problem was to find a way to exclude all water from the connectors before putting power to the cable.

Before the divers entered the water, Navigator Barry Jacobs, who had the Deck watch, floated *Teuthis* a foot off the bottom. Guided by the Basketball, he repositioned *Teuthis* fifteen feet away from the *Alfa's* starboard side, with the shore sockets facing each other.

ON THE SEAFLOOR—AT THE *ALFA*

Ham put the two engineers, Ski and Jer, into the water along with Jimmy, who had been kept on standby for the last several dives in case his medical skills were needed. Before dropping the shorepower cable through the lock, Harry completely packed both connectors with silicone grease. Ski grabbed one end of the cable, and Jer grabbed the other. Jimmy floated above them, keeping a wary eye out for unforeseen problems, such as visiting Orcas.

My guys were not particularly concerned about Orcas because no human had ever been attacked by an Orca in the wild. They *were* concerned about the presence of narwhals and belugas because these were the staple diet of Orcas in the Arctic. In a feeding frenzy, an Orca might not be able to distinguish a small whale from a human in diving gear. So, Jimmy stood watch, so to speak.

Before pushing the shorepower connector into its socket, each diver packed his receptacle with silicone grease, forcing out all the water. Ski had the *Teuthis* side. He jammed the cable connector into the socket on Ham's signal, forcing out grease, but keeping water out of the connection. The *Teuthis* connection was secured with a twist locking ring. If the two subs drifted apart during recharging ops while resting against the underside of the ice canopy, the *Alfa* side was free to pull out. With both subs resting on the bottom, it was not a problem this time. Jer jammed his connector home and signaled to Ham that they were ready to charge.

✳

In the protocol we had worked out, *Teuthis* would supply power to their side of the cable first, putting power through the cable, through the *Alfa* socket, up to the load switch that would feed power into the *Alfa*'s system. This seemed simple enough, and in the *Alfa*, we were ready to receive power. That was when Jimmy called out an emergency hold, and *Teuthis* removed power from the cable.

In the *Alfa*, we did not have direct communications with the divers, so all we knew was that the voltage indicator for the incoming side of the shorepower switch suddenly showed zero volts.

I called Barry, who was still on watch. "What happened?"

"A couple of belugas showed up and started nosing around the connectors. Jimmy feared they might grab the cable and pull out the connector. That would short the cable with seawater—something we want to avoid."

"How long a delay?" I asked.

I could picture Barry grinning with his response. "Ham just sent out a couple of four-by-four pieces of lumber. It looks like both belugas are playing fetch."

"Perhaps you should keep a couple of divers in the water for the duration," I suggested.

"Ham's already on that," Barry said.

"I should have known," I said. "Let me know when you're ready to charge."

THE *ALFA*—BOTTOMED NEAR *TEUTHIS*

It only took about ten minutes to lure the two belugas away from the cable. Ham replaced Ski and Jer with Whitey and Jake, and brought Jimmy back as well. This probably was one of Whitey's and Jake's easiest dives ever—basically two hours of playing catch with a couple of fifteen-foot belugas.

Bert and Dokey opened the *Alfa* power circuitry to the incoming power slowly and carefully. They wanted no surprises. After about a half-hour, Bert reported to me, "The battery bank is charging. You can power up your consoles, but take it slow—one console at a time. Let's see how much drain they put on the system."

Not much, it turned out. The Soviet design engineers could not have anticipated our current situation, but their circuit design was efficient and very well put together. I couldn't help likening it to the difference between a high-end German Mercedes and an Italian Fiat. I don't mean in comparison to American subs but in comparison to earlier Soviet subs.

Within another half-hour, in the Control Room I had effective control of all ship's systems. Bert and I played around with different configurations, keeping an eye on the battery charge level as we did so.

The primary system was *Akkord*, the combat information and control system. It received and processed sonar, television, radar, and navigation data from the other systems. It deduced the location, speed, and predicted trajectory of itself and other ships, submarines, and torpedoes. It displayed the resulting information on control terminals, along with recommendations for operating a single submarine, both for attack and torpedo evasion, or commanding a group of submarines. Obviously, we didn't need all of its capabilities, and furthermore, the damaged sonar dome severely restricted its passive sonar capabilities. The watch officer would sit in front of *Akkord* during our transit.

The *Ritm* system controlled the operation of all onboard machinery, including atmosphere control, and fed their status to *Akkord*.

The *Sozh* navigation system and *Boksit* course control system integrated course, depth, trim, and speed control, for manual, automated, and programmed maneuvering and fed its data to *Akkord*.

We would not be able to make much use of the *Okean* automated tactical sonar system. It normally provided target data to other systems, eliminating the need for crew members working with detection equipment. With the damaged sonar dome, it was of little use to us; besides, we would not be hunting other subs. *Teuthis* would do that for us. On the other hand, with the replacement of the *Alfa's* fathometer with the secure depth-sounder, we could feed depth-under-the-keel info to *Akkord*.

For obvious reasons, we also would not be using the *Sargan* weapon control system.

Working in the background, the *Alfa* radiation monitoring system kept track of potential radiation, but with the reactor shut down, none was being produced, at least none that could reach us.

A final system was a complete surprise not only to me but to the DIA *Alfa* experts. The *TV-1* television optical system accessed several external TV cameras that we knew nothing about. We could see forward and aft, above and below, and to both sides; all six cameras could pan and tilt. I activated the starboard camera and zoomed in on Whitey's and Jake's antics with the two belugas. A polynya must have been close-by, because when they left together for air—always together—they were gone for only a few short minutes.

❋

"It's time to put an official veneer on all of this," I told Bert.

I reached into my bag and pulled out a fresh Navy Bridge Logbook.

The cover displayed the Navy seal, and right below it the words:

DECK LOGBOOK

of the

U.S.S. ___________________

COMMANDED BY

____

I crossed off the "U.S.S." and filled in LYRE and put my name and rank in the "Commanded by" line. Lyre? That's the transliterated Russian name of the *Alfa* sub—*Liré*, the ancient harp-like stringed instrument.

I made the first entry: *Charging ship's batteries using an external charging cable from* USS Teuthis. And added the *Lyre's* location and depth. Then I entered the date and time, and that's when I realized that I had completely lost track of the time. It was midnight. I needed to set up a watch list that would keep the five of us functional.

Bert pulled me out of my reverie. "We need to do one more thing," he told me, pointing to a gauge on the *Akkord* console. "Highpressure air is getting low. I think we need a full charge before we get underway."

ON THE SEAFLOOR—AT THE *LYRE*

During our transition from the "*Alfa*" to the *Lyre*, Special Ops Officer Franklin James had assumed the *Teuthis* watch from Barry.

I let him know that our battery bank was fully charged and that we needed to recharge our HP air banks. I asked to speak with the skipper.

"You know what time it is, right?" Franklin asked.

"I do, but I think he's expecting to hear from me."

Shortly, the skipper was on the line. "Give me your status," he said. I did, including informing him that we were now the *Lyre*, and finished by saying, "We still have to do four things before getting underway. First, we need to disconnect shorepower. Second, we need to lift off the bottom and approach the ice canopy so we can drain the pod and bring it to one atmosphere. Third, we need to top off our HP air banks. This means we'll have to poke through the ice sufficiently to expose the snorkel. I don't intend to run the diesel, just the fans to pull air inside. The boat could use an airing, anyway. And fourth, we should top off our batteries just before we get underway." "You got your watch list done?"

"Working on it. We're going to do overlapping five-hour watches. Until we are underway with a couple of charge cycles completed, we will just have to feel our way forward."

✳

As before, Ham put the three divers in the water who had connected us together initially, Ski and Jer with Jimmy hovering above them. With our new-found knowledge of the *TV-1* system, I monitored their actions. Jimmy held the two short lengths of 4 x 4.

Ski placed his finned feet against *Lyre's* hull and pulled the shorepower cable straight out. The connector slipped out of the socket. Jer released the shorepower cable twist-ring on the *Teuthis* side and then repeated Ski's action.

Although I could not hear the divers' communications, I saw both look sharply at Jimmy. Jimmy dropped slowly toward the gap between the subs while keeping his body squarely facing what I reckoned to be a thirty-foot-long male Orca. The Orca's six-foot mouth was partly open—it almost looked like he was grinning at Jimmy. Gently, he nudged Jimmy's chest. Jimmy released the 4 x 4 pieces. The Orca backed away two feet and took one of the wood pieces into his mouth. He crunched it, breaking it into several smaller pieces.

Ski and Jer moved under *Teuthis* toward the DDC hatch. As Jimmy dropped, the Orca moved down with him so that he nestled between the two hulls. There was sufficient room for him to lie there, but no room for any maneuvering. When Jimmy slipped under *Teuthis*, the

Orca rose, quickly passed over *Teuthis*, and poked its nose under the port side. It was a tight squeeze, but it managed to get its head near the hatch. The divers pushed the cable through the hatch, and then Ski and Jer left the water, leaving Jimmy with the Orca.

Driven by Derrick, the Basketball slipped under *Teuthis* away from the Orca with a good view of everything. The Orca was not aggressive, simply curious, like a very big puppy. He stuck out his tongue, and Jimmy reached out and rubbed it with his gloved hand. Then he pulled himself up through the hatch, but before he could close it, the Orca left briefly and returned with the 4 x 4 length, pushing it through the hatch.

USS Teuthis & Lyre at the hole off Pt. Barrow

CHAPTER NINE—The *Lyre*

THE *LYRE*—AT THE SURFACE OFF PT. BARROW

The first thing Franklin did was lift *Teuthis* several feet off the bottom and move her about 100 feet to port. He used the outboards, so there was virtually no noise output. *Frisco* and *Swordfish* were keeping *Shchuka* and *Carp* at bay, but the Soviet subs were diligently searching for us. Our decoy had lured them to the edge of the Arctic Basin, and our guys were keeping them there for now. Sooner or later, however, they would return to the hole. When that happened, we wanted to be long gone.

My immediate task was simple—lighten *Lyre* with a couple bursts of HP air into her ballast tanks, just enough to lift her off the bottom, and then let her slowly rise to the underside of the ice canopy. No heroics, just slow and easy.

My inclination was to station my guys around the sub to monitor the process. On reflection, however, I concluded that the Soviets had purposefully automated this beast to make that unnecessary. I sat at the *Akkord* combat information and control console controlling the maneuver. Bert manned the *Ritm* console, but it was automatically feeding pertinent data to *Akkord*, so all he did was observe. The *Sozh* navigation and the *Boksit* maneuvering consoles were to my left and right, respectively. I could manipulate them if necessary, but their data also fed to *Akkord*, so I could focus on the *Akkord* screen. Spook manned the *Okean* automated sonar console, but we were in passive mode only with a damaged sonar dome. We had not yet activated the under-ice sonar, so he had nothing to do but monitor. Besides, *Okean* fed its data to *Akkord*, where it was integrated into my overall display. Pots manned the *TV-1* console, and he actively monitored our external environment, especially the upward-looking camera. Dokey moved from console to console, familiarizing himself with how they operated and watching what each operator was doing.

The four DIA guys and Sergyi were all over the place, checking out how my actions at the *Akkord* console affected things throughout the sub.

It took *Lyre* a couple of minutes to overcome bottom suction along most of her keel. Then, with a sucking sound we could hear inside the sub, she lifted slowly off the bottom. I cracked the fore and aft ballast tank valves to release some of the air as she rose. There probably was an automated way to do this, but I didn't know that routine, and I wanted to get a feel for how the sub acted in the water column.

As we rose, the air bubble in each ballast tank expanded, forcing water out through the opening at the bottom of each tank. This increased our positive buoyancy so that I had to release more air. It was somewhat like a snowball rolling downhill. I kept our ascent slow so that a full five minutes passed before we bumped gently against the ice canopy. Pots gave me a good view of the ice immediately above us. *TV-1* was a pretty slick system. I knew I would be putting it to good use during our transit. I couldn't help but wonder how *Lyre* managed to sustain such damage to her bow during her transit of the Prince of Wales Strait at the Princess Elizabeth Islands.

I intended to crack the ice just enough to push the snorkel through the ice into the air. We were not moving horizontally, and there was no wave action to speak of, so just a few inches above the ice surface was all I needed. Bit-by-bit, I added air to both ballast tanks. The sail pressed against the canopy with increasing pressure until a loud crack signaled success. Immediately, I vented air from both ballast tanks until *Lyre* no longer pressed against the ice. Then, I added just enough air to keep her resting against the ice.

It took a moment to locate the snorkel mast switch. Apparently, the snorkel mast normally operated automatically in conjunction with diesel ops at periscope depth or on the surface. When I activated the switch, bypassing the automation, I was then able to set the height with a slider.

Bert commenced charging the HP bank from the *Ritm* console. The compressor was a high-capacity unit that compressed air from inside the sub while the atmosphere system sucked fresh air into the sub through the snorkel. The HP bank was fully charged in a half hour, and the internal temperature of the sub had dropped to near freezing. We were glad we had extra clothing with us so we could layer it and keep warm.

While the HP bank was charging, I located the drain valve switch for the escape pod. The pod was filled with water at about 200 psi. When I flipped the switch and opened the valve, the pod pressure dropped to just over one atmosphere. Then I opened the pressurizing valve, forcing the water inside the pod to sea. When the pod was dry, I shut both valves. We were ready to return to the bottom.

THE *LYRE*—BOTTOMED NEAR *TEUTHIS*

By the time we settled on the bottom, the XO had assumed what would have been my watch on *Teuthis*. It had been a long night, and I was exhausted. I turned the watch over to Spook, who would spend the next five hours making sure we were ready to get underway, and at the end, top off our batteries.

I directed everybody to catch up on their sleep—for five hours, anyway. I told Spook to wake me for any problem, no matter how slight. Several of the guys chose to grab a meal first, intending to heat water in one of several electric hot-water pots the Dev Group had included with the LRP shipment. As I drifted off to sleep, I heard Bert swear in the small galley.

"Shit! Can you believe it? We don't have any adaptors or transformers to plug in these suckers and use them."

With the certain knowledge that Bert could solve the problem, I zonked out.

※

While I slept, Bert spoke with Doug Watson, explaining the problem. Doug's people set about winding a reduction transformer, 220 V to 120 V, with sufficient capacity to handle our four hot-water pots. They didn't bother with the frequency, since the pots didn't care whether the current was 60 Hz or 50 Hz. They also kludged up four adaptors to change the standard two-prong plugs on the pots to the Soviet version—two round posts a bit farther apart than our standard flat prongs.

I slept right through topping off of the batteries and the other preps for getting underway. I found out later that Sergyi had made sure I wasn't awakened. There was nothing, he insisted, that the nine of them couldn't handle. Finally, as *Teuthis* was preparing for *Mystic* ops, Sergyi awakened me with a hot cup of coffee. I didn't ask him how he managed to pull that off, but it was a godsend.

I arose, splashed a bit of water on my face, and carried my cup of coffee up the ladder to Control. The rest of the crew was sitting around the consoles eavesdropping on Spook's conversation with *Teuthis*. The divers had returned to the DDC after topping off *Lyre's* batteries and spending a few minutes with their new best friend, the curious Orca, who brought a female with him this time. *Teuthis* had moved back to her position a hundred feet off *Lyre's* starboard side.

Sergyi volunteered to remain behind in *Lyre* while the rest of us went back to *Teuthis* for a final visit, a meal, and a shower. Instead, I made the command decision for five of us to go first, and then to make a second trip for the second five. We would be stuck for thirty-one days with only LRPs to eat and sponge baths for cleanliness. I figured a final meal and shower would do everyone good.

ON THE SEAFLOOR—*MYSTIC* OPS

Even though we had replaced virtually all the air in *Lyre* when we topped off our HP Bank, when Flanger opened the hatch, Bob Taggert wrinkled his nose at the stench.

"I'm glad it's you guys and not me," he said with a grin. "Let's get you back for some chow and a shower."

I sent Sergyi with the first group and remained back with the DIA team. I was surprised when, just an hour and twenty minutes later, the XO called to say that *Mystic* was on her way back with the first five guys. There are showers, and then there are *showers*. I cannot remember when a shower felt so good. I stood under the hot stream for as long as possible, allowing just a few minutes for a steak and potatoes meal, complete with popovers.

Before we returned to *Lyre*, the skipper called me to his cabin. He gestured for me to sit.

"I wanted to spend a few minutes with you before you get underway," the skipper said with a smile. "First, do you have any questions? Is there anything you wish to discuss with me privately?"

"Not really, Skipper. We know what we are doing—we think. Everything but the reactor seems to be working, although the sonar is limited because of the sphere damage." I told him about the *TV-1* system and how it should significantly help us in tight situations. I finished up by saying, "Thank you again for giving me this opportunity. I never imagined I would be doing this when we got underway last fall."

"Mac, I chose you because you are the best man I have for the job. I was initially somewhat reluctant to relieve you of your diving responsibilities, but you convinced me that Ham can handle the job.

"You will be driving a special sub with unique capabilities. I suspect you will undergo a long, detailed debriefing when we finally arrive at EB. Learn everything you can, but don't take unnecessary chances. The Soviets will do everything they can to stop our delivery. I would not put it past them to attempt sinking *Lyre* if they find you. Be alert, but don't take offensive action. Leave that to *Teuthis* and me.

"Finally, remember that we are close by. We can get to you on short order for any problems you can't resolve." The skipper rose to his feet and held out his hand. "Good luck and God's speed!"

THE *LYRE*—UNDERWAY OFF PT. BARROW

Mystic had left our afterdeck and returned to *Teuthis*. We were topped off—batteries and HP air, food and water, oxygen candles, even toilet paper. We were ready to go and eager to be underway.

I gathered my nine companions in Control. "It's time, guys. This may not be what you signed up for, but here we are. We Navy boys will keep us on track and moving forward. You DIA guys and Sergyi will make sure everything continues to work. We will be at ultra-quiet for the entire journey, so get used to it. *Teuthis* will be within several miles of us at all times, but I want us to be invisible.

"One more thing. I know it is tempting to wolf down the LRP stuff, followed by some water. *Please* don't do that. The nutrition boys tell me that's a good way to mess up your gut. We don't need that kind of problem out here."

Sergyi raised a hand while digging in his duffle bag. "I brought these," he said, holding up a handful of Hershey Bars. "They not Belgium chocolate, but they damn good!"

✳

I took the first five-hour watch. I pumped water to sea and lifted *Lyre* off the bottom. I took her to a depth of 100 feet[11] over the bottom and set a course of 081 degrees at five knots. My big concern was that both *Shchuka* and *Carp* were on this approximate bearing eighty or so nautical miles out. *Los Angeles* and *Swordfish* were between us and them, but I could think of no reason to alert the Soviets to our presence as we crept northeast toward deeper water. *Teuthis* was ahead of us. Our passive sonar system couldn't hear her, but I was confident that she was tracking our position. I was concerned about a shallow spot some forty-seven nautical miles out, just a bit to the right of our track where the water was only seventy feet deep. I intended to pass to the north of it, but charts in this region were notoriously unreliable—thus

---

11 We had to get used to meters instead of feet because all the indicators were in meters, but to avoid confusion, I will continue to use feet in this narrative.

my five-knot speed. Bumping into that seamount at five knots would not harm us.

I leaned back in the comfortable seat facing the *Akkord* console. We had about nine hours before we needed to worry about the seamount.

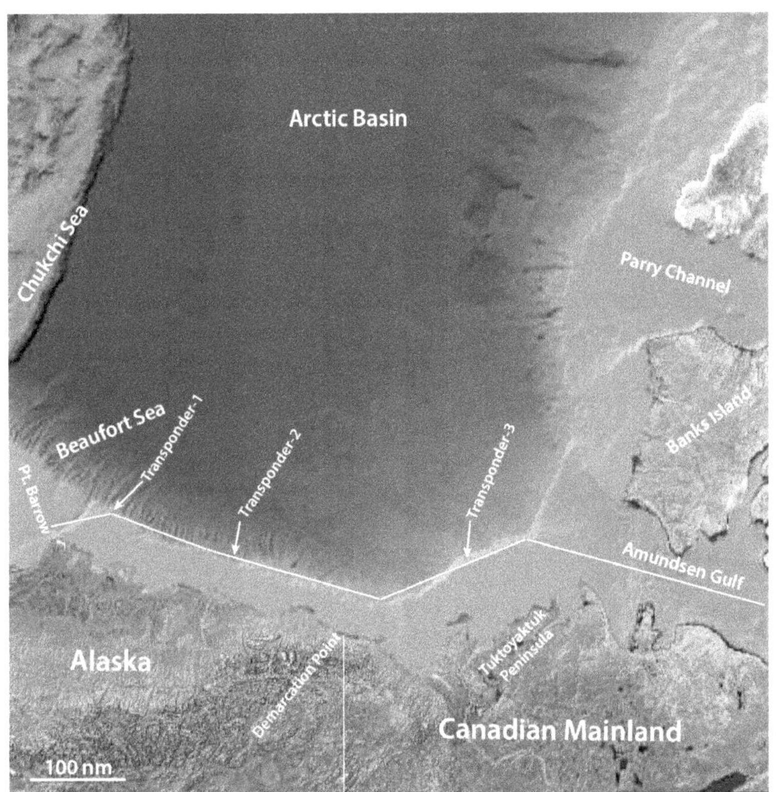

Track of USS Teuthis & Lyre from Pt. Barrow to Amundsen Gulf

CHAPTER TEN—Beaufort Sea

THE *LYRE*—BEAUFORT SEA

I was reasonably confident that Frisco and Swordfish were tracking *Teuthis* and *Lyre*. I was also confident that they knew our ultimate destination and probable track. With the aid of the first transponder, they would keep the two Soviet subs off our tails until we lost them in the sweeping canyons that formed the drop from the Alaskan continental shelf into the Arctic Basin.

Ahead of us lay forty-eight nautical miles of water that started out fairly shallow for most of my watch and then got increasingly deeper. As soon as we left the hole, I changed the automatic height-over-bottom setting to fifty feet because the average depth going forward was about 120 feet. That didn't give us a lot of room.

Near the end of my watch three hours later, the secure bottom sounder began to show some variability to the bottom as we cut across the incipient canyons. *Akkord* moved us up and down in the water column to maintain fifty feet above the bottom. I reset the depth to seventy feet below the ice canopy, which stopped the ups and downs, but also made us more susceptible to detection. Traveling at only five knots, I considered that very unlikely.

*

For the next five hours, Spook moved us forward into the canyons that dropped into the Arctic Basin. As we got closer to that shallow spot just off our track to the right, Spook moved us up to sixty feet. This put our sail sufficiently close to the ice that a large downward pressure ridge could cause problems.

"What do you think?" Spook asked me. "Do you think we'll be okay at this depth?"

"Pressure ridges don't usually form this close to shore," I answered, "but I'm far from an expert." I looked at the chart, for whatever it was worth. "Keep us at five knots, and let me know if I'm not around when we're within a mile of the spot."

"That's gonna be Warrant Officer Cobb," Spook said. "Oops, you're right. Pass the instruction on to him, please."

That's when I realized that I needed to establish a Night-order book. I checked the duffle bag of supplies that Ship's Yeoman Brad Roman had sent with us. Sure enough, along with spare pens and pencils, he had included a couple of spare Ship's Logs and two blank Navy-issue hard green covered lined books. I retrieved one, labeled it prominently *Night-Order Book*. I wrote out the order and handed the book to Spook.

"That works," he said.

*

An hour into Bert's watch, he called me to Control. "It looks like we're shallowing up a bit," he said. "How soon to our course change?" I asked.

"'Bout an hour," he answered.

"Okay, let me know." I turned to look at Sergyi, busy on the *Okean* automated sonar console.

"I think I got this *Okean* figured out," he said, his Ukrainian heritage still showing in his pronunciation. "Reception no so good here," he said, pointing to the port bow sector. "It fine everywhere else." He pointed at two spots on his screen. "*Swordfish* and *Frisco*," he said with a grin. "And those—*Shchuka* and *Carp*," pointing to two others. "I guess range based on what we know," he said. "*Okean* automatically refine and update."

"You've turned out to be quite a sonar tech, my Ukrainian friend," I said.

He grinned his acknowledgment.

THE *LYRE*—DEMARCATION POINT

"The bottom's dropping off, Mac," Bert told me near the end of his third hour on watch.

"When you hit the twelve-hundred-foot curve, drop down to two hundred feet, increase your speed to ten knots, and come right to course zero-nine-seven," I told him. "Then set the automatics to take a secure sounding every five minutes, average the last three soundings, and adjust our course to follow the twelve-hundred-foot curve." I pointed to the chart that had I pulled up on his *Akkord* console. "One more thing," I added, "we should commence baffle clearing hourly just like we did on *Teuthis*. Randomize commencing the figure eight within fifteen minutes before and after the hour, and randomize the initial turn direction—right or left. Make sure that during the baffle clear, either Sergyi or Matt is on the *Okean* looking for anything behind us."

"I thought *Teuthis* was doing that."

"Sure, and if they find something, they'll let us know by Secure Gertrude. It never hurts to have another set of ears. That's what we will be doing."

✳

During Bert's second baffle clear, Matt called me to Control. "Look at this, Mac." He indicated five sound sources on the *Okean* screen. "This is *Teuthis* off to our port. These guys behind us are probably our two guys and the two Soviets. By the sound levels, I'm guessing that our guys are closer, but the Soviet subs are so noisy that relative sound levels are unreliable."

"Let's get some ranges from *Teuthis*," I said. "We can feed that info into *Okean*, and it should keep things relatively clear for several hours, at least."

✻

Sam's five-hour watch was uneventful. The *Akkord* panel worked flawlessly. It even selected the random hourly intervals and the initial turn direction. In effect, Sam's real job was to be present and aware of what was happening if *Akkord* screwed up. It didn't.

When Sam turned over the watch to Potts, he finished up with, "Piece of cake!"

✻

"*Lyre*, it's *Teuthis*," came clear as a bell through our Secure Gertrude.

We were near the end of Potts' third hour on watch. He had just completed a baffle clear with Sergyi manning the *Okean*. Sergyi got me out of my bunk with a steaming cup of coffee, and I joined them in Control. The *Okean* screen displayed three contacts, *Teuthis*, about six nautical miles off our port bow, and both *Swordfish* and *Frisco* behind us to port several miles, but Sergyi had no way to distinguish which was which.

"What about *Shchuka* and *Carp*?" I asked.

"No detection, Mac," Sergyi said. "I don't got King's fancy equipment."

"Grammar lesson, my friend. It's *don't have*, not *don't got*." I grinned at him. "Your English is coming along just great. You're just picking up some common errors from the guys."

Potts handed me a hand-held mike. "*Teuthis*, this is *Lyre*, over," I said.

On the old Gertrude, it would have been impossible to recognize an individual voice, but I clearly recognized the XO's voice. I glanced at the watch section chart I had posted on the Control bulkhead. Sure enough, he was on watch.

"XO, it's Mac."

"Mac, we have located an appropriate spot for transponder-two. *Lyre* is about an hour away from a battery charge. Head toward our position at two hundred feet. In the meantime, we are preparing for *Mystic* ops. When you reach our position, we will set up for your battery charge."

✳

It was a bit frustrating not to be part of the *Mystic* transponder-laying operation, but that paled when compared to what we would commence in about an hour.

"Slow to six knots," I told Potts. With nothing to do, I hung around Control as Potts brought us to our rendezvous.

About fifty minutes later, I said, "Potts, put us D-I-W and trim to stay at two hundred feet."

"Roger that, Mac. Now we get to see just how well this sucker hovers."

I just grinned. I knew Potts could handle any deviation the *Alfa* automatics screwed up.

"*Teuthis*, this is *Lyre*. We're at your location, two hundred feet below the canopy."

"Roger, *Lyre*. We will be back with you shortly. Stand by."

And so we waited. I guessed *Mystic* was either underway or about to get underway. My guys—Ham's, I corrected myself—would have placed the transponder into the grip of *Mystic's* manipulator arm. Then they would set up the shorepower cable.

"Potts," I said. "Activate the external lights and cameras." "Got it, Boss."

"*Lyre*, this is *Teuthis*. We're ready for battery ops. I have you three hundred yards to starboard. Present your starboard side and then ease *Lyre* upward until your sail rests against the canopy. Notify me when you are stable."

"*Lyre*, aye." I nodded to Potts.

While Potts brought us up, I entered the details in the Ship's Log.

The rest of the crew joined us in Control to watch the proceedings.

It took about five minutes. This was our first time in open ocean. *Okean* said the ice was six feet thick, so there was little chance we would break through the canopy.

"Make sure we are slightly positively buoyant, Potts," I said as *Lyre* bumped gently against the canopy.

"*Teuthis*, this is *Lyre*. We are in position."

✳

Over the next few minutes, as Potts finished his watch, *Teuthis* placed her sail twenty feet below the ice and inched her way toward us until she hovered just twenty feet from our starboard side. As she got closer, we were able to watch her progress on our monitors. The Basketball appeared and dropped to our shorepower connection to ensure it was clear.

As the divers appeared on our monitors, I officially assumed the watch from Potts. The divers plugged the cable into our socket following the same procedure they used on the initial charge—packing the socket with silicone grease before making the connection. It was a slip connection, of course, so it would disconnect should we drift apart.

"*Lyre*, this is *Teuthis*." I recognized Waverly's voice. He had assumed the watch on *Teuthis* from the XO. "We're connected."

Bert, Potts, and Gilbert Edwards (the *Alfa* reactor specialist) stood by in the engineering space.

"You guys ready?" I asked over the intercom.

"Here it comes," Bert said as he threw the main breaker.

I had an eye on the *Ritm* console that showed the state of onboard machinery. My current interest was the state of the battery charge. It hovered just below 20%. When Bert threw the breaker, the needle jumped momentarily and then settled back to its original position.

I watched. There was no apparent movement. I turned to Wyatt Cook, the senior DIA *Alfa* specialist, and then turned back to the console. To my relief, the needle had moved a fraction of an inch.

Our schedule allowed two hours for the charge, but so far as I was concerned, I would let the schedule slide to ensure a full charge. Once again, I was impressed by the Soviet engineering. The initial charge was rapid, and Potts reported that the battery cells did not seem to be heating up appreciably.

An hour later, we were three-quarters charged. Bert explained that the charge-rate would slow down as we topped off the batteries. He was right. The remaining charge took another full hour.

✳

"*Lyre*, this is *Teuthis*. How is your HP air charge?"

"We're topped off," I answered. "We used no air since our last charge off Point Barrow. Our battery bank is charged. We have opened the circuit."

"Roger that, *Lyre*. Divers will disconnect shortly. We will let you know when to proceed."

On our monitors, we watched the divers disconnect the shorepower cable from both subs—the water was transparently clear with a couple hundred feet visibility—and stow it in the DDC…well, at least we watched them take it beneath *Teuthis* and disappear. I guess, technically, we didn't see them push the cable into the DDC.

About thirty minutes later, *Teuthis* released us. "*Lyre*, this is *Teuthis*. You are released to proceed at two hundred feet on a course of zero-nine-five, generally."

✳

As I've written in my previous mission reports,[12] submarining is often characterized as endless hours of tedious boredom interrupted by moments of sheer panic. For the next fourteen hours, we most definitely were on a tedious boredom leg. The *Akkord* automatics were so efficient at keeping us at depth and on our general course of 095 degrees that the watch officer had virtually nothing to do.

From my fourth hour to Sam's third, we slipped silently under the canopy, covering 113 nautical miles with nary a peep from anything behind or ahead of us. Each hour, either Sergyi or Matt manned the *Okean*. We knew that *Frisco* and *Swordfish* were somewhere behind us, but *Okean* could not pick them up. Every now and then, *Okean* got a hint of either *Shchuka* or *Carp*. It didn't get enough, however, to identify either one of them. Had we not known they were back there somewhere, their detection would have been meaningless.

Only one marginally significant event happened during this fourteen-hour leg: About 100 nautical miles into the leg, we passed Demarcation Point, the point on the coastline where the United States and Canada meet. At this time of year, it was all ice-covered. It occurred to me that we may have been the closest humans to this point, there being no reason at all for anyone else to be near—on land or sea.

I made an appropriate log entry.

______

12 *Operation Ivy Bells* and *Operation Ice Breaker*.

THE *LYRE*—NORTH OF THE PINGOS

Those of you who read my previous mission report[13] will already be familiar with pingos. They do not really have much bearing on this mission report, but they are so interesting that I decided to include a short description.

On land north of the permafrost zone, pingos are a type of frost heave where ice forms beneath the surface layer on top of the permafrost, pushing the ground above it into a mound that can rise as high as 180 feet. The Tuktoyaktuk Peninsula, roughly south of our position, is home to a very large number of these formations.

Just offshore of Tuktoyaktuk Peninsula, extending for fifty nautical miles right to the edge of the drop-off into the Arctic basin, is a large number of gas-hydrate pingos that bubble methane from the tops of their structures. They are not very well understood but might indicate the presence of oil beneath the seafloor. The ice surface above these pingos is mostly smooth and fairly thin—six to eighteen inches for the most part.

We expected to pass just north of this large pingo field, right at the continental break—the drop-off into the Arctic Basin. We intended to lay the third transponder about eighty nautical miles north of the eastern-most point of Tuktoyaktuk Peninsula.

Other than a course change to the left to 085 degrees and an eighty-three nautical mile leg that took all of ten hours, this leg was much like the last—tedious boredom. This was about to change, however.

THE *LYRE*—CONTINENTAL BREAK

"*Lyre*, this is *Teuthis*." I was in the second hour of my watch, and I recognized Waverly's voice. The Secure Gertrude was as clear as ever.

"This is *Lyre*."

"We are eight nautical miles off your port bow over the location where we will emplace Transponder-three. Approach my location slowly at two hundred feet while I obtain a sat fix."

---

13 *Operation Ice Breaker.*

"Roger, wilco," I responded.

I guess I'm repeating myself, but the *Akkord* is truly remarkable. I dialed-in the parameters, and *Akkord* guided *Lyre* to our destination. We arrived an hour later.

※

"*Teuthis*, this is *Lyre*. We have arrived."

"Roger that, *Lyre*." Waverly still had the watch. "We got a good sat fix. Stand by for position coordinates."

I received the coordinates and put them into *Akkord*. *Akkord* had us several nautical miles from our actual position. I noted the difference in the log and made a mental note to keep a closer eye on our *Akkord* position—get a manual update hourly from *Teuthis*. Obviously, the Soviet dead reckoning system did not match ours.

"*Lyre*, this is *Teuthis*. We are setting up *Mystic* ops. Remain where you are until *Mystic* is well away from *Teuthis*. When I notify you, ease your way up to the canopy, starboard side to *Teuthis*. When you are stable, let me know, and we will approach you for the battery charge." About twenty minutes later, *Teuthis* told me to ascend to the canopy. "Don't worry about breaking through," Waverly told me. "The ice is about five feet thick."

※

This was the second time we had done this—charging our batteries just beneath the canopy. As we ascended with lights bright and cameras on, instead of a smooth undersurface like we had experienced before, a jumble of jagged ice filled our monitors.

I slowed our ascent and moved us around, looking for a relatively smooth spot to settle against. The jumbled ice spikes pushed down as far as thirty feet. For fifteen minutes, I crept below the jumble, looking for a clearing. Finally, I settled for an upside-down canyon about fifty feet wide. I eased *Lyre* up between the ice walls until her sail rested against the ice above us.

"*Teuthis*, this is *Lyre*," I transmitted. "I'm against the canopy, but you will have some difficulty getting next to me. My bow is at zero-five-zero, wedged between two downward-thrusting ridges. I think there is room beyond the ridge to my starboard."

Because she was not carrying *Mystic* right then, *Teuthis* could be more aggressive in clearing out a space on my starboard side. *Mystic* would just have to wait to return until *Teuthis* dropped down to deeper water after the battery charge.

It was a full half-hour before divers appeared to starboard on our monitors. They dragged the shorepower cable under the ridge and came up short by three feet.

"*Teuthis*, this is *Lyre*," I transmitted again. "The cable is three feet short. You may be in a better position to drop several feet and hover than I. The *Akkord* is good, but I'm not willing to trust it to maintain my depth to the precision we need."

"Roger that, *Lyre*. We're descending five feet and moving closer to you."

As they did, on the monitors I watched the divers struggle with the cable, and then one gave a thumbs up.

"We got it, *Teuthis*. Hold your position."

The divers disappeared as Sam threw the breaker, and we commenced sucking up *trons*. Two hours later, with the charge complete—we had sucked up all the *trons* the batteries could hold—the divers showed up on our monitors as Spook assumed the watch from me, and Barry took over from Waverly on *Teuthis*.

Once we were disconnected from *Teuthis*, Spook dropped us to two hundred feet and set our general course to 085 degrees. Ahead lay what we hoped would be nine hours of quiet as we ran toward the entrance to Amundsen Gulf and then another fifteen hours to Dolphin and Union Strait.

THE *LYRE*—AMUNDSEN GULF

As things turned out, our nine-hour transit to Amundsen Gulf and the following fifteen hours to Dolphin and Union Strait were without incident—another boring leg of the submarining formula. I got some well-deserved sleep, but before I fell asleep, I pulled out the ivory capsule Kate had slipped into my hand as *Teuthis* was getting underway following our first night together. As I unscrewed the cap, her faint spicy smell filled my nostrils. I pulled out her silk panties and held them against my face for a moment. Then I restored them to the capsule before their *Kate aroma* could dissipate. I drifted off with images of Kate floating through my mind and filling my dreams.

I must really have needed my sleep because I slept through nine full hours, whereas I usually need only four or five hours a night. I popped awake, splashed some water on my face, and climbed the ladder to Control. Sam was on watch.

"Hey, Sam," I said as I poured a cup of coffee. "Want one?" "Yeah, black," he said.

As I handed him a cup, I scanned *Akkord* and *Okean*. "Who are your contacts?" I asked.

"*Teuthis…*" he pointed to a relatively close contact off our port bow. "*Frisco…*" he pointed to a distant contact out ahead of us. "I lost *Swordfish* somewhere behind us. Sometimes back here," he pointed to the edge of the monitor in our baffles. "I think I picked up either *Carp* or *Shchuka*. Not enough to identify, but whatever it is seems to be headed the same way we are."

"What's this?" I pointed to a smudge at the right side of the screen. "I think it's near-shore ice sounds," Sam said. "King would know."

Then he looked at me with a grin. "Hey, you're an ex-sonar type. What do you think?" He handed me a headset.

I listened for a moment. "Could be," I answered, "but it could also be one of the Soviet subs trying to make a run-around. Keep an eye on it." I picked up the Secure Gertrude mike. "*Teuthis*, this is *Lyre*." Franklin on *Teuthis* responded. I told him about our possible contact. "I'll check it and get back to you," Franklin said. A couple of minutes later, he came back up on the circuit. "Drop down two hundred feet. You're blocking the contact's sound."

Sam dropped us down, and ten minutes later, Franklin said, "It's *Carp*, about twenty-seven nautical miles south, so watch yourselves. I'm going to put *Teuthis* between *Carp* and you."

"Bring us back to two hundred feet, Sam," I said, "and keep a close watch on *Carp*."

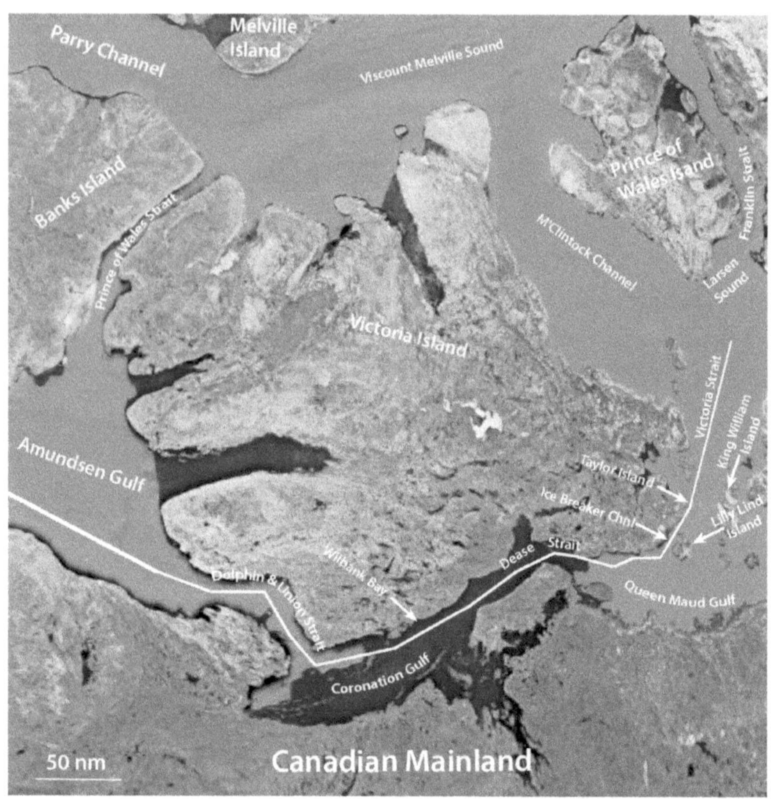

Track of USS Teuthis & Lyre from Amundsen Gulf to Victoria Strait

CHAPTER ELEVEN—Amundsen Passage

THE *LYRE*— DOLPHIN & UNION STRAIT

In 1903, Roald Amundsen commenced the first successful north-west passage through the Canadian archipelago in his 45-foot herring-cutter *Gjøa*. He crossed the Atlantic, up the west coast of Greenland, westward through Parry Channel, south through Peels Sound between Somerset Island to the east and Prince of Wales Island to the west, around the east coast of King William Island, and through Simpson Strait to follow westward our eastward path through the archipelago.

Amundsen took the northern route through Parry Channel and Peels Sound because he was entirely uncertain about the shorter, southern route we would be taking through Bellot Strait and Fury and Hecla Strait, discovered in 1852 and 1822 by Capt. William Kennedy and William Parry, respectively. He suspected that ice conditions and tides and currents through both straits would be an insurmountable barrier to his little herring-cutter, and looking back on it, he wouldn't have made it.

I assumed the watch ten hours into our push through Amundsen Gulf. My watch would end as we set up for our next battery charge. I kept an eye on *Carp*, who seemed to be hugging the coastline south of us. To the east, *Frisco* took station patrolling the entrance to Dolphin and Union Strait to protect our six as we entered the narrow passage. Rather than remain silent as she would normally do, *Frisco* announced her presence as a deterrence to *Carp* and *Shchuka*.

✳

Battery charging had become fairly routine. This time we were in deep water with a smooth overhead ice canopy. First, Barry on *Teuthis* broke through the canopy to get a sat fix. Then, Spook actually completed the two-hour charge a half-hour early because the divers had learned to be more efficient in connecting and disconnecting the shorepower cable. We were a long way from shore, and there were no nearby polynyas. This meant we had no cetaceous visitors. Nevertheless, the divers kept one person on lookout just in case.

Polar Bears had not been an issue since we departed the Pt. Barrow area. They roam over the entire Arctic ice cap, but they predominate near shore, where the presence of game for hunting and polynyas for fishing makes life much easier. Once we moved down into Dolphin and Union Strait, we expected to see more Polar Bear activity from there through the rest of our Arctic transit.

✳

Ten hours later, near the end of Sam's watch, we were in our fifth day as we passed *Frisco* and entered Dolphin and Union Strait.

"Slow to nine knots," I told Sam. "We have a lot of maneuvering to do as we move through the strait." I checked the chart. "We've got one hundred sixty-five nautical miles of strait ahead of us—one hundred four before the next battery charge. That's fourteen hours."

I checked the *Okean* display. *Frisco* had moved south of us, and I couldn't see *Carp*. "Looks like *Frisco* chased *Carp* away," I said.

"Or she just went quiet to wait things out," Sam rejoined. "Any sign of *Shchuka*?"

"None that I can tell," I said.

"Maybe she headed up the west side of Banks Island or north through Prince of Wales Strait."

"Around Banks—maybe," I said, "but through Prince of Wales…I doubt it. It's pretty ice jammed by now. Remember the mess we passed through."

"And the damage this baby sustained," Sam said, patting the *Akkord* console in front of him. "That's why we're here, I guess."

"Just keep a sharp eye, Sam," I said as I turned and headed for the mess.

Z

Sergyi was in the mess preparing a LRP meal for himself—pork and scalloped potatoes.

"Hey, Mac…You gonna eat?" Sergyi asked. "Yeah, toss me a Beef Hash."

We each poured 1 ½ pints of boiling water into our LRP bags and then settled down on opposite sides of a mess-table to set up our chessboard. Sergyi and I started playing chess together during our joint decompression in *Halibut* on Operation Ivy Bells.[14] We picked up the game again once we had settled into our underway status on *Lyre*. Back on *Halibut*, I had reached a point where I won about half the games. Not anymore. I suspect that Sergyi now let me win on those occasions where I prevailed.

I had five hours before my next watch, enough time for Sergyi to give me a couple of lessons—in chess and humility.

✳

My watch passed without incident. I turned over to Spook with just three hours remaining before our next battery charge, this time with a sat fix. We were headed into a part of the strait with lots of shoals and rocky protrusions. Furthermore, their charted positions carried a lot of uncertainty.

---

14 See *Operation Ivy Bells*, the first book in the *Mac McDowell Mission Series*.

Thus far, I had pretty much ignored the built-in charts in *Sozh*. *Teuthis* was doing the navigating, and I was following. Now, however, things were different. We would be pressing through the canopy with about seven nautical miles to the cliffs north of us and seventeen nautical miles between us and the land to the south. I needed to know as precisely as possible the location of the small islands and shoal areas in our path.

"Spook," I said, pointing to Harkness Island two nautical miles ahead of our position on *Sozh* and its slaved image on *Akkord*, "creep up on this island until you detect its upslope on the secure bottom sounder. I want to compare *Sozh's* position with its position on our chart."

"Roger that. This ought to be fun."

We slowed to bare steerageway and crept forward, our depth seventy-five feet with the bottom two to three hundred feet below us. About three hundred yards out from the island, the bottom surged upward sharply. Spook brought us to sixty-five feet and crept to within a hundred yards of the steep cliff-like shoreline. I plotted our position on the paper chart based upon our recent Sat fix and the *Sozh* DR trace since then. The paper chart position was a mile west of Harkness. *Sozh* has us nestled up against the western edge of Harkness—our actual position. The implication was clear. I picked up the Secure Gertrude mike.

"*Teuthis*, this is *Lyre*." "*Teuthis*, aye."

I explained our discovery and my belief that the Soviets had mapped out much of the Canadian archipelago and stored this info in the *Sozh* memories.

"Based on our findings, the Soviet charting in this region is much more accurate than what we received from the Canadians."

"Roger that." It was the skipper. "Use the *Sozh* but keep a parallel track on your paper charts. We don't want any nasty surprises.

"We're three nautical miles off your port bow. We'll push through the ice for a sat fix, and then we'll set up for the battery charge."

It sounded routine. In subs, that's what you want.

✳

We were in the middle of Spook's watch as we readied for charging ops. We hung out while *Teuthis* pushed her sail through the ice for a sat fix. Barry had the watch over there, and he was good at it. He took twenty minutes for the entire operation. When he finished, he submerged and moved *Teuthis* a hundred feet away from the broken ice.

"My head is due south," Barry told us over the Secure Gertrude. "I'm three hundred feet off your starboard beam, up against the canopy. It's a bit jumbled, but nothing extends down more than ten or twelve feet. You should have no problem coming alongside."

And Spook didn't. In less than a half-hour, we were ready to receive *trons*. It wasn't like we hadn't done it before. With our lights ablaze, on our monitors we watched the divers approach our starboard side with the shorepower cable, two dragging the cable, and one remaining aft and above as lookout. The Basketball surveyed the entire scene. Pure routine.

Because we were not connected to the diver talk network, we could not hear what happened next—only watch in horror.

Out of nowhere, a large, white body flashed from above behind the lookout, who we learned later was Ski. Ski must have sensed water movement behind him because he turned to confront the largest Polar Bear I ever saw: a male nearly ten feet long and massing just under 1,000 pounds. We determined these numbers later, but at that moment, it was just one damn big bear almost certainly mistaking Ski for a seal.

Ski propelled himself backward with furious fin strokes and fired a dart into the bear's massive chest. The creature didn't seem to notice it. An excellent swimmer, the bear caught up with Ski in moments and grabbed his right fin and foot in its mouth. Ski shot off another dart, this time directly into the bear's left eye. The bear opened its jaw, releasing Ski's foot. The fin was gone, and we could see blood oozing through Ski's punctured hot water suit, spreading like a black cloud through the icy water.

The bear pulled back, swiped at its left eye several times with both enormous paws, and then lunged back at Ski, who was doing his best to open up space between himself and the giant creature. The other two divers, Harry and Whitey we learned later, approached the bear from either side, trying to distract it so Ski could swim to safety.

Without a moment's hesitation, the bear lurched toward Harry, who launched a dart and dropped rapidly down under *Lyre*. Instead of heading for safety, Ski turned to confront the bear as it focused its attention on Whitey.

All of this took place in the eerie pantomime of total silence, except the divers could hear each other through their comms. From my point of view, there seemed little the divers could do except try to save themselves. Ski could have, and Harry was out of immediate danger, but both divers returned to Whitey's predicament.

With the loss of its left eye and probably in a lot of pain, the Polar Bear—normally a remarkable hunter—seemed disoriented, unable to decide whom to attack first. That was the moment another player joined the fracas.

Out of the darkness, a black and white fury three times the bear's length slammed into the hapless creature, ripping out its entire stomach with one massive swipe. The Orca dragged the carcass away from the divers and then returned, Polar Bear entrails trailing from its massive jaws. Ten thousand pounds of Orca gently nudged each diver with its snout and then darted off to check its prey.

Immediately, Harry and Whitey pulled Ski back to the Egress Lock, where Jimmy commenced treating his mangled foot. Jer replaced Ski, and the three wet divers returned to the task of connecting the shorepower cable. As they finished, the Orca returned, watching closely but maintaining its distance.

Not knowing what the Orca would do to the shorepower cable, Harry and Whitey remained near the shorepower connector on *Lyre*. The Orca stayed nearby for the full two hours except when it returned to the hole in the ice left by *Teuthis* to grab a lungful of air. About halfway through the charge, Jer spotted another Polar Bear approaching their activity. Before he could raise the alarm, however, the Orca charged, and the bear got the hell out of Dodge.

When *Lyre's* battery bank was fully charged, Harry and Whitey disconnected the cable and returned it to the Egress Lock, closely monitored by the Orca. Once the three divers were safely inside the Egress Lock, the Orca swam to the hatch and placed its left eye against the opening, rolling back and forth to take in the entire interior. As the Orca departed, the divers noted a bite-size piece missing from the trailing edge of his dorsal fin, probably the remnants of a long-forgotten encounter with a shark.

Ski was unable to say *goodbye* to his rescuer because he was sedated, while Dr. Janus Everest, *Teuthis* surgeon, carefully reconstructed his mangled foot.

✳

Oh, by-the-way…that was when I suddenly realized that it was December 25—Christmas! I reached into my pocket and fingered Kate's cylinder. *What is she doing?* I thought. *Who's she with? Is she safe?* Kate's cylinder was distracting me. I couldn't allow that. Too much rested on my shoulders. I let the cylinder go and pushed it deep into my pocket. I pulled myself together and announced throughout *Lyre*, "Merry Christmas! Bet you never dreamed you would spend Christmas like this!"

THE *LYRE*—CORONATION GULF

As soon as Ski was able to talk coherently, I arranged to speak with him over the Secure Gertrude.

"What happened, you crazy Polock?" I asked.

"I dunno," Ski answered. "I guess I got into a fight with a Polar Bear, and the bear won."

"Seriously, Ski, how are you doing?"

"Doc Everest done good, Sir. Says I'll be good as new by the time we get to EB."

"You in a cast?"

"My lower leg and foot, yeah." "How's your chess?" I asked.

"Shit, Sir, Sergyi's with you, and the other guys don' play." "What about Jake? I'm pretty sure he plays." To me, it seemed unlikely that our electronics genius didn't play chess.

"I didn' think about that. I'll check with him." Then Ski's voice cracked into a grin I could hear over the circuit. "That fuckin' Orca sure saved my ass, you know. He the same one we saw back at Point Barrow?"

"Not likely," I said. "I don't think there are sufficient polynyas between there and here for him to get air. I think this guy lives around here."

"Yeah…yer probably right. Thanks for calling, Commander. I really appreciate it. Ham's doing great, you know, but we all miss you. You guys be careful over there. There's a lot of shit going on!"

✳

We moved through the strait at seven knots, faster than steerageway but not by much. In the best of times, with well-charted waters, we would not have moved much faster. There simply were too many objects in our way. As the skipper suggested—ordered, really—we kept a running track on our paper charts. Every rock, every islet was precisely located on *Sozh*, while they were just far enough off on the paper charts to make precise navigation impossible. One had to wonder just how long the Soviets had been at this charting task right under the Canadian noses.

I kept the skipper appraised of our *Sozh* findings, and while we agreed that *Sozh's* accuracy was astonishing, we were unwilling to rely on the system without full paper backup. Whoever had the *Lyre* watch dutifully plotted the proper position of each obstacle we encountered so that our paper charts became increasingly valuable as we continued our journey. One of the things a ship's captain always takes with him when he abandons ship is the ship's log. It occurred to me that I now had something else equally valuable. I made sure our completed charts were readily available should the worst happen before we reached our destination.

※

We had a total of eleven hours on this leg, eleven hours of slow walking at seven knots through the second half of Dolphin and Union Strait. Having to pay such close attention to everything out there, however, kept this leg from falling into the boring camp. Bert, Sam, and Potts kept busy identifying and charting all the obstacles the strait threw at us. As we departed the strait in Potts' third hour, he called me to Control. "What do you make of this, Mac?" he asked, pointing to a contact in Coronation Gulf several nautical miles ahead of us.

I called *Teuthis*. Waverly had the watch and picked up.

"What do you know about that contact out ahead of us in Coronation Gulf?" I asked.

"It's *USS Drum*," Waverly told me. "She's been guarding our front door, so we could concentrate on transiting the strait safely."

The *USS Drum* (SSN 677) was a *Sturgeon class* fast-attack sub commissioned in 1972. This boat and crew had a lot of under-ice experience. It was gratifying to know she was out there looking out for us.

※

Coronation Gulf is a continuation of Dolphin and Union Strait, sort of. This entire part of our passage lay between Victoria Island to the north and mainland Canada to the south. Coronation Gulf differed in that it was much wider and shallower than the straits at both ends. We planned to hug the northern edge of the gulf, keeping to the deepest water available. As with Dolphin and Union Strait, we had to keep a careful watch for rocky and islet obstacles that very well might be incorrectly placed on our official charts. I was hoping that *Sozh* would continue its valuable assist.

Potts drove us into Coronation Gulf and, on my order, increased our speed to 8.5 knots. *Sozh* continued to be more accurate than our charts, so we relied on it more and more while continuing to keep the paper track. My watch was uneventful, as was Spook's. Toward the end of his watch, however, Spook had to transit a four-nautical-mile-long gap between Edinburgh and Murray Islands that narrowed to just one nautical mile at its midpoint. Fortunately, both islands were accurately placed on our charts as well as on *Sozh*. With bated breath, we passed through safely. Then Bert took over to bring us past Richardson Islands to Wilbank Bay.

We were protected out front by *Drum* and to our rear by *Frisco*. Right here, at the entrance to Wilbank Bay, we had the opportunity to catch our breath, so to speak. I wanted to flush *Lyre* with fresh air. Onboard, we were nose blind, but I was sure we stank like hell. We had a pretty good idea of our exact location since both *Sozh* and our charts placed Edinburgh and Murray Islands at the same place. But, we were about to enter Dease Strait between Victoria Island and Kent Peninsula. The strait itself was wide enough, but halfway through lay the Finlayson Islands with shoals, rocks, and islets all over the place. If we were going to negotiate this treacherous water safely under the ice, we needed to know exactly where we were.

✳

"*Lyre*, this is *Teuthis*." It was Franklin. "We are two nautical miles off your starboard bow. Stand by while I get a sat fix."

"*Teuthis*, this is *Lyre*. While you get your fix, I will flush my atmosphere. Give me your exact position and heading after your fix, and I will cross your bow and come alongside starboard to starboard."

"*Teuthis*, aye."

This would be another first.

"Okay, Bert, set us up for flushing our air, and then bring us up against the underside of the canopy," I said, watching the monitor view of the water above us. Bert threw a couple of switches on *Ritm*, lining up the snorkel system for sucking in air with the blower, and in less than a minute, I could clearly see the smooth ice surface above us. Bert stopped our slow ascent as we came up against the ice.

"Okay…drop down five feet and pop it up," I ordered.

The ice was about a foot thick, so *Lyre* broke through easily. I raised the scope and swung around. Other than the surprisingly large phosphorescence-illuminated open polynya we had just created, I saw nothing. I scanned the ice off our starboard bow but did not see *Teuthis'* antenna in the darkness. In the pale phosphorescent light, I watched the snorkel rise.

"Start the blow," I ordered.

The air we sucked in was cold, ten or fifteen degrees below zero—that's Fahrenheit. Sergyi brought parkas to Bert and me. After fifteen minutes, the temperature in Control was near freezing. I decided we had had enough fresh air and secured the blow.

Bert dropped the snorkel, and I swept around with the scope one final time—nothing but phosphorescence. Bert eased down to a hundred feet while I contacted *Teuthis*.

"*Teuthis*, this is *Lyre*. Transmit your updated coordinates, and I will swing around to your starboard side."

Franklin got back to me a few minutes later. I guess he first had to get to a stable position up against the ice cover. He had moved a bit closer to our position—just over a nautical mile off our port bow. I reset *Sozh* and verified that *Akkord* had synched properly.

"Let's do it, Bert," I said, hunching into my parka.

Bert blew on his fingertips to warm them and set the coordinates into *Akkord*. Twenty-three minutes later, we rested against the canopy, our starboard side twenty feet from *Teuthis'* starboard side, external lights ablaze.

✳

Three divers appeared in what I now considered standard configuration, two carrying the cable and one watching over them from above. I was frustrated by not knowing each diver's identity and made a mental note to solve that problem. When I realized that the lookout was excited by something, I added a second note: Tap into the divers' comms.

The lookout's excitement became apparent immediately thereafter as two diving Polar Bears appeared from *Lyre's* port side, making a beeline for the other two divers. They were much smaller than the bear that had attacked Ski—my guess, litter twins still under mama's care. Before anyone could react, however, an Orca appeared, quite literally eating one bear whole and scaring the second off. Then the Orca approached the divers who had clumped together to ward off the bears. "Look!" Sergyi said, pointing to the monitor that displayed the Orca's dorsal fin. "That exactly the same bite that the other Orca had."

"I'll be damned," I said. "I think that big guy followed us here. There are plenty of polynyas along our route. It's possible."

Briefly, we observed a much larger Polar Bear nose around the edges of our lighted area—probably mama looking for her cub—but our Orca chased her away. I suspect that when she saw the Orca, she knew what had happened to her cub.

"You think the Orca really swallow little bear whole?" Sergyi asked. "I think little bear scratching and biting in stomach not good for Orca." "I've watched Orcas eat seals from close-up," I answered. "It sure looks like they swallow them whole, but logic dictates that somehow the Orcas crush the critters before swallowing."

"So, we got us an Orca for a mascot," Bert said. "That does beat all." We finished the battery charge as we completed our sixth day underway on *Lyre*. Bert, Sergyi, and I watched the divers complete their task and disappear beneath *Teuthis*. Our Orca—Sergyi had named him *Borysko*, a Ukrainian name that means fighter and warrior—watched them and even followed them to the Egress hatch. "I wish to be diving," Sergyi said wistfully.

"I know," I answered, "but we need you here for your Russian expertise."

"*Da*...but I like dive better!"

THE *LYRE*—DEASE STRAIT

Ahead lay more of the same, except for the Finlayson Islands. For nearly seven hours, we cruised along happily on course 082 degrees at nine knots until we neared those treacherous obstacles. As I had come to expect by then, *Sozh* placed them accurately, whereas, on our chart, they were misplaced by nearly a nautical mile. The skipper and I decided to let *Lyre* lead both of us through the Finlaysons. *Teuthis* kept abaft our starboard beam for the entire passage.

We took nearly an hour to pass the islands. Then we "sprinted" at ten knots on course 098 degrees into Queen Maud Gulf.

As we left the strait behind us, Potts had the watch. He called me to Control.

"Look at this, Mac." Potts pointed to his *Okean* display and its counterpart on *Akkord*. Ahead of us, a contact faded in and out as *Okean* attempted to isolate the incoming signal supplied by our damaged sonar dome.

I got on the Secure Gertrude. "*Teuthis*, this is *Lyre*. We hold an intermittent contact ten nautical miles on bearing zero-nine-six."

"Roger, *Lyre*," it was Waverly, "that's *Ohio*. While we transited Dease Strait, she sprinted around us to protect our front door. *Ohio* commented on the tight squeeze at the Finlaysons. Says she could have used your *Sozh*."

"They know about *Sozh*?" I asked.

"We told them when we gave them the corrected positions for the islands. That's how they were able to get out ahead of us so quickly."

THE *LYRE*—QUEEN MAUD GULF

"Queen Maud Gulf…Where the hell did that name come from?" Potts asked as I assumed the watch from him and commenced the seven-hour run along the gulf's northwestern edge toward Ice Breaker Channel.

"Actually, that's an interesting story," I answered, digging into my accumulated store of absolutely useless historical trivia. "Before 1905, Norway and Sweden were one country with one king, although they still carried their separate names. In England, Princess Maud Charlotte

Mary Victoria of Wales was the third daughter of Albert Edward, Prince of Wales. In 1896, she married Prince Carl of Denmark, becoming Maud, Queen of Denmark. Then, in 1905, on a nearly one-hundred percent-vote, the Norwegians decided to separate from Sweden to form their own independent country. Against some opposition by Socialist partisans, the Norwegians decided on a monarchy. They asked Prince Carl of Denmark to be their king, and he accepted, naming himself Haakon VII. Thus, in 1905, Maud Charlotte Mary Victoria of Wales became Queen Maud of Norway.

"While all this was happening, Norwegian Roald Amundsen had set up and was undertaking the world's first successful Northwest Passage by sea. He wintered over twice on King William Island, on the other side of Jenny Lind Island, about seventy-two nautical miles due east of where we are right now, before moving westward on the route we just traversed. When he reached Nome, Alaska, in 1906, he found out about the event I just described. He wired his new king, stating, "My traversing the Northwest Passage was a great achievement for Norway," and signed the wire, 'Your loyal subject, Roald Amundsen.' Then he named the area we occupy right now after his new queen: *Queen Maud Gulf*." I grinned at Potts. "One more thing… British explorer John Rae named Jenny Lind Island after his favorite Swedish opera singer. Now that's probably more than you ever wanted to know."

"Actually, Sir, that's fascinating. How do you remember all that crap?"

"I don't really know, Potts. I read something interesting, and then I move on. At some later time, when it seems pertinent, that stuff just bubbles up into my mind. I don't have a clue how I do it." I grinned again. "You guys must get pretty tired of my stories."

"Shit no! How else we gonna pass the time down here?" Now Potts grinned at me. "Seriously, Sir, you tell good stories."

✳

Spook picked up the last hour of our Queen Maud transit and took us through ten-nautical-mile-wide Ice Breaker Strait between Victoria and Lilly Lind Islands. Bert took over and shepherded us northeastward through lower Victoria Strait for four hours. He brought us to a stop fifty feet over the bottom in 150 feet of water, just four nautical miles southeast of Taylor Island. Both *Sozh* and our chart agreed on Taylor Island's position.

"*Lyre*, this is *Teuthis*." It was the XO, taking what would have been my watch. "We are three hundred yards off your bow."

"This is *Lyre*. We have perfect agreement between *Sozh* and our chart and have our position accurately marked. Sat fix appears unnecessary. Suggest you approach us starboard to starboard and reset your SINS accordingly."

"Roger, *Lyre*. Stand by for our approach."

Bert lifted us straight up against the canopy. In the brightness from our beams, we could see the jumbled underside of the canopy at our location. It looked like ice in a frozen river—large chunks three or four feet thick tumbled in all directions and then refrozen. It presented no obstacle, but its appearance was as wild as anything we had yet seen. Within a few minutes, *Teuthis* had come alongside, and the divers were in the water. I had not yet discussed my thoughts with Ham about diver identification, but Jake had kludged a method for us to monitor divers' comms. It was akin to the OOD placing an open Secure Gertrude mike in front of the diver comms speakers.

Our charging ops were entirely routine this time. We were too far from shore and the polynyas near Taylor Island to be visited underwater by Polar Bears, although I would not have dismissed the possibility that a bear or two were above us on the ice. The divers had hooked us together.

We were just about to commence the charge when the lookout diver shouted, "Hey! There's Borysko!"

I checked the monitors. Sure enough, if it wasn't Borysko, then this Orca was his twin, right down to the shape of the bite out of his dorsal fin. Borysko approached each diver in turn, gently nudged him, and then backed off and swam in circles around our submarine sortie. One of the divers, it turned out to be Harry, returned to the Egress hatch, got a piece of 4 x 4, and pushed it toward the Orca. Borysko took the wood into the front of his jaws, swam around with it for several minutes, and then returned to the two divers. He gently poked Harry with the 4 x 4 and then left it nearby. When it rose, he retrieved it and again brought it to Harry. This time, Harry grabbed it. Borysko whipped his massive tail up and down, much like a dog wagging his tail. Harry pushed the 4 x 4 toward the canopy so that it rose and wedged itself between two pieces of ice. Borysko followed it, worried it loose with his front teeth, and brought it back to the divers.

Both we and the Basketball were able to record this remarkable play behavior.

When the charge had finished and the gear was stowed, all three divers joined Borysko for a few minutes of play. Thirty feet of 12,000-pound Borysko hovered in the clear water with three divers floating around his massive head, rubbing his dome, patting his snout, and scratching his tongue. They might have kept it up for hours, but Ham finally recalled them. They reluctantly returned to the Egress hatch, and *Teuthis* slowly pulled away from our starboard side.

A few minutes later, Sam got us underway for our remaining twelve-hour run through Victoria Strait.

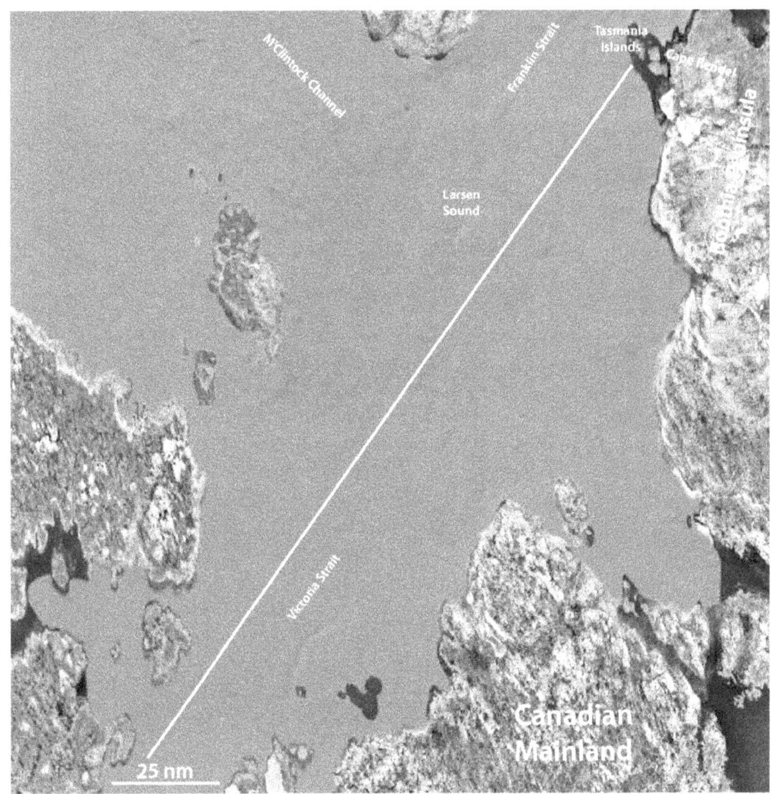

Track of USS Teuthis & Lyre from Victoria Strait to the Tasmania Islands

CHAPTER TWELVE—The Tasmania Islands

THE *LYRE*—VICTORIA STRAIT

We were six hours into our eighth day when Sam got us underway through Victoria Strait on course 071 degrees. Our immediate goal was Larsen Sound and then Franklin Strait stretching north between Prince of Wales Island to the west and the Boothia Peninsula that pushed northward from the Canadian mainland into the Canadian archipelago.

According to our chart, our route was fairly shallow—722 feet at the deepest part of Victoria Strait, but otherwise typically less than 400 feet. The canopy was nearly six feet of solid ice—old ice. This shit hadn't broken up in decades.

Sam drove us for two hours. Then Potts took the next five. I had the final five and brought us into Larsen Sound. This was a straight run at ten knots. We did not stop for anything. My one regret was that Borysko probably would not be able to follow us. He could break through fairly thin ice, but five or six feet was totally beyond him. He was too smart to trail us without known breathing holes.

As we passed through the northern reach of Victoria Strait, Barry contacted me from *Teuthis*. "*Lyre*, this is *Teuthis*. We have picked up a Soviet sub intermittently ahead of us. Not sure if it is in M'Clintock Channel or Franklin Strait. Insufficient data to determine type or range. We designated this contact Sierra-seven."

"Could be *Shchuka*," I responded. "She could have headed west of Banks Island up to Parry Channel and could now be working her way south through either M'Clintock or Franklin."

"It's not *Carp* because *Frisco* has kept her well south," Barry said. "The captain thinks the Soviets have put more submarine resources than just *Carp* and *Shchuka* on our tail. He suspects they will be monitoring all three north-south channels we might access—M'Clintock Channel, Peel Sound-Franklin Strait, and Prince Regent Inlet-Boothia Gulf. The captain says that when they do not find us in M'Clintock, they'll assume we are either heading to Parry Channel to cross over and head south down the east side of Baffin Island, or we'll transit Bellot Strait to go south through Fury and Hecla Strait."

I turned to Spook, who was preparing to relieve me. "You get all that?"

Spook nodded. "I'll play around with *Okean* to see if we can come up with something." He turned to examine the *Okean* console. "My guess," he added, "is it's another sub altogether."

THE *LYRE*—LARSEN SOUND

Larsen Sound is actually the confluence of M'Clintock Channel to the northwest, Franklin Strait to the northeast, and Victoria Strait to the south, from whence we had just come. Typically, according to our charts, its average depth is 300 to 500 feet, but it has a 700-foot depression near its center. The northern reaches of both M'Clintock and Franklin drop down to more than a thousand feet.

Our immediate destination was just south of Wrottesley Inlet on Boothia Peninsula—the Tasmania Islands, projecting into Franklin Strait from Boothia Peninsula. We intended to take a few hours on the bottom at the Tasmania Islands to allow my crew to return to *Teuthis* for a shower and a "home-cooked" meal and for Barry to transfer our track info to his charts.

✳

Spook was not able to pick up the Soviet sub—Sierra-7— on *Okean*. He tried throughout his watch but got nothing. By the time Bert took over, we had begun to lose a clear line of sight to M'Clintock Channel. Halfway through his watch, Bert got a couple of hits on *Okean*, nothing to hang our hats on, but enough to decide that Sierra-7 was in Franklin Strait. This was both good and bad—good because we knew where he was and bad because he was where we needed to go.

Shortly before Sam assumed the watch, we got a Secure Gertrude call from *Teuthis*. It was the XO.

"*Lyre*, this is *Teuthis*. We have firm contact info on that Soviet sub—Sierra-seven. She's a recent *Victor III class*—the *Volgograd* (K502). She's hanging out west of Pemmican Rock, the entrance to Bellot Strait. *Swordfish* transited west of Banks Island and is dropping down through Peel Sound to investigate."

An hour into Sam's watch, the XO called us again.

"*Lyre*, this is *Teuthis*. We've picked up a second *Victor III class* sub north of us. Designate Sierra-eight. This one is not in our books." The XO paused. "Sierra-eight, the unknown *Victor III*, appears to be heading toward the Tasmania Islands, so watch yourself!"

THE *LYRE*—BOTTOMED AT THE TASMANIA ISLANDS

The Tasmania Islands are somewhat of a mystery. They sit atop a mound jutting out from Cape Rendel on the Boothia Peninsula surrounded by about a hundred feet of water that drops to 500 feet over a range of one-third to one-and-a-half nautical miles—a slope of 2.5 to 12 degrees. This was in sharp contrast to the 30-degree slope and vertical cliffs we experienced at Hecla and Fury Islands when we placed the transponder when we were trying to lose the *Alfa* during

Operation Ice Breaker.[15] Although they are charted, all but two remain unnamed. Toms Island, the second largest, lies 0.8 nautical miles due west from the largest, that is unnamed. Graham Island lies three nautical miles northeast from the largest island, just 0.8 nautical miles north of Cape Rendel.

A three-quarter nautical mile wide tongue-like canyon pushes north between Toms Island and the largest island. It stops one-third nautical mile south of a small islet between the two larger islands.

Our intent was to bottom both subs, commence the charge, and bring half my crew at a time to *Teuthis* for a shower and a steak and baker dinner. The skipper decided to bottom both subs at the lip of the canyon. Sam brought us up the canyon, placing us crosswise at the lip with our starboard side facing downslope. Waverly brought *Teuthis* alongside, starboard to starboard.

Within a few minutes, Ham put three divers in the water—Harry, Whitey, and Jake. Ham had solved the diver identity problem with Storekeeper First Class Frank Ender, *Teuthis'* senior Storekeeper under Lt. j.g. Wilson Ferrer, the Supply Officer. Ender created cloth badges that attached to each diver's helmet displaying a bright letter representing the diver's surname. So, Harry, Whitey, and Jake wore *B* for Blackwell, *F* for Ford, and *P* for Palmer, respectively.

Harry and Whitey swam the shorepower cable from the Egress Lock to our external connector while Jake and the Basketball watched from above. Suddenly and unexpectedly, Borysko appeared from the canyon behind *Teuthis*. The giant cetacean whipped his tail around like a joyous puppy—a 12,000-pound puppy.

"Where the hell did he come from?" Harry barked.

Sergyi looked at me. "How is this possible? He has to breathe. We just crossed under one hundred eighty nautical miles of solid ice."

"Well…" I said, giving myself some time to come up with a meaningful answer. "Orcas roam all over the world. Any specific Orca has a territory of several hundred to thousands of miles. This is Borysko's home territory—he knows it well. Orcas have

---

15 See *Operation Ice Breaker*, the second book in the *Mac McDowell Mission Series*.

excellent sonar. I think Borysko tracked us sonically while he headed east to Boothia Peninsula. Then, tracking our sound, he followed the coast northward from polynya to polynya until he found us right here. He seems pretty happy. If that isn't joy, then I don't know what joy is."

After his greeting, Borysko swam around both subs, carefully inspecting everything, perhaps to ascertain that things were normal. He paid particular attention to *Mystic* moving independently through the water. I am sure this gave the crew plenty of opportunity to kid Bob Taggert and his crew about Borysko's intentions toward *Mystic*.

The Tasmania Islands are home to a large number of Polar Bears. The thin ice and currents under the ice give the bears an endless supply of fresh fish, and both the seal population around the islands and muskox herds on Boothia supply nearly endless game. Because they looked so much like seals, the divers were on continuous alert for swimming bears. With Borysko around, they felt much safer.

Mystic had taken half my crew to *Teuthis*—Bert, Spook, Dokey, Hart (the DIA sonar specialist), and Sergyi. Potts had the watch, and a half-hour later, he called me to Control.

"What do you make of this, Mac?" he asked, pointing to three blips on both *Okean* and *Akkord*. Each was accompanied by a small Cyrillic character. The outside blips displayed *II-1* and *II-2*. The middle larger blip displayed *C*.

I called *Teuthis*. "This is an emergency! Get me Sergyi!" Moments later, Sergyi answered. "Yes, Boss…"

I described the three blips and their Cyrillic letters. Sergyi interrupted me. "This is very important, Mac. Those are Russian diver carriers.

The *IIs* are Protei-five one-man diver carriers. Protei is simple machine. Has large battery container against which diver lies prone, two hinged braces in front that press against diver's shoulders, hinged bar that swings up between diver's legs, and shrouded electric propeller near diver's feet. It also carries transponder, a simple homing indicator that points to a beacon, and on/off switch. No accelerator, brake, or steering. To stop, rider turns it off. He changes depth and steers with his fins.

A Morskoy Spetsnaz diver riding a Protei-5 carrying an APS underwater rifle

"The *C* is two-man Sirena torpedo; it has double warhead. Sirena has small homing readout—no range, just direction. Also magnetic compass, but that useless up here.

Two Morskoy Spetsnaz divers riding a Sirena two-man torpedo

"We are under attack by Soviet *Morskoy Spetsnaz*—Naval Spetsnaz. Very good…very dangerous. I suit up and get into water immediately! Get armed divers in water fast. Watch out! These guys armed with APS underwater rifle and SPP underwater pistol. APS fires twenty-six darts in full automatic—lethal range forty feet. Pistol fires four darts in double-action—lethal range twenty-five feet."

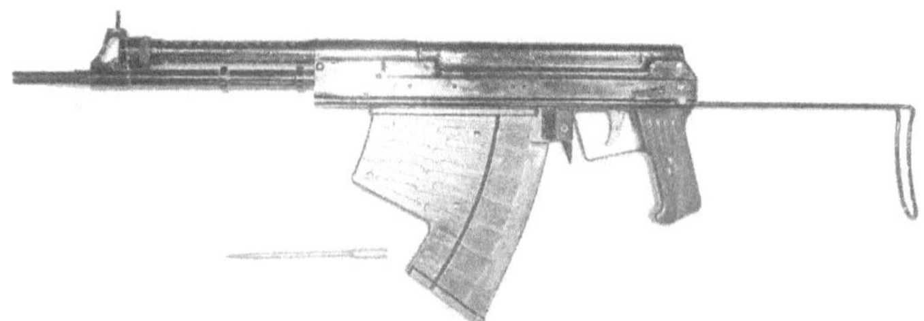

APS Underwater fully automatic Assault Weapon and dart. Magazine holds 26 darts

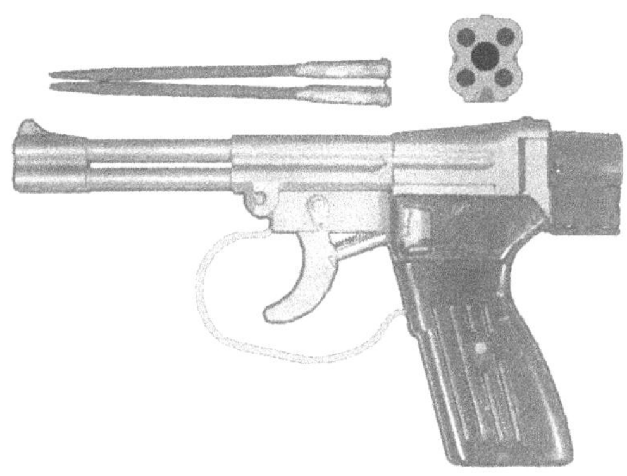

SPP-1 Underwater double-action pistol and darts.
Darts load in a cartridge of four

Sergyi left to prepare for the dive. I asked for the skipper.

"What is it, Mac?" the skipper asked several seconds later. I told him about the approaching divers.

"I recommend," I said quickly, "that you put all the divers into the water on rebreathers with dart guns and ammo, break off the charge, and slide *Teuthis* into the canyon. Drag the shorepower cable with you. If possible, leave the Basketball above the lip. These Spetsnaz guys don't know what they are getting into. My guys can handle them."

"Your divers are entering the water now," the skipper said. "Sergyi is with them. Let me worry about *Teuthis'* disposition. You concentrate on gaining control of the in-water situation."

ON THE SEAFLOOR—THE TASMANIA ISLANDS

I had an immediate decision—to turn on my external lights or not. We were mid-winter in the high Arctic. Above the ice canopy was dark 24/7. Even were there daylight above, very little light would have penetrated to our 100-foot depth. We were below the canyon lip, and the water was crystal clear. If I turned on only those lights that shined downward, I suspected that the incoming attackers might not see the glow. On the other hand, each of my divers wore a helmet light he could turn on or off as necessary. The incoming divers certainly would be wearing helmet lights and possibly lights on their vehicles.

I decided—no external lights and extinguished them.

Ham had instructed each diver to give frequent updates on his position and surrounds.

The five crew members still onboard *Lyre* joined me in Control. "Gil," I said to Gilbert Edwards, the DIA reactor specialist, "terminate the battery charge." He left to carry out the order.

I checked the monitors. *Teuthis* was still alongside; I had no idea whether or not the skipper would move down into the canyon. There was nothing he could do where we were. All the divers were deployed. I suspect they took with them all the darts they could carry—perhaps all we had. *Teuthis'* only potential task would be to accept wounded divers, should that become necessary. With the double warhead coming toward us, I relegated diver safety secondary to *Teuthis'* safety.

Teuthis lifted several feet off the bottom and commenced drifting downslope into the canyon. Harry, Whitey, and Jake were already in the water. Jimmy, Jer, and Sergyi joined them. I saw a seventh diver, but before I could ask Ham, he told me over the Secure Gertrude that Bill had requested to get wet for this fight. Then I spied two more divers that Ham identified as Wyatt Cook, the DIA supervisor, and Kendrick Long, the hull specialist.

"They both insisted on joining the fight," Ham told me.

On word from Ham, the divers extinguished their lights. My monitors showed pitch black, but I could detect a faint glow over the lip to the north.

Borysko had remained with the divers below the lip but seemed subdued, almost as if he could pick up their vibes. On the monitor, against the glow from the oncoming divers, I could see silhouettes of Harry, Whitey, and Jake aligned in a spaced-out line along the lip. Then Borysko's bulk blocked my view as he checked them out.

That's when a machinegun-like chatter shattered the silence. At the time, it was pure chaos, although we pieced it together afterward. Apparently, the lead rider on the Sirena suddenly spotted Borysko peeking over the canyon lip about thirty feet distant. He emptied his APS in Borysko's direction, twenty-six darts super-cavitating their way out of his barrel. Several lodged in Borysko's blubber, causing no permanent harm, but seriously pissing him off. Both Harry and Whitey took darts in their arms—painful but not serious. Jake took a dart through his faceplate into his brain. He died instantly.

Jake had established a rapport with Borysko. The Orca always seemed to favor Jake when they both were in the water. Borysko sensed something about Jake. He briefly nuzzled Jake's body and then streaked toward the Sirena. He slammed into the manned torpedo, knocking both divers out of their cockpits. A deadman switch activated, and the Sirena settled gently to the bottom. Borysko tore into the two divers, killing them and scattering their body parts left and right.

The two Protei-5 riders turned their attention to Borysko, firing their APS darts in quick three-shot bursts. All that accomplished was to anger Borysko even further. My divers turned on their headlamps and rushed to the aid of the attackers, but Borysko was having none of that. He methodically took out both riders and then checked each of my divers one-by-one, making sure they were okay, including Harry and Whitey, who had hunkered down at the lip, nursing their wounds.

Bill, Jimmy, and Jer cautiously approached Borysko and commenced pulling the smooth darts from his skin. He seemed to understand their intent and let them do it. Sergyi, Wyatt, and Ken joined them. All six divers later exclaimed about what an awesome experience that was.

Teuthis returned upslope to her former position beside us, and the divers got Harry and Whitey into the DDC for treatment. Jake's body was placed in a body bag and brought into the DDC. Bill, Jimmy, and Jer then reattached the shorepower cable so we could complete the charge. The mood inside both subs was somber and increasingly angry.

Everybody wanted revenge, nobody more than Sergyi. After the first half of my crew completed their ablutions and partook of a hearty steak and baker meal, they assembled in *Mystic* for the short return trip. As the five men dropped into *Lyre*, their normal jocular repartee was missing. Instead, a somber atmosphere permeated the captured Soviet sub. Sergyi was more than somber; he was livid.

"Mac, can we talk?" Sergyi asked almost as soon as his feet hit the deck.

"Sure," I said and walked with him to the Mess Deck.

"Jake's death was NOT necessary," he said as soon as we were alone. "Those Spetsnaz guys bastards. Their reputation is shoot first and apologize after. They are taught that Orca is not dangerous, and they would not normally attack Orca. They are very smart. The shooter must have surmised that Borysko had risen from a depression. Based on their reason for attack in first place, he presumed presence of armed divers at the lip of the depression. He was not shooting at Borysko. He was shooting at divers he *knew* were there. It was unprovoked… unnecessary…abomination!" Sergyi took a deep breath. I could tell he was shaken.

"*Victor III* not normally carry *Morskoy Spetsnaz*. But their purpose is find and destroy *Lyre*. For that, they decide they need *Morskoy Spetsnaz*. Somehow, they figure we bottom at Tasmania Islands and decide to destroy *Lyre* with Sirena. I train on Sirena and Protei-five." He paused again and looked me deep in my eyes.

"I think Borysko not damage Sirena, maybe also not two Proteis. I have proposal," he said quietly. "Doc says Harry and Whitey okay for diving. I take them outside with two heated paraffin drums. We find Sirena and both Proteis. We rig drums to draw power from Serina to melt paraffin. I take Sirena and sling drums over back. Harry and Whitey each take Protei. I rig Sirena with delay detonator. We locate *Victor III* and pump paraffin into intake. Then delay-detonate Sirena at screws and ride Proteis back to *Teuthis*. I hitch ride back with Harry or Whitey."

"What will the Sirena do to the *Victor III*?" I asked.

"Damage propulsion, perhaps force Victor to use auxiliary screws on stern planes. Not sink sub, but plenty scare."

Sergyi had a point. I gave what he said some thought and then said, "Okay, Sergyi, you return to *Teuthis* with me, and we will talk with the skipper. If he approves, we'll do it."

✳

Cmdr. Roken asked Sergyi several penetrating questions. Perhaps the most pertinent was, "What are the odds of there being more Spetsnaz divers on the *Victor III*?"

"*Morskoy Spetsnaz* units on subs usually consist of four divers," Sergyi answered, holding up four fingers. "Just four."

In the end, the skipper approved the excursion. Sergyi went back to the machine shop in the Auxiliary Machinery space to kluge together a mechanical delay-timer for detonating the Sirena.

The skipper and I both agreed that I should return to *Lyre* in case we needed to move the *Alfa* from its present location. I managed to get in a shower and a quick medium-rare with a buttered baker before taking the short ride back to my new command. Part of me really wanted to be with Sergyi and the others. I had full confidence in their abilities, but I still yearned to be with them.

By the time *Mystic* had clamped into her cradle on *Teuthis*, we had completed our charge. Earlier, in preparation for such an event, we had set up two paraffin drums like we did with *Carp* off Pt. Barrow.[16] Each drum was wrapped with heating coils and covered with thick insulation. Instead of the waterproof extension cord we used with *Carp*, however, we rigged both drums to draw power from the Serina. We also replaced the hand pumps with electric pumps that would speed up the process enormously. As before, each drum also carried a couple of diving weights to bring it to neutral buoyancy.

Sergyi, Harry, and Whitey entered the water and took charge of the drums with their makeshift harness. The three divers kept close to the bottom as they topped the lip and headed toward the carnage Borysko had caused. They found the Sirena on the bottom, undamaged, surrounded by the torn body parts of the two Spetsnaz divers. The Protei divers had their heads ripped off, and both sets of Protei shoulder braces were bent, but otherwise, they still functioned. Nearby, the divers located four APS underwater weapons with empty magazines and four extra magazines with twenty-six darts each. They also found two SPP underwater pistols with four four-dart loads on the two Protei riders, but they never located the two pistols probably worn by the unlucky Sirena riders. They didn't find any extra four-dart loads.

The three divers headed toward the *Victor III*, presuming that it rested on the slope immediately opposite *Teuthis* and *Lyre*. The Sirena's homing readout indicated the *Victor III*'s general direction—no range, just direction. That sufficed to get them within visual range of the sub.

"They will see us coming," Sergyi said over the underwater circuit, "but they will think we are their returning divers."

"No matter," Harry said, "but we need to hustle."

---

16 See *Operation Ice Breaker*, the second book in the *Mac McDowell Mission Series*.

They worked directly off the Sirena's back. Sergyi and Whitey manipulated the Sirena so the heated drums were directly beneath the starboard intake. While Sergyi stabilized the Sirena, Harry and Whitey held the hoses inside the intake, and Sergyi activated the pumps. They emptied the drums about ten minutes later. Suction at the intake ceased, and the *Victor III's* reactor scrammed. The divers could hear the alarms right through the hull.

"Now!" Sergyi said as all three pushed the Sirena aft under the giant tandem four-bladed props.

Sergyi armed the Sirena's double warhead and attached his makeshift timer to the detonate button. Harry and Whitey mounted their Proteis, and Harry moved his so that Sergyi could grab hold of the bracket that passed up between his legs.

"Now!" Sergyi said, activating the timer. Both Proteis sped off in the direction of *Teuthis* and *Lyre*. One nautical mile later, the double warhead exploded. Since Protei steering control was provided by the divers' fins, the explosion's shockwave drove both Proteis into the muddy bottom. Harry and Whitey extricated themselves from the soft bottom after the shockwave passed and checked themselves and their mounts.

"Everyone okay?" Sergyi asked. When the shockwave hit, he had let go of Harry's brace and thus was spared the indignity of being slammed into the mud.

Other than ringing ears, the three seemed unharmed. They mounted up, and five minutes later, they brought their mechanical steeds to a standstill directly below the Egress hatch. They passed their three APSs and two SSPs through the hatch along with the full magazines. Using the block and tackle they had used to lower the paraffin drums through the hatch, they hoisted both Proteis into the DDC.

At that moment, a large Orca head appeared next to the three divers. Borysko nudged them gently and opened his mouth for a tongue scratch. They spent the next five minutes giving their total attention to the 12,000-pound cetacean.

It was only later that we all realized the Sirena explosion could have caused serious injury to Borysko. That was when we decided that somehow Borysko had figured this out and had distanced himself from the explosion before it happened.

✳

We still had a problem before moving on to Pemmican Rock and the entrance to Bellot Strait. We did not know the status of the damaged *Victor III*. Sergyi was fairly confident that he had damaged but not disabled the Soviet sub. According to him, the worst-case scenario was that the *Victor III* had lost use of her main shaft. That left the two small propellers on the stern stabilizers right next to the hull. Together, they could move the sub at five knots. The skipper decided to send divers to assess the situation. "If the *Victor III* still there," Sergyi said, "she will be able to detect our divers. That not good." Sergyi then explained that he could disable the two Protei transponders and sneak up on the *Victor III* without her being any the wiser.

"What about other Spetsnaz divers?" the skipper asked.

"Not likely," Sergyi answered. "*Morskoy Spetsnaz* not normally on subs. When there, four-man team normal."

The skipper briefed me over the Secure Gertrude. "What's your opinion, Mac?" he asked.

"I have a lot of faith in Sergyi's assessments," I said, "but my instinct says they have more Spetsnaz divers. I think we should deactivate the transponders like Sergyi said, and Sergyi and Bill should go well armed with the confiscated weapons."

"I concur," the skipper said.

"BUT," I added, "I want to go with them. Sergyi knows the *Victor III* and Soviet diving procedures. Bill is our most qualified diver—that's why he will soon be our next sat dive supervisor." I paused. "And me… I'm more devious than the lot of them."

"Really?" the skipper said. "Do I have to be concerned about that?"

I decided he was kidding and didn't respond. Instead, I asked, "Will you put Sergyi and Bill under my in-water command for the excursion?" I waited for a minute while I suspect he checked with Bob. "*Mystic* will be on *Lyre* in fifteen minutes," he said. "Be ready to board and return here for the dive excursion."

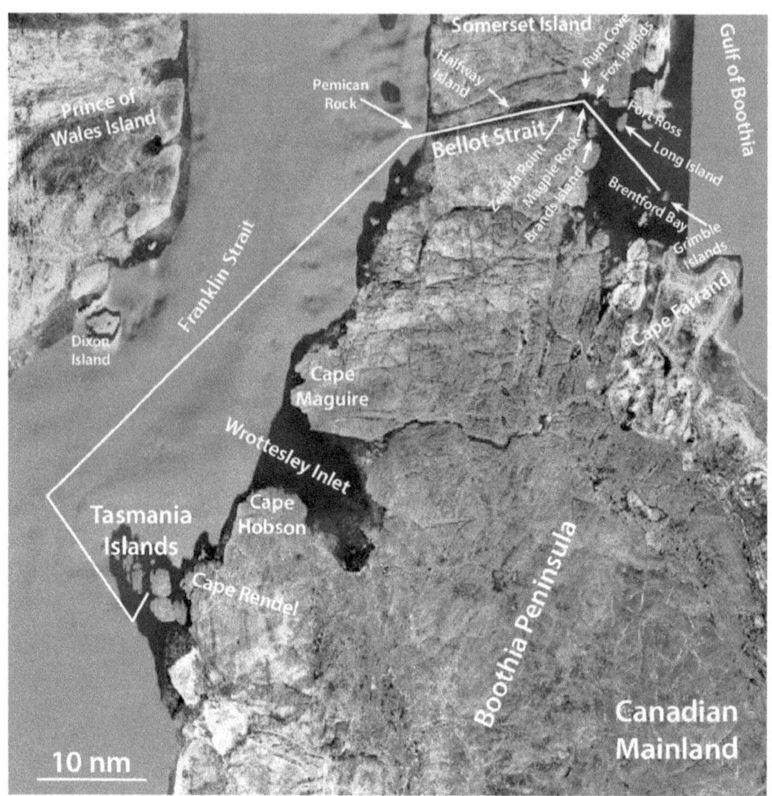

Track of USS Teuthis & Lyre from the Tasmania Islands through Bellot Strait to Gulf of Boothia

CHAPTER THIRTEEN—Threading the Needle

ON THE SEAFLOOR—THE TASMANIA ISLANDS

Bob Taggert and his crew had become really good at launching and retrieving *Mystic* and moving between *Teuthis* and *Lyre*. No more than thirty minutes following my Secure Gertrude conversation with the skipper, I joined Sergyi and Bill in the Egress Lock. We had the two Proteis, batteries fully charged, three APSs with three filled magazines (twenty-six rounds each), and two SPPs. Furthermore, we each had one of our own gas-powered dart guns strapped to our backs with ten darts each in leg bandolas. We were rigged for bear, although hopefully, not the polar kind.

Thinking ahead about possibilities, I obtained fifty feet of high-strength, stainless steel reinforced, jacketed cable from Eng and a handheld cutter that could slice through it. I looped the cable over my head and right arm and stuffed the cutter in a leg pocket.

We dropped through the hatch, where Borysko immediately greeted us, checking each diver carefully. He recognized Sergyi but did not recognize either Bill or me. Sergyi scratched his tongue; Bill and I followed suit. That seemed to settle things for Borysko. He backed off and let us proceed.

I drove one unit, Sergyi, the other with Bill hanging on to the bar between Sergyi's legs. Borysko accompanied us, although he darted to his polynya every few minutes for a breath of air. We had about a mile to go.

We proceeded without lights because we had no idea what lay ahead. About a half mile out, my homing indicator began to give me a reading. That meant two things: The *Victor III* was still there, and we were headed in the right direction. Our total distance was about one-and-a-half nautical miles. I figured we were doing about four knots, so we had fifteen minutes left, give or take. Ten minutes later, I called a halt. I couldn't see anything. It was like we were swimming in pitch black ink.

We huddled together, listening as carefully as possible. Borysko joined us after getting a gulp of air. He could not have understood what we were doing, but he was a natural hunter who excelled in coordinated stalking with other Orcas. That gave me an idea. I quietly explained my thought to Sergyi and Bill. Then we implemented the plan.

We parked both Proteis where we were, and then Sergyi circled around to the left and Bill to the right. I headed down the middle, swimming slowly with Borysko cruising slowly right above me. After about two minutes, Borysko darted to Sergyi and then to Bill, and then he returned to me for a moment before darting straight ahead, chittering as he swam.

Several seconds later, I saw a glow about ten feet over the bottom. Borysko stopped and watched me as I circled to my left and approached the light. As I moved closer, the bulk of the *Victor III* loomed over me to the right. We had come on the massive sub nearly bow-on. The glow was down the starboard side, probably at the tandem screw. I held my

APS at the ready but killing an unsuspecting diver who probably was just inspecting damage to his sub was not exactly on my bucket list.

The diver was outfitted like the other Spetsnaz divers we had encountered. An APS was slung over his rebreather backpack, and an SPP was holstered on his right leg. To my left, I caught a glimpse of Sergyi approaching cautiously. Borysko hovered above us at deck level, not making a sound. Bill was probably on the other side of the *Victor III*. I was concerned about using our comms this close to an adversary. I suspected that our transmissions would be audible, although nonintelligible, close-up. I signaled Sergyi to circle behind the diver off the sub's stern. I looked up to see what Borysko was doing and caught a glimpse of Bill hugging the upper side of the sub's tapered stern. He was slowly moving past the giant rudder toward the tandem props. He spied me and indicated that he could see two divers.

That changed the calculus. I was not about to risk another of my divers, especially Sergyi or Bill. I held up my right clenched fist, signaling the guys to hold where they were. I faced Sergyi and drew my hand across my neck, and pointed to the diver he and I could see. He acknowledged. Then I drifted up until I could see the second diver. I trained my APS on him, pointed to my chest and my right arm, and then at Bill and my left. I held my clenched fist high and dropped it.

Three percussions sounded as one. Sergyi put a dart through the back of his diver's head, killing him instantly. Bill and I sent darts into each of our diver's arms, just below the shoulders. Seconds later, I jerked our diver's full-face mask off and disabled his comms, hopefully preventing a report to his dive controller. Before he had a chance to react or breathe in water, I pressed his mask back against his face. Bill activated his headlamp. In the reflected light, I could see both pain and relief in the diver's eyes. No panic—this guy was a pro.

Borysko drifted down to our level and opened his mouth for a tongue scratch. The Spetsnaz diver's eyes widened with astonishment, but he maintained his composure. The diver clearly was in a lot of pain. I could tell that my dart had pierced his right humerus. Bill's seemed to have penetrated muscle only.

I retrieved both divers' APSs, handing them to Sergyi and Bill. Each diver also carried two spare APS magazines and an SPP with three spare four-dart loads. I strapped one SPP to my left leg, and

Sergyi took the second. We added the spare loads to our own dart bandolas.

"Let's get to the torpedo tubes," I said on the circuit, feeling free to talk now that the divers had ceased being a threat.

We moved forward smartly, Sergyi and Bill escorting the wounded diver between them. It took us a bit under two minutes to reach the bow. In our head beams, we clearly saw the top starboard torpedo tube door open. That was how the divers exited the sub. Torpedo tube doors are mechanically interlocked so that it is physically impossible to open both the outer and inner doors simultaneously. I slipped several turns of my high-strength cable from the coil, retrieved my cutter, and cut a ten-foot length. I pointed to the open door hinges and gestured for Sergyi to assist me. Together, we intertwined the cable around the hinges so that the door would not close unless someone removed the cable.

"I think they normally use those tubes for diving," I said, pointing to the open tube and the opposite one on the port side. "They're the best level for entering and exiting from inside the sub." I cut off another length of cable and handed it to Sergyi. "They lost comms with their divers. They will send out another diver to check on them. When they discover the starboard door jammed, they'll use the port, but they will be highly suspicious and ready for anything." I placed myself in a hover just above and behind the port door. "Sergyi, you take control of our wounded prisoner. Bill, you be ready to fire at the emerging diver, but not unless absolutely necessary."

Shortly thereafter, we began to hear mechanical sounds coming from the tube I was watching, and the outer door opened. The first thing I saw was the muzzle of an APS. As the diver moved out, I reached down and jerked off his full facemask. He was startled but didn't drop his weapon. I disabled his comms and knocked the APS from his grip. This guy was trained Spetsnaz—he was good. Rather than attempt to retrieve his facemask, he reached back to grapple with me. I wrapped a length of cable around both his hands and looped it around his rebreather backpack. Then I grabbed my knife from its chest sheath and placed the blade against his throat. That settled him down.

I waited a few seconds more and then pressed his facemask against his face, snugging the cup over his nose and mouth. He gulped a couple of breaths, and I pulled the facemask away again. I called Bill to the open door. "Take control of him and see that he remains subdued. Don't give him more than two breaths at a time."

While Bill dropped down to the seafloor with the captured diver, I wrapped another length of cable through the port door hinges. This would definitely slow them down. If they had more Spetsnaz divers at the ready, within minutes, we could expect them to emerge from one or the other of the remaining tubes.

I heard them attempt to close the port door. I could only imagine what was going through their minds. They had just lost three Spetsnaz divers after losing four earlier. Their reactor had scrammed, and their main shaft was damaged—possibly by external forces. They were bottomed in shallow water in the remote Arctic, and the crew was terrified of a possible radiation leak. The Soviet mantra had always been the many over the few. The sub slowly lifted off the bottom and began to slide backward as the small stern plane propellers took a bite. Then, with a loud rush of air, the *Victor III* lurched toward the ice canopy.

I dropped off the bow and joined my companions and our two prisoners on the seafloor. Borysko hovered over us, apparently more interested in our safety than what was happening with the *Victor III*. "Let's get back to the Proteis pronto!" I said. "They're going to vent the sub to calm the crew's fears. What they do after that is anybody's guess, but we need to be long gone."

THE *LYRE*—PEMMICAN ROCK

While I sat in *Lyre's* Control Center making a mental inventory of our acquired weapons, Spook, who had the watch, moved *Lyre* down the canyon and then set a course of 290 degrees.

About five nautical miles distant on the north side of the Tasmania Islands, the *Victor III* was using her diesel to vent the sub's atmosphere. We could almost hear her through our hull. She was totally blind to her surroundings, so we were able to move along smartly for an hour before we turned north to course 071 degrees for our forty-eight nautical mile leg to Pemmican Rock, the entrance to Bellot Strait. Toward the end of Spook's watch, our track took us through the middle of Franklin Strait, halfway between Dixon Island and Cape

Maguire. We were on the edge of Franklin trough that dropped to over 1,300 feet. With the bottom dropping off like that, you can get an idea of the rugged land on both sides of the strait.

We had four APSs from the original Spetsnaz divers and three more from my excursion, plus 338 APS darts. We had two SPPs from the original Spetsnaz guys and three more from my trip with their twenty darts plus seventeen four-dart loads for a total of eighty-eight SSP darts. That was a lot of firepower. Out of an abundance of caution, I turned the lot over to the COB for storage in the ship's armory. I obtained the skipper's permission for the COB to issue the underwater weapons directly to me, or Ham in my absence, without clearing it with him.

✳

Our major concern was *Volgograd*. At last report, she was hanging out west of Pemmican Rock. Since *Swordfish* was headed her way for several hours now, we didn't know what we were getting into. Plus, of course, we had to worry about the damaged *Victor III*. We had left her venting with her diesels on the surface just north of the Tasmania Islands. By the time she completed venting, her reactor would have come back online, which should have mollified the crew. Her main shaft had sustained damage, and her skipper was not stupid. He had deployed the Spetsnaz divers in an attempt to surprise us and disable the *Alfa*. He had to know the *Alfa* had a titanium hull, so sinking us with the Sirena was not a realistic option.

Doc Everest had patched up the captured Spetsnaz diver, Aleksandr Alexeyev, who was wounded in both arms. Despite my dart having penetrated the Russian's humerus, he was mending quickly. Both he and Boris Kuznetsov, the second captured Spetsnaz diver, were being held in Dive Control. Sergyi remained on *Teuthis* to help secure and supervise these guys. I reminded everyone that they were highly trained special operators, like our SEALS. They were dedicated to their mission and would take every opportunity to carry it out.

We considered building a cage because submarines don't have brigs. That turned out to be impractical. Ham came up with a better solution. We locked them into the DDC Main Lock under two atmospheres pressure. They could move about, eat and sleep, and communicate with us. When we needed the Main Lock, we transferred them into the Entry

Lock for the duration. Our own corpsman, Jimmy Tanner, maintained a medical watch over Alexeyev. When the wounded diver needed medical attention, Jimmy entered the lock, breathing pure oxygen with a mask so he wouldn't subject himself to any decompression.

Earlier, when we captured the *Carp* diver, Leonid Volkov,[17] Sergyi extracted a promise of good behavior from him. Unlike our present captives, Volkov was *not* Spetsnaz. These guys would resist to the death. We cleared our baffles hourly during our transit, but the unknown *Victor III* was undetectable while on his auxiliary props until we were very much closer. In the third hour of Bert's watch, *Okean* finally picked up *Volgograd*, quietly hanging out two nautical miles west of Pemmican Rock. We knew *Swordfish* was out there, but she was too quiet. We knew that *Carp* was somewhere to the south, kept there by *Frisco*, but we expected *Frisco* to join us for the Bellot Strait transit. Obviously, that would free up *Carp* to rejoin the fray. *Shchuka* was still AWOL, but since the Soviet sub north of us turned out to be *Volgograd*, *Shchuka* could be anywhere. Of one thing we were certain, she had not returned to the barn. My guess was she was hanging out in the south end of the Gulf of Boothia.

Why was *Volgograd* just hanging out? She had to know that our subs were aware of her presence. Could she be waiting until she detected the *Lyre* in order to blow us out of the water? Apparently, that was what the *Swordfish* skipper thought because he moved his sub between us and *Volgograd*, informing us of his intent by Secure Gertrude. Then he commenced pinging directly at the Soviet sub. Apparently, that was more than *Volgograd* could handle. She headed north at flank speed.

That left the damaged *Victor III* somewhere south of us. Obviously, she had a role to play, or she wouldn't have been here in the first place. Since our intent was to transit Bellot Strait, I had Sam, who had been on watch for a half-hour, carefully move *Lyre* north, placing us between Pemmican Rock and the strait entrance.

"Mac…look at this," he said once we were in position, pointing to the *Akkord* display.

Akkord clearly showed Pemmican Rock and the bluffs defining the entrance to Bellot Strait. *Frisco* appeared about ten nautical miles

---

17 See *Operation Ice Breaker*, the second book in the *Mac McDowell Mission Series*.

south. What had caught Sam's attention, however, was a flashing string of the Russian letter м stretching between the bluffs all the way across the entrance to Bellot Strait. Although I suspected what it meant, I grabbed the *Okean* manual to look it up. Sure enough, the м indicated ммина—Russian for mine.

"*Teuthis*, this is *Lyre*," I transmitted on the Secure Gertrude. "*Okean* has detected a string of mines across the entrance to Bellot Strait. Apparently, *Okean* is programmed to pick them up."

"Stand by, *Lyre*."

A few minutes later, *Teuthis* called. "The strait entrance is just over a half mile wide and a thousand feet deep a bit south of the centerline. The canyon is a sharp V-shaped trench at the bottom. Can the *Akkord* display a three-D view?"

I checked the manual. To my surprise, it did, and I switched to that mode. I called *Teuthis* back. "*Akkord* has a fully integrated three-D display with navigation and contacts. Thirty-six mines cover the entire entry from ten feet above the trench floor to about forty feet from the surface. The mine density near the trench bottom is double."

"Roger that. Stand by, *Lyre*."

A few minutes later, *Teuthis* called again with the outline of a battle plan.

✸

My job was simple. I proceeded to a point about a quarter mile west of the entry and dropped to a few feet from the bottom—980 feet exactly. I had never taken *Lyre* this deep. I knew she was capable of at least 3,000 feet, perhaps as much as six. Interestingly, her titanium hull compressed very little—virtually no creaking or other stress-related noises that we normally experienced when taking a submarine deep.

Five hundred feet above us, *Teuthis* readied a wire-guided torpedo, opened a torpedo tube outer door, and fired the fish—which meant activating the fish so it swam out the tube. Under the watchful eye of Senior Chief Firecontrol Technician Ogden Winder (good old Oggy), a firecontrol technician steered the fish to its destination using a joystick. When the fish was directly in the mine swarm near the trench bottom, the skipper ordered the detonation.

My *Akkord* display showed the results. Twelve of the mines disappeared, leaving a gaping hole at the bottom of the mine curtain. I was not immediately aware of what happened next. I learned about it afterward. *Teuthis* had gone to Battle Stations to fire the torpedo. Shortly after the explosion, King detected the nearby presence of the damaged *Victor III*. Immediately thereafter, he heard two torpedo tube doors open. Without hesitating a moment, Cmdr. Roken got a single-ping range and snap-fired a torpedo. Then he released two noisemakers port and starboard, snap-fired a second fish, and dropped toward the bottom and the hole he had just blasted through the mine curtain.

The *Victor III* fired two torpedoes. The first diverted toward one of the noisemakers and detonated harmlessly. The second locked onto *Teuthis* just as *Teuthis* passed through the hole. The Soviet torpedo was programmed for an intercept course. It had no way of detecting the mine curtain. It struck a mine 600 above the bottom and detonated, taking another eight mines with it. At virtually the same time, the skipper's first torpedo slammed into the *Victor III's* torpedo room, ripping a gash in the submarine's hull. Before the concussion subsided, the second fish found its mark, the twin screws on the stern planes. It ripped off the stern planes, opening the engine room to the sea. The explosions took out both the forward and after main ballast tanks, causing the doomed *Victor III* to drop toward the seafloor, slamming into the bottom 300 feet from my location.

*

My thoughts turned to the men trapped in the doomed *Victor III*. Sure, I was aware that they had attacked us first at the Tasmania Islands and again at Pemmican Rock. That didn't change the fact that, depending on how many men perished from the breach of the forward and after compartments, sixty or more men were still alive inside the hulk. The *Victor III* had a large escape pod, but the surface above them was ice-covered, and there was no other sub nearby to rescue the survivors.

That wasn't strictly true, of course, since *Volgograd* was somewhere to our north, and we thought *Carp* was down in Victoria Strait, probably headed in our direction. *Teuthis* was already well into Bellot Strait, but both *Frisco* and *Swordfish* were nearby. Since *Frisco* was not really capable of breaking through the heavy ice, I decided to call *Swordfish* on the Secure Gertrude.

"*USS Swordfish*, this is *Lyre*, over."

"*Lyre*, this is *Swordfish*. To verify your identity, where did Roger Staubach attend college? Over."

"U.S. Naval Academy," I answered.

"Why did he go Supply Corps?" *Swordfish* asked.

"Red-green color blindness," I answered, hoping I remembered correctly. "This is Lt. Cmdr. Mac McDowell, commanding," I added.

"Okay, Commander, it's your dime."

I explained the need to break up the canopy over the downed *Victor III*.

"Roger, *Lyre*. Follow *Teuthis* into Bellot Strait. *San Francisco* will tail you, covering your six. *Swordfish* will break the ice as you requested and will guard the Bellot Strait entry until you enter the Gulf of Boothia."

THE *LYRE*—BELLOT STRAIT

Bellot Strait is a thirteen nautical-mile-long, scant half-mile-wide cut between Boothia Peninsula to the south and Somerset Island to the north. The north side rises steeply to 1,500 feet, and the south to 2,500 feet. Tidal currents reach eight knots and reverse with the tide. A thousand-foot trench runs for six-and-a-half nautical miles along the strait from the western end to Halfway Island. The remainder of the strait is about 500 feet deep, terminating at Fort Ross on Somerset, an abandoned Hudson's Bay Company outpost.

Fort Ross was established in 1937 and abandoned in 1948 due to continual heavy icing and difficulty reaching the outpost. The fort, actually two small buildings, overlooks a quarter-mile wide, very shallow impassable slot between the fort and Long Island to the south. Our path would take us south of Long Island—still shallow water, but passable, especially at high tide.

※

Potts had the watch as we entered Bellot Strait, but I remained in Control to handle anything unexpected. We were two hours ahead of high tide, which gave us about five knots of current going our direction. "Activate the secure depth-sounder," I told Potts, "and take us down to a hundred feet above the bottom. Maintain that depth until we reach Halfway Island. Remember," I told him as an afterthought, "the tide is giving us an extra five knots right now. It will slow for the next two hours until it reaches zero. That's about the time we should be navigating through Brentford Bay south of Long Island." I showed him the paper chart. "It gets pretty shallow here, but these depths are for mean lower low tide. We will be at the opposite end of the tide scale." *Akkord* had made passing through the hole in the mine net simple.

Akkord also displayed both sides of the strait, making our navigation easy as we whipped along at fifteen knots thanks to the tide. We reached

Halfway Island in a half hour. From there, the bottom shallowed until we reached Zenith Point.

"Make your depth one-zero-zero feet, Potts," I ordered. "Make your course zero-nine-zero degrees and slow to five knots."

We were two-and-a-quarter nautical miles from some very shallow water, and I didn't want to be surprised. I checked *Okean's* upward-looking beam. The ice canopy was mostly brash—shattered floes because of the eight-foot tide difference. It never really got a chance to consolidate. There were no serious underwater ice impediments because the constant ice motion kept breaking up the floes.

After two miles, I ordered, "Potts, bring us to periscope depth and watch the bottom carefully. We're at high tide. Total depth ahead of us is about eighty-six feet. That puts twenty feet between our keel and the bottom."

I checked *Akkord* and my paper chart. "We're one-point-four miles from Magpie Rock." I pointed at the *Akkord* display. "We want to pass Magpie down our starboard side. Set course zero-nine-four." I pointed again. "Keep a sharp eye. We've got twenty feet under our keel from here to Magpie." That was twenty feet with the high tide.

It was a nail-biting seventeen-minute trip, made more difficult because Magpie Rock was misplaced several hundred yards on our paper chart. Once we cleared Magpie Rock, I dropped us down to eighty feet and ordered course 110 degrees that took us into Brentford Bay through a mile-wide gap between the Fox Islands to the north and Brands Island to the south. Several minutes later, *Frisco* appeared behind us, slipping past Magpie Rock, still watching our six. We began to pick up traces of what turned out to be *Drum,* keeping our front gate clear. For the moment, at least, we did not have to be concerned about the three remaining Soviet fast-attacks.

My battery charge meter indicated less than ten percent. We really needed to recharge *Lyre's* batteries. Seven-and-a-half nautical miles directly ahead lay horseshoe-shaped Grindle Islands, with a two-and-a-half nautical mile, eighty-foot-deep, protected basin between the horseshoe arms. Cmdr. Roken and I agreed to take advantage of this protected spot for the charge.

From our perspective, the Grindle Islands offered a safe haven from the Soviet submarine wolfpack that seemed intent on hunting us down. Despite our now fairly expansive Arctic experience, I guess we still did not really understand the many danger sources in this remote part of the world.

THE *LYRE*—BOTTOMED AT THE GRINDLE ISLANDS

Cmdr. Roken and I discussed our options over the Secure Gertrude. "The water between the arms seems to be about eighty feet deep, according to both *Sozh* and my paper chart," I told the skipper. "I suggest that *Lyre* enter the basin first and bottom near the end pointing west.

Then you can follow to bottom alongside. *Drum* can maintain station a mile or so to the northeast as insurance while we charge."

"I think your plan is good," Cmdr. Roken told me. "Do we know anything about Polar Bear activity around here?"

"Nothing except our general understanding that they prefer land-sea ice combinations to just land or sea ice," I answered. As I thought about it, I added, "Since bears will certainly be present, I recommend that all three divers carry APSs with a spare magazine."

"I'll order it," the skipper replied.

※

Potts brought us to the end of the basin during the last hour of his watch. Barry followed up on *Teuthis,* settling next to us on their skids a half-hour later. The ice cover above us was about two feet thick but broken into ten to twelve-foot floes. Since the water surrounding the Grindles was relatively deep, tidal currents tended to flow around the island complex rather than through it. Consequently, as the tide changed, the floes above us jostled in place more than moved past us. Even though we were headed into a low tide, the ice noise was tolerable, and on *Teuthis*, Benny Simms was able to keep watch on the basin entry.

With Ski still out of commission and both Harry and Whitey not fully recovered, Ham was left with only Jimmy, Jer, and Sergyi, who had remained on *Teuthis* at my direction for just this eventuality. Harry and Whitey pressed down but did not dress out. They were to tend the divers.

I felt odd not being part of this decision process, but I realized that the skipper had put Ham in charge. Since I had full confidence in Ham, I reconciled myself to the matter…but it still felt odd.

In the glow of *Lyre's* lights, with APSs slung, Jimmy and Jer— identified by *T* and *R*, respectively—attached the shore-power cable to *Teuthis* and dragged the other end to *Lyre*. Sergyi—identified with an *A*—hovered over them, his APS at the ready. The divers said they missed Borysko's presence, both for the pure enjoyment of playing with a six-ton cetacean and the protection the Orca provided.

Apparently, the night sky above the ice was clear because, as the floes above the divers shifted, the open water areas between them were brighter than the floes. Sergyi scanned the canopy, paying particular attention to the nearby open areas. As he did, a dark shape appeared in an open area directly above the divers, eighty feet above. As he watched, the Polar Bear—for that is what the shape was—twisted and headed straight for him.

On *Lyre's* monitors, I watched this bear, not so large as the first one we had encountered—more like 700 pounds, dive toward Sergyi. I knew that Polar Bears typically dive within fifteen feet of the surface for thirty to sixty seconds. Sergyi was three times that depth, but the bear kept coming. When it was twenty feet away, Sergyi let go a short burst of darts directly at the bear's face. Several penetrated the bear's upper body, probably only the blubber. Several missed altogether, but one struck the bear's left eye. The bear stopped momentarily, swiped at its eye with its left paw, and then advanced again, its mouth open wide as if it were trying to bellow underwater.

Sergyi fired another deafening burst, concentrating on the right eye, striking it twice. The massive bear stopped, swiping at its face with both paws while twisting in the water, rising slowly due to its inherent positive buoyancy. Sergyi dropped the empty magazine, slammed his spare into the weapon, and cycled the receiver. By this time, the bear was bobbing against a large floe. Then it slipped past the edge and clambered to the surface. Almost immediately, a second bear splashed into the opening, diving straight for Sergyi. As I watched him bring his APS into firing position, Sergyi seemed to surge to his left. A moment later, a large Orca nearly filled my screen. The cetacean twisted and turned toward the second bear, and a moment later, there was no second bear—at least not one that was living.

Sergyi shouted, "It's Borysko! It's Borysko!"

Unbelievably, as the Orca moved away from my cameras, I could clearly see the bite out of his dorsal fin—it really was Borysko. We last saw him at the Tasmania Islands. I guess he followed us to Pemmican Rock, and then, somehow, he survived the explosions. Following us through Bellot Strait would have not been difficult because, for the most part, the ice was broken into floes and even brash along the entire passage. What an amazing thing; this 12,000-pound killer whale at the top of the oceanic food chain had befriended us and seemed to have assumed the task of protecting us in the water from anything—even other humans.

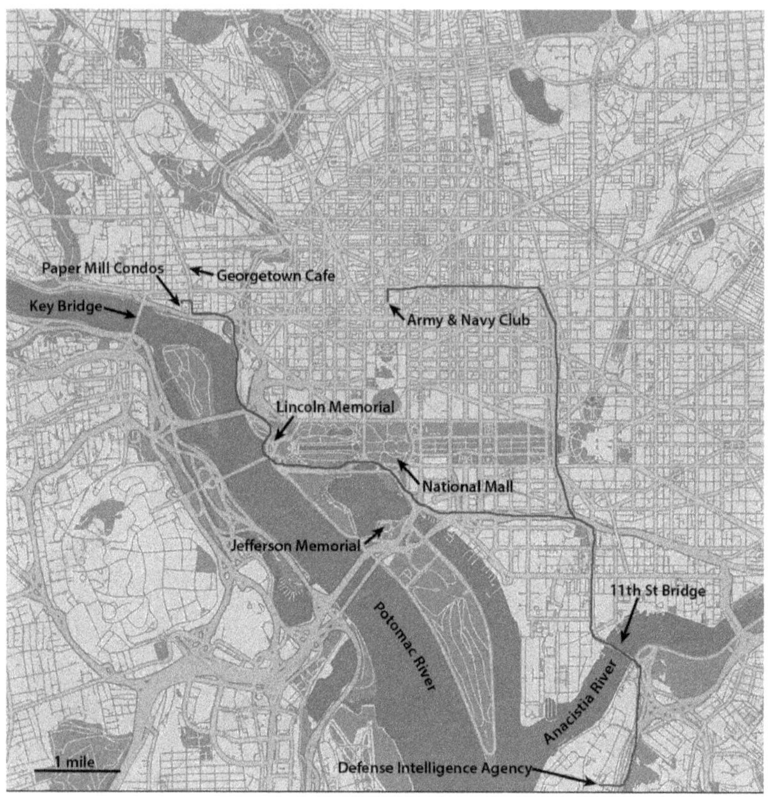

*Washington, D.C. routes between DIA and Paper Mill Condos
and between DIA and the Army and Navy Club*

CHAPTER FOURTEEN—Kate's Journal 2

DIA HEADQUARTERS—ANACOSTIA, DC

I drifted awake the next morning out of a sensuous dream where I was wrapped in Mac's arms, protected from the entire world. My eyes came into focus just inches from Jennifer's face. She was still sleeping, breathing softly, her breath sweet and fresh. I can't really explain why, but I moved closer and kissed her lips gently. She moaned quietly, still asleep, and parted her lips. On impulse, I pressed my lips to hers, probing gently with my tongue. As she came awake, Jennifer responded, and we drifted into a sensuous cloud.

Later, as we showered, I said, "Jennifer, you know I'm still completely crazy about Mac."

"I know, Hon," she said back, "I'm not jealous. Besides, you needed that release." She winked and kissed me quickly. "We gotta hurry. A DIA car will be here in a half-hour."

✳

The car looked entirely normal—no markings, no government plates. Tinted windows made it impossible to see inside the back. I didn't recognize the driver, but Cappy was in the front seat beside him. Jennifer kissed his cheek through the open side window.

"Hi, Cappy!" she said lightly. "Anything I should know about?"
"Naw…get your butts in the back so we can get underway."

I giggled at the friendly repartee. "Hey, Cappy," I said, "how's Arty?"
"Fine…got the day off, lucky sucker."

Jennifer and I climbed into the back, and as we got underway, I grabbed her hand.

"Thanks for being my friend," I told her.

✳

About a half-hour later, we passed through Arnold Gate into the Joint Base Anacostia-Bolling. A short distance farther, we parked in a marked slot near the entrance of the large, glass building I had visited two days earlier. Cappy got out, cast his gaze about, and then opened the back door for Jennifer and me.

"See you, Cappy," Jennifer said, kissing his cheek lightly.

He grinned and looked at me. "Have fun, Kate. You'll do fine; I know it."

With that, he got back in the passenger seat, and the car left the lot. "Let's go," Jennifer said, adjusting her jacket and then reaching over to fluff my collar. "You look pretty this morning. Let's get you checked in."

The check-in process was much more elaborate than I had expected. The guard at the entrance to the still-unfinished building clearly recognized Jennifer, but he still checked her ID. Once inside the grand lobby, we went down a hallway and entered a room with a sign on the door: SECURITY. Inside, I was fingerprinted and photographed, and then the clerk gave me a DIA ID card similar to the card Josh had carried for the Coast Guard. He told me that I was granted a provisional Top Secret clearance, based upon my situation and the preliminary results of my background investigation that had commenced the moment I stepped aboard *Teuthis*. He explained *Need to know*. The only Top Secret material I would see, he said, would be material directly connected with my research. I also received a badge on a lanyard that had my photo and a bunch of other stuff.

"Wear this badge at all times when you are in the building," the clerk told me. "It will grant you access to every area where you are authorized. If you attempt to gain entrance to an unauthorized area, Security will be notified immediately." He grinned. "That's a big no-no around here."

"Okay," Jennifer said, "let's find your new home."

✳

We went up three levels, down several hallways, and finally arrived at a door labeled *Section 9*. Jennifer pointed to my badge, and I slid it through the slot by the door. I heard a quiet buzz, and Jennifer pushed the door open. As we stepped inside, a woman in her forties dressed in somewhat severe business attire left her cubicle and met us. She took us to a cubicle with a wide desk, three computer screens, two keyboards, and a telephone.

With a faint smile, she said in a business-like manner, "This is your cubicle, Ms Perry. Your desk is stocked with whatever we think you may need." She handed me a card. "These are your login credentials. Memorize them and then shred the card." She pointed to a small cross-cut shredder on top of a waste can. "The bathroom is down there. When you leave your cubicle for any reason, blank your screens. We have a small kitchen over there. Feel free to use it. If you have any questions, you can reach me at three-one-three on the intercom line."

She turned and departed, leaving Jennifer and me to wonder what had just happened.

"Wow!" Jennifer said. "You gonna be okay?"

"I'll figure things out," I told her. "How difficult can it be?"

✳

It turned out to be more challenging than I had expected. I was generally familiar with computers; I had purchased a Macintosh a year ago and used it for my shop inventory and my accounting, such as it was. The computer or computers (I wasn't sure yet) on my desk were way beyond my little Macintosh, and they were much more difficult to use, but I got the hang of it. I had access to virtually every database on Earth. Once I figured this out, I really had to exercise restraint to focus on my task instead of roaming over the globe.

I'm a pretty organized gal, which is why I was able to keep going after Josh was killed. It didn't take me long to narrow my focus to the events that happened in Kodiak. I must admit to taking a little side trip into Mac's background. That's how I found out about the *Alfa* and the role he played. That's also how I learned about his current activities in the high north.

"Oh my God," I prayed, "keep him safe. He's all I have…please don't let anything happen to him!"

✳

I took lunch in the small section kitchen. I grabbed a sandwich from the vending machine for 50¢ and made a mental note to bring something the next time. I met a couple of the gals and a guy who worked there, but they seemed standoffish, and I decided not to press it on my first day. Later, I figured out that they resented my coming in from *nowhere* to an apparently senior analyst position when they had been required to jump through several hoops to get to where I started. I saw no reason to tell them anything about why I was there. I remembered too vividly the incident in Kodiak and then Oakland. The bad guys seemed to be everywhere, and I was not about to give them any advantage. So I kept my own counsel and focused on the reason I was there.

As I dug deeper into Jack Petrikoff's life, I discovered that his parents came from eastern Siberia and shipped out to Kodiak with a wave of Russian immigration shortly after the Bolshevik revolution. Jack's father was tasked by the new Soviet regime to set up and maintain a cell of fellow travelers—men and women secretly loyal to the Soviet regime but outwardly happy to be American citizens. The cell turned out to be more of a social club than anything else. They had no contact with the Soviets and were obligated only by their oaths and their sense of duty.

When Jack was in his late teens, his father initiated him into the cell along with the boys of several other cell members. The younger men carried on the tradition as their parents passed away until the cell consisted only of the second-generation participants. For a while, Jack was their elected leader, but as time passed, he became more and more disillusioned with the cell's stated goals. He turned down any further leadership role but continued to participate in their mostly social activities.

The cell was activated for the first time ever when the *Alfa* crew returned to the Soviet Union. Jack and the other members knew nothing about the circumstances surrounding their activation. Their orders were to kill Lt. Cmdr. J.R. McDowell and anyone associated with him in Kodiak and attempt the destruction or disabling of *USS Teuthis*.

How the Soviets were able to identify Mac was still a mystery. When the cell was activated, Jack had not yet met Mac, but he rebelled against destroying a U.S. submarine. Apparently, Jack didn't tell anyone. He just decided not to carry out the orders. His meeting Mac at the Breaker's sealed the deal. He introduced Mac and me and then laid plans to sabotage the cell's task.

I did not discover all this in one day, of course. I pieced it together over several weeks. On that first day, all I really did was learn how to use a command-prompt-driven computer to access the mass of data that I discovered as I moved forward.

✳

Following Friday's close of work, Jennifer picked me up in a Datsun roadster, much like the one I lost in Kodiak. That endeared her to me even more. We drove back to Papermill through heavy Friday afternoon traffic. As we passed the Jefferson Memorial, she reached over and squeezed my hand.

"Tomorrow, Girl, I'm going to take you to the National Mall, and you and I are going to play tourist—all day."

What neither of us knew was the extent of Soviet infiltration into the Defense Intelligence Agency.

THE NATIONAL MALL—WASHINGTON, DC

We roused ourselves early Saturday morning, did our ablutions together, and got ready to go out. Jennifer didn't even offer me a cup of coffee.

"I've got a special treat for us," Jennifer said, "but we have a ten minute walk. It's cold this morning, so bundle up."

We stepped through her door into a crisp, sunny morning. The brick edges of the empty flower beds were covered with frost. My breath formed a white cloud as Jennifer took my hand and led me out a side entrance to Papermill court. We turned right onto Grace Street and then left on Wisconsin, crossing over the Cambridge and Ohio Canal. Five minutes later, we arrived at one of Georgetown's oldest coffee shops—Café Georgetown.

We stepped inside, found a table by the fireplace, and shucked our outer coats. We sat opposite each other, letting the fire's warmth seep through our chilled bodies.

"May I order?" Jennifer asked. "Sure. You know what's good here."

Jennifer ordered sweet mocha, crepes with strawberries and cream (imagine, fresh strawberries in the winter!), little mild, sweet Italian sausages, and oven-fresh popovers. Oh my…was it tasty! We lingered for an hour enjoying each other's company, and then we strolled hand-in-hand back to Jennifer's condo.

Twenty minutes later, snuggled in Jennifer's Datsun, we drove to a parking area near the National Mall set aside for government officials.

"Can you do this?" I asked.

Jennifer pointed to a government decal on her windshield. "Yep," she said.

✳

We did a lot of walking, but I didn't mind. I had never been here before, and I wanted to see everything. Two things impressed me more than anything else. When we climbed the steps to the Lincoln Memorial, and I gazed at the white marble statue and read the inscriptions, I teared up. We must have remained there for a half-hour or more. I simply couldn't pull myself away.

Finally, Jennifer said, "C'mon, Girl, I'm gonna show you something that's even better."

We walked around a basin for a few minutes and entered the Jefferson Memorial. Jennifer was right. I was completely blown away. The bronze statue of the man who wrote the Declaration of Independence was utterly magnificent. As we strolled around the interior hand-in-hand, reading excerpts from his writings, I never felt more awe, more reverence. No wonder Mac was what he was. No wonder Archie Desmond did what he did. No wonder Jennifer chose to be a DIA agent.

We returned to Jennifer's Datsun and picked our way home through side streets. Jennifer pointed out this or that building, explaining its significance, a statue here, a fountain there, until I was completely saturated with everything Washington, D.C. I was glad to pull into her carport and finally settle down in front of her gas fireplace with a hot toddy and some soft rock in the background.

"What a day," I said, between sips. "Thank you, thank you, thank you!"

"What are friends for?" she asked as the phone rang. Jennifer picked it up and listened. Then she handed it to me. "It's Kate," I said.

"Kate, it's Archie Desmond. I'm in town and would like to see you."

My heart started to pound. I swallowed and said carefully, "Commander Desmond, how wonderful to hear your voice."

"Come on, Kate, it's Archie. I need to know you're okay, and I want to spend some time with you."

I told him about Jennifer and her protection role, and I told him about our friendship, leaving out some specific details. I guess I gushed a bit, like a daughter to her father.

"Can we meet tomorrow?" he asked. "Perhaps I can take you both out for a late brunch at the Army and Navy Club, where I'm staying." I explained to Jennifer. Her eyes widened when I mentioned the Army and Navy Club. "By all means," she said. "That's absolutely the nicest place in town."

"We'd love to," I told Archie.

"Great! I'll have a car pick you both up at eleven tomorrow morning."

I gave him the address. "I so look forward to seeing you again," I told him as I hung up the phone. Of course, that was before the events that happened later that evening.

＊

I followed Jennifer up the spiral staircase to the loft, where we quickly undressed and cast ourselves into her bed, exhausted from our long day. We snuggled for warmth and friendship and drifted into a happy sleep.

Sometime later, how long I do not know, Jennifer gently shook me awake.

"Shhh," she said. "Someone's in the house. Quickly, get under the bed."

She pushed a multi-featured phone at me. In the glow from a nightlight, I saw a pistol in her right hand with what I later learned was a silencer attached to the end. "Dial star-one," she whispered. "As soon as the phone answers, dial pound-one and lay the handset on the floor. Don't say a word!" She squeezed my hand. "No matter what happens, don't make a sound!"

As I slid under the bed, I saw her grip the pistol with both hands and point it toward the top of the staircase. I picked up the handset and dialed *1. It answered immediately and soundlessly. I dialed #1 and placed the handset on the floor beside me. I could just see the top of the staircase from under the bed. As I watched, a man's head appeared. He held a silenced pistol in his right hand. Then I heard a soft *pfsst* from the top of the bed. A hole appeared in the intruder's forehead, and he tumbled back down the staircase.

I heard some noise from below. Either the shooter wasn't dead— but he had to be; Jennifer hit him square in the forehead—or there was a second shooter. I heard a soft scraping sound followed by a slight tap at the right front of the loft, where it dropped into the living room. I felt Jennifer shift on the bed above me. Then I saw a hand appear above the edge, holding what I later learned was a silenced Uzi automatic. The weapon sprayed a swath of bullets across the entire width of the loft and dropped below the edge. I heard a grunt from the bed above me, and Jennifer's pistol fell to the floor.

I didn't have any firearms training, but I grabbed the pistol, held it the way Jennifer had, and pointed it where the hand had been. A moment later, a dark head eased up above the edge. I waited until I could see enough to aim at and squeezed the trigger. The pistol recoiled back, striking my face painfully. I heard a crash and a loud thump.

I waited a full five minutes and then whispered, "Jennifer…" No answer. "Jennifer, Jennifer…" Still no answer.

I cautiously crawled out from under the bed. To my horror, Jennifer lay sprawled on her back across the bed, a row of jagged holes crossing her chest, piercing both her breasts. Her mouth and eyes were open wide. She wasn't breathing.

I stifled a scream and peeked over the edge of the loft. Both intruders lay on the floor, apparently dead. A flimsy aluminum ladder lay across the chest of the one I had shot. I pulled the phone out from under the bed and whispered into the handset, "Can you hear me?"

"Who is this?" a voice said in my ear.

"I'm Kate Perry. I'm at Special Agent Jennifer Coolerage's condo. Intruders shot Jennifer while she tried to protect me. They're both dead."

I started sobbing. "So is Jennifer…" I lost it completely, throwing myself over her body, sobbing in despair.

✻

I lost track of time. Perhaps I fell asleep—I don't remember. The first thing I recall clearly is a soft, soothing woman's voice and something warm being draped across my naked shoulders. The loft lights brightened, but not fully.

A woman in black tactical gear said, "I'm Special Agent Sally James, DIA. These," she pointed to three other people in tactical gear, a woman and two men, "are my colleagues."

"How…what…" I stammered.

"We got your emergency call," she told me. "We heard everything that happened. Jennifer was my friend. You are incredibly brave, but now we need to get you out of here. Put on something warm…we gotta leave!" She turned to the two guys who were watching our exchange. "Hey! Face away…Assholes!"

Five minutes later, they helped me down the staircase and out the door. Holding both my hands, the two female agents ran with me through the courtyard in the opposite direction Jennifer and I had taken just that morning. We crossed a narrow street, ran under the Whitehurst Freeway, crossed another street, and ran to a chopper with idling rotor, waiting on the open space of Waterfront Park.

Moments later, we lifted into the black night sky over the Potomac River.

✳

I'm not entirely sure what happened next. I thought we were flying to DIA Headquarters. Instead, there was some kind of exchange between the pilot and his dispatcher that ended with a contrite "Yes, Sir!" from the pilot. Shortly thereafter, we landed in Farragut Square across the street from the Army and Navy Club. Archie—Cmdr. Desmond—was there to greet us. I ran to him and threw my arms around his neck.

"They killed Jennifer," I sobbed, "they killed Jennifer."

He held me close without saying a word. Then he picked me up, cradling me in his arms, and carried me across the street into the Club, through the lobby to the elevators, and up to his room. There, he removed my coat and laid me gently in his bed, covering and tucking me in. He turned down the lights, and as I drifted off to sleep, I heard him order a cot for himself.

DIA HEADQUARTERS—ANACOSTIA, DC

"What kind of a chicken-shit outfit are you running here, General?"

I could hear Rear Adm. Austin B. Scott's voice right through the closed door of Lt. Gen. Eugene Tighe's top-floor office in the DIA Headquarters building. Special Supervisory Agent Darrell Capland and I were waiting outside the general's door to meet with him. I had learned enough to know that Gen. Tighe outranked Admiral Scott, but it was obvious to anyone nearby that mattered little to Admiral Scott. "I leave my girl Kate in your care, and you almost get her killed.

Shit, General, her bodyguard and friend, Jennifer, was killed. I want her protected one hundred percent of the time. I want her driven in a bullet-proof sedan anytime she's outside this building or the Army and Navy Club. I want at least two agents with her twenty-four/seven. I want her to have a federal carry permit, and I want her trained to shoot straight." Admiral Scott paused and lowered his voice a bit. "If you can't make this happen, General, I'll bring my goddamn fleet up the Potomac and enforce it myself!" He stormed out the door, slamming it behind him.

✳

"Perhaps we should come back later," I suggested to Cappy. "Naw," Cappy said, "they will be sharing drinks at the Club this evening." He rapped on the door, and we entered.

"Kate!" Lt. Gen. Tighe said, rising to his feet and stepping toward us, hand outstretched. "I'm so sorry about Jennifer. I know you two were close." He waved us to his couch and took the easy chair opposite.

"Nice work you've been doing down in Section 9, Kate. How're they treating you down there?"

"Could be better," I answered, "but they're getting used to me. I really enjoy the work."

"It's important, too," he said. "Commander Dennison has arranged for you to reside at the Army and Navy Club until we can find something that we know is safe. Special Supervisory Agent Capland will ensure you have at least two special agents either with you or directly outside your door at all times. We don't want a repeat of last night. A car and driver will move you between here and there." He slid a card across the coffee table. "This is a Federal Concealed Firearms Permit. Special Agent Capland will assist you in choosing an appropriate handgun and will train you in its use." He stood up with a warm smile. "I want you to know that my door is always open for you. I mean that. If you need to see me for any reason, any reason at all, call my front desk, and I will make time for you."

I thanked him warmly. He seemed entirely unaffected by his exchange with Adm. Scott. Cappy and I left, and I went to my cubicle in Section 9. The day passed normally as I continued my deep dive into Soviet activities in and around Kodiak for the past several decades. At quitting time, Cappy and Archie—Cmdr. Desmond—met me outside the Section 9 door.

"We need to pick you out a weapon," Cappy said. The commander, here, collared me and said he wanted to tag along."

Archie grinned his affirmation. "Let's go to the armory," Cappy said.

✳

Cappy explained the difference between various ammunition calibers. He said that if a person is an expert shot, even a .22 will do the job, but if you miss, you just anger the aggressor. Typically, the larger the bullet, the larger the pistol.

"You will learn to shoot, I promise," Cappy told me. "The difference is that if you use something relatively small, like a three-eighty, you will need to put three bullets into an attacker to ensure he stops." He showed me a .380 cartridge. "A well-placed nine-millimeter or larger will do the trick. With someone your size, it might be easier to place a nine-millimeter than a forty-five." He showed me both a 9 mm and a .45 caliber round. "The main difference here is that a nine-millimeter weapon is typically significantly smaller than a forty-five or larger."

He laid on the table a Colt M1911, a SIG Sauer P220, and a Glock 17. The Colt was a .45 caliber and was big and heavy with an 8-round capacity. The SIG Sauer was a bit lighter, more compact, and used either 9 mm or .45s with up to a 10-round capacity depending on several factors. The Glock was half the weight of the other two, and was available in 9 mm, .45, and other calibers. It had a seventeen-round capacity.

I started out with the Colt. It was easy to fire, and after several rounds, I began to hit the target with a bit of precision—*small groups*, as Cappy said. I tried the SIG in both calibers. I liked the 9 mm better. It had less recoil, and I was able to group my shots after the second round. I thought the SIG was better than the Colt. Then I shot the 9 mm Glock. What a difference! I was spot on from the very first round. "I never saw a girl shoot so good the first time out," Archie said.

"That's not fair," I said with a mock pout.

"Seriously," he fired back, "I mean it. I've coached a lot of young officers. You're as good as any of them, and this is your first time…right?" "Except for Saturday night," I said, losing some of my enthusiasm as I remembered.

Cappy put a hundred-round box on the counter and loaded a spare magazine. "Keep shooting," he said, "until these are all gone."

As I cleared each magazine, Cappy handed me another. He had me do slow fire, rapid-fire, intermittent fire, and even so-called quick-draw single shots. When we did these, he said, "The idea is to get off your first shot as rapidly as physically possible—a snap-shot. Hit or miss, speed is the most important thing…although a hit is better than a miss." He grinned. "Then, make your second shot count…and your third and fourth, if necessary."

Two hours passed almost unnoticed. Finally, I had shot all hundred plus rounds. Cappy showed me how to break down—disassemble—the Glock, and we took a few minutes to clean it. Then he handed me the

Glock with a full magazine and one in the chamber, a second magazine, 500 rounds, a holster, and a cleaning kit. Archie carried the ammunition and kit. I carried the rest.

"We'll practice the break-down tomorrow until you can do it in your sleep, and we'll shoot another hundred rounds. We'll do this every day until it becomes second nature."

"Join us for dinner?" I asked.

"No thanks, I got something goin' tonight," Cappy said with a wink.

Archie and I left for the Army and Navy Club in the chauffeured limo the general had made available.

THE ARMY AND NAVY CLUB—WASHINGTON, DC

Archie is wonderful, and I don't want to make too much of this. Ever since we met, he has been like a protective father to me. I think I am the daughter he never had. For the record, I love it! On the other hand, I'm an adult woman with my own needs and wants. I've been on my own longer than most women my age—even married and widowed. I don't always need or even want a protective arm around my shoulders.

I loved living with Jennifer. We had an easy-going relationship that took the hunger off my missing Mac without guilt. Jennifer was more than capable of protecting me, although the night I lost her might be interpreted differently. The thing is that the Army and Navy Club, grand as it was, was not my cup of tea. Archie was back on *Los Angeles* playing sub boat captain again, and that's where he really belonged. I filled my days with esoteric research that never failed to fascinate me. Every evening I increased my firearms proficiency. That was fun too. Before Cappy introduced me to my Glock, I had no idea just how much fun it could be, not to mention that it might come in handy.

I didn't much care for being chauffeured everywhere in a bulletproof limo, and I really disliked staying at the Club, as it was called. I figured I had three weeks or so before Mac finally arrived at Electric Boat. I didn't really think it was a good idea to upset the whole system just so I could be on my own for these days. So, I made the most of it. Fortunately, Cappy made sure there were always two DIA agents in the Club lobby—usually two guys, occasionally a guy and a gal, never two gals.

Somebody was paying for my stay, including my meals. I don't know for sure, but I have a suspicion it came from ComSubPac's slush fund. I tried not to abuse it, but occasionally, I would invite one of the agents to dine with me. Never both, because they told me someone had to cover the lobby. There were no incidents, at least that I knew of. I don't think the agents would have told me if there were unless they had to take immediate action to get me out of danger.

I was still a bit self-conscious about carrying my Glock 17. I did it religiously, but since I don't wear a bra, I could not carry it between my boobs the way some of the gals did. One of the female agents turned me on to a holster that fit into the small of my back when I wore either pants or an appropriate skirt. With that arrangement, I could make a snap-shot in less than a second. Otherwise, I just carried it in my purse. A lot slower, but the only way if I wasn't wearing something that covered the small of my back. I wasn't out and about enough to make that an issue anyway. My DIA protectors were always there, so I really could have kept my piece in my panties drawer for all the good it did me.

*

Christmas was especially lonely. I spent last Christmas with Jack Petrikoff. He did more than anyone could have expected to make my holiday meaningful, and I loved him for it. Now that I have Mac—oh, God, I miss him!—I feel more alone than ever.

Gen. Tighe invited me to join him and his family for Christmas dinner. It was delightful. His beautiful Georgetown mansion was filled with grandkids, and even several great-grandkids, running around, screaming and yelling, filling the house with Christmas cheer. Dinner was a traditional roast goose with all the trimmings and mincemeat pie for dessert. It was as nice as I had ever experienced—ever.

The general's generosity and kindness made Christmas tolerable for this lonely, lovesick girl.

＊

Three weeks—I marked them on my calendar. In three weeks, I would hold my beloved in my arms again. I really did not anticipate how needy I was—physically and emotionally. The only thing that kept me going was my research. For a few hours each day, I lost myself in the history of Kodiak, Soviet sleeper cells, and the general international communist movement—the fellow travelers.

When I surfaced from my research, my emotional hunger took over to carry me through the rest of the day. When I finally fell asleep, I dreamed of Mac and our future life together. When my hunger overwhelmed me, I would remember Jennifer and cry myself to sleep.

＊

About New Years—it came and went. That's about all I can really say about it.

PART THREE

The Sting

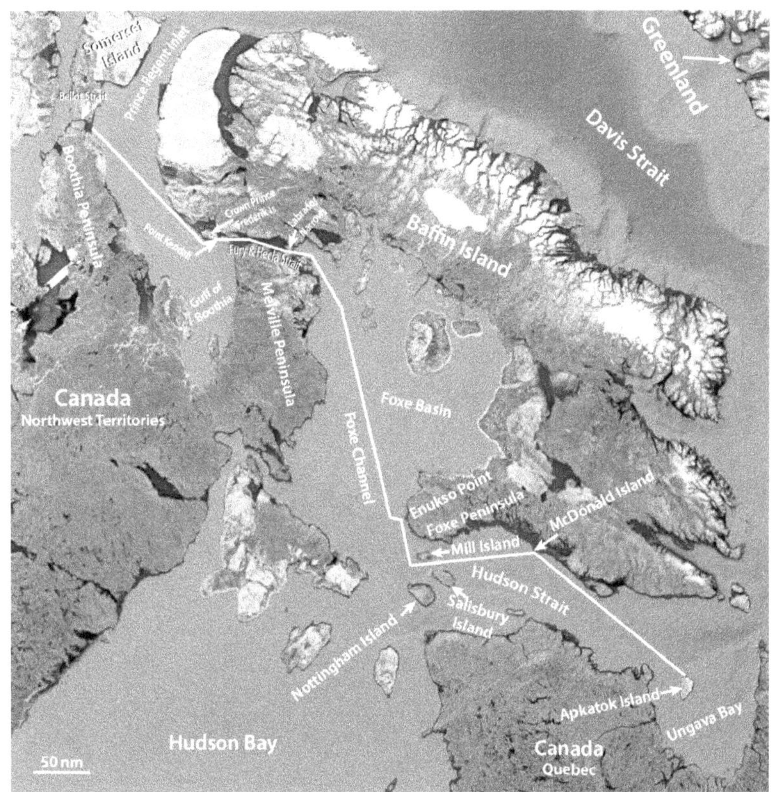

Track of USS Teuthis & Lyre from Bellot Strait to Akpatok Island in Ungava Bay

CHAPTER FIFTEEN—Current Express

THE *LYRE*—GULF OF BOOTHIA

I had the watch as we followed Teuthis away from the Grindle Islands. As soon as I got away from the near-shore ice racket, I picked up *Drum* out ahead and *Frisco* back toward Brentford Bay. I figured that *Swordfish* was still near Pemmican Rock, making sure the *Victor III* survivors were rescued by *Volgograd* and *Carp*, making it unlikely that either of them would slip past into Bellot Strait to tail us. We still had no word on *Shchuka*, but as I indicated earlier, I was pretty sure she was lurking south near the entry to Fury and Hecla Strait. She was probably a bit confused by the transponder we had placed at the base of Hecla and Fury Islands on our transit around

Baffin Island at the beginning of this whole thing.[18] There might have been other Soviet subs, but I did not think so since we had not picked up anything but the four we had already encountered—three now, I reminded myself.

As we moved into the northern Gulf of Boothia, the ice canopy consolidated into a solid sheet about four feet thick. There were sufficient floes and brash along the western edge to raise the noise level and, I thought with a certain degree of pleasure, maintain enough open water for Borysko to follow our progress.

I set a course of 108 degrees and settled back for the remainder of my watch. We had 174 nautical miles to cover, which would take us right to the start of my next watch. *Drum* scooted out ahead of us to make sure *Shchuka* would not pick us up as we transited south. *Swordfish* hung back, covering our six and keeping watch on the east end of Bellot Strait since sooner or later, we could expect *Volgograd* or *Carp*—or even both of them—to exit the strait.

On the other hand, if *Swordfish* pulled it off, both of them might take the long way around the north end of Somerset Island. *Frisco* would catch them either way, coming south through Prince Regent Inlet or directly through the strait. Once the Soviet subs left the west end of Bellot, *Swordfish* would dart through the strait to give our back door more coverage.

By now, the Soviet subs knew we intended to transit Fury and Hecla Strait. That left us only one option, to exit the archipelago through Hudson Strait. That presented an interesting scenario. *Carp* had a top submerged speed of about thirty-four knots. She could easily power around the north end of Baffin Island and wait for us at the mouth of Hudson Strait. To retain control of the situation, therefore, I figured that *Drum* would have to transit Fury and Hecla Strait ahead of us and power her way at her best speed to where Hudson Strait emptied into the Labrador Sea. It wouldn't be a flank-speed trip because the waters of Foxe Basin were too shallow. My calculations showed that *Drum* and *Carp* would arrive at the mouth of Hudson Strait about the same time. The big difference would be that *Drum* was way quieter

---

18 See *Operation Ice Breaker*, the second book in the *Mac McDowell Mission Series*.

than *Carp*. Very likely, *Carp* would be unaware of *Drum*, and that was good for us.

*

As I assumed the watch twenty-two hours later, I changed course to 089 degrees, pointing to a spot off Point Kendall on the southeast end of Crown Prince Frederik Island. Two hours later, right after grabbing a sat fix, *Lyre* and *Teuthis* settled side-by-side in eighty feet of water to recharge our batteries.

Although Polar Bears abounded around this area, none chose to visit us this time. That didn't change the divers' watchfulness, however. As I watched on the monitors, I actually was more tense than I had been when Polar Bears really were present.

At this time of year at our position, the sun stayed below the horizon for the entire day, but there actually were eight hours of semi-twilight. We had missed that period by two hours, so it was pitch dark above the canopy.

To my delight, and everyone else's, Borysko showed up as we were wrapping up. We had gotten so efficient at the charging process that we were completely finished an hour early. Instead of calling the divers back, Ham allowed them to play with the big guy for a while. I certainly didn't object, and neither did the skipper. Spook had the watch for that final hour, so I could relax and just enjoy the activity outside our hull.

THE *LYRE*—FURY & HECLA STRAIT

As we prepared to get underway, we started to get intermittent but clear indications of *Shchuka* about thirty nautical miles to the south. She was heading generally to the west, probably trying to track the location of the transponder. Since that was the whole idea, we didn't do anything to discourage her.

We crept into the mouth of Fury and Hecla Strait under strict ultra-quiet conditions—both Lyre and Teuthis. Over the next fifteen hours, we covered only fifty-nine nautical miles. At first, the current helped us, but then it died away. By the time Sam brought us to the shallow ridge just west of Liddon Island, we were moving over the bottom at a bit more than walking speed. Liddon Island lay about three nautical miles ahead of us as Sam turned his watch over to Potts.

The canopy had thinned to just a few inches as Potts eased us up against the ice. It cracked and broke effortlessly.

"Okay, Potts," I said, "I'm raising the scope." To my surprise, I saw the polynya's quiet surface in the dim twilight. We were near the middle of an eight-hour twilight at this latitude. The sky was overcast, and there was no specific light source, just a general dim skyglow. As I swung around, off our starboard bow I saw several brief white flashes. "What's *Teuthis'* location?" I asked.

"A bit over a mile off our starboard bow," Potts answered, supplying information from the *Akkord* console.

"Okay, I got her scope visually," I said. "She's flashing a white light." I took my eye from the scope to look at Potts. "Can we do that?"

"Sergyi," Potts called. "To control, please." "He's not here, remember…" I grinned at him.

"The DIA guys speak Russian, don't they?" Potts asked. "Wyatt does. Call him."

When Wyatt appeared, I asked, "How can I flash a light from the periscope?"

Wyatt grabbed one of the manuals and flipped the pages. "There's a switch for that near your right hand," he told me a couple of minutes later.

Sure enough…I flashed the light several times and got back a responding flash. That was Waverly, finishing up his watch. With that, we concluded our informal comm test using periscopes.

"*Lyre,* this is *Teuthis.*" It was the secure Gertrude, and I recognized the skipper's voice.

"This is *Lyre,*" I responded.

"We intend to float with the current through Labrador Narrows ten hours from now. In the meantime, we can both bottom, and we can bring half your crew at a time to *Teuthis* for a hot shower and a meal. That is, of course, only if your guys want to do this."

By the end of this short conversation, all eight of my guys were in Control, grinning from ear to ear.

"It looks like my crew has decided," I said. "Oh, by-the-way, Happy New Year!"

I fingered Kate's ivory cylinder in my pocket, wondering what she was doing on this special night.

✳

First things first. We pulled around to Liddon Island's southwest side and set down gently on the mud bottom with clear water overhead. We were just inside a relatively permanent polynya. *Teuthis* bottomed alongside starboard to starboard—our normal protocol. I turned on *Lyre's* lights only to find visibility very low because of the mud we had stirred up. For the most part, the currents that raged through Fury and Hecla Strait bypassed the south side of Liddon Island. Even so, by the time the divers had connected us to *Teuthis*, and we were sucking *trons*, the surrounding water had started to clear.

While we definitely were in Polar Bear country, I did not expect any close encounters this time. Polar Bears prefer jumbled pack ice relatively close to land. They avoid large flat expanses of ice because they cannot easily break through the ice to fish. Continuously open polynyas often have Orcas, one of the few predators that Polar Bears avoid. The ice in the strait was quite broken up, although jammed together. It would have been fine for the bears, except for the recurring swift currents. The jostling floes and smaller bergies were hazardous for a swimming Polar Bear. Not even a 1,000-pound male can survive being crushed between two large floes or a couple of large bergies.

Borysko didn't show either.

"Where's Borysko?" Sergyi, who was one of the deployed divers, asked.

"Borysko can cruise all day at ten knots," I answered. "If he followed us from the Grindle Islands, he would have had to circumnavigate the south end of Boothia before following us through Fury and Hecla Strait— some five hundred nautical miles. He should have been able to track our progress until we entered the strait, so—if he followed, and we don't know that—he should be showing up before we leave." Then I added, "Don't let my thoughts about Polar Bears lower your awareness."

"No Ukrainian food for Polar Bears today," Sergyi said as I watched him scan the surface above them.

✳

"Stand by for *Mystic* ops," Barry, who was on watch by this time, announced over the Secure Gertrude.

I had already decided to send the DIA team first along with Bert, so he could relieve me when they returned. The DIA guys had not been sharing watchstanding duties with the five *Teuthis* crew members, but they had spent virtually all their time when not sleeping or eating, studying the *Lyre* systems. Even Kendrick Long, the hull specialist, kept himself busy assisting his teammates. As we were awaiting *Mystic*, I asked Wyatt about it.

"You guys have been keeping pretty busy learning the *Alfa* systems," I said.

"Yeah," he replied, "this is the most advanced sub ever built. It has some flaws, but it beats the shit out of anything we got. The automation alone…my God!" He shook his head. "No reason we couldn't do this—even if we didn't use titanium. A fleet of these boats built to American standards, using one of our reactors, manned by American submariners…we would be invincible."

"We pretty much are right now," I said.

"Not if the Soviets build a bunch of these," Wyatt said. "They'll eat our lunch, dinner, and breakfast!"

We heard *Mystic* making a seal above our after-hatch.

"Okay, guys," I said to the DIA team and Bert. "Get your butts over there and enjoy a shower, some real chow, and a bit of relaxation. We'll see you in about three hours."

❊

Potts was finishing up his watch, and I was next. Other than monitoring the charge and what was happening outside our hull, we didn't have a lot to do. I called the guys into Control.

"Spook, you will be taking us through the Labrador Narrows. I'll be here in case you need me, but you will be in the driver's seat. This will be the most difficult seventeen nautical mile stretch we have done thus far. We're traveling ultra-quiet—engines shut down, screw not turning. Since we will be moving with the water, your rudder and planes will not work. All you will have are the two little screws on the tips of the stern plane stabilizers. Remember, these guys don't tilt. *Alfa* stern planes are like aircraft elevators, moving flaps in a horizontal stabilizer.

The auxiliary props are at the outer ends of the stabilizers, so they don't tilt. You can use them to accelerate, decelerate, and turn. If you gain sufficient forward momentum beyond the current, then you can use the control surfaces." I stopped to let him absorb what I had said.

"This is gonna be trickier than setting neutral buoyancy on *Teuthis*. I don't know how much help *Boksit* and *Akkord* will be. If Wyatt is correct, Ivan designed this system to handle something like the Labrador Narrows, but we better be on our toes in case it loses the bubble."

I could tell that Spook was a bit nervous about the forthcoming assignment. He tried not to show it, but I saw it. "Senior Chief Jones," I said, putting as much sincerity as possible into my words, "if anyone can do this, *you* can!" I grabbed his shoulder and grinned at him. "Besides, if we do hit bottom, this baby's made of titanium. Shouldn't cause any damage, especially at the slow speed we will be traveling."

"You'll do fine," Sam said. "Yep," Potts added

I thought they both were happy it was Spook and not them.

"Seriously, Spook," I said, "this will be a feather in your hat. Don't worry. I'll be right there to help if things get crazy."

✳

We finished the charge without Borysko making an appearance. The divers were disappointed, but that changed when they found several Greenland Halibut camouflaged by the muddy bottom. Their find was highly unusual since these fish usually stay in much deeper water—over 1,200 feet. They brought three seventy-pound fish for Cedric and his crew. The divers completed their short decompression and were hanging out in Dive Control when I arrived about three hours later. I had left Bert in charge, but despite my having full confidence in him, I found myself a bit nervous at not being aboard *Lyre*.

I spent a half-hour with the divers, shooting the bull and generally reestablishing our warm rapport, with high-fives for the three halibut. Then I hit the rain locker and must have spent a full fifteen minutes luxuriating in the hot spray.

Cedric Hurst went out of his way to give my crew a great meal. He made it diner's choice, steak or halibut. Everyone opted for the Greenland Halibut, some of the best eating fish in the world. Cedric baked up a batch of cornbread that we consumed slathered with butter and honey, or in my case, maple syrup. It was definitely good eating and outclassed our LRPs every which way from Sunday.

Just as I sat down for my meal, Ham knocked at the Wardroom door and stuck his head inside.

"What is it, Ham?"

"Borysko just showed up. The captain has given permission for several divers to pay him a visit. I thought that since you have not yet had the pleasure, you might like to join them." He grinned at me.

There is no doubt—Ham knew his boss. I checked with the skipper.

"Just make sure you are back and decompressed in time to transfer back to *Mystic*," he told me.

※

A half-hour later, I was in the water with Sergyi and Borysko—thirty feet of 12,000-pound friendly killer whale. Borysko recognized Sergyi, probably by his bright white ID letter—*A*. Borysko opened his huge mouth, and Sergyi reached in and scratched his tongue. Then he pulled back with me and pointed to my ID letter—*M*. Borysko approached me and nudged me with his snout. He swam around me, examining me from every angle. Then he approached me front-on, mouth wide agape.

Sergyi gave me two thumbs up, and I heard his voice in my ears. "Go ahead, Mac. Scratch his tongue."

I did, after which Borysko closed his mouth, put his snout against my chest, and gently pushed me around a large circle bounded by the light from *Lyre*. I have experienced a lot of things in the water, but this was a first, an absolute first. When we were done, Borysko approached me again and opened his mouth for a tongue scratch.

I was running out of time. Sergyi and I headed back to the DDC. Before we closed the Egress hatch, Borysko squeezed himself under *Teuthis* and pushed his left eye against the Egress hatch, peering around the lock.

"Don't close it yet," I said, as I doffed my helmet and rig so Borysko could see my face. As he watched, I pulled off my hot water suit and stood free in the lock. Borysko rolled over and stuck his tongue through the hatch. I reached down with my bare hand and scratched it, and then pressed my flat hand against his tongue. We remained that way for about a minute, creating an eternal bond between us.

Suddenly, without warning, Borysko moved so that his blowhole was in the hatch opening. He let go a furious blow that covered the entire lock and all of us with a faintly fishy spray. Then he sucked in a lungful of the compressed air from the Egress Lock. It was fortunate that we were using air and not mixed gas. I have no idea what the helium might have done to him. I was worried about the two-and-a-half atmospheres of air he took in, but he didn't seem to notice. He moved his eye back to the hatch and then stuck his tongue in again. We all scratched his tongue, and then I once more pressed my hand against his tongue. After a minute or so, Borysko pulled back, and we shut the hatch.

I surfaced from my short decompression with five minutes to spare and hurried to join the rest of my crew for the return trip to *Lyre*. The entire crew had watched my antics with Borysko. As I hurried aft, high-fives slapped my hands the length of the sub. It was kind of fun, but I didn't have much time to dwell on it as my thoughts turned to our forthcoming passage through Labrador Narrows.

What I didn't know, what none of us knew, was what actually lay ahead of us.

THE *LYRE*—LABRADOR NARROWS

After we safely transited to *Lyre* and *Mystic* was secured in her cradle, I relieved Bert, and we all assembled in Control.

"Some of you have already heard this," I said, "but Bert and the DIA guys have not." I took a deep breath. "Spook is next up on the watchbill, so he's going to take us through the narrows." I noticed that Spook winced slightly.

I then explained what I had earlier gone through with Spook. "You all are welcome to hang out in Control. Just don't get in our way. Things may get exciting. Spook, you've got it!"

Teuthis took the lead, moving with her outboards. Ten minutes later, I signaled to Spook, and he lifted us off the bottom and moved us on the auxiliary props into the main channel. As we poked into the stream, water pressure pushed our bow to starboard, and we straightened out in the middle of the flow. I checked the *Akkord* display. We were moving along at a smart seven knots, a hundred feet above the bottom, with 500 feet of water above us.

"Bring us up to two-hundred feet," I told Spook. "Let's keep away from the bottom."

Things were going well, and Spook was doing a good job. He set our parameters into *Akkord*, and *Akkord* automatically fired the props and manipulated our buoyancy so that we remained at 200 feet over the deepest part of the channel. Every now and then, *Lyre* would swerve a bit to one side or the other, pushed by the current. Spook's hands hovered over the *Akkord* console controls, ready to change things manually, but

Akkord always seemed to recover quickly. It was pretty impressive. And that's when things got crazy.

At one hour and forty-three minutes into the run, *Lyre* went into a wild, counterclockwise spin. One moment we were pointed at 097 degrees. The next, our stern overhauled us to starboard, and the next thing we knew, we were headed backward toward our destination.

I opened my mouth to tell Spook to take *Akkord* offline, but he did it before I could utter the words.

Spook looked at me with a shocked expression. "Wha' happened? Wha' do I do?"

That was a good question, one for which I was not sure I had a good answer. "Try moving us to starboard," I said, "away from whatever spun us—I mean port the way we are pointed now." I looked at the *Akkord* display. "Go back on the port screw and forward on the starboard."

He did. Not much happened, though the current quickly straightened us out.

"Full power on both screws—port back, starboard forward," I said. He did, and after an agonizing minute of ever-so-slow twisting, the current caught our starboard bow and swept us back around. "Okay, Spook, well done! Now bring us to one hundred feet and steady us back on course."

Spook grunted a couple of times and then grinned with satisfaction. "Got you, you sonofabitch!" He turned to me, relief evident in his features. "Back under control, Mac."

✳

Afterward, we reconstructed what must have happened. As accurate as they were, the Soviet charts were not perfect. Trying to map out a narrow, deep canyon that is constantly ice-covered and subject to extreme currents is a difficult task under any circumstances. Simply stated, they got it wrong. The *Sozh* navigation system missed a finger of shallower water intruding into the otherwise deep channel. We struck it with a glancing blow. No damage to *Lyre*, just enough to slow us so the current could spin us around. I have no idea whether or not *Akkord* could have corrected the situation. Spook and I didn't give it a chance. We preferred to rely on good old seamanship to solve the problem.

Later, when Spook and I explained the matter to the skipper in his cabin, he looked at me and said, "Mac, you continue to amaze me with how you react to emergency situations. Bravo Zulu!"

"Spook had the conn," I tried to interject.

"No, sir!" Spook interrupted. "I just followed your orders!" "Seriously," I said, "Senior Chief Morris played a significant role." "I know," the skipper said. "I know."

THE *LYRE*—FOXE BASIN

As we swept out of the Labrador Narrows, the bottom shallowed to about 160 feet and would remain so for the next 440 nautical miles. The canopy consisted of smaller floes and lots of brash, with occasional bergies forming anchor points for pressure ridges topside and downward projecting obstacles that we needed to avoid. The entire mass moved southeast with the tidal current. It would reverse to jam Labrador Narrows in twelve hours as the current-driven ice tried to force its way through the narrows into Fury and Hecla Strait.

Bert assumed the watch as we exited the narrows. While I laid out our track for him, I said, "Set your depth to seventy-five feet so long as you have at least seventy-five feet of water beneath you. Where the bottom deepens, drop to a hundred feet. Keep an eye on the canopy." I paused, thinking how to say the next. "Now, here's the thing. I have to believe that Borysko is following us. He seemed at home in Boothia, but I have no idea whether or not he knows anything about Foxe Basin and Foxe Channel. So long as the canopy is loose and slushy, he can follow us, grabbing a breath whenever he feels the need. Once it's solid, he will drown if we don't help him out. He can cruise at about ten knots and will need to breathe every forty-five minutes or so."

Bert grinned at me. "You want to make periodic blowholes," he said with a chuckle.

"Yeah, it's gotten kinda personal for the divers and me." I smiled. "Just slow to a stop for your baffle clear and bump a hole through the ice with the sail. Borysko's smart. He'll quickly figure out what we are doing."

"What does the big guy eat?"

"Anything that swims," I answered. "I suspect it's mostly pelagic fish, fish swimming around in the water, and probably demersal fish near the bottom. He just opens his mouth while underway and swallows whatever enters."

"What about sharks, large tuna, and other bigger ones?"

"He prefers those, but when they are not present, I think Borysko is perfectly satisfied with the little guys. Near shore, there are seals, walruses, and even Polar Bear—we've seen that." I grinned. "Food is not a problem. If we ensure he has air, he'll do just fine."

✳

Twenty hours later, just as I completed my watch, I slowed to DIW and communicated with *Teuthis*.

"*Teuthis*, this is *Lyre*," I transmitted over the Secure Gertrude. "I'm pretty sure Borysko has been following us. I've been punching through the canopy every forty-five minutes or so when it was too heavy for him to break so he can breathe. I'm about to punch a hole here and then slide over a hundred feet to settle against the canopy for a battery charge."

"Roger that." It was Franklin. "Is he here?"

"Don't know, but the divers will know as soon as they enter the water," I answered.

"The captain wants a fix, so we're gonna crack ice, too," Franklin said.

Forty minutes later, we were side-by-side resting against the ice.

The view with my monitors was pitch black until I turned on the lights. A minute or so later, the Basketball appeared following three divers—Harry, Jimmy, and Sergyi. Whitey remained in the Egress Lock tending Harry and Jimmy, who were on umbilicals. Sergyi wore a rebreather and acted as lookout, armed with an APS. The other two carried APSs slung over their backs just in case.

As far away from land as we were, I thought it unlikely that we would be bothered by Polar Bears, but better safe than sorry. I was glad Ham had armed them.

"Wish we were with them," Wyatt said, draping an arm around Long's shoulder. "You're working them to death."

"It's what they live for," I said. "We would have a mutiny on our hands if we kept them out of the water any more than absolutely necessary." I grinned.

"Really…?" Wyatt said.

"Naw, but they would definitely be an unhappy bunch." "Hey! There's Borysko," Long said. "Look at that!"

Borysko was rubbing his snout against each diver in turn and then asking for a tongue scratch. To everyone's total astonishment, he produced a length of 4 x 4.

"You guys gotta know," I said to the assembled crew in Control, "Borysko has carried that piece of wood with him for several hundred nautical miles."

✳

Spook had the watch during the battery charge, and over on *Teuthis*, the XO had relieved Franklin for the last two hours. The divers were wrapping up and spending a bit of playtime with Borysko and his 4 x 4. Frankly, I wished I could join them.

Out of the darkness off our bow and *Teuthis'* stern, a very large, dark shape emerged.

"What the fuck is that?" Sergyi yelped as he backed away from a 20-foot-long, 2,000-pound shark that approached him slowly. He brought his APS to bear on the giant.

"Sergyi…NO!" I transmitted through our local comm system for divers on rebreathers. "That's a Greenland Shark. What you see is as fast as it can swim…just stay away from its mouth. It can create a suction that will draw you right into its gullet."

My crew crowded around the monitors.

"We dealt with one of these fuckers on our way out here," Jimmy said, his comment forwarded through our hookup. "He chopped Harry's fins off right at his toes. Those suckers are hangin' in Dive Control."[19]

Our monitors were filled with the monster's head, gaping mouth a full four feet top to bottom. It had a double row of smooth, razor-sharp teeth in its upper jaw. They looked like two-inch daggers, the front row pointed slightly outward, the back row slightly inward. The lower jaw seemed a bit disjointed and also held two rows of teeth. Unlike the top row, these teeth each had two cross members, looking so much like little saws.

Borysko kept away from the shark's mouth, but he didn't seem intimidated by the giant. Instead, he nudged Sergyi away from the shark and placed his larger body between the predator and Harry and Jimmy, who had moved to the open Egress hatch. Borysko didn't attack the Greenland Shark at first, but he drove his snout into the shark's flank several times with enough force to have rocked the *Lyre* had he struck the sail. It became obvious that he was shoving the monster away from the vicinity of the divers. The Basketball followed the struggle, looking down from above, shining its spots on the shark.

When Borysko had driven the shark to the edge of the volume illuminated by *Lyre's* lights, he backed off, clearly preparing to strike again. This time, however, he rammed into the shark with his mouth wide open. His fifty conical teeth, twenty-five upper and lower, tore into the Greenland Shark's side, ripping a six-foot piece of flesh out of the hapless creature. Blood and guts spewed everywhere.

"Into the Egress hatch…all of you!" I shouted into the rigged comm system. The divers complied with more speed than I thought them capable of.

I turned to my crew in Control, glued to the monitors. "Borysko is one of the good guys," I said, "but there are blood and guts in the water. He may not be able to control himself. Even a one-Orca feeding frenzy would be extremely dangerous."

To my surprise, however, instead of going crazy the way we had seen when the Orcas attacked the belugas off Point Barrow, Borysko

---

19 See *Operation Ice Breaker*, the second book in the *Mac McDowell Mission Series*.

left his feast and swam to the Egress lock. He peered into the lock with his left eye, then rolled over to use his right. Then he whistled several times and headed to the surface for a breath of fresh air.

A minute later, he was back, clearly trying to coax the divers back into the water. I held my breath, wondering what Ham would do. This was entirely unprecedented. I would match his judgment against mine any day, so I waited.

A minute later, the three divers appeared, still carrying APSs. Harry and Jimmy disconnected the shorepower cable and stowed it. Then all three divers clustered around Borysko's huge head, rubbing his dome, scratching his tongue, and generally bonding with their six-ton playmate. Had I not actually seen it with my own eyes, I simply would not have believed it.

✳

Spook had the watch for the first hour as we got underway. I was with him in Control.

"Spook," I said, "before putting it into gear, drop to the bottom to see what Borysko is doing. He still has a two-thousand-pound meal waiting for him down there."

Spook took us down 168 feet to the bottom. Sure enough, Borysko was feeding leisurely on the Greenland Shark carcass. He looked up at *Lyre*, gave a squeal, and rose about thirty feet to rub the bottom of our sail. He watched us depart before turning back to his meal.

We would be angling southeastward for twenty-two hours toward Enukso Point, the westernmost extension of Foxe Peninsula near the southern end of Baffin Island that we had circumnavigated before we laid the Carey Øer SOSUS array near the start of this whole venture.[20] We intended to recharge our batteries just offshore of Enukso Point.

I modified our routine as during the previous leg so that we stopped every forty-five minutes or so to clear our baffles and punch a hole through the canopy for Borysko. As we neared Baffin Island, the ice became more jumbled—a mix of smaller floes and brash. For the last eight hours of our transit, we could forego punching the holes.

---

20 See *Operation Ice Breaker*, the second book in the *Mac McDowell Mission Series*.

At hour twenty-one, I turned the watch over to Spook, and an hour later, he came left to 104 degrees for our twenty-nautical mile run to a bay just south of Enukso Point. He put us on the bottom in 148 feet of water with light brash overhead on the surface. Borysko showed up just as Harry, Whitey (who had replaced Jimmy), and Sergyi completed hooking us to *Teuthis*. He seemed to understand to keep away from the shore cable, so the divers concentrated on finishing their task so they could play with him.

We were definitely in Polar Bear territory, but they don't particularly like brash and would have no reason to swim out to our submerged location. Nevertheless, Sergyi kept his eyes open for an unwanted visitor.

Bert finished the charge and got us underway almost due south on the final forty-nautical mile leg of our transit to Hudson Strait.

THE *LYRE*—HUDSON STRAIT

Three hours into the leg, Sam took over and passed several nautical miles west of Mill Island, one of three islands guarding the entrance to Hudson Strait—the other two were Nottingham Island and Salisbury Island. Sam passed north of both into the Hudson Strait main channel, aiming for McDonald Island, a God-forsaken, stretched-out island several miles northwest of the strangely named Islands of God's Mercie. I pitied the guys who determined this was an appropriate name for these rocks. There were so many hundreds of small islands scattered along the southwestern edge of Baffin Island that I was certain the Soviets had not yet surveyed them all from underwater. The *Sozh* console indicated many of these islands, but I suspected that they were present courtesy of the Canadian Hydrographic Service—the guys who make the Canadian charts.

When I relieved Potts eight hours later, we were about halfway along the track to McDonald Island. Potts looked a bit pale, almost as if he were a bit seasick—something that does not normally happen on subs.

"You okay, Potts?" I asked him.

"A bit tired, I guess," he said without his usual enthusiastic nature.

"Try to get some sleep," I answered. "You got twenty hours before your next watch."

He grunted and headed below. That's the last I saw of him for a while. I could hardly blame him. Our routine was about as boring as it gets on submarines. It had been a while since we had done anything but cruise and charge. We were in the middle of our fifteenth day, and the only real distraction recently had been Borysko. I suppose you could add the Greenland Shark, but that did more for the divers than for us in *Lyre*. We didn't even have any activity on *Okean*.

Frisco was guarding our back door, probably lurking south of Nottingham and Salisbury Islands, so *Okean* could not see her. By now, *Swordfish* had transited Fury and Hecla Strait and should have been covering Foxe Channel to the northwest. Foxe Peninsula would be shielding her. *Drum* was out ahead of us, monitoring the entrance to Hudson Bay. Although we had a line-of-sight to *Drum*, she was 300 nautical miles distant and much too quiet for us to pick her up. *Carp* was somewhere near *Drum*—at least that was our presumption. As a Sierra-I, she was a capable submarine but relatively noisy, like *Lyre*. We couldn't see her on *Okean*, but I was confident that *Teuthis* had identified her.

Bert had the last hour of watch as we arrived at McDonald island for our battery charge. The surface was completely ice-covered, but it wasn't solid—small to medium floes and brash.

"What do you think?" Bert asked me. "Will Polar Bears be comfortable here?"

"Everything I know," I answered, "tells me this is ideal bear country." I pulled out the paper chart so we could see a larger area. "All these islands will keep the ice from moving in any specific direction for very long. It just sloshes around like in a big bathtub. These floes," I pointed to the under-ice display, "are big enough for the bears. They'll take to the water to move from floe to floe, and thus from one island or rock to the next. Hudson Bay, to our south, is home to the world's largest Polar Bear population. The southern end of Baffin Island, where we are right now, takes second place."

Bert bottomed us in eighty feet of water, and Waverly moved *Teuthis* alongside. By now, our daily chargings were about as routine as something gets on subs. I don't mean to minimize what the divers did, their critical role, and the dangers they faced each time. But when you face danger often enough, even danger becomes routine.

Borysko had become another routine part of our daily battery charge. He never seemed to tire of his frolics with the divers. His presence was even more important this time because his being there seemed to keep the big white bears away.

We had two hours of morning twilight and an hour with the sun above the horizon—barely—at the end of our charge operation. We had no bear visitors, perhaps because Borysko took several breaths through the brash right above us. That may have been enough to keep the bears away.

Sam got us underway on a course of 124 degrees at 500 feet to mask our sound from the lurking *Carp*. We were stretching things a bit on this leg. We would remain on course and depth for 210 nautical miles, just before the shelf that held Akpatok Island. Then we planned to come up to 100 feet for another thirty nautical miles. If necessary, we would bottom for a charge on the shelf at some 200 feet. If possible, we wanted to push our batteries another eight miles past the 240, so we could bottom close-in to the rocky cliffs of Akpatok.

Potts was supposed to relieve Sam, but he couldn't get out of his bunk. He had a fever and a fast pulse. His stomach was rock-hard.

"What have you been eating?" I asked. "LRPs," he said.

"You been mixin' them like I said?"

"Mostly, except for the last few. We were busy, so I tossed them down and drank some water."

"Really?" I grabbed his shoulders and said with mock ferocity, "You dumb fuck! That shit has plugged your gut like a bottle stopper."

I shook my head. "Doc's gonna give you a whole glass of mineral oil to clear that out. Before this is over, you're going to be shitting your guts out for a couple of days."

"Sorry, Boss. Just trying to be efficient." He sounded glum.

"At least, we're not going to lose you, Potts." I smiled. "You remain in your rack till we can transfer you to *Teuthis*."

"So, I'm off the *Lyre* crew?"

"Sorry, Potts."

I took his watch and called *Teuthis* on the Secure Gertrude. "*Teuthis*, this is *Lyre*."

"Go ahead, *Lyre*." It was Barry.

I briefed him on the situation. "We'll want to transfer him first thing and get a replacement—someone with Control Room experience," I said.

I turned the watch over to Bert, who would squeeze the last *trons* from our batteries to get us to the shallow water off the east shore of Akpatok.

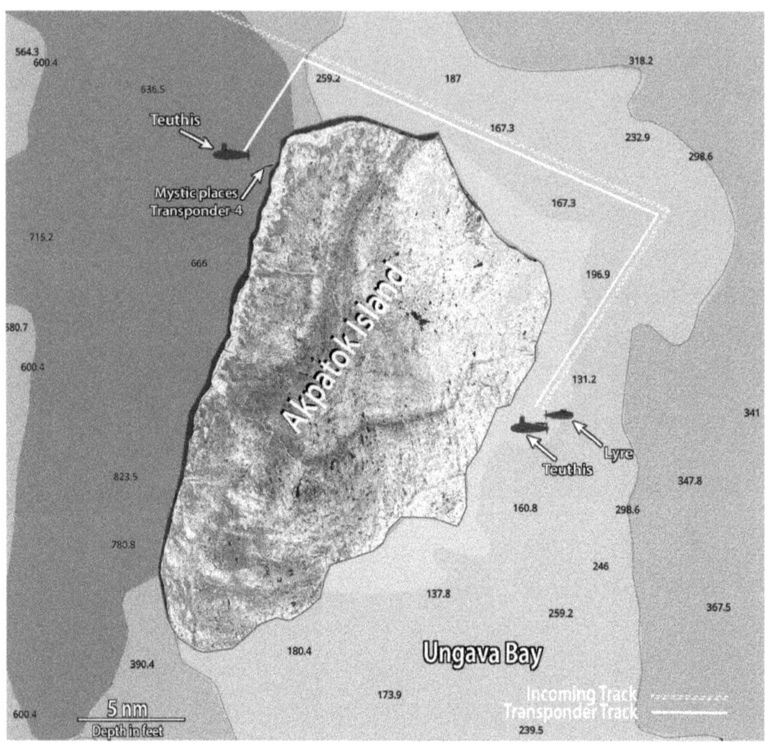

USS Teuthis & Lyre at Akpatok Island in Ungava Bay.
USS Teuthis & Mystic placing Transponder-4

CHAPTER SIXTEEN—Akpatok Island

THE *LYRE*—BOTTOMED AT AKPATOK ISLAND

In record time, Bert on *Lyre* and Waverly on *Teuthis* placed both subs on the bottom in eighty feet of water just twelve feet apart. The moment both deck officers announced they were stable, *Mystic* unlatched and lifted off *Teuthis*. Five minutes later, she made a seal against *Lyre*. We were standing by below *Lyre's* after-hatch. *Mystic* crew members

Senior Chief Abelé and Petty Officer First Class Flanger hauled Potts into the DSRV in a hastily improvised sling. The rest of my crew remained behind to facilitate Pott's rapid transfer into Dr. Everest's and Chief Corpsman Gunderson's capable hands.

The canopy was solid ice except for brash alongshore all around the island—mid-winter in Ungava Bay, subject to forty-foot in-out tidal currents. Borysko joined us for our initial *Mystic* ops. I'm guessing he followed eastward along the south shore of Baffin Island and then cut south across Hudson Strait, where the ice was beginning to break up as it emptied into the Labrador Sea. While *Mystic* transported Potts to *Teuthis*, Borysko paid close attention to the DSRV. It was some fifteen feet longer than he and about the same diameter. He kept his distance but watched closely.

"Maybe he thinks it's a long-lost girlfriend," Bert said as we watched Borysko on our monitors.

"He's way too smart for that," I said. "He recognizes each diver by their ID letters; he tracks us across hundreds of nautical miles; he guards the divers diligently—he's way too smart."

"Too bad," Sam said. "I'd love to see a killer whale try to fuck a DSRV." "Not with you inside," Spook said with a grin. "Borysko would make short work of the fiberglass fairing."

Bert added, "The titanium spheres would be unscathed, but the piping and electrical would probably suffer."

"Whadya think, Mac?" Sam asked. "You've driven one of those things." "We'd survive and probably be operational—sort of; enough to get back to *Teuthis*," I said, wondering what I would do if it really happened with me inside. "Let's be glad Borysko is as tame as he is."

The DIA guys watched each of us during our exchange. Then Wyatt said, "You guys are a bunch of crazy fucks…and I'm damn glad you're on our side."

✳

"*Lyre*, this is *Teuthis*. Doc Everest has Potts. He's gonna be fine." That was Waverly, getting ready to turn over to Barry.

"Once he gets past the effects of the mineral oil," I transmitted back.

"Stand by for dive ops." That was Barry. "We'll send *Mystic* over in fifteen minutes to bring half your crew here for dinner and a douche."

ON THE SEAFLOOR—AT THE *LYRE*

While *Mystic* prepared for her second trip in an hour, the divers showed up outside, much to Borysko's obvious delight. He bounced around, flipping his tail, popping to the surface for a breath, zooming up and pulling back, so much so that the divers took longer to hook up the shore power cable than they normally did. Ham put his four available divers in the water this time—Harry, Whitey, Jer, and Sergyi, with Jimmy tending. By the time they had hooked up shore power, *Mystic* was settling back on our hatch.

I sent Bert with the DIA team so he could relieve me on his return, and I kept Matt, the DIA sonar guy, to even us out—and because he played a pretty good chess game. We set things up so they would return in about seventy-five minutes.

"Bring the chessboard to Control," I told Matt.

✳

The highest Polar Bear population in the Arctic is probably around Hudson Bay—certainly for the Canadian Arctic. This includes Ungava Bay. As I mentioned earlier, the south end of Baffin Island, where we just were, has the second-highest population. We were sitting on the bottom, close to shore, in the middle of a host of Polar Bears as large as any on Earth. True, they typically didn't dive to our depth, but the tops of our sails were twenty feet or so below the canopy. It wasn't a situation that made me feel warm and fuzzy. I fingered Kate's cylinder in my pocket and thought about her, us, and what was going on around me.

Matt mated me more quickly than usual. I guess I was distracted, not up to my best game.

"Hey, Mac, you okay?" Matt asked as I tipped my king on its side. "Yeah, just a bit distracted, and I'm worried about Potts."

"But Doc Everest said he would be fine."

"Yeah, I know. But why didn't I see it coming?" I put my head in my hands. "It isn't as if we were overworked down here."

"Maybe not, Mac, but it's constant focus. No way I could do what you guys do every day."

"Thanks, Matt. Let's get ready for the guys to return."

✳

It was good being back on *Teuthis*. I stopped to see Ham and the divers. While in Dive Control, I spoke with Aleksandr Alexeyev and Boris Kuznetsov, the two captured Spetsnaz divers we continued to hold inside the Main Lock. Alexeyev was still recovering from the wounds in both his arms. They were both polite but reserved.

In Russian, I said, "I understand that you were doing your jobs. Neither I nor my men hold that against you. You must understand that you are inside an operating submerged submarine. I know your orders are not to cooperate and to escape as soon as possible. You both have to know that escape is impossible."

Alexeyev spoke up. "We will sabotage your sub and sink it if we can. It will be our honor to carry this out in death." He spoke politely but firmly.

Kuznetsov simply nodded and said, "*Da!*"

I waved Sergyi over. "Have you been able to reach these guys?" I asked.

He shook his head. "Never happen," he growled. "I say, kill and dump overboard. Best way."

"We don't do things that way," I said. "You know that."

"*Da*—still best way!"

✳

After a wonderful fifteen minutes in the rain locker and an excellent meal of crispy Southern Fried Chicken and fries better than anything you could get at Micky-Ds, accompanied by mounds of steaming fresh cornbread and butter, all washed down with *vintage* bug juice, the skipper called me back to his cabin. He was in a chair at his desk.

"Mac, we're preparing to leave *Lyre* on the bottom here while we go around the north tip of Akpatok so *Mystic* can place a transponder near the bottom at the island edge. I want you aboard *Mystic* to assist Lieutenant Taggert and his crew in placing the transponder." He smiled at me. "I'm not expressing any lack of confidence in Lieutenant Taggert; he's the *Mystic* pilot. *You* know more about placing transponders than anyone else onboard, so it's got to be you.

"Conduct a formal temporary relief of command with Chief Warrant Officer Cobb, and log the transfer." He stood up. "One more thing. I'm replacing Chief Panner on *Lyre* with Chief Jackson for the remainder of the trip."

TEUTHIS—MYSTIC OPS

The *Lyre* log entry read: *Lt. Cmdr. J.R. McDowell, Commanding, relieved by Chief Warrant Officer Bert Cobb.*

Should something drastic happen on *Lyre*, it was no longer my personal responsibility. For better or worse, Bert had the bag until I returned. *Mystic* docked long enough to pick me up. Shortly, we locked down on *Teuthis*, and I dropped into the Engine Room and went forward to report to the skipper.

The next step was to place the transponder firmly into the manipulator grip. Ham continued to be in charge of diving operations, and I overheard Ski arguing with him.

"C'mon, Master Chief. I'm fine for a short dive."

"Not according to Doc Everest, Ski. You're gonna have to stay dry for the time being." Ham's voice took on a fatherly tone. "Look at it this way. You'll make first-class by the end of this run, and think of all the bragging rights you'll have with the chicks."

That seemed to cheer Ski up a bit, but his unhappiness was obvious.

"Whitey and Jer—you guys get out there and handle this little task." Borysko was right in their faces when the divers exited the Egress hatch. Whitey showed the transponder to the cetacean, and for a moment as we watched with the Basketball, we thought Borysko would take it from him. Instead, Borysko scooted away, returning a minute later with his 4 x 4.

"He wants to show us he has one too," Whitey said.

"And it's bigger than yours, Bro," Jer said with a laugh. "Much bigger than yours!"

"And the whale you rode in on," Whitey answered as they turned to place the transponder firmly into *Mystic's* manipulator grip, the bright white stripe facing toward the hinge.

When they finished, they backed off to admire their work. Borysko brought his 4 x 4 right up to the manipulator as if to say, "Take mine, too!"

Jer placed himself between Borysko and the manipulator and pushed both hands away from himself as if pushing Borysko back. Borysko seemed to get it and backed off. The divers waited until Taggert had safely tucked the manipulator and transponder under *Mystic* before returning to the Egress hatch.

Ten minutes later, *Teuthis* lifted off the bottom for our four-hour trip to the northwest end of Akpatok Island.

✳

Barry followed our inbound track for two hours. Franklin relieved him and continued until we were off the northwest corner of Akpatok Island. Then we headed southwest for some three nautical miles while dropping to 600 feet. We settled on our skids at 660 feet with a broken canopy overhead. The sandy bottom sloped gently to the west, and 200 yards to the east, a thousand-foot cliff rose from the bottom, through the brash to 400 feet above ice-covered Ungava Bay.

It had been several years since I piloted a DSRV. As we unlatched and lifted off *Teuthis*, I crouched in the opening between the pilot-sphere and the mid-sphere.

"You piloted this baby back when, right?" Bob Taggert asked. "Want to give it a go now?"

No way I was going to turn down that offer. Jim Deckhart slipped out of the Second Pilot chair, and I climbed in. I hovered my hands over the controls.

"You got it," Bob said, lifting his hands off the controls, and I gripped the controls lightly.

I turned toward the cliff and moved forward, scanning my monitors in the pitch blackness. As we approached the cliff, our beams picked it up, a towering massif, terminating in fine grey sand.

"We want to place it vertically in the cliff between ten and thirty feet from the bottom," I said, although I was aware that Bob had already been briefed.

"With the white stripe facing out," he said, finishing my sentence. "That's why you're here—to keep us honest."

"If the truth be known," I said with a grin, "I think he just wanted to give me one more chance to pilot a DSRV. Did he talk with you about it?"

"Naw, but we all know your exploits. It's worth a couple of drinks at the O-Club[21] to be able to say that I allowed the great Mac McDowell to take over the controls of *Mystic* at six hundred feet under the ice in the Arctic!" He gave me a wide grin. "Seriously…it may not seem like a big deal to you 'cause you do these things all the time, but it makes a hell of a sea story and is worth drinks at every O-Club I ever been to." We found a good spot twenty-four feet from the bottom—a nice vertical V-shaped notch. I turned the control back over to Bob and relinquished my seat to Jim. As Bob extended the manipulator, rotating it so the transponder was upright, Borysko suddenly appeared in the monitor about ten feet from the transponder, carrying his 4 x 4 in his massive jaws.

"We gotta pull prints of that off the tape," Jim said. "Without the evidence, no one will ever believe us."

Borysko didn't interfere; he just watched. When Bob finished and backed off, Borysko nosed up to the transponder and whistled at it. Then he swam over to the open manipulator grip and placed one end of his 4 x 4 inside the grip.

"Why not?" Bob said and closed the grip. He pulled slightly, and the cetacean released the wood from his jaw. As we watched in astonishment, Borysko slipped to the surface, presumably to take a breath, and then he showed up again and started gently pulling at his 4 x 4.

"You gonna give it to him?" Jim asked. "I don't want him getting pissed at us."

Bob released the 4 x 4, and Borysko took a firm grip on his prize. Bob motioned to the Second Pilot's seat.

"Before we return," I said with a wide grin, "we are in ideal Greenland Halibut territory. Shall we go fishing?"

"Why the hell not?"

I took *Mystic* to about ten feet over the bottom and began a slow one-hundred-foot grid transit. In about five minutes, we located a big one hunkered beneath the sand.

"You need to sneak up behind him," Bob said, "and use the manipulator to grab him around his gills. It's a bit tricky. Want me to do it?"

"Are you kiddin'?" I growled at him.

---

21 Officers' Club.

I placed *Mystic* behind and above the five-foot-long flatfish. I eased the manipulator out to about three-quarter extension with the forward arm angled down. I opened the grip and slid down so that I could close the grip above and below the halibut's gill area. The halibut wasn't happy, but my grip was firm.

Borysko was very interested in my actions. I feared he might snatch our catch, but he just examined it closely with both eyes and his clicking sonar. Without letting it go, I moved the manipulator so the halibut was tucked beneath *Mystic*.

"Do you think you can dock her?" Bob asked.

"It's been a while, so keep your hands near your controls," I said, feeling confident I could do it.

As I headed back to *Teuthis*, I couldn't see Borysko, but when I arrived at the cradle, he was patiently waiting several yards away.

"Do you hear that clicking sound?" I asked generally.

Bob pointed to a sonar screen display that displayed apparently random noise spikes.

"He's examining the cradle in detail with his high-resolution sonar. That stuff's so detailed," I said, "that he can distinguish a Coho Salmon (his favorite) from Sockeye or Chinook. He's making a mental blueprint of the whole thing." I grinned. "Is that something, or what?"

I settled us into the cradle like I had been doing it for ages. I think I impressed Jim, but Bob just said, "I knew you could do it."

We made a seal to *Teuthis* and dropped into the sub. We were still four hours from mid-rats, but Cedric mixed us up some tuna sandwiches that we washed down with mint tea. All-in-all, not a bad eight hours.

THE *LYRE*—UNDERWAY

When we returned, I stopped by the Goat Locker to check up on Potts. Several chiefs were drinking coffee at their small wardroom table. One of them, Chief Torpedoman Cedrik, looked like he had just awakened to go on watch.

"Hey, Commander, haven't seen you in a while," he said.

"Naw, Tubes," I said as I accepted a cup of proffered coffee and squeezed into a seat at the crowded table, "Been busy on *Lyre* twenty-four-seven takin' care of the lap-dancers and working girls." I grinned. "How's Potts doing?"

"Been shittin' his guts out for the past three hours."

"Doc says he's gonna be okay," I said. "You guys taking good care of him?"

"When we can get past the smell," Tubes said, drawing a long face.

"Back in my college days," I said, "I was the bottom-man-on-the-totem-pole grunt for a shipboard Arctic expedition. I came down with something that stopped up my gut as tight as Potts'. Ship's Doc tried everything—nothing worked, so he made me drink a full glass of mineral oil. I spent the next day-and-a-half on the shitter." I grinned at the chiefs. "I know what Potts is going through. Wouldn't wish that on anybody. Tell Potts I stopped by." I stood and opened the door into the passageway. "Gotta go take care of the dancing girls."

✳

Ham sent a couple of divers out—Jimmy and Sergyi—to retrieve what turned out to be a 120-pound big guy. This gave Jimmy some time with Borysko to his great delight.

A half-hour later, I was back in Control on *Lyre*, and *Mystic* was latching down in her cradle on *Teuthis*. Chief Electronics Technician Rusty Jackson accompanied my group, replacing Potts.

"Glad you're back, Mac," Bert told me. "Everything's shipshape. Nothing happened during the last nine hours, but I'm glad you're back to take over the responsibility. The more I thought about it, the heavier it weighed on my shoulders." He grinned at me. "I like being master technician, making machines do what I want. This command shit ain't what it's cut out to be."

We conducted a brief, formal Change-of-Command, and I logged it. Shortly thereafter, we lifted off the bottom and set course for the Button Islands at the northeastern end of Labrador, where Hudson Strait empties into the Labrador Sea.

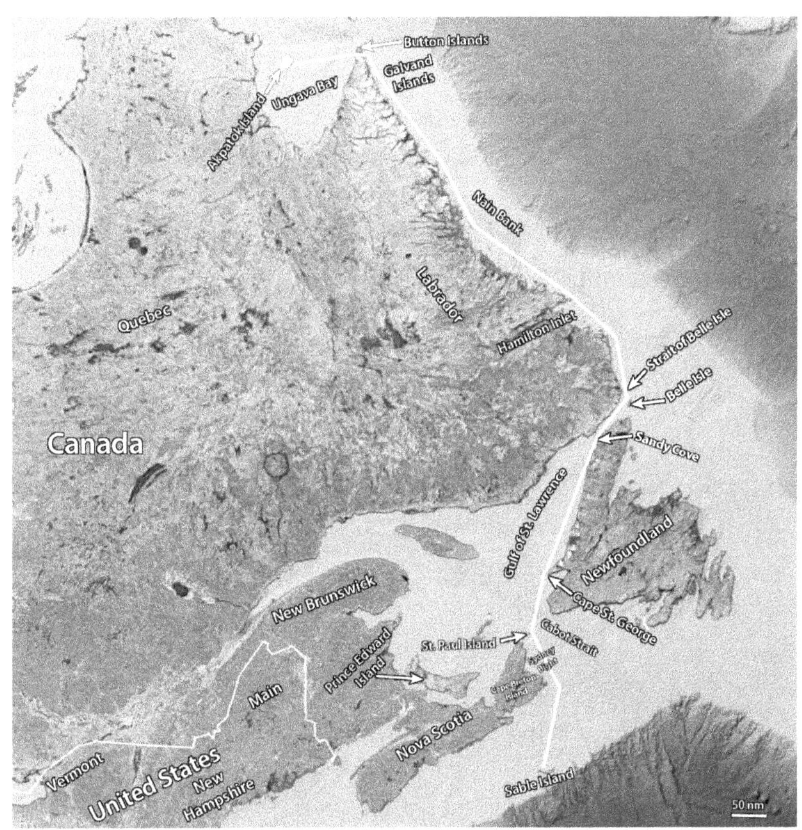

USS Teuthis & Lyre transit from Akpatok Island to Sable Island off Nova Scotia

CHAPTER SEVENTEEN—Labrador to Nova Scotia

THE *LYRE*—SOUTHWARD ALONG THE LABRADOR PENINSULA

We were in mid-winter east of Akpatok Island. The ice canopy above us was about as thick as it gets. Occasionally, old ice from a previous year hangs around near the east and west ends of Ungava Bay. During the winter, they become upward and downward projecting ridges that are hard enough to damage a sub sail. We were headed right toward them—if they were present this year.

We traveled at a hundred feet for over fifty nautical miles of increasingly deeper shelf off the east side of Akpatok Island. Bert took us to 200 feet when the bottom dropped to a thousand feet. This formed a deep-water ring around Akpatok Island and the shelf it sat on, separating it from the otherwise shallower Ungava Bay. The deep water extended through Gray Strait between Labrador and the Button Islands, where it linked with the Hudson Strait channel out into the Labrador Sea. A hundred nautical miles farther, the bottom dropped to the abyssal plain, 6,000 feet or deeper. Somewhere out there, but close by, lurked *Carp*.

Back on *Teuthis*, Barry and I had discussed taking a shortcut to the Labrador Sea through eighteen-nautical-mile-long McLelan Strait between the northern tip of Labrador and Killiniq Island.

"We save twenty-two nautical miles. That's more than two hours," I said.

"Look," Barry told me, "McLelan narrows to less than a third of a nautical mile here and here." He pointed to two places about equally spaced, dividing the strait into thirds. "And the water shallows to about thirty feet here and here," pointing to two other spots.

"But the tide range here is forty feet." I had checked *Sozh's* tables. "The westward current is about ten knots and follows high tide by fifteen minutes or so. That makes depth a non-issue."

"Do you really want to sweep through eighteen nautical miles of narrow, shallow near-rapids with heavy ice floes and brash overhead?" He grinned at me. He knew when he had won a debate.

Gray Strait also ran at ten knots with a heavy ice cover, but it was ten times wider and 800 feet deep. That trumped two hours every time. Sam took us through Gray Strait at 500 feet. We did not even notice the massive flow of ice above us. *Carp* lurked somewhere ahead, but *Drum* was nearby, probably between us and *Carp*. Not very far behind, *Frisco* had our six. *Swordfish* was back there, too, monitoring both *Shchuka* and *Volgograd*.

As he exited the strait, Sam brought us up to 200 feet and turned south, aiming for the Galvano Islands. The Torngat Mountains dominate the eastern side of Labrador's tip. They form deep fiords into the peninsula and jagged ridges jutting out into the coastal waters of the Labrador Sea. The Galvano Islands are the tips of some of these ridges. They were charted on our Canadian charts, and they showed up on *Sozh*, but I trusted neither.

Rusty followed Sam's watch, and I stayed with Rusty while he got his feet wet piloting *Lyre*. We planned to recharge near the Galvanos, so Rusty shallowed us as the bottom began to creep up. He eased us past two islands so they could shield us from *Carp* to our rear. We bottomed with *Teuthis* in eighty feet of brash-covered water inside another island to shield us from seaward.

"Well done, Rusty," I said, as he settled us on the bottom. "Thanks for staying with me," he answered. "Watching you guys and doing it myself are very different." He grinned nervously. "Do you ever get used to the tension?"

"Sure," I answered, "but you stay focused. If a lot's going on, it can be pretty exhausting, believe me." I assumed the watch. "You might want to hang around for a bit. Our monitors give us a good show outside."

※

I turned on our outside lights. The water was crystal clear. We could easily see the Egress hatch on *Teuthis* bottomed on her skids a few feet away. Borysko was right there, nosing around the hatch, waiting for the divers. To his surprise, and ours, the first thing through the hatch was the carcass of the large Greenland Halibut Bob and I had brought back from our transponder-laying trip on the west side of Akpatok. Cedric had collected the head, skeleton, and all the remains into a large garbage bag—forty or fifty pounds worth, for the divers to give to Borysko. They dumped the contents through the hatch. A one-knot current was running north to south. As it carried the mess away from the hatch, Borysko managed to suck it all into his gullet in two gulps. Then he returned to share some playtime with the divers, his ever-present 4 x 4 protruding from his mouth like the stump of a cigar.

Halfway through my watch, we entered our nineteenth day since we had departed Pt. Barrow. I reached into my pocket and fingered Kate's ivory cylinder. While the batteries charged, I let my thoughts roam back to Kodiak and the girl who had captured my heart like no one before.

Two hours later, with everything tucked away and shipshape, I let go of the cylinder, pushed it deep into my pocket, and refocused. I lifted *Lyre* off the bottom, the XO retracted *Teuthis'* skids, and we got underway for Nain Bank.

✳

Nain Bank forms an unusual feature along the northeastern coast of Labrador. For most of the large peninsula, the land more or less slopes to the sea and then drops off gradually to the continental break, where it plunges to the abyssal plain. At Nain Bank, a 1,600-foot deep trench runs for a hundred nautical miles between the shoreline and the bank. It's about thirty nautical miles wide and sports a hefty, southward-flowing current.

The Nain Trench is not a chasm like the Grand Canyon. Instead, it is a depression that drops from the bank at about a two-degree rate over eight nautical miles to the 1,600-foot floor. The floor averages about fourteen nautical miles wide, and then it slopes back up at about ten degrees to the shore. It has no cliffs like those we experienced at Akpatok Island. Nevertheless, it still cuts a wide swath between the peninsula and the bank. Our goal was the eighty-foot level on the bank's trench side, protected from prying Soviet ears. It would take us a day to get there.

We stayed close to *Teuthis* and avoided the islands poking up from the coastal mountain ridges extending into the sea. As we moved south, the ice above us began to clear. Our big concern was icebergs moving south with the current.

We picked up submarine sounds occasionally off our port side, and once we thought we saw *Swordfish* behind us on the *Okean* display. Just before we tucked into the Nain Trench, *Okean* displayed an entirely different object beyond the bank out in the Labrador Sea. I called *Teuthis* on the Secure Gertrude. Franklin had the watch.

"We picked up something new about fifty nautical miles east of Nain Bank. *Okean* displays the Russian letters И-С-А—I-S-A in English. It has to be a Soviet ship that *Okean* identified."

"Yeah, we saw a blip out there, too. Stand by," Franklin said.

About five minutes later, Franklin transmitted, "That would be the *Admiral Isachenkov*, a Soviet *Kresta II class* large anti-submarine cruiser. She's probably on routine North Atlantic patrol. Her presence offshore may be coincidental."

"I don't believe in coincidences," I said. "We need to keep an eye on this bitch. She carries the best towed-array sonar the Soviets have." I figured the Soviets were getting desperate and had brought in their big guns. With that bad girl out there, we were bound to find a destroyer or frigate nearby. Combined with *Carp*, *Shchuka*, and *Volgograd*, we were faced with a formidable task force whose only focus was finding and sinking *Lyre*.

✳

Spook and Bert split the battery charge at Nain Bank, while I managed a rare chess win against Matt. Nestled against the bank's western slope, the charge was as routine as any during our transit. The one surprise was that the overhead ice cover had increased again, consisting mainly of medium-size floes. When we finished, and *Teuthis* was wrapped up and ready to go, Bert lifted us off the bottom, dropped down the slope until we were 200 feet over the bottom, and then headed us south on course 120 degrees. On the next watch, Sam kept us below the trench's edge until we ran out of trench—sort of.

Rusty had a bit of a challenge during his watch. He examined the chart and *Sozh*, and then he called me.

"How do you want to handle this?" he asked, pointing to a convoluted deep-water path to the west of Makkovik Bank, Harrison Bank, and then Hamilton Bank.

"What do you suggest?" I asked, "and don't forget about *Admiral I* out to the east somewhere."

"I guess we keep our heads down," Rusty said. "So, you want me to navigate as necessary west of these banks."

"Yep…keep us west of the banks no shallower than two hundred feet, but no closer to the bottom than eighty feet."

I hung around but let Rusty take charge of his watch. I had no complaints. When I assumed the watch five hours later, we were passing Harrison Bank, well out of sonic view of *Isachenkov's* towed array. Spook took us behind Hamilton Bank, and Bert parked us safely for our next charge.

I had been giving a lot of thought to *Admiral Isachenkov's* presence. I wanted to sit with the skipper in his cabin and discuss the matter in some detail. I called Waverly on the Secure Gertrude.

"*Teuthis*, this is *Lyre*." "*Teuthis*, aye."

"This is Mac. Please arrange for a quick *Mystic* transfer so I can speak with the skipper about an urgent matter."

After three minutes, Waverly responded, "Roger. *Mystic* will seal to your hatch in twenty minutes."

✳

I settled onto the skipper's couch with a cup of hot coffee delivered with a warm smile by Petty Officer Rivera.

"What's so urgent, Mac, or did you just want a hot shower?" Cmdr. Roken smiled at me.

I got right down to business because I didn't want to hold things up by coming to *Teuthis*. "The Soviets have to know we have *Lyre*, and they know that her reactor is frozen. It follows that they know we are charging the *Alfa* every twenty-four hours or so." I took a sip of the scalding liquid; it was much better than what we could make on *Lyre*.

"Yeah, I figured that," the skipper said.

"They have tracked us one way or the other all the way across the Arctic," I said. "They threw everything at us at Bellot Strait, but it didn't work. I think they know our location within fifty to seventy nautical miles. It's no coincidence that *Admiral I* shows up just when the ice is disappearing.

"They know about the lost *Victor III*…"

"And that we saved the crew," the skipper added.

"Yeah, I agree. And *Isachenkov* is not alone. I'm certain that a destroyer or frigate is somewhere to the south, waiting for us to appear.

"The two surface ships along with their three advanced subs are about as formidable as it gets." I looked at the skipper earnestly while sipping my cooling coffee. "They will have a trawler off New London, too," I added.

"So, what are you telling me, Mac?"

"That these guys are dead serious. They want their *Alfa* back, and I suspect they will do anything short of war to retrieve it…or sink it." The skipper nodded. "I reached your conclusions and sent a burst message to SubLant and SubPac during our last charge. CincLantFlt is sortieing a destroyer squadron off the New England coast to complicate things for the Soviets."

"The *Admiral I* has an excellent towed sonar array," I said. "Even though she's fifty or so miles out there, she can easily pick us up if we aren't careful. We're transiting well outside Canada's 12-mile territorial limit but well inside her exclusive economic zone. How bold are the Soviets? They know we have their sub. Does that justify a physical attack? Pemmican Rock was out of sight for most of the world. We had the upper hand there, and they have kept a low profile since then. But *Isachenkov*, her inevitable escort, and three state-of-the-art subs present a formidable challenge. Even with *Swordfish*, *Drum*, and *Frisco*, *Lyre* is a crippled *Alfa*, and *Teuthis* is hampered with *Mystic*."

"I understand, Mac, but we have something they do not have." I lifted my eyebrows.

"I'm talking about you and your TOG team, Mac." The skipper smiled warmly at me. "You and your guys keep doing your jobs, and I am confident that we will bring *Lyre* home to EB without serious incident." He looked at the clock on the bulkhead over the door. "Time for you to return to *Lyre*. Stop by the Galley on your way. I had Cedric toss together a bag of sandwiches for your crew."

THE *LYRE*—GULF OF ST. LAWRENCE

Sam stayed behind Hamilton Bank and the cover it afforded for sixty-one nautical miles, and then Rusty came right to 215 degrees, pointing us at the Strait of Belle Isle. We remained on this course for twelve hours until Bert angled us across the strait to Sandy Cove, where we bottomed with *Teuthis* in eighty feet of water for a battery charge. We were well inside Canadian territorial waters, away from prying Soviet ears. Overhead was clogged with brash and medium-size floes, all of it seemingly flowing into the Gulf of St. Lawrence.

Nevertheless, Borysko had no trouble finding us, no trouble grabbing air whenever necessary, and no trouble feeding. I hung out in Control for the charge preps.

"What do you suppose Borysko eats here?" Sam asked.

I dredged up some information from my oceanography studies. "The Gulf of St. Lawrence has a lot of Atlantic Cod, Greenland Halibut, Redfish, and Northern Shrimp—Borysko likes them all. In the late sixties, they were pulling more than one-and-a-half-million tons of halibut from these waters each year. It's probably less now, but there's more than enough for our pal."

I left for the Galley and a chess game with Matt, fingering Kate's cylinder as I descended the ladder. I kept the ivory container clenched in my fist throughout the game, allowing it to distract me. Matt won—or rather, I lost…again. I had trouble focusing on the game.

❋

Sam got us underway, generally following Newfoundland's coastline for fifty nautical miles, into the last hour of Rusty's watch. Rusty pointed us toward Long Point, the southernmost point of Cape St. George. We remained on this course for eighteen hours. Then we stopped for another charge.

We tracked more surface traffic during our charge than we had seen for our entire journey thus far. Much of this traffic was entering or exiting the Gulf of St. Lawrence through Cabot Strait to our southeast. Every so often, we detected the distinctive sound profile of an icebreaker, keeping Cabot open for marine traffic. Rusty assumed the watch as the divers commenced removing the shore power cable.

"Any chance of a Soviet sub inside the Gulf?" he asked me.

I pulled out a paper chart. "Technically," I said, "a small portion of the Gulf could be considered international waters." I indicated this in pencil. It encompassed a narrow strip through Cabot Strait and the deepest part of the Gulf—about 1,000 feet deep. "In the real world, the Soviets avoid places like this. Too easy to trap them inside. The Canadians patrol the area with a couple of frigates carrying ASW gear, but the last time there was any serious penetration of the Gulf was during World War Two, when German U-boats sank twenty-three ships in the Gulf."

"So we don't really have to clear baffles in the Gulf," Rusty said.

"You want to bet your life on it?" I asked.

THE *LYRE*—ST. PAUL ISLAND

Following the charge, Rusty put us on a course of 214 degrees at 200 feet for St. Paul Island on the south side of Cabot Strait. During my watch, the bottom dropped off to nearly 1,500 feet, while the surface continued to be ice-covered—brash and small floes, probably due to the clearing efforts of the icebreakers. During the third hour of Spook's watch, the bottom began to shallow up to the steep cliffs of St. Paul.

St. Paul Island, nicknamed the *Graveyard of the Gulf*, is a mile wide and three miles long, sitting across the southern side of Cabot Strait, the main entrance to the Gulf of St. Lawrence. When not icebound, from late spring through early autumn, St. Paul is normally shrouded in fog. Without radar and other modern navigation aids, in and out-bound sailing ships and early steamships frequently found themselves in trouble up against the rocky cliffs of St. Paul. During World War II, more than one German U-boot found the island the hard way.

As we approached the island, the mid-winter ice cover was as noisy as it gets. Billions of ice chunks rubbing and jolting against each other generated a racket that drowned out nearly everything. Spook and Waverly, respectively, brought both *Lyre* and *Teuthis* into protected MacDougall Cove near the northwestern end of St. Paul Island. We settled to the bottom in eighty feet of water and commenced preparing for our charge.

Spook still had the watch as the divers entered the water to hook up the shore power cable. I joined him in Control. Borysko, as frisky as ever, joined the divers with his 4 x 4, now showing a lot of wear where he clamped it in his teeth.

The divers entered the water just before local twilight commenced. By the time the charge was underway, the sun was above the horizon and would stay there for over nine hours.

Borysko noticed them first. He started darting around like an excited puppy. Then Sergyi saw them—two bright lights descending slowly, directly toward our lighted space on the bottom. Derrick was driving the Basketball. He moved it up, revealing two descending divers wearing orange Unisuits, twin-90s, with full facemasks. One carried an underwater camera and the other a video rig.

I got on the Secure Gertrude.

"Franklin, put me in touch with Ham immediately!" Shortly, Ham answered. "Yes, Sir."

"Do you know about the two descending divers?" "I do."

"What are your plans?"

"I was just about to call you, Mac."

"There must be something around here that interests them. Have Harry or Whitey escort them to the Egress hatch. Bring them into the lock with their masks and hoods removed. Then call me."

"Aye, Sir."

Harry and Whitey, with APSs slung across their backs, approached the divers as they reached the bottom. Harry gestured for them to follow him. On my monitor, I watched them swim beneath *Teuthis* to the Egress hatch and disappear inside.

"We're ready," Ham announced.

"Gentlemen," my voice reached them via our jerry-rigged comm system. "I'm Lieutenant Commander Mac McDowell. I'm in the second submarine you saw as you descended. Please identify yourselves."

"John Peel," the older spoke up, mid-thirties, short dark hair, clean-shaven, under six feet. He carried the still camera.

"Marchand Baptiste," said the second with a French accent, twenty-something, blond, shorter. He sported an underwater Sony Handycam CCD-M8. It had come out just last year and was state-of-the-art. He sounded nervous.

"Thank you. Why are you diving in this remote location?"

Peel answered. "We are amateur archaeologists—wreck divers, actually. We tracked down a lost German U-boot to Mac-Dougall Cove— here where we are. We rented a motorized scow that can navigate the ice around here to check it out ourselves. We arrived yesterday afternoon, surveyed the cove's bottom with our wreck-finding fathometer, and we think we found the U-boot. We anchored over the spot and got a full night's sleep. We arose early this morning, intending to get some video and stills before heading back to announce it publicly. Instead, we found you guys. Are you investigating the wreck, too?"

I grinned at my shipmates, who had all gathered in Control. "We did not know about the wreck," I said. "We have other business here." I paused for a few seconds. "What is your dive profile?"

"Ninety feet for thirty minutes with a safety stop at ten feet for five minutes."

"Conservative and smart," I commented. "What is your current bottom time?"

They both looked at their dive consoles. "Fifteen minutes," Baptiste said.

"Whom do you have topside on your boat?"

"Ah…no one. We wanted to keep this site a secret for the time being."

"What have you recorded thus far?"

"I took a video of our descent," Baptiste said. "Both subs are in it." His voice quavered a bit. "Are we in trouble?"

"I got several shots of you guys," Peel said, "probably not a lot of detail." "You have two options," I said. "I realize you stumbled upon us quite by accident. We have a couple of hours before we depart. You're still inside your profile, so you can exit the way you came, surface, and wait us out on your scow. Or, you can strip off your gear, lock into the sub, and one of the crew will give you the grand tour. You can meet with the captain, and I suspect our cook, Cedric, will be happy to give you something to eat. When we've completed our work in two hours or so, you can press back down into the DDC, don your gear, exit into the water, and make your ascent as you normally would. Either way, be sure to greet Borysko, the Orca you saw outside. He's friendly, safe, and loves having his tongue scratched. After we depart, you can explore that German U-boot. In any case, you will have one hell of a story to tell at your local pub."

"That's a no-brainer," Peel said enthusiastically to Baptiste's nodding concurrence.

"There is one more thing," I added. "Peel, how many still shots did you take?"

"Four."

"Here's the thing," I said. "We can't let you have any images of our activities. Baptiste, we'll need to wipe your videotape. Peel, we will either need to confiscate your film or flash the first four frames. If we flash, you will have the rest for shots of the Orca.

"Are you guys okay with this?"

✳

First thing, the ship's photographer flashed Peels four exposed frames and erased Baptiste's 8mm tape. Our visitors were pretty equanimous about this. I guess the excitement of their unexpected adventure more than compensated for their loss.

Cedric actually fixed them steak and eggs with hash browns. They washed it down with hot coffee. I didn't bother to ask the skipper to send *Mystic* to bring me to *Teuthis*. It would just have complicated things even more. Besides, I don't think he would have done it anyway.

Two-and-a-half hours after they entered the Egress Lock, Peels and Baptiste dropped back into the icy water of MacDougall Cove. Sergyi and Whitey accompanied them to ensure they took no surreptitious photos or videos of our two subs. Our visitors actually exercised care not to do this, obviously going out of their way to eliminate either sub from the background of their Borysko shots. Predictably, our cetacean mascot put on a delightful performance.

Peel and Baptiste were friends who had met on a previous diving excursion in the Gulf of St. Lawrence. Peel lived in Halifax, Nova Scotia, on the North Atlantic, and Baptiste was from Chicoutimi, at the head of Saguenay Fjord in Quebec, north of the St. Lawrence River. They were avid wreck divers, but I suspect that this particular dive in MacDougall Cove was the highlight of their diving history. Should you ever visit a dive shop anywhere in Nova Scotia, you are likely to spot a photo of an Orca with a 4 x 4 protruding from his mouth like a stubby cigar. I have not verified this, but you may even find it if you visit a dive shop in one of the towns at the head of Saguenay Fjord.

Borysko with his well-worn 4 x 4 in MacDougall Cove

THE *LYRE*—CABOT STRAIT TO SABLE ISLAND

As soon as our visitors had safely surfaced through the brash, Cobb lifted *Lyre* off the bottom, headed around the north end of St. Paul, and pointed us to Sydney Bight off the northeastern coast of Cape Breton Island. Eleven hours later, with some of the overhead brash finally clearing, Rusty set a course of 212 degrees for Sable Island, right on the Continental Break about 200 nautical miles due south of St. Paul.

Shortly after his course change, Rusty called me to Control. He pointed to the *Okean* display.

"What do you make of this?" he asked, indicating two blips to our southeast. One displayed the Russian letters И-С-А—I-S-A in English—that we already knew was the *Admiral Isachenkov*. The other displayed the Russian letters З-А-Д—Z-A-D in English.

I called *Teuthis* on the Secure Gertrude, describing the new indiction. A few minutes later, Franklin called back. "We think that is the Soviet Frigate *Zadornyy*. She is an ASW ship with anti-sub rockets and torpedoes. Her sonar is second-rate with a maximum range of less than twenty nautical miles. Keep in mind that *Isachenkov's* towed sonar range is more than a hundred miles under the right conditions. *Zadornyy* will stay close to *Isachenkov* and work off her sonar solution. Together, they are quite formidable."

I passed the word to my crew—no unnecessary noise. With just ten of us onboard, that wasn't a problem anyway. Then I took a close look at our tactical situation. The Soviets pretty much knew our destination, and they knew that we had to charge *Lyre* periodically. If I were positioning the available forces, I would place *Carp*, *Shchuka*, and *Volgograd* on our path to Groton. As best as possible, I would keep *Isachenkov* and *Zadornyy* east of us, constantly trying to get a good position. Then there was the perennial Soviet *trawler* in international waters off New London Harbor. To the best of my knowledge, the Soviets had put one of their better-equipped so-called trawlers in position—the *Vega*. I knew that *Vega* had a sophisticated sonar suite and state-of-the-art electronic surveillance equipment.

I called *Teuthis* on the Secure Gertrude. Franklin still had the watch.

"I think *Carp*, *Shchuka*, and *Volgograd* are ahead of us on our track to Groton. I recommend you guys keep a close watch. They will be lurking—as quietly as they are able."

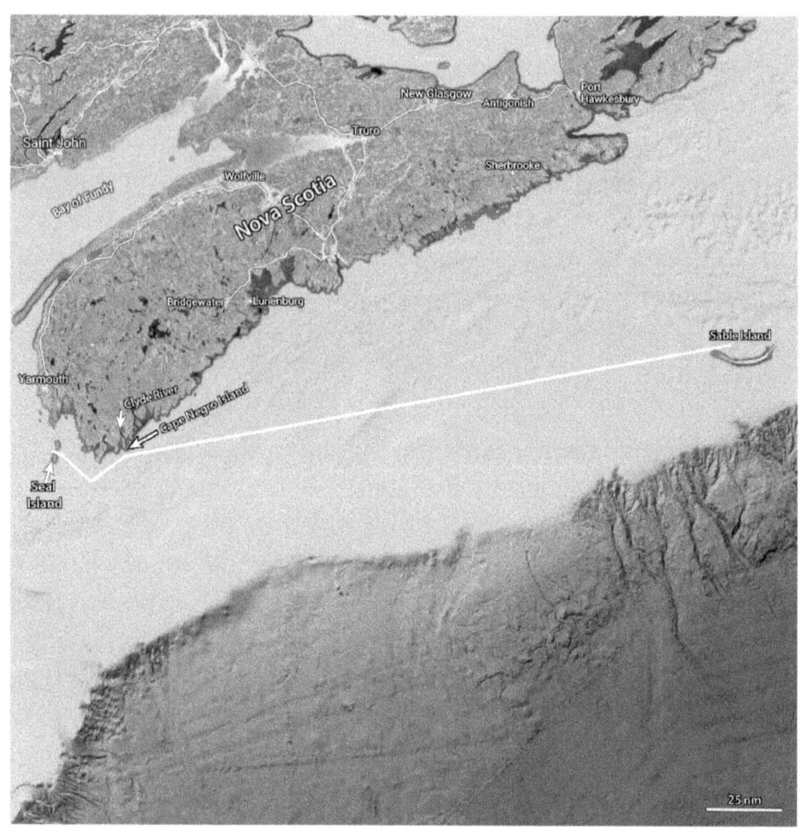

USS Teuthis & Lyre transit from Sable Island to Seal Island
off southwestern Nova Scotia

CHAPTER EIGHTEEN—Fire!

THE *LYRE*—PORT OF CLYDE

Sam got us underway for the Port of Clyde on the southwestern tip of Nova Scotia. Barry picked this spot for no other reason than it was twenty-four hours away at ten knots with our periodic baffle clearing.

I would like to tell you that it was uneventful, but I can't. Perhaps *Admiral Isachenkov* got a piece of us or *Teuthis* on her towed array—if so, it probably was us. *Teuthis* is way too quiet. It was really difficult to tell what happened. But suddenly, in the middle of Rusty's watch, out of

218

nowhere that big Soviet cruiser commenced pinging. We didn't have a very good track on him. I'm sure *Teuthis* had a better one, but they did not always keep us informed of every element of the other guys' behavior. The thing was, she was surprisingly close—close enough to pick us up on her active sonar.

It took me three seconds to arrive in Control. I glanced at the *Akkord* display. "How deep is the water?" I asked. "One hundred sixty, getting deeper," Rusty said.

"Okay, take us down to twenty feet over the bottom. Maintain your course. She's making a lot of racket, so she cannot hear us. She's looking for a ping return, not a sonar signature."

"*Teuthis*," I called over the Secure Gertrude, "can you get between us and *Isachenkov*? We're hugging the bottom."

"Roger," Franklin answered, "We're there now, about midcolumn."

I turned to Rusty. "*Teuthis* is tracking us and *Isachenkov* full-time—and *Zadornyy* as well. Barry calculated the depth she has to be to intersect the pings from *Isachenkov*. *Teuthis* will maintain the shield until *Isachenkov* gets tired of the game…or her active sonar breaks. The *Kresta-II class* cruisers are notorious for their active sonars breaking down when used for more than a half-hour or so."

"*Lyre*, this is *Teuthis*," on the Secure Gertrude. "*Zadornyy* has crossed your track and is paralleling you off your starboard bow about fifteen nautical miles."

"This is *Swordfish*," a Secure Gertrude transmission interrupted our conversation. "We have placed ourselves between *Zadornyy* and *Lyre*. We will push her aft of your stern and outboard of your track."

Rusty and I scanned the *Okean*. Every once in a while, we could see a bit of *Zadornyy*. Of *Swordfish*, there was nothing—as if she were invisible.

"What a sea story this would make, Rusty!" I said. "Here we are in a stolen Soviet *Alfa*, surrounded by a Soviet cruiser, frigate, two *Victors*, and a *Sierra*, and not only can they not get to us, but they don't even know where we are for sure. It's a real shame we can't tell the story."

✳

Frisco was good to her word. *Zadornyy* dropped back, crossed our track behind us, and rejoined *Isachenkov* somewhere off our port beam.

I relieved Rusty and remained near the bottom as we continued toward Clyde. Finally, sixteen hours later, Sam eased us to the bottom shoreward from *Teuthis* in 90 feet of water just off Cape Negro Island. Some land ice clung to the rocky shore, but except for a bit of brash, the water overhead was clear of ice.

Apparently, *Isachenkov* fixed her active sonar because we heard her pinging from time to time from due south. We were miles beyond her acquisition range—safe and secure for the time being. We were eager to commence our next leg to Seal Island, where we planned to attach the false sail to *Lyre*. Even on my monitor, I could tell that the divers were moving more quickly. They didn't stop to play with Borysko even though he inserted himself into their activities as much as possible. Sergyi grabbed his 4 x 4 and sent it to the surface a couple of times. Borysko happily retrieved it and pushed it at each of the divers in turn, trying to get them into the game. When they failed to respond, rather than getting discouraged, the cetacean created his own game where he pushed his 4 x 4 under *Teuthis* and then hurried around to the other side to catch it before it escaped to the surface.

We finished the charge an hour early, and Sam headed us toward Seal Island on a course of 235 degrees at eighty feet. An hour later, Rusty took over for two more hours. Then he slowed to five knots and turned northward.

I had the next watch and would be bringing us through the shallows to our designated sail conversion location. I joined Rusty early to make sure he didn't run us into the shallow bottom accidentally. He kept us off the bottom without my help, but I suspect he was glad I was there, just in case.

THE *LYRE*—SEAL ISLAND

Seal Island lies almost fifteen nautical miles due west of Cape Sable, the southernmost point of Nova Scotia. Water depth between Cape Sable and Seal Island is mostly under one hundred feet, although it reaches 130 feet at one point. Our track took us south of the shallows and then angled to the entrance slot for Seal Island and its four companions, Noddy, Mud, Round, and Flat Islands.

Our destination was a seventy-five-foot-deep hole, two-and-a-third nautical miles west of a line connecting Seal and Noddy Islands. Why does that matter? Because there were only two ways out, the way we came, or ahead to the west or southwest. Between the two westbound paths was a shallow spot we would need to avoid. That bump protected us from ears to the west, Noddy Island protected us to the north, Seal Island protected us to the south, and to the east, nobody could get close enough to matter.

"*Teuthis*, this is *Lyre*. What is the disposition of the Soviet subs?" "This is *Teuthis*. As of an hour ago, we lost all three. *Carp* was headed in your general direction. *Shchuka* was pointed at Georges Shoal, and *Volgograd* seemed to be headed toward the south end of Cape Cod.

Isachenkov and *Zadornyy* are steaming together about halfway between you and the Continental Break."

We were in our twenty-seventh day since leaving Pt. Barrow. We had stopped twenty-seven times to charge the *Lyre* batteries. Despite not being able to track us directly, the Soviet subs knew our destination, knew how fast we could go and how far between charges. Furthermore, by this time, they had to have a sense of where we liked to charge. Obviously, it didn't matter under solid ice, but where the bottom was reasonably available, we chose protected spots that tended to be shielded from them. They had to have figured this out by now.

We were nearing our ultimate destination. If the Soviets were to have any chance of stopping us, it would be in the next three days. What would I do were I controlling their operation? *Carp* was most familiar with us. We had actually forced her to the surface through the ice off

Pt. Barrow toward the end of Operation Ice Breaker.[22] I don't think her skipper knew that *we* had done that to her, or that we were even there. His divers clashed with ours—we killed three and captured two. As far as Carp was concerned, they simply disappeared. Nevertheless, *Carp* still had the most experience with this entire matter.

---

22 See *Operation Ice Breaker*, the second book in the *Mac McDowell Mission Series*.

So, if I were they, I would assume we would bottom somewhere near Seal Island. I would position *Carp* to take advantage of our limited maneuverability during the charge.

As for the other two, I would place one at Georges Shoal, halfway between Seal Island and Cape Cod, and the other near Cape Cod. I would keep the two surface combatants somewhere off Seal Island. I got on the Secure Gertrude with the XO, who had the watch on *Teuthis*. After detailing my thoughts, I said, "I am shifting *Lyre* to her auxiliary props. I recommend *Teuthis* run on the outboards at ultra-quiet.

We really don't need to advertise our position to *Carp*, assuming she is waiting in ambush for us."

"The captain is listening and agrees with you. We already initiated a shift to the outboards and are at ultra-quiet."

"Roger. Which way will you point?"

"To the west."

"Roger. I will bottom off your starboard side pointing east."

THE *LYRE*—BOTTOMED OFF SEAL ISLAND

Normally when we have maneuvered next to each other, we were in water sufficiently deep that I could position *Lyre* appropriately, and then *Teuthis* could come alongside and bottom with little difficulty, using the Basketball if needed. Things were different here. The Basketball was virtually useless because visibility was only ten feet or so. The water was too shallow for one of us to come in from above as *Teuthis* normally did. And, *Teuthis* got there first, so I had to find my way without the maneuverability the outboards afforded *Teuthis*.

The XO planted *Teuthis* on the bottom in the hole without problems. We were sufficiently close that *Okean* gave me a position for *Teuthis*. I couldn't bring myself to trust the display enough to come within ten feet of *Teuthis*. I set *Lyre* on the bottom about a hundred feet away. On the Secure Gertrude, set to the lowest possible output, I said, "*Teuthis*, you need to locate me with the Basketball and then edge *Teuthis* sideways until we are sufficiently close."

A good thirty minutes later, the XO called me. "*Lyre*, we are crossing the gap. Visibility remains ten feet or less. We'll take our time, so we don't bump into you."

※

The XO was right—it took another thirty minutes before he was satisfied with our relative positions. He let me know by Secure Gertrude. I answered back, "It's going to be several hours. Whadya say we rotate my crew to *Teuthis*? I want to be with Ham for the false sail installation, and we all could use a break from LRPs."

"We can do it," the XO said, "but we need to retain a responsible party aboard *Lyre* to get her underway if necessary."

"Bert and I will rotate so he can spend time aboard *Teuthis*. We'll work it out."

※

Seal Island experiences high tide approximately every twelve-and-a-half hours, followed by low tide six hours later. Tidal range is about thirteen feet, but that doesn't tell the whole story. High tide was eleven feet or so, but low tide was about minus two feet. So, high tide gave us more room, but low tide made our margin even tighter. The tidal flood current flowed eastward toward Nova Scotia and should have brought in clearer water, but the shallow water and muddy bottom worked with the current to keep visibility really low. The tidal ebb current brought even more muddy water from the shallows. I guess that when we planned to use this spot for installing the false sail, we didn't take this into consideration. Too late now…the divers would just have to make the best of it.

We settled into position at low tide, which gave us about three hours before the flood current made handling the false sail materials difficult. Ham, Bill, and I worked out a plan together. Ski, with his still-healing foot, was off diving duty. That left Harry, Whitey, Jer, and Jimmy, along with Sergyi.

"I want Jimmy to remain out of the water as much as possible," I told Ham and Bill.

"But he needs water time," Bill objected.

"Conditions out there are much more hazardous than we're used to," Ham said. "Jimmy stays in the pot unless we need him outside."

I agreed, but since Ham still had official control of the divers, I said nothing.

"There is the matter of umbilicals or rebreathers," Bill said. "Given the conditions, I like umbilicals, but they will interfere with flexibility. I think they will interfere with the false sail installation."

Both Ham and I agreed. We laid out a plan for the frame and Kevlar sleeve.

"What's our window?" Bill asked, glancing at the bulkhead clock. "We're about an hour into flood. We have two more before the current becomes a problem," I answered.

"The four divers are at depth and ready to deploy," Bill said, glancing from Ham to me.

"Ham's the official boss here," I said with a grin. "I'm going to grab a shower and a bite."

✳

I actually spent only ten minutes in the rain locker, and for chow, I grabbed tuna sandwiches and washed them down with bug juice. Fact is, I really wanted to get back to Dive Control. This was a big operation, and despite Ham's competence, I wanted to be present.

During my twenty-minute absence, the divers had moved the frame pieces from the DDC into place on both sides of *Lyre*. They laid out the pieces for easy assembly. Borysko had shown up as soon as the divers entered the water, 4 x 4 firmly clamped in his jaw. Wally had the Basketball and did his best to show the main action centered in our monitors. Even so, it was challenging to keep the whole picture in mind.

The frame for each side consisted of a thirty-foot bottom beam with four sections that folded like a carpenter's rule, and similar beams for the middle and top, each about a foot shorter, and three vertical beams, one at the sail's back and two evenly spaced along the sides. The folding vertical beams bolted together at the intersections with the horizontal beams. The after vertical beams for each side bolted together. The frame front consisted of a folded vertical beam bolted to three curved horizontal beams that bolted to both side frames. The fairwater planes were four folding sections that unfolded to the shape of a fairwater plane, with a fifth piece that extended down along the middle vertical beam of the side frame. It was bolted in place along the vertical and horizontal middle beams. The top consisted of two curved cross-pieces that bolted to the side-frame vertical beams and one lengthwise folding beam extending forward twenty-three feet from the back. Each folding joint was made rigid with a bolt. All the bolts screwed directly into the frame pieces and did not need nuts.

The frame designers supplied custom one-piece titanium ratchet wrenches designed not to freeze-up in sandy or icy water.

Harry and Whitey picked up the bottom beam for the starboard side. Borysko approached and eyed it curiously. It was about his length, and he seemed to know that. He nosed around the other pieces and then wedged his 4 x 4 under one of *Teuthis'* skids and picked up one of the curved top pieces about as long as his 4 x 4. It was light, and he swam away with it effortlessly. Jer and Sergyi jumped into action and gripped both ends of the curved piece. Borysko shook his massive head, throwing both divers away from the beam.

One of Borysko's games was to let go of his 4 x 4 in mid-water, watch it rise to the surface, and then fetch it. In another, he handed it to a diver and indicated that the diver should let go of it. Then he would chase it to the surface and fetch it back. Borysko let go of the titanium beam, expecting it to rise to the surface. Instead, it dropped to the bottom, half-buried in the mud. He retrieved it and tried again, with the same results. Then he picked it up, swam to the surface, and dropped it. Then again…and again.

I grinned at Ham. "Looks like Borysko has outsmarted them. Tell them to finish the construction and then try to coax it from him. As long as they're in the water, Borysko's not going very far."

Bill took mike in hand. "Keep building the frame, guys. We'll figure out how to get that piece back when you are done."

It took another hour, but the design was beautiful. Every piece fit as designed. The frame and extended fairwater planes were rigid and stable. If push came to shove, we would be able to operate without Borysko's new toy.

The current was picking up from the west, clearing the water a bit. Visibility now extended to fifteen feet. Borysko was still playing drop-the-titanium-beam when the divers finished. Sergyi waved the other three divers toward him.

"Guys, let's push the four-by-four under *Teuthis* and coax Borysko into fetching it on the other side…you know, the other game he likes to play."

They pulled the 4 x 4 out from under the skid where Borysko had stashed it and shoved it under *Teuthis*. Borysko watched intently and then dashed to the other side to retrieve the piece of wood, but he took the beam with him. When he returned, he carried both in his mouth. He opened his jaws to drop them, but the wood rose while the beam sank. Borysko hesitated a moment and then dashed up to retrieve the 4 x 4.

Harry and Whitey grabbed the dropped titanium piece, swam it to the top of *Lyre's* sail, and bolted it in place. While they did so, Borysko stuck his nose into the matter and tried to grab the now attached beam. He pulled several times without effect and then gave up. Not being one to hold a grudge, at least against my guys, he opened his huge mouth for a tongue scratch.

As the tidal current increased, the four divers returned to the DDC to wolf down some sandwiches and grab some z's.

✳

Four hours later, the divers were struggling to push the folded Kevlar cover through the Egress hatch. By any measure, it was a tight fit. The package was a five-foot-long roll slightly narrower than the hatch opening—theoretically. Either somebody goofed, or the package had swollen since we received it. The divers pushed it through about a foot, and that was it. They tried silicone grease, WD-40, nothing worked. Finally, Jer and Sergyi exited through the Main Lock and pushed from below to force the package back into the Egress Lock.

They remained outside while Harry and Whitey unrolled the package inside the DDC. They pushed one end through the Egress hatch, and Jer and Sergyi swam it out and away from the hatch. We wasted a half-hour with this silliness. Borysko was fascinated by the stretched-out black fabric, but the divers discouraged him from testing it with his teeth.

Harry and Whitey joined Jer and Sergyi, placing themselves around the bottom of the sleeve. Without opening it, they swam it to the top of the sail. While Harry and Whitey held the fore and after ends, Jer and Sergyi opened the sleeve, and all four divers slipped it over the frame. The frame had appropriately placed Velcro loops. The sleeve had corresponding hooks on the inside with small straps opposite the hooks on the outside. As they slipped the cover down the frame, the divers pulled the hooks out sufficiently far to pass over any intervening loops. Once the cover was properly positioned, they pressed the hooks into the loops, effectively fixing the sleeve's position. The fairwater plane covers were attached to the sleeve where they extended out from the sail. Flaps hung from both the fore and after edges with Velcro strips along their lower ends. Harry pushed the starboard after flap up against the frame, and Whitey folded the forward flap up against it, sealing the Velcro. Jer and Sergyi did the same on the port side.

"Okay," Bill said on the circuit, "get the belly straps and lay them out."

Jer retrieved the straps from the Egress Lock, while Sergyi got a twenty-foot length of line. The straps had a clip at one end that hooked over an embedded bar at the bottom of the sleeve. The other end sported a cam buckle similar to a cinch for a trailer load tie-down.

"Here, Jer," Sergyi said, "take this end to the after connector."

When Jer placed his end against the connector, Sergyi stretched the line and cut off the end at the forward connector.

"Okay, guys," Harry said, "let's do this before the current fucks up our visibility completely."

Harry and Whitey carrying one strap and Jer and Sergyi the other, they swam them forward of *Lyre* and laid them out on the bottom across *Lyre's* beam, separated by the length of Sergyi's piece of line. The clip ends were to the port side.

It was time for Bert's big moment. On my signal through the Secure Gertrude routed to Dive Control, Bert lifted *Lyre* five feet off the bottom and inched her forward on the auxiliary props. Wally monitored the move closely, with the Basketball a mere foot away from the sleeve's forward connector.

When the connector and the strap lined up, I ordered, "Stop!" Bill told the divers to check the alignment of the after strap. "It's two inches off," Harry said.

"Okay, you and Whitey move it from both sides until it aligns perfectly," Bill told them.

Four minutes later, Harry said, "Okay, we got it."

Wally checked out both straps and connectors on both sides and gave his concurrence.

"Ease her to the bottom," I told Bert. "Take your time, so we don't dislodge the straps."

Once *Lyre* rested firmly on the bottom again, Bill ordered the divers to hook up the port fixed connectors.

"Done," Harry said five minutes later.

"Okay, now Jer and Sergyi, attach the starboard connectors and cinch the cam buckles hand tight. Then, stroke the cam buckles together," Bill told them.

"Can't see one another," Jer said. "Visibility's too low."

"Alright, count your strokes out loud over the circuit. Count as you stroke."

Jer started. "One—stroke…"

Sergyi picked up the count. "Two stroke…three stroke…"

At seventeen, Sergyi said, "No more can stroke!"

"I still got some," Jer said.

Bill looked at me. I nodded. "Continue stroking," Bill told Jer.

Jer completed six more strokes. When he finished, the sleeve was taut as a drumhead.

"Okay, guys, secure the cam buckles."

And with that, *Lyre* looked ever so much like a U.S. fast-attack submarine—at least the part we could see.

USS TEUTHIS— BOTTOMED OFF SEAL ISLAND

I was relaxing in the Wardroom while Bob Taggert and his crew readied *Mystic* to transport me and my partial crew back to *Lyre* so Bert and the rest of the crew could return to *Teuthis* for a stretch. The skipper stepped into the Wardroom with the XO. I started to rise, but he waved me down and handed me an official Navy message from SubLant. Apparently, the powers that be had gotten antsy about the buildup of Soviet seagoing forces off the New England coast. I already knew about three subs, a cruiser, and a frigate, but it seems there were more forming a shield around the ones we knew about.

Basically, the message informed us that several destroyers with Sikorsky SH-60 Seahawk helicopters had been deployed from Norfolk to form a screen around our operation. The Seahawks would be dropping sonobuoys to locate and herd the Soviet subs farther into the North Atlantic. We were to continue our operation to arrive at EB as soon as we could without endangering ourselves and our prize.

"Thought you would want to know about this," the skipper said. "It's going to get complicated out there."

The Wardroom sound-powered phone trilled. The XO picked up the handset.

"Lieutenant Taggert is ready to go," he told me.

✳

I went to the Crew's Mess to grab the rest of my crew. Potts and Sam were snacking on sandwiches and coffee.

"Hey, Potts," I said, "how are you doing?"

"Better…I think I lost ten pounds. Doc Everest really did a job on me." He grinned. "Serves me right for not following protocol. How's Rusty doing?"

"He picked up the slack pretty quickly…for an ET." Everyone chuckled. "Seriously," I added, "he started carrying his own weight in a day."

At that moment, I heard a loud *Whoosh!* From the Galley followed by a scream. Then black smoke billowed from the Galley door.

"Sam! Get to Control! Tell them there is a fire in the Galley," I ordered as I grabbed EAB masks from under one of the benches and tossed them to everyone in the mess.

A mess cook stumbled out of the Galley, his face a black blistered mess—it was Seaman Randolph Zimmerman. Potts grabbed him, sat him in the forward corner away from the Galley door, and called for the medic.

"Greg's still in the Galley. He's hurt bad!" Zimm said.

"Toss me a blanket," I yelled to no one in particular. I knew there were plenty in the Torpedo Room, just a few feet forward. One of the guys, I don't know who, dropped the blanket over me and splashed a full pitcher of water over it. "Extinguisher!" I yelled.

Someone pushed a purple-K cylinder into my right hand. I rushed into the Galley. It was full of flames. If I didn't get Seaman Patterson out in the next few seconds, he would die. The deck was slippery with burning grease, and I skidded to my knees, hot flames licking at my wet blanket cover. I found Greg's arm. Through the smoke and flames, he seemed on fire. I hit him with purple-K, dragged him under my blanket, snuffing the flames with my hands, and slid out of the Galley backward on the deck, pushing with my feet against bulkhead protrusions. By this time, my blanket was on fire. The guys in the mess grabbed me, threw off my burning blanket, and snuffed it out.

Chief Gunderson, our ship's medic, took charge of Greg, cutting off his clothing and treating his extensive burns. Doc Everest was in the corner with Zimm, treating his face.

Two guys on the fire-fighting crew, I'm not sure who, grabbed purple-K bottles and entered the Galley. They extinguished the fire in less than a minute after that.

The whole thing was over in less than five minutes after I first heard the *Whoosh!* Other than minor burns to both hands, I was fine. Zimm's face was in bad shape. Greg was in serious condition. Both needed way more than the Docs could supply onboard.

✳

The skipper showed up in the Crew's Mess, spoke briefly with Doc Everest, and then made the only decision possible under the circumstances.

Moments later, the 1MC blared "Surface! Surface! Surface!" followed by three long *Aoogahs!* from the Klaxon.

I remained in the Mess while Doc Gunderson treated my hands. Like I said, it wasn't serious, but it doesn't hurt to be careful. He bandaged both my palms and a couple fingers on each hand. Looked much worse than it was.

While this was going on, Barry, the current OOD, surfaced *Teuthis* and commenced ventilating the sub to get rid of the smoke clogging the Control Compartment. Seth Beaumont was in Radio with the skipper transmitting an urgent medevac request for the injured seamen. One of the destroyers patrolling nearby radioed back that his Seahawk would be onsite in fifteen minutes.

The COB—Master Chief Brock Davis—hustled his deck gang topside with a wireframe stretcher for Seaman Patterson and a sling for Seaman Zimmerman.

The Seahawk chopper arrived a couple of minutes early and lowered its lift cable. The COB touched the lift cable with his grounding rod, and then one of his guys hooked up the four stretcher lift-pennants. Patterson, who was sedated, had no idea what was happening to and around him. Then the chopper lowered the cable again. Brock grounded it, and his guys hooked up Zimm's lift harness. Zimm waved as he disappeared into the Seahawk, and the chopper headed for the barn.

On the open bridge, Barry shouted, "Clear the deck!"

Five minutes later, *Teuthis* was back on the bottom 300 feet from *Lyre*, creeping sideways to reach her former position, fifteen feet from *Lyre's* starboard side.

What nobody saw was a periscope just above the surface a mile to the southwest, just on the other side of the mound that protected *Teuthis* and *Lyre* from prying ears in that direction.

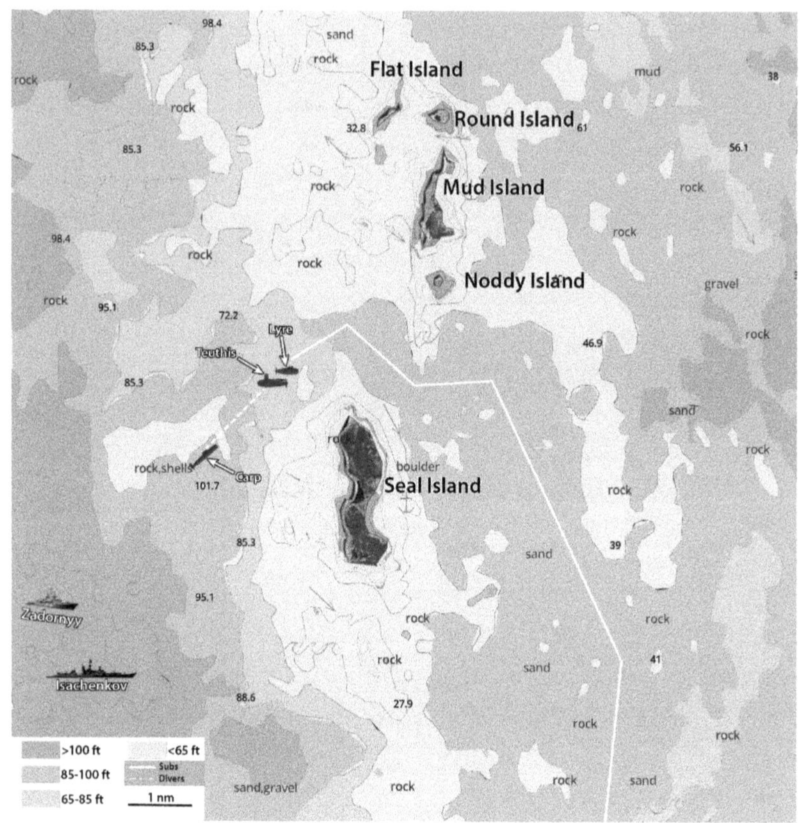

USS Teuthis & Lyre bottomed at Seal Island.
Divers interact with Carp.

CHAPTER NINETEEN—Battle for The *Lyre*

ON THE SEAFLOOR—AT *USS TEUTHIS*

Although we did not know it at the time, the Seahawk that medevacked our injured seamen laid a passive sonobuoy x-pattern on its way back to the destroyer. Almost immediately, these sonobuoys picked up the sounds of the *Carp* that had worked its way toward us from the southwest. *Carp* had bottomed in the depression behind the mound to the southwest that we thought would shield us from that direction. We were able to communicate over short distances from our shallow depth. Cmdr. Roken informed our shield that he would handle *Carp*, and for them not to interfere until it was obvious that their presence was needed. He called me to his cabin.

"How are your hands, Mac?" he asked as soon as we were alone. "Nothing serious, Skipper. Another day or so, and the wrappings come off."

"Take a look at these." The skipper handed me several dispatches. They were intelligence reports about Soviet submarines that had experienced radiation leaks in the past several months. There were several evacuations, even some deaths, and at least one lost sub. The crews were skittish. Anything reactor related would set them off.

"We forced *Carp* to surface on a reactor scram off Pt. Barrow," he said.

I was well aware of this because I had engineered that particular scram and played a significant role in pulling it off. The skipper pulled out a chart.

"*Carp* is bottomed about a mile away, here," he said, pointing to her location behind the mound. "What do you think would happen were we to scram her reactor again?"

I grinned at the thought. "Crew's already skittish," I said. "Might force the skipper to evacuate—tow her home on the surface."

"That would never happen on *Teuthis* or any American sub," the skipper said, "but Soviet subs have had a lot of reactor problems lately." He pointed to the stack of dispatches. "Captain might not have a choice…" He smiled at me. "What are your thoughts?"

"How would her crew react? No clue, Sir. That's above my pay-grade." I paused. "Can we force her to surface? Absolutely!"

✴

I got with Ham in Dive Control, and together we laid out a plan to tackle *Carp*. We had two paraffin-filled drums left. The divers wrapped each drum with heating coils and covered that with thick insulation.

After liquifying the paraffin, they rigged each drum to draw power from a Protei and installed electric pumps to force the liquid paraffin into *Carp's* intakes. As before, each drum also carried a couple of diving weights to bring it to neutral buoyancy.

Ham assembled all the divers in Dive Control, where I addressed them.

"We're in the short strokes, guys. The Soviets have maybe two days left to take *Lyre* back—that ain't gonna happen! They have a lot of firepower out there, and *Carp* is just a mile away. We have a large protective screen that will absolutely keep the major players away from our immediate vicinity, but like I said, *Carp* is already under our nose, and the skipper waved help away—said we would handle it. And *we* means you guys—specifically, Harry, Whitey, Jer, and Sergyi. If we still had the Serina, Bill and Jimmy would join you, and Ham would run the dive with me backing him up. *If.* right?

"So, Harry and Whitey—you guys team up on one Protei, Jer and Sergyi on the other. Harry and Sergyi will drive. Whitey and Jer, clip a drum to your Protei frame, hook up the power, and hang on. Each of you carry an APS with two extra mags. Harry is in charge of in-water ops.

"Visibility sucks…"

"No shit, Sir," came back at me in several iterations. "Yeah… really sucks, so use your compasses and remain close together. *Carp's* gonna be listening hard, so secure the Protei motors when you reach the ridge and swim them over. We don't know *Carp's* orientation, but I suspect you will come upon her broadside. Locate the intake on that side, and then Jer and Sergyi swim over *Carp's* deck to the other side. Time yourselves so you start pumping paraffin at the same time.

"One more thing. No matter how well we plan, no plan survives the commencement of hostilities. Expect *Carp* to put divers into the water. Be ready! Follow Harry's lead!

"And like Patton said in the movie, *Your job is not to die for your country, it's to make the other poor dumb bastard die for* his *country.*" I let that sink in. "Hooyah!" I barked, finishing the briefing.

Hooyahs! all around.

ON THE SEAFLOOR—AT *CARP*

It was more difficult than I could have imagined as I watched Ham and Bill conduct the dive. I was aboard *Teuthis*, so technically, the ball stopped with me. There was no reason for me to interfere with Ham, however, since he was entirely on top of the matter. If the truth be known, I really wanted to be out in the water with the guys.

The four divers dropped into the water. Jimmy lowered the Proteis and the drums through the hatch, and the divers set themselves up for their trek to *Carp*. Derrick was on the Basketball, but with the low visibility, there was little we could see…except for a momentary black and white flash as Borysko made his presence known.

The divers set out on a southwest tack with Borysko bouncing along beside them. Derrick followed them for a while and then lost them in the haze.

✳

Harry took the lead with Sergyi three feet to the right and back. Borysko hung around, keeping pace with them. They stayed close to the bottom, leaving a silt trail behind them. The Protei had no speed control, only an on-off switch. Left on, it could travel three knots with an equipped diver. These were carrying two divers and a drum of paraffin. They did two knots at best.

A half-hour after departure, the bottom started to rise, and Harry stopped their progress. He inched forward, switching his unit on and off several times. He reached the crest and found the water clearer on the other side. He waved the other three to his position. Before them, some thirty to forty feet distant, *Carp* sat on the bottom, presenting her port side through a fog of suspended silt. Borysko darted off to investigate.

Not wanting to use their comms so close to *Carp*, Harry signaled to find the port intake scoop. They found it about five minutes later. Harry signaled Jer and Sergyi to swim their Protei over the top of *Carp* and set up for pumping paraffin into her starboard intake. He pointed to his watch and showed ten fingers. Then he pointed two fingers at his eyes, pointed toward the bow, then his eyes again, and then pointed at each diver. He unslung his APS, pointing it at the bow. Each of them understood to be on the lookout for deployed divers from the bow and indicated his understanding with a thumbs-up. Jer and Sergyi noted the time and headed over *Carp's* after deck, followed by Borysko.

When Harry's watch indicated the passage of ten minutes, Whitey poked his hose into the intake and started the pump. Simultaneously on the other side, Jer and Sergyi did the same. Five minutes later, reactor scram alarms sounded right through the hull as turbine sounds disappeared and human shouts erupted. The noise from within seemed to excite Borysko. His darting activity increased.

On the port side, Harry and Whitey moved along the bottom under the curve of *Carp's* hull, each with APS at the ready. On the starboard side, Jer and Sergyi did the same. As they approached the bow, the keel began to curve upward, allowing the two teams to see each other. They moved together, hugging *Carp's* hull, adjusting their buoyancy to compensate for their depth change. A loud noise above and forward of their position caught their attention as a torpedo tube outer door opened. Harry signaled a halt with clenched fist. They flattened themselves against the hull.

Following a scraping noise, an inverted diver's torso pushed out of the open torpedo tube and dropped toward the seafloor. Harry and Sergyi fired their APSs nearly simultaneously, one dart shattering the diver's faceplate, the other penetrating his belly. He was dead before he hit the mud. Borysko swam to him, nudging him with his snout. Harry waved his divers to approach the torpedo tube from both sides and above. He placed himself directly below.

A second diver exited the torpedo tube, reacting with surprise when he saw Borysko. He failed to see Harry, who grabbed him, pulled off his full-face mask, and placed his knife at the diver's throat. The diver went limp in surrender, and Harry ripped off the mask strap and pressed the strapless mask back against the diver's face. He placed the diver's right hand against the mask to hold it in place and tied off his other hand with a short line.

Scraping noises indicated a third diver, but he seemed to delay his exit from the torpedo tube, possibly fearing the Orca. Sergyi reached into the tube and grabbed the diver from the side, but before he could immobilize him, the third diver fired a dart from an SPP underwater pistol that appeared in his hand. The shot was poorly aimed, but it caught Sergyi in his lower leg. Without missing a beat, Sergyi pressed his APS barrel against the diver's shoulder and fired. Then he immobilized the diver, following Harry's lead. Harry grabbed his captive by his buoyancy compensator with one hand and pointed to the seafloor with his other. Sergyi secured his captive, and all six divers floated to the mud.

As they hit the seafloor, above them, *Carp* activated her main ballast blow as air rushing into her main ballast tanks drowned out all other sound. Harry spread out his hands, pushing them repeatedly toward the seafloor, telling the divers to make themselves heavy. The *Teuthis* divers deflated their buoyancy compensators while Harry and Sergyi let the air out of their prisoners' BCs.

With a mighty lurch that nearly pulled the six divers off the seafloor, *Carp* broke her bottom tension and popped to the surface a hundred feet above them.

Harry broke comms silence. "Find your rides and return to *Teuthis*," he ordered. "Hang onto the drums, keep control of the prisoners, and stay together." He looked up as Borysko bumped him gently from behind with his 4 x 4. Through their masks, the captured divers appeared terrified. Borysko moved around to face them and opened his huge mouth. With a grin, Harry reached in and scratched his tongue and then said, "Back to *Teuthis*, guys."

USS TEUTHIS—SURFACED AT SEAL ISLAND

I called the skipper on the handset from Dive Control. "Skipper, can you come down here? You need to hear Harry's report directly from him."

"Be down shortly," the skipper said and disconnected. Five minutes later, he walked into Dive Control.

Harry briefed him generally, taking him through their timeline. Then he said earnestly, as much as a person can when in a chamber under pressure, "When their reactor scrammed, Captain, we heard the usual alarms, but there was something else…we could hear it right through the hull. It was like panic had overtaken the crew. They were yelling and screaming like they were all dying. This was back aft—the Engine Room. They deployed divers in a normal fashion from their Torpedo Room, but then, all of a sudden, they blew to the surface. They abandoned their divers. I know the water's not that deep, so they could have expected the divers to surface and swim to the sub, but the whole thing was crazy, absolutely nuts!"

"Thank you, Petty Officer Blackwell." The skipper replaced the chamber handset and looked at me. "What do you think, Mac?"

"I'm speculating, Sir, but I think they panicked. This was the second time their reactor scrammed while they were submerged, apparently for no good reason. These crews are already antsy about radiation leaks." I looked at the skipper with a serious demeanor. "I think the Control

Room crew panicked and surfaced without their skipper's approval. It's not mutiny, but it's pretty damn close." I grinned glumly. "I think the *Carp* crew is topside on the deck. Nothing will make them reenter the sub. They think it's a death sentence."

"I agree," the skipper said and picked up the Dive Control telephone handset. "Commander James, surface *Teuthis*. Put men topside ready to render assistance to *Carp's* distressed crew. Have Lieutenant Beaumont meet me in Radio." He gave me the handset and left Dive Control.

✳

As I replaced the handset, the 1MC blared "Surface! Surface! Surface!" followed by the Klaxon's three long *Aoogahs!*

I met the skipper on the bridge. The water was pitch black, but the nighttime sky was clear and filled with stars. *Carp* was less than a mile away, deck brilliantly floodlit and filled with lifejacketed Soviet sailors. The skipper handed me a bullhorn. "Ask in Russian how we may be of assistance."

"*Eto amerikanskaya podvodnaya lodka* Teuthis. *Chem my mozhem vam pomoch?—[This is the American submarine* Teuthis. *How may we assist you?*] I asked over the horn while the skipper moved *Teuthis* slowly in their direction.

A man I identified by his uniform as an officer wearing a lifejacket over his overcoat answered in Russian by bullhorn. I translated for the skipper. *The* Zadornyy *is nearby. Please inform her by radio that the submarine* Carp *has experienced a severe reactor casualty. The crew requires immediate evacuation, and the* Carp *must be taken under tow.*

The skipper sent me to Radio to coordinate the transmission with Seth. He called me from the Bridge.

"Mac, tell *Zadornyy* that we have four soviet divers onboard, three with non-life-threatening injuries."

"Skipper," I responded, "the captured divers know that we had divers on the bottom near that *Victor III* and *Carp*. The last two saw our empty drums. They're not stupid—they can add two and two. I strongly recommend NOT revealing their presence."

The skipper was silent for nearly thirty seconds. "You're right," he finally said. "Good call, Mac. Say nothing about them."

That's one of the things I liked about Cmdr. Roken. He surrounded himself with the best officers he could get, and he listened to them. He wasn't afraid to reverse himself when the situation dictated. My recommendation got me a bonus point with the Old Man.

The skipper turned the Bridge Conn back over to Franklin. "Are the divers out of the DDC yet?" he asked me over the circuit.

I checked with Ham. "Just surfaced," I answered.

"Put Sergyi on the Bridge with Commander James in case Russian is needed. I want you with me in Radio."

✳

A few minutes after the skipper joined Seth and me in Radio, Franklin called on the Bridge phone. "Captain, the *Zadornyy* is approaching from the southwest, directly off our bow. She's about a half mile away from the *Carp*. She's shadowed by two of our destroyers, and five of our choppers are hovering nearby. The *Isachenkov* is holding position about five miles beyond the *Zadornyy*. It looks like the *Isachenkov* may be launching a bird."

The skipper acknowledged and then said to me, "Inform *Zadornyy* that she's free to maneuver in any way she must to enable evacuation of *Carp's* crew and take *Carp* under tow. Tell her we can assist the evacuation with helicopters if they wish. Warn her of the shallow water between *Carp* and us."

I sent the message. They thanked us for our generosity but declined our immediate help.

Franklin called by phone from the Bridge again. "*Isachenkov's* chopper is flooding the entire area with bright light. The *Zadornyy* has launched two motorized small craft. They're heading for the *Carp*. I see three men on the *Carp* Bridge. They seem to be holding her head steady but not otherwise moving her."

The skipper acknowledged and then asked Seth to reach SubLant.

While he was briefing the high command, I called Franklin. "Has anyone told Bert what is going on?" I asked.

"I had my JOOD give him a full briefing right after we surfaced. His instructions are to remain absolutely silent. There must be no hint of his presence."

✳

It took an hour and then some to get all the Soviet personnel except the deck gang off *Carp* by small-craft and onto *Zadornyy*. It took another hour-and-a-half to couple *Zadornyy* and *Carp*. It was pretty obvious that neither deck crew had a lot of experience setting up towing or being towed, especially at nighttime. There were several starts and stops, including one Soviet lad from *Carp* falling into the drink. They got him out of the water and had the courtesy to inform us he was okay.

Finally, after nearly five hours of frustration for the crews of both Soviet vessels, *Zadornyy* took a strain on the quarter-mile-long towline and slowly put on speed to about five knots, with *Carp* meekly following behind. It would be a long and frustrating trip around Norway to the Polyarnyy shipyard, only to discover that there was absolutely nothing wrong with *Carp's* reactor. This would certainly spell the end of her captain's naval career. I cannot say that bothered me very much.

But we were not yet home free. *Isachenkov* sent a thank you message as her lights disappeared over the horizon. I suspected she would not go far. And *Shchuka* and *Volgograd* were somewhere nearby.

No… it was not yet over.

ON THE SEAFLOOR—*MYSTIC* OPS

Cmdr. Roken kept Teuthis in position until Zadornyy and tow disappeared into the night. The XO, who had relieved Franklin by this time, moved us close to Lyre's position, submerged us, and brought us alongside *Lyre* to top off her batteries.

Just as *Teuthis* settled on her skids fifteen feet southwest of *Lyre*, King in Sonar called Control.

"Conn, Sonar. I have an active pinger, but this is not your routine active sonar. The ping lasts fifteen seconds and seems modulated in some weird way that I have never encountered."

I was passing through Control to grab a bite in the Mess before returning to *Lyre*, so I stepped into Sonar.

"Whatcha got, King?"

King handed me a headset. "That's a signal if I ever heard one," I said. "You tell Control. I'll get the skipper."

While the skipper and I stood in Sonar, King analyzed the pings. They consisted of a musical signal heterodyned onto the ping's base frequency. Its source seemed to be *Shchuka*, located some twenty nautical miles to the southeast. *Teuthis* was located directly between *Shchuka* and *Lyre*. Bert reported that *Okean* did not receive anything.

The strange pinging stopped after five minutes and did not resume.

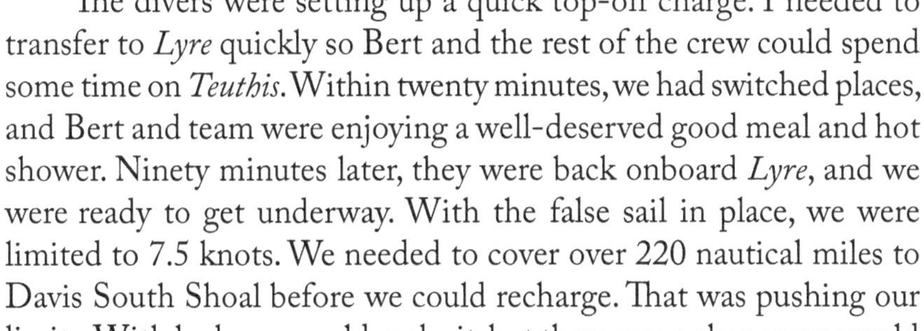

The divers were setting up a quick top-off charge. I needed to transfer to *Lyre* quickly so Bert and the rest of the crew could spend some time on *Teuthis*. Within twenty minutes, we had switched places, and Bert and team were enjoying a well-deserved good meal and hot shower. Ninety minutes later, they were back onboard *Lyre*, and we were ready to get underway. With the false sail in place, we were limited to 7.5 knots. We needed to cover over 220 nautical miles to Davis South Shoal before we could recharge. That was pushing our limits. With luck, we would make it, but there was a chance we would have to recharge in deeper water, putting the divers into a multi-day decompression.

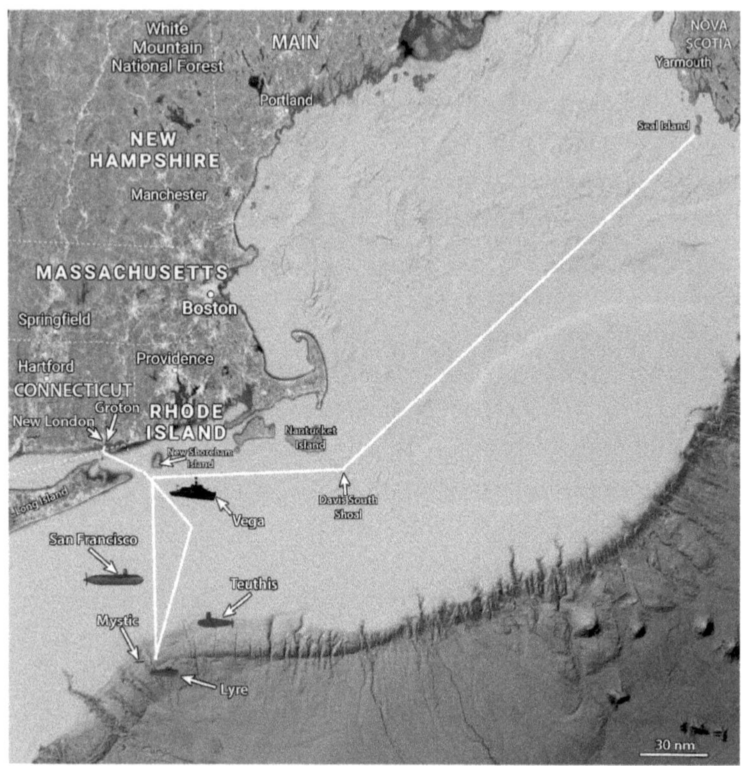

USS Teuthis & Lyre transit from Seal Island to New London Harbor. Lyre and Mystic approach the Continental Shelf Break.

CHAPTER TWENTY—The Trawler & the Wayward *Alfa*

THE *LYRE*—DAVIS SOUTH SHOAL

In this journal several times, and in previous ones, I have described submarining as endless hours of tedious boredom interrupted by moments of sheer panic. Our transit to Davis South Shoal south of Cape Cod certainly qualified for this definition. *Zadornyy*, with *Carp* in tow, was gone—headed for her Polyarnyy barn, east of northern Norway.

Isachenkov was gone too—big surprise. I had figured she would hang around for one last try at retrieving *Lyre*. *Shchuka* and *Volgograd*

242

were somewhere nearby, of that I was certain, but they had gone to ground, hiding somewhere at ultra-quiet. Following that last, strange active ping—nothing, nothing at all.

We chugged along at 200 feet and 7.5 knots, *Teuthis* keeping between us and the open ocean. We picked up some fishing boats, a couple of trawlers—genuine, and several cargo vessels, but no Soviet anything. *Frisco*, *Swordfish*, and *Drum* formed a shield along the Continental Break, but if they heard anything, they didn't tell us. With nothing else to do, the divers concentrated on their sub quals.

My guys on *Lyre* kept a close eye on our charge level as it dropped lower and lower. Fortunately, we still had an hour or so of charge remaining when Bert set us on the bottom in ninety feet of water in Davis South Shoal about seventy nautical miles due south of Nantucket Island. The water was crystal clear with hundred-foot-plus visibility.

Ham put Jimmy in the water again, to Jimmy's great delight, along with Harry, Whitey, and Jer. He kept Sergyi in the DDC even though his injury was relatively minor.

"After you get the charge underway," Ham told them, "inspect every inch of the false sail. Cinch the belly straps if necessary. Check the Velcro closures—Fuck…check everything you can think of. We don't want any surprises when we surface and sail up Thames River."

Jimmy was so happy to be in the water once more that he checked everything twice before the others had finished setting up the charge. He took time to reacquaint himself with Borysko, who remembered him but hadn't seen him in a long time. By this time, Borysko's 4 x 4 was nearly chewed through. Jimmy had Ham send out a fresh length of 4 x 4, but Borysko would have nothing to do with the new piece. He ignored it completely, apparently preferring his old, trusted toy.

The divers took several additional turns on the belly strap cinches and reported that *Lyre* was indistinguishable from her namesake, the *USS Sculpin*, complete with the hull number 592 emblazoned on each side. I doubted that it was an exact match, since the *Alfa* hull was shorter and squatter, but I let it go. No reason to make an issue of something that could not be changed anyway.

Where are the Soviets? I asked myself. *These guys don't give up easily. Where are they?*

THE *LYRE*—OFF NEW LONDON HARBOR

As we got underway from Davis South Shoal, we picked up the distinct sound of a working trawler ahead of us. Sam had the *Lyre* watch, and Franklin was the *Teuthis* OOD. Sonar Tech Don Forge identified the trawler as none other than the Soviet spy trawler *Vega*, notorious for her continuous presence off New London Harbor. Photos of *Vega* showed her bristling with antennas, and she was purported to have excellent sonar as well. A formidable adversary.

We needed to enter New London Harbor on the surface. We had done everything possible to ensure that *Vega* or any other observer would not recognize *Lyre*. In twelve hours, we would be at the harbor entrance. If the Soviets could prove with hard evidence that we had their *Alfa*, international repercussions could be severe. It could bring us to the brink of war.

We were in our eighth hour of the transit. I had the watch. Bert Cobb and Wyatt Cook were hanging out in Control with me. It was our thirtieth day since departing Pt. Barrow, and with a bit of luck, we would dock at EB late tomorrow.

I noted *Vega's* position on the *Akkord* console. "That sonofabitch is tracking everything we send to sea, everything that returns," I commented. "She often places herself in the track of our subs and violates the International Rules of the Road at every turn. She records the sounds our vessels make, records their electronic emanations, collects as much info as possible."

"Why don't we drive her away?" Wyatt asked.

"She's in international waters," I answered. "We demand that every nation respect our right to operate in all international waters everywhere. We really have no choice but to respect that right for any other nation, including the Soviets."

"So, we have to put up with her," Bert said. "That sucks a big one." "Is she armed?" Wyatt wanted to know.

"We're not sure. For certain, she carries small arms. She displays no missile launchers, but nothing says she doesn't carry a load of torpedoes," I said.

That gave me food for thought. I picked up the Secure Gertrude and called *Teuthis*. Waverly answered. He was just relieving the XO.

"Let me speak with the XO," I said. "What's up, Mac?" the XO said.

"We're about three hours from our surfacing point," I said. "I need to discuss an urgent matter with the skipper, but I don't want to do so over this circuit. It has to be face-to-face. Once we reach the surface zone, I want to bottom *Lyre* and have *Mystic* transfer me to *Teuthis* so I can have that conversation with the skipper. I don't mean to be mysterious, but once the skipper approves my idea, I'm certain he will brief you fully."

THE *LYRE*—OFF NEW LONDON HARBOR

At 0900 hours, I set *Lyre* on the sandy bottom in 190 feet of water about 12.5 nautical miles southeast of Shoreham Island and a nautical mile north of *Vega*. *Teuthis* bottomed nearby, both of us as quiet as we could possibly be.

A few minutes later, *Mystic* made a seal to our after-hatch, and I climbed aboard. In fifteen minutes, I sat on the red Naugahyde couch in the skipper's cabin. He occupied his chair backed against the fold-down desk. Petty Officer Rivera had just delivered a pot of fresh coffee with two mugs and a warm "Nice to see you, Commander."

"So, what's the mystery—the one you couldn't divulge to the XO over the Secure Gertrude?" His tone was friendly, but I sensed that he did not entirely approve.

"It's about the *Vega*, Sir. We know about her electronics and think we know about her sonar. She doesn't have a sonar dome, so we have to assume she carries some kind of dipping sonar. That would be primarily active." I paused.

"I have no quarrel with your comments thus far, but where are you taking this?"

"Why does any surface vessel have active sonar?" I asked. "The only reason I can think of is to target a submarine." I paused again. The skipper nodded his head. "When a ship operates alone, her only reason to target a sub is to take the sub out."

"So, you're assuming that *Vega* carries one or more torpedoes." It was a statement, not a question.

"I've studied photos of *Vega* carefully, Sir. She has no mechanism for launching torpedoes over the side. That means she launches them underwater." Again, the skipper nodded. "There's not a lot of below-deck room, so I'm assuming *Vega* has a moonpool of sorts. She can launch a torpedo by lowering it through the opening, probably the same one she uses to lower her dipping sonar for range info."

"You make an excellent argument, Mac. Where are you taking this?"

"*Vega* is on station. She is expecting us to show up with the *Alfa*. Skipper, I think *Vega's* job this time around is to detect and destroy the *Alfa*."

The skipper's eyes widened at this, but before he could respond, I continued. "Remember the strange transmission *Shchuka* transmitted? That was a modulated signal laid over the underlying sonic carrier. No way it could have been meant for us. I propose it was sent in the blind to *Lyre*. To me, that means *Lyre* has some kind of self-destruct mechanism that can be activated by that signal." I paused to take a sip of my cooling coffee. "Obviously, *Shchuka's* signal didn't reach *Lyre*. I think the ridge and *Teuthis* blocked it or attenuated it sufficiently that *Lyre* didn't respond." I took another sip. The coffee really was getting cold. "If *Vega* sends that signal here, whatever it is supposed to trigger will happen!" I leaned back against the red Naugahyde. I had spoken long enough.

The skipper refreshed our coffees from the thermos pot and sat silently, sipping his coffee while thinking. Finally, he leaned forward and looked earnestly at me. "I can't find a flaw in your argument. I presume you've worked out a counter for this."

"Sort of, Sir. You bring *Teuthis* close enough so the Basketball can examine *Vega's* underside. What we do depends on what we see." I paused, thinking about it. "Worst case, *Vega* has deployed both the sonar and a torpedo. If whatever the signal triggers doesn't work, she launches the torpedo. If *Lyre* blows herself up, or whatever she's supposed to do, *Vega* retracts the torpedo and reports a successful mission to Moscow." I shrugged. "Otherwise, she launches the torpedo to do the job."

The skipper stood up, and I joined him. "First things first. Let's check *Vega* out."

"Skipper, ever since I thought my way through this, my guys have been scouring *Lyre* for any explosives. The only thing we found, and I mean the *only* thing, is a double rack of torpedoes in the forward room. We have disconnected every wire, fitting plug—anything at all that could possibly lead to a detonation. Right now, you couldn't fire a torpedo from *Lyre* if your life depended on it." I took a deep breath. "I am confident that if the signal is designed to trigger an explosion on *Lyre*, it is now ineffective."

As it turned out, I was right…but only partly so.

✳

The skipper called Barry and Franklin in conference mode. "Barry, assume Waverly's watch and bring *Teuthis* beneath *Vega* with sufficient clearance so Franklin can scan the bottom with the Basketball. Franklin, you be ready to get me a clean picture of *Vega's* underside. *Do not* allow us to be detected!"

Then he called the XO and Waverly to his cabin. The skipper retained his desk chair, Waverly joined me on the couch, and the XO took the lounge chair. The skipper looked at me.

"Take them through what we just discussed, Mac."

I walked them through the argument, step-by-step. When I finished, they greeted me with quiet astonishment.

"You're certain *Lyre* is clean?" Waverly asked. "Absolutely!"

We sat quietly while Cmdr. Roken put his considerable intellect to the problem.

"If you are wrong, Mac," he said slowly, "and I really hope you are, we fade away and carry on with our planned parade through New London Harbor. If you're right, he will send the signal, it will fail, and he will go to Plan B. The big unknown is how long will the *Vega* captain wait before launching his torpedo?" He turned to Waverly. "What are your thoughts?"

"We know nothing about that fish. Don't know how it's armed, how it's steered. We know that a torpedo can explode if triggered by another explosion or if subjected to a large electric charge." He reached for the phone. "With your permission, Captain."

The skipper nodded. Shortly, Chief Torpedoman Jasper Cedrik knocked on the cabin door.

"Tubes, can you rig a large capacitor that can deliver a delayed high-voltage charge to a torpedo suspended in the water?"

Cedrik looked at Waverly in astonishment as the phone warbled. "Thank you," the skipper said into the handset. He looked at us. "Barry reports *Vega* has an open moonpool with a suspended six-foot torpedo and a dipping sonar device. *Vega* is moving at bare steerageway."

He turned to Waverly. "Well?"

Waverly raised his eyebrows at Tubes, who stammered, "Y…yes, Sir, I got something that'll work. I need to get with the ETs for the delay circuit."

"How long?" Waverly asked. "Half-hour…maybe a bit more."

"See to it!" the skipper said as Tubes left the cabin. "I need to return to *Lyre*…"

"You do," the skipper interrupted.

"But I need to speak with Ham first…make sure the divers know what is at risk."

✳

Mystic launched in mid-column while *Teuthis* maintained station beneath *Vega*. I took Sergyi with me so I would have another Russian speaker. Since we were preparing to run on the surface into the Thames River, I had Bob set *Mystic* on the hatch aligned with *Lyre's* axis.

"Do you and your crew want to hang out down here?" I asked.

Taggert told me that either he or Jim and one of the crew would remain in *Mystic* all the time—just in case, he said.

We settled down to wait out whatever sequence would take place.

✳

On *Teuthis*, Waverly and Tubes handed Harry and Whitey a package half the size of a briefcase—about twelve inches square by three inches thick. One side was marked with a bright "X." A stainless wire with a grip handle large enough to accommodate a diver's gloved hand extended out one end.

Tubes addressed them. "Place the case with the 'X' against the torpedo with the wire unobstructed. Duct-tape the case around the torpedo about ten times. The number of turns isn't critical. Just make sure it is snug as possible."

"Then stand by," Waverly said. "Do you both have ear protection?" The divers nodded.

"Stand-by near the torpedo…we don't know how long…until the sonar sends a ping. Then wait exactly two minutes, pull the handle, and hustle back to *Teuthis*. Try to get under her hull ASAP, and then get inside soonest." He turned to Wally Dubbs. "Follow the divers back to *Teuthis*, but stow the Basketball right away." He turned to Ham. "Let the OOD know the moment the divers are secure."

✳

We caught most of it on tape through the Basketball. Harry and Whitey mounted the case against the torpedo like they had been doing this all their lives. The worst part was the wait. They hung near the torpedo, keeping pace with the barely moving *Vega*, for a full hour and ten minutes. When the sonar finally pinged, they both slapped their hands to their ears. Two minutes later, Harry pulled the handle sharply, and they dropped like rocks to *Teuthis* a hundred feet below. Wally followed with the Basketball barely able to keep up with them.

Five seconds after Ham reported the divers secured, Barry dropped *Teuthis* to within a few feet of the bottom and ordered a few seconds of flank speed to get the hell out of there.

Five minutes later, the kludged delay circuit inside the waterproof case fired, releasing the megavolt charge across the massive capacitor, transferring the charge directly into the torpedo's steel body. A microsecond later, the PBX warhead exploded, breaking *Vega's* keel, sending her to the bottom.

✳

On *Lyre*, *Okean* picked up the modulated ping from *Vega*. At first, nothing seemed to happen. After a couple of minutes, the *Sozh* display shifted to a larger scale. Spook had the watch, but I jumped in to monitor the *Sozh* more closely. I called Sergyi, Wyatt, and Matt to Control. As they arrived, the *Ritm* machinery control console lit up, and the main screw started turning. Then *Boxit*, the course control system, went into action. *Lyre* lifted off the bottom and came to heading 180 degrees. I got on the

Secure Gertrude. "*Teuthis*, this is *Lyre*. We figured that modulated signal out. Something has taken control of *Lyre's* systems. They are completely non-responsive to us. *Lyre* is picking up speed and driving straight toward the Continental Break, course one-eight-zero.

We are doing everything we can to slow her down, drive her into the bottom—whatever it takes to stop her.

"I think she is headed to deep water where she will drop to crush depth. We will stop her if we can."

⁕

Swordfish and *Drum* picked up my transmission and altered course to intersect *Lyre*. Without a DSRV to slow her down, *Teuthis* chased us at flank speed. When she caught up, she paced us a hundred yards off our starboard beam.

Wyatt and Matt were deep into the Russian manuals, looking for clues about how the control worked.

"Look," Matt said, "*Okean* gets the enabling signal and sends it to *Akkord* right here on this line. From somewhere, *Akkord* conjures up a destination and sends signals to *Boxit* and *Ritm*. See…look!" He traced out the signal path with a finger.

I jumped in. "Guys, we got six hours on our present course and speed. If you can find a way to slow us down, we gain more time to solve the problem."

They both grunted.

In the Engine Room, Sergyi and Gilbert traced out power lines. Power to the electric motor was physically protected. They couldn't access it without appropriate power tools, which they didn't have.

"Gilbert," Sergyi said. "why not disconnect the batteries?" "Okay, you inform Mac, and I will do it."

Sergyi came to tell me, and we both returned to the disconnect panel.

"Okay, Gil, throw the switch." Nothing happened.

"Their override seems to have cut the disconnect out of the circuit," Gil said. "Shit!"

After three hours, we had made no progress.

Wyatt and Matt were frantic. "We've checked every circuit three times," Wyatt said.

"Let's take a different tack," I suggested. "Wyatt, if you were going to design a system that could surreptitiously take over this nearly autonomous machine, how would you do it?"

Wyatt turned to Matt, and they began brainstorming this concept. "I would hide it in plain sight," Matt said.

Two hours left.

"How do you do plain sight without someone seeing it?" Wyatt asked in exasperation.

Matt pointed at an *Akkord* circuit board. "What's on the other side?" he asked.

They pulled it out and turned it over.

"That circuit's not on the schematic," Wyatt said, excitement coloring his voice.

One hour left. The bottom was 500 feet below us and dropping. "Look, Wyatt, another one, and another!"

"Mac, come here. Look…there is a complete set of hidden circuitry under all these boards." I could feel Wyatt's excitement.

I checked the depth. 1,000 feet and dropping. I looked at Wyatt. "What happens if you simply pull a board, turn it over, and plug it back in?" I asked.

Matt looked at me in astonishment. "Hide it in plain sight… It'll run that circuit."

"Everybody…to control!" I shouted.

They were there in five seconds. I glanced at the depth. 2,500 feet! "Here's the deal," I said, pulling and flipping boards as I talked. "*Mystic's* test depth is five thousand feet. We're getting there fast. I want everyone inside *Mystic* except me and Sergyi. We're gonna flip boards until the last minute…"

"I'm staying with you, Boss," Bert said. "You need a couple more hands."

Others started to protest that they wanted to stay, too.

"Stop it, people! We don't have time for this. Get your butts into *Mystic* NOW—That's an order!" I turned to Taggert. "Lieutenant Taggert, when your depth indicates five thousand feet, you break your seal and move away."

"But…but…" he stammered.

"That's an order, Bob. Just do it!"

4,000 feet!

Sergyi flipped a board at the bottom of the *Akkord* console. The display commenced oscillating between the imposed setting and those we had set before all this started. Quickly, we flipped the remaining boards along the console bottom.

5,000 feet—slowing the descent! *Mystic* broke seal and pulled away. I reached for the depth control knob and cranked in 4,000 feet.

Lyre assumed a ten-degree up angle but still dropped.

5,500 feet—still slowing the descent—only dropping half as fast! I tried the rudder control. The rudder responded. I tried the speed control and cranked it up to fifteen knots. *Lyre* responded, sucking power from the batteries.

6,000 feet—holding, almost!

I came to my feet, and Sergyi threw his arms around me in a bear hug. Draped against the *Akkord* console, Bert grinned at me.

"What the fuck!" I said. "I thought I told you to get your ass on *Mystic*."

"I must not have heard you, Boss," he said quietly.

5,500 feet—rising.

"Looks like we got damn control back," Sergyi said. "You want to drive her?" I asked Sergyi.

"You bet, Boss."

"Make your depth two hundred feet, speed seven-point-five knots."

✳

At 1,000 feet, we picked up a Secure Gertrude call from *Teuthis*. "*Lyre*, this is *Teuthis*."

"Roger, *Teuthis*, we hear you."

"What is your status?" I recognized Franklin's voice.

"We are okay, coming to two hundred feet. *Mystic* is independent with most of the crew. Recommend you take her aboard *Teuthis* until we figure out what to do next."

"Are you certain?" It was the skipper. "We don't need any more heroics."

"Yes, Sir. We have sufficient power to reach the two-hundred-foot curve on course zero-one-six. We can bottom there, recharge the batteries, and check out any damage to the false sail. We were doing ten knots for longer than I would have wished."

"Roger. We will watch your six until we arrive at the two-hundred-foot curve."

✳

The transit took eight hours. The three of us remained in Control the entire time—just in case something else went wrong. Sergyi put us on the bottom at 195 feet with two percent of batteries remaining.

A half-hour later, *Teuthis* slipped up to our starboard side, and *Mystic* made a seal to our after-hatch. My entire crew came with her.

After the hugs and back-slapping, I sent Sergyi and Bert back to *Teuthis* to get cleaned up and have a meal.

Outside, the divers hooked up the charge and then inspected every inch of our false sail. To everyone's surprise, it had withstood the harrowing journey at least as well as those of us inside the *Alfa*. All the divers did was to cinch up the belly straps again. The divers played with Borysko, who had finally accepted the new 4 x 4 when his old one broke in two.

For most of this, I pulled away from the others. I didn't need any more praise. It was my job to anticipate the take-over possibility and prepare for it. I fingered Kate's ivory cylinder, wondering how she would have reacted to learning that I had perished at sea.

One more thing. While Sergyi, Bert, and I were fighting for our lives, as *Lyre* plunged toward the abyssal deep, Borysko tried to keep up with us, as reported by Bob Taggert from *Mystic*. According to my sources, Orcas generally remain shallower than 1,000 feet. I think Borysko knew we were in trouble and tried to help. *Mystic* picked him up at nearly 4,000 feet. Bob said he ended up staying on the surface for several hours following that deep dive. I suspect his massive body was warding off mild decompression sickness.

✳

Bert returned to relieve me so I could freshen up. I expected to see Kate soon and wanted to look my best. My circadian cycle was all screwed up. It was 0930, and all I wanted to do was sleep. I figured Kate would get my rhythms straightened out.

THE *LYRE*—ELECTRIC BOAT

For a final time, the 1MC blared "Surface! Surface! Surface!" followed by the Klaxon's three long *Aoogahs!* I did not hear it because I was aboard *Lyre*. We simply surfaced and trimmed ourselves to sit low in the water. I was on the Bridge with Bert. Sam and Rusty posed as lookouts on the port and starboard fairwater planes. It was 1400 hours on a bright, sunny winter afternoon outside the channel buoys.

Frisco took the lead. We followed 300 yards back, with *Mystic* sitting proudly on our after-deck. *Teuthis* was last, behind us by 300 yards. To any observer, we were obviously three nuclear submarines returning to port after DSRV exercises at sea.

The temperature was in the low forties with a slight easterly breeze. Driving *Lyre* from the Bridge was child's play. The bridge box was only superficially similar to ours, but I had direct control over everything with appropriate switches and knobs. In the water alongside us, and sometimes ahead or behind, Borysko cruised easily, fully recovered from his deep dive experience. He carried his 4 x 4 like a cigar stump sticking out of his mouth.

We passed the channel buoys and somewhat later Race Rock. *Frisco* refused the Pilot. So did we and *Teuthis*. A Navy tug accompanied *Frisco* upriver to her berth. Two Navy tugs met us. Spook and Wyatt handled the lines down on our foredeck, snugging the tugs against our port and starboard bow. *Teuthis* lowered her outboards but had a tug stand off her port bow as a precaution.

When we reached the EB assembly building, our tugs swung *Lyre's* bow sharply right, pointing us to the open space between the jutting wharves. Navy personnel on both wharves tossed lines to Spook and Wyatt, lines that disappeared into the open building front. The tugs tossed off their lines and headed downriver while winches inside the assembly building quickly pulled *Lyre* into the submerged drydock, away from prying eyes.

Teuthis followed us between the wharves but tied up starboard side to the downstream one. Someone pulled the heavy steel pontoon across the opening between the wharves. Divers positioned wood blocks beneath *Lyre* to cradle her as the dock lifted her from the water. Once she was high and dry, dock workers slid a brow across the gap, and we walked across the brow and off *Lyre* for the last time.

I looked up to see the skipper standing at the foot of the brow. I saluted, and he returned my salute. Then he stepped aside to reveal Kate, flushed and beautiful. I ran the last few steps and folded her into my arms as she sobbed against my shoulder with joy.

✳

"I got your Vette out of storage, Mac," she said, her words tumbling over each other in her excitement. "I got us a reservation at the Mohican Hotel in New London—the Bridal Suite." She took my hand and pulled me forward. "Come on—I can't wait!"

*The Club exterior, The Dining Room, Kate's Room, The Library at
The Army and Navy Club in Washington DC*

CHAPTER TWENTY-ONE—Kate's Journal 3

ARMY AND NAVY CLUB—WASHINGTON, DC

In my last journal entry, I complained a lot about the Club. That really wasn't fair. At the beginning of this entry, I posted four photos showing the Club exterior, the dining room, my stateroom, and the library. They will give you some idea of what I had during my stay. The library was super but unsuitable for my research, so I didn't make use of it.

Finally, on January 19, I received a call from Gen. Tighe's office that Mac was arriving at EB the following afternoon. Just as I was scrambling to purchase a plane ticket, there was a knock at my door. It was Cappy.

"Hi, Kate! How soon can you be packed and ready to go?" "Why? What do you mean?" I asked.

"General Tighe's executive jet is waiting at Washington National Airport. His pilot will fly you to New London." He grinned from ear to ear. "Oh yeah—his chopper is waiting outside in the park for you."

Oh my gosh! Can you believe it? I'm riding a chopper to the airport and then taking a private jet to New London!

I never imagined!

UNDERWAY—WASHINGTON NATIONAL AIRPORT TO NEW LONDON, CT

A nice soldier escorted me into the helicopter and strapped me in. We took off, and it seemed like just a few minutes, and I was climbing back out. The chopper landed only a few yards from a gorgeous small passenger jet. The nice soldier told me it was a Rockwell business jet. I gave Cappy a warm hug and climbed the staircase into the jet interior. Oh, wow! Being the general in charge of the DIA definitely has its perks. A pleasant female airman offered me a glass of champagne.

Can you believe it? Little ol' me?

The trip didn't take very long—less than an hour. An official, unmarked DIA vehicle met me on the tarmac and whisked me to the Mohican Hotel. The driver patiently waited for me to set things up—you know, the Bridal Suite, the wonderful celebration dinner. Then he told me to meet him in the morning at the front desk at 0900—that's 9 AM. He left two agents in the hotel lobby who promised to remain there on watch until he picked me up in the morning.

I awakened early and had a nice breakfast. Before I went to the lobby to meet the DIA driver, my phone rang.

I picked up the handset and said tentatively, "Hello?"

"It's Archie, Kate. Archie Desmond. I heard that Mac's on his way in. I just wanted to congratulate you and wish you the best."

"Where are you, Archie?" I couldn't believe that he had called. "In Hawaii—Pearl Harbor. We have several days in port before heading out for another exercise. I wanted to make sure you were okay and wish you much happiness."

"Thank you, thank you for thinking about me. I hope to see you again soon."

We hung up, and I went down to the lobby to meet my driver. He drove me to where Mac had stored his Vette. Again, someone from the DIA had taken care of everything. All I had to do was take the proffered keys and drive away. It was late morning, and I had some time to kill before driving to EB to meet Mac around 1500 (I like telling time this way.) My DIA guy was always within a few yards of me, no matter where I went. He made me feel safe.

I decided to explore the Submarine Base. The guard at the gate saluted me as I slowed to drive through. "Good afternoon, Ma'am," he said.

I drove up one street and down another, imagining all the months Mac had spent here—as an enlisted sailor and then an officer. All the energy, all the excitement. I had to be careful not to be late at EB.

Finally, I drove out the same gate, along the river, under the Gold Star Memorial Bridge, and then along the river again until I arrived at EB—General Dynamics Company Electric Boat Division. I drove to the gate, identified myself, and parked where the guard indicated down along the Thames facing the water.

I walked out on the wharf to watch Mac and everyone else sail upriver and into the dock.

While I waited, I took a few minutes to complete this journal entry. It's probably the last one I will be making for quite a while.

Oh…one more thing. To my total surprise, as the submarines arrived, out in the river, apparently accompanying them was a huge Orca—a killer whale. He was carrying a long piece of wood in his mouth and frolicked like a many-ton puppy. Double wow!

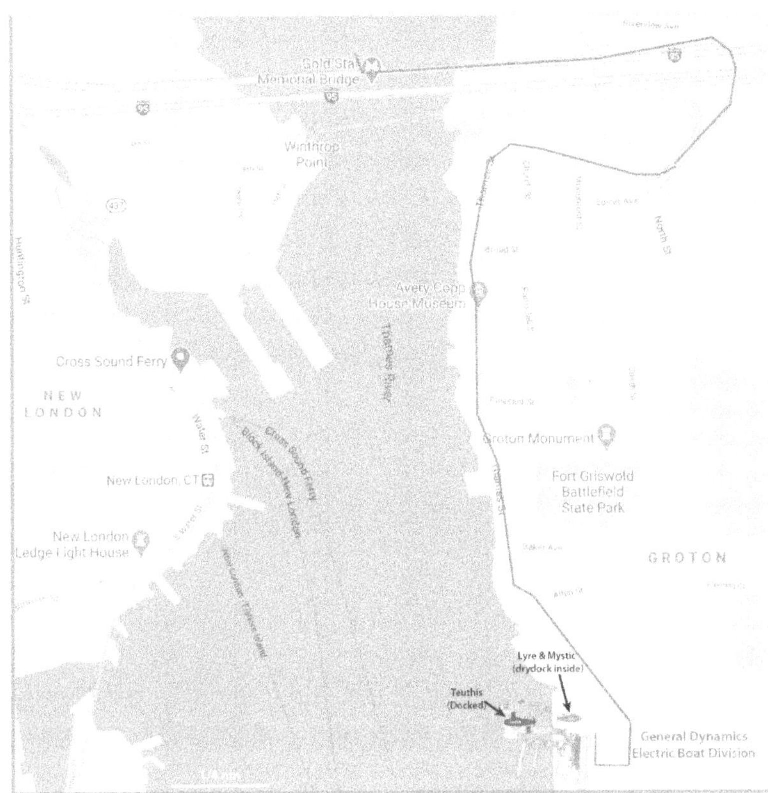

USS Teuthis docked at EB & the Lyre drydocked undercover.
Mac and Kate's path to the Gold Star Memorial Bridge

EPILOG

GENERAL DYNAMICS, ELECTRIC BOAT DIVISION— GROTON, CONNECTICUT

Kate pulled Mac toward the parking lot, urging him to hurry. "We don't have any time to waste!" she said, excitement filling her voice.

"Wait a bit, Kate," Mac said. "I want you to meet someone."

He took her hand and walked her out to the downstream wharf where *Teuthis* was moored. They didn't stop at the brow but instead walked right to the end of the wharf. Mac put his fingers to his lips and whistled loudly.

Kate squealed with delight as Borysko whipped to the wharf, extending his upper body so his fins rested on the wood planks.

"Borysko," Mac said, "I want you to meet the girl of my dreams, Kate." Borysko opened his mouth, deposited his 4 x 4 on the planks, and stuck out his tongue. Mac reached into his giant mouth and scratched, and then laid his flat hand against the tongue for several seconds.

"What are you doing?" Kate asked, laughing nervously, and then she got it and gingerly reached out to touch the tongue that was nearly her size. It was soft and pliable, so she scratched and then imitated Mac and placed her flat hand against it, bonding with the giant.

Mac picked up the 4 x 4 and pointed it upriver. "We're going that way," he said to Borysko. "You can swim along with us."

"We picked him up around Amundsen Gulf," Mac told Kate as he took her hand. "He saved our lives a couple of times—for real, from Polar Bears." Mac grinned at Kate. "I'm with you now because Borysko made it possible."

He tossed the 4 x 4 into the river. Borysko whistled, grabbed the wood, and backed off into the water.

GOLD STAR MEMORIAL BRIDGE—GROTON TO NEW LONDON, CONNECTICUT

Kate and Mac walked off the wharf and around to the parking lot next to the river. Borysko followed and watched them climb into his Corvette—something he recognized as another human machine.

"Too cold for the top to be down," Mac said with a wink.

Inside the cockpit, Kate took his face in her hands and kissed him deeply. When they came up for air, she said, "That's a foretaste of more to come!"

Mac started the engine, honked his horn twice at Borysko, and backed out of the parking spot. Borysko pushed up out of the river and watched as they drove through the gate. The Corvette engine produced a distinct rumble that Borysko could hear easily. When he submerged, it reached him through the water. He associated it with Mac and Mac's companion.

The happy couple waved at the guard and turned north along Thames Street, their DIA escort following discreetly behind.

"Look!" Kate said, her voice filled with excitement. "There's Borysko. Do you think he can see us?"

"I don't know," Mac said, "but I suspect he can hear the Vette through the water. His hearing is incredible. Up in Victoria Sound under the ice pack, he tracked us a hundred miles away."

As they passed Broad Street, four blocks to the east, two loaded semis turned slowly onto North Street, heading for Interstate 95. The first one pulled out ahead. The second held back until Mac's Corvette whipped around the curve onto the on-ramp. As soon as Mac negotiated the initial bend, the second semi pulled onto the ramp behind him. The semi ahead of Mac slowed for the steep curved ramp.

"Dammit!" Mac muttered. "He could have let me go ahead." The two semis and Mac merged into the heavy afternoon traffic.

The DIA escort followed the second semi, trying to work his way forward but without success. Within a half mile, traffic speed increased, but Mac had no opportunity to pull out from the right lane and pass the semi ahead of him, and their escort was still trapped behind the second semi. Suddenly, the driver of the semi in front of Mac hit his brakes and turned his cab sharply left so that his trailer twisted right, slamming through the bridge rail.

Mac braked hard, skidding toward the broadsided trailer. Kate screamed as the semi behind them slammed into their left rear, spinning the Corvette to the right. In the blink of an eye, the second semi pushed the sports car through the broken railing. The Corvette and its two passengers plunged 135 feet to the river below.

"Brace yourself! I love you, Kate!" Mac yelled through her screams as they fell through the cold air.

In the river below, Borysko had lost the machine carrying his friends when Mac turned right to reach the Interstate 95 ramp. He was confused and worried. He swam in circles beneath the bridge, trying to locate them by sound. Then he heard the machine and looked up to see the plunging sports car in the air. He recognized Mac's yells and Kate's screams before the machine struck the water. Borysko raced to the entry point and dove sixty feet to the bottom, searching for them with his fine-tuned sonar. In a mangled mess of fiberglass and steel, he found Mac struggling weakly and Kate not moving at all.

Gently, ever so gently, Borysko picked them up in his massive jaws and brought them to the surface. As astonished onlookers watched from 135 feet overhead, Borysko raced downriver to EB. In the time it took him to cover the two miles, word had reached the submarine manufacturing facility and the *Teuthis* crew. Mac's divers crowded the end of the wharf as Borysko pushed himself out of the water and gently laid Mac and Kate on the platform. Kate was still, but Mac stirred a bit. "Mac's alive!" Jimmy shouted. "Make a hole! I need to get to him."

Sergyi rushed over to help, looked at Kate, her neck twisted at an odd angle, and burst into tears. "Oh my God…they got her. The sonsofbitches got her…" He buried his face against her torso, unabashedly crying his heart out.

A few yards away in the river, Borysko held his upper body out of the water, watching and listening. Something had gone terribly wrong; he knew this with every fiber of his being. Machines with flashing lights arrived. They took his friend and his friend's companion, the one who had touched his tongue and who did not now move.

The giant cetacean dropped back into the river with a whimper and a long whistle. Driven by the stream, his 4 x 4 bumped into his snout. He pushed it away with a drawn-out, low-register note that echoed across the river. He didn't want it anymore.

❋ ❋ ❋

CBC News article from November 2, 2016

—byline Jimmy Thomson[23]

Hunters in a remote community in Nunavut are concerned about a mysterious sound that appears to be coming from the seafloor. The "pinging" sound, sometimes also described as a "hum" or "beep," has been heard in Fury and Hecla Strait—roughly 120 kilometers northwest of the hamlet of Igloolik—throughout the summer.

Paul Quassa, a member of the legislative assembly, says whatever the cause, it's scaring the animals away.

The sound appears to come from the seafloor in Hecla and Fury Strait.

Boaters aboard a private yacht passing through the area also say they heard the mysterious sound. The noise can apparently be heard through the hulls of boats.

"The Department of National Defense has been informed of the strange noises emanating in the Fury and Hecla Strait area, and the Canadian Armed Forces are taking the appropriate steps to actively investigate the situation," a spokesperson wrote in a statement.

"As of today, we're still working on it," he said. "We don't have a single clue."

---

23 Actual news article from CBC, dated November 2, 2016

RESEARCHERS HAD 'NO IDEA' KILLER WHALES COULD DIVE THIS DEEP

British Columbia-based marine researcher Jared Towers witnessed a tagged killer whale diving 3,566 feet to snag some toothfish off a long commercial fishing line. More than 60 killer whales and 40 sperm whales were studied, though just one of each was tagged because whales aren't particularly cooperative, said Towers.

"We had no idea they were physiologically capable of diving this deep," said Towers.

Killer whales, depending on size, can eat between 200-400 pounds of fish a day. They also often share food with their kin. Toothfish in the south Atlantic are a particularly energy-dense and highly desirable food for whales of all types.

The killer whales observed for this study dove quickly and then had to spend hours recovering. One whale spent four hours at the surface trying to fight off the bends.

Fisheries may be aghast at the discovery. Typically they set out longlines, measuring 2.5-7.5 miles in length with hooks every 10 feet or so, to haul in multiple fish at once.

---

24 Actual news article from Motherboard—Tech by Vice dated October 4, 2018.

A Note about Saturation Diving

The air you breathe is about twenty-one percent oxygen and seventy-nine percent nitrogen. When you dive on SCUBA, your equipment supplies you with compressed air that matches the pressure of the water around you, and this increases by about one atmosphere every thirty-three feet. So, at a thousand feet, air enters your lungs at about thirty atmospheres or 450 pounds per square inch (psi).

Normal air becomes toxic under too much pressure. When you inhale more oxygen than about twice the amount you would when breathing pure oxygen at the surface, the oxygen becomes toxic. This happens at about two-hundred feet when breathing compressed air. Furthermore, nitrogen becomes narcotic at about the same depth. This is a lethal combination: You're breathing toxic gas and are so narked by nitrogen that you don't know what to do about it.

We solved this problem by reducing the total amount of oxygen in the breathing gas mix so that the actual amount in each breath is about the equivalent of the twenty-one percent we breathe on the surface. We replaced the nitrogen with helium that does not become narcotic. It made us talk funny, but we didn't get narked.

The formula for the resulting oxygen percentage at any depth is

$$\%O_{2\,(at\,depth)} = \frac{.21}{\left(\dfrac{depth_{feet}}{33}\right) + 1}$$

Consequently, at 1,000 feet, oxygen in the gas mix is 0.7 percent. At 470 feet, oxygen in the gas mix is 1.4 percent.

Right now, your body is saturated with all the nitrogen it can hold. Your cells, bones, organs, everything, have absorbed all the nitrogen possible. If you dive to thirty-three feet (one atmosphere) and stay there long enough, you will become saturated at thirty-three feet. If you stay at a hundred feet, five-hundred feet, same thing—stay long enough, and you saturate; you can't take up any more nitrogen or helium if you are breathing a mixed gas.

If you are saturated to thirty-three feet, you can come right to the surface without suffering any consequences. But if you saturate at forty feet, you cannot come shallower than about seven feet without suffering the bends, when the dissolved nitrogen or helium in your body comes out of solution to form bubbles. The bends are very painful and can be fatal. A body can tolerate a one-atmosphere difference between its saturation level and the ambient pressure. That's the background information. In practice, we have discovered that there is increasing leeway as the saturation depth is deeper.

An Upward Excursion Limits Table in the Navy Diving Manual lists the excursion limits for any saturation depth.

Please post a review for
Operation Arctic Sting

Authors rely on reviews, so I really appreciate your posting a review on Amazon and Goodreads. To post a review, scan the pertinent QR code below and follow the prompts. You will be prompted to log onto the platform. If you are not a member, you will need to sign up. It's free. Amazon will require a minimum $50 purchase volume during the past twelve months. Goodreads has no requirement. Thank you very much for going through this effort!

Scan to review on Amazon

Scan to review on Goodreads

Excerpt from Operation White Out

by

Robert G. Williscroft

PROLOG

COMSUBPAC—PEARL HARBOR, HAWAII

Commander Archibald Desmond focused on two semis speeding across a high bridge with a Corvette sandwiched between them, surrounded by traffic front, back, and left, with railing on the right. Suddenly, the front semi braked and turned sharply left. The trailer twisted right, slamming through the bridge rail. The Corvette braked hard, skidding toward the broadsided trailer as the semi behind the Corvette slammed into its left rear, spinning the little sports car to the right. Despite the grittiness of the monochrome satellite image on the RCA KP-5040 projector TV, Desmond saw the second semi push the Corvette through the broken railing of the Gold Star Memorial Bridge, 135 feet above the Thames River, in Connecticut.

"Rewind, please," Desmond said softly.

Rear Admiral Austin B. Scott, Jr., manipulated a control on his desk and glanced at R. Adm. Jack Darby, who was there to relieve him as Commander, Submarine Force Pacific—Com-SubPac.

After watching the Corvette for the second time plunge off the bridge into the river 135 feet below, Desmond uttered softly, "I'll be a sonofabitch! Those fucking assholes deliberately forced them off. It *wasn't* Mac's fault. *They* killed my Kate!"

In the ensuing silence, Scott said, "You might want to mention that to Mac."

NATIONAL NAVAL MEDICAL CENTER—BETHESDA, MARYLAND

"It's me, Jack," Master Mariner Jack Petrikoff said as Mac opened his eyes and squinted at the sunlight flooding into his hospital room through the upper floor window. "Jack Petrikoff…I come as soon as I hear—red-eye, Kodiak, Seattle, DC." Petrikoff looked at Mac warmly. "You alive, my friend. You alive!"

"Wha' happened? Where am I?" Mac asked weakly.

"Don' know, Mac, don' know. Just got here from Kodiak, but you in the Bethesda Naval Hospital, Washington, DC."

"Where's Kate?"

As Mac struggled to sit up, a white-uniformed nurse with lieutenant bars on her collars hurried into the room. "Easy does it, Commander. You can sit up, but you have to be careful. You suffered two broken legs, three broken ribs, and a chipped vertebra." She smiled while adjusting his IV drip. "Push the call button if you need me." She placed the console in his left hand and departed.

Mac's blue eyes focused on Petrikoff's. "What the fuck, Jack? Where is she?"

✳

A knock on the door, and R. Adm. Scott entered, followed by Cmdr. Desmond. Mac lifted his right hand in an attempted salute.

"You're uncovered and indoors, Commander, so knock it off!" Scott said with a chuckle. "You know Archie, and I know Master Mariner Petrikoff. So much for the preliminaries."

Desmond stepped to the foot of Mac's bed, wondering how the admiral would handle this.

Scott pulled up a chair and turned it around, straddling it while leaning forward against its back. "Glad to see you're still with us and conscious." Scott's demeanor turned serious. "I've got some bad news for you, Son, and there's no way to soften this." He cleared his throat and swallowed. "You got pushed off the Gold Star Memorial Bridge by a couple of semis—part of a sleeper cell in New London. Borysko pulled you and Kate from the wreck on the bottom, but Kate didn't make it."

"What…?"

Desmond felt his own stomach drop…again.

"I am terribly, terribly sorry, Mac, but Kate's gone." He turned to Desmond with a slight nod.

"I watched the satellite video, Mac. You were sandwiched between two semis with no way to get away because of the traffic. Your DIA[25] escort was stuck behind the second semi the whole time. They deliberately crashed the front semi and pushed you off the bridge." A catch filled his voice. "The water impact broke Kate's neck; it's a miracle you survived." He paused to regain his composure. "Borysko brought both of you back to EB.[26] You've been in a coma until just a short while ago." His voice trailed off.

"I'm working with DIA Director General Gene Tighe," Scott said. "We'll get those bastards, I promise you."

✳

Petrikoff remained in the background during Scott's and Desmond's conversations with Mac. *So, that's how it happened. Oh, Kate, my poor wonderful girl.* He felt himself tearing up, sniffled, and blew his nose. *At least you had some happiness before the bastards got you.* He stepped to the bed and gripped Mac's right hand.

"I'm here for you, Diver Boy. You know that." He peered through his lashes at the look the two naval officers exchanged.

Mac squeezed his hand.

"Thanks, Jack."

✳

Scott cleared his throat. "I still have some official business with the commander."

---

[25] Defense Intelligence Agency.
[26] General Dynamics Electric Boat Company in Groton, Connecticut, the builder of many US submarines.

"Sorry, Admiral, we been through a lot together, me and Mac." Petrikoff stepped to the side of the small room.

"I understand." Then Scott turned his attention to Mac. "Commander McDowell, you are being assigned as Executive Officer to *USS Teuthis*."

"Commander…?"

The admiral placed a set of silver oak leaves on Mac's pillow.

"TOG…," Mac started to say, referring to his old team, the Test Operations Group.

"Is being assigned to newly commissioned Warrant Officer Hamilton Comstock," Scott interrupted with a smile. "*Teuthis* has a new, complex assignment, and CNO wants to keep the team together," referring to the Chief of Naval Operations.

"Nuclear Power School…?" Mac started to ask.

"I'm getting to that. Admiral Kinnaird McKee has replaced retiring Admiral Rickover as Naval Reactors. He's tentatively agreed to let you do the classwork here at Bethesda while you recover. Somewhere along the process, he will personally visit you to assess your progress. That's when the final decision will be made." Scott stood up and shook Mac's hand. "Good luck, Son. I wish I had a couple dozen officers like you."

Desmond leaned across the bed and took Mac's hand. "Kate was not your fault, Mac. You gotta believe that." He placed his left hand over their clasped right hands. "We'll get the bastards, I promise!"

NATIONAL NAVAL MEDICAL CENTER—BETHESDA, MARYLAND

"You are eligible for a medical retirement with full pay and benefits," Mac's Navy detailer, a captain, told him by phone. "You've given more than just about anyone. You're a genuine hero whose exploits are already a legend here at BUPERS."[27] The caller paused. "Hell, Commander, I outrank you, but I'll come to my feet any time you enter a room."

"Thank you, Captain. You made my day, but I don't deserve your kind words. My team did all the hard work, and they deserve all the

[27] Bureau of Personnel.

accolades, not me. Mostly, I was along for the ride, and when I got back, I managed to get my girl killed. Some hero I am. Besides, I got to get my Nuke quals done so I can ship out with the real heroes." Mac disconnected the call.

Working through the Nuclear Power School curricula was as difficult a task as Mac had ever undertaken. The theory wasn't difficult—he already knew most of that stuff. It was the application on a submarine that required all his attention. *Difficult* probably didn't describe it so much as *challenging*. Since 1958, when the *USS Nautilus* launched, the Navy had experienced zero nuclear reactor incidents. That was an extraordinary accomplishment brought about by strict adherence to a set of procedures that never changed, ever. Learning those procedures was not particularly difficult, but making them a part of his person, a part of his inner being, was a major accomplishment.

Every day, Mac did three things: Rehab for eight hours, study for eight hours, and eat and sleep for eight. Kate was gone, and there was nothing Mac could do about it. So, he concentrated on beating the odds—in rehab and his off-campus studies.

✳

Mac's hospital room no longer looked like one. Free weights, a treadmill, a stationary bike, and a small trampoline for in-place running occupied one side of his room. A desk and study materials took up the other side. Just the evening before, he had completed the last of his Nuclear Power School Assignments.

Mac strolled down the hallway and took the staircase down to the second-floor cafeteria, where he consumed a protein-rich meal. A half-hour later, while running a measured five miles on his trampoline, a knock on the door interrupted his concentration.

A four-star admiral in uniform stepped into his room. "I'm Admiral Kinnaird R. McKee, Naval Reactors." He held out his hand.

Mac wiped his with a towel and shook. "Commander J.R. McDowell, Sir."

Adm. McKee sat on the edge of Mac's immaculately made bed.

"It's time I met you, Commander. From what I hear, you walk on water…but I doubt that. I understand that an Orca had to retrieve you from the bottom of the Thames." He offered a brief smile. "But that's not why I'm here. I wanted to meet you to see if I want you to join my cadre of nuclear-trained submarine officers." He paused. "I've reviewed your training. You are at the top of your class despite not being able to attend classes personally. ComSubPac[28] wants you as XO of *Teuthis*, and I understand his reasons. I know you lost your girl when you went off the bridge. Is this going to impact your critical thinking when you are EOOW[29] on *Teuthis* at five hundred feet and something goes wrong?" The admiral locked eyes with Mac.

What the fuck! Mac thought as he kept his gaze steady. "You've studied my record, Admiral," Mac answered. "What do you think?" Mac took a deep breath. "I know my priorities, Admiral. That's why I'm alive, and my team is still functioning."

Adm. McKee sat quietly, apparently contemplating what Mac had said. "Okay," he finally spoke up, "complete your EOOW quals on *Teuthis*, and I'll certify you as fully nuclear qualified."

You have just been reading from the Prolog of Operation White Out, *the next book in Robert Williscroft's* Mac McDowell Missions. *Purchase this book from your favorite online bookseller.*

---

[28] Commander Submarine Force Pacific.

[29] Engineering Officer of the Watch—in charge of the nuclear plant and propulsion systems.

Other Books by this Author

Please visit RobertWilliscroft.com to discover other books by Robert Williscroft. Scan for more information.

Current Events:

The Chicken Little Agenda: Debunking "Experts'" Lies

Children's Books:

The Starman Jones Series:

Starman Jones: A Relativity Birthday Present

Starman Jones Goes to the Dogs (2026)

Biographies:

Mission Possible (by Gladys L. Williscroft)

Sŭbmarine-ër (by Jerry Pait; compiled by Robert G. Williscroft)

Short Stories:

Reality Hack

First Contact

The Cold Spot

The Virus

Novels:

Mac McDowell Missions

Operation Ivy Bells

Operation Ice Breaker

Operation Arctic Sting

Operation White Out

Operation Vela Redux

Operation Alfa Rogue (2026)

The Starchild Saga:

Slingshot

The Daedalus Files

The Starchild Compact

The Iapetus Federation

The Oort Chronicles:

Icicle: A Tensor Matrix

The Oort Federation: To the Stars

RAN: A Civilization in Hiding

KEID: A Lost Civilization

Beyond the Beyond (2025)

Connect with Robert G. Williscroft

I really appreciate you reading my book! Here are my social media coordinates:

Facebook: *https://www.facebook.com/robert.williscroft*
X/Twitter: *@RGWilliscroft*
Amazon author page: *https://buff.ly/2N5ZnlG*
Blog: *https://ThrawnRickle.com*
LinkedIn: *https://www.linkedin.com/in/argee/*
Book website: *https://RobertWilliscroft.com*
Newsletter: *https://eepurl.com/guZ5uv*

About the Author

Dr. Robert G. Williscroft is a retired submarine officer, deep-sea and saturation diver, scientist, author, and a lifelong adventurer. He spent 22 months underwater, a year in the equatorial Pacific, three years in the Arctic ice pack, and a year at the Geographic South Pole. He holds degrees in Marine Physics and Meteorology and a doctorate for developing a system to protect SCUBA divers in contaminated water. A prolific author of both non-fiction, Cold War thrillers, and hard science fiction, he lives in Centennial, Colorado.

Dr. Williscroft is a member of Colorado Author's League, Independent Association of Science Fiction & Fantasy Authors, Science Fiction Writers of America, Libertarian Futurist Society, Los Angeles Adventurers' Club, Mensa, Military Officers Association, U.S. Sub Vets, American Legion, and the NRA, and now spends most of his time writing his next book, speaking to various regional groups, and hanging out with the girl of his dreams, Jill, and her two cats.

Scan for more information

Glossary for Operation Arctic Sting

1MC—Ship's announcing system.

Akkord—The general control console on the Soviet *Alfa* submarine.

Alfa—The radiation monitoring console on the Soviet *Alfa* submarine

***Alfa* Submarine**—A Soviet nuclear submarine (Project-705 Lira) with the NATO reporting name *Alfa class*. It was the fastest military submarine ever built. The *Alfa* had a unique design with a titanium hull and a small but powerful lead-bismuth cooled fast reactor. This reduced the overall weight and size of the submarine and allowed for very high speeds; however, the reactor had a short lifetime and had to be kept warm when it was not being used. The *Alfa* was very automated and carried about 25 crew members, unlike other fast-attacks with crews of about 100. It had an escape pod in the sail that could hold 35 people.

APS—Underwater fully automatic Assault Weapon. Fires 26 darts in full automatic—lethal range forty feet. Magazine holds 26 darts. Was made in the Soviet Union for use *underwater* by Soviet frogmen as an *underwater* firearm. It was developed in the late 1960s and accepted for use in 1975. Under water, ordinary-shaped bullets are inaccurate and very short-range.

ASR—Submarine Rescue Ship (Auxiliary Submarine Rescue)—Ships specially designed to rescue crews from downed submarines. They originally carried McCann Rescue Bells. Later, two catamaran ASRs (the *USS Ortolan* and *USS Pigeon*) carried the DSRVs.

ASW—Anti-submarine Warfare.

Baffles—The area in the water directly behind a submarine or ship through which a hull-mounted sonar cannot hear. This blind spot is caused by the noise of the vessel's machinery, propulsion system, and propellers.

Basketball—A slightly larger than basketball-size, camera-carrying remotely operated vehicle (ROV) on a tether.

BCP—Ballast Control Panel; the console from which water is pumped into and out of a sub, and distributed fore and aft in the sub. The Chief of the Watch occupies this position, under the control of the Diving Officer or the OOD.

Bergie—A large chunk of sea ice that projects both above and below the water's surface.

Boat—Slang term for submarine. Officially. All modern nuclear subs are called *ships*, but in practice, most submariners call them *boats*.

Boksit—The course control system console on the Soviet *Alfa* submarine.

Bollard—A short, thick post on a pier or wharf, to which a ship's line may be secured.

Boomer—Ballistic Missile Submarine.

Bottom—Bottom of the ocean, the seafloor. As a verb as in *to bottom*, putting the submarine on the seafloor.

Bow—Front of a ship or sub.

Brash—Small, floating fragments of sea or river ice typically near the ice edge in the ocean and in narrow straits with high tidal currents.

Bridge—The place on a ship from which it is driven. On a sub, it is the conning station at the top of the sail. (See *Conn.*)

Brow—Gangway onto a vessel from the pier or another vessel.

Butter bar—Military slang for the insignia of an Ensign or Second Lieutenant because the golden bar looks like butter. Also used as slang to refer to those officers. They're affectionately called "butter bars," both because their rank insignia looks like one, and because they have about the same value as a stick of butter.

Capstan—A revolving cylinder with a vertical axis used for hauling in a rope or cable.

Captain—The officer in command of the ship or sub. He is an absolute dictator, subject only to the Uniform Code of Military Justice and the orders of his superiors in the chain-of-command.

CDMA—Code division multiple access. (See *Secure underwater telephone.*)

Chief of the Boat—COB; the senior enlisted man on a submarine who serves as advisor to the commanding officer and executive officer. When a new enlisted sailor joins a boat's crew, the COB is usually one of the first people the new sailor will meet.

Chief of the Watch—COW; the enlisted watchstander (usually a chief petty officer) who sits at the BCP and controls the ship's load of ballast water and its distribution throughout the submarine. The COW is also the senior watchstander for all the non-engineering spaces.

CINCLANTFLT—Commander-in-Chief, Naval Fleet Atlantic; the commander of all naval forces in the Atlantic.

CINCPACFLT—Commander-in-Chief, Naval Fleet Pacific; the commander of all naval forces in the Pacific.

Clear the baffles—A submarine tracking another submarine can take advantage of its quarry's baffles to follow at a close distance without being detected. Periodically, a submarine will perform a maneuver called clearing the baffles. The boat will turn left or right far enough to listen with the sonar for a few minutes in the area that was previously blocked by the baffles.

Cleat—A T-shaped piece of metal or wood, esp. on a boat or ship, to which ropes are attached.

COB—see Chief of the Boat.

Column—(water column) All the water above and below.

Come-home bottle—A small gas bottle that gets a diver back to the PTC/DDC in an emergency.

COMSUBLANT—Commander, Submarine Force Atlantic; the commander of all submarine forces in the Atlantic.

COMSUBPAC—Commander, Submarine Force Pacific; the commander of all submarine forces in the Pacific.

Conn—(1) The location from which the sub is controlled by the OOD (Officer of the Deck)—also called Control. (2) The Conning Officer (Conn), the watch position for the person who controls the sub's direction, speed, and depth. The OOD usually has both the Deck and Conn, but can pass off the Conn to another qualified officer. Sometimes the captain will assume the Deck, leaving the Conn with the officer watchstander.

COW—see Chief of the Watch.

Crazy Ivan—A baffle-clearing maneuver practiced by Soviet submarines.

CRC—Cable Reel Compartment.

DDC—Deck Decompression Chamber; a pressure chamber on a ship's deck or just below the deck that contains a side lock for entrance and egress, a top lock to mate with the PTC, a small lock for passing in food or medical supplies, emergency equipment, and depending on how it is being used, bunks, lavatory facilities, etc.

Deck—The watch position of OOD (Officer of the Deck); the person in-charge of the sub when the captain is not in the Control Room or has not assumed the Deck while in the Control Room.

Dev Group—SubDevGruOne.

DIA—Defense Intelligence Agency.

Dive Control Console—A console with gauges, valves, and indicators from where a saturation dive is controlled.

Diving Officer—The officer or specially qualified Chief Petty Officer controlling the submarine depth. Works directly under the OOD. The COW works directly for the Diving Officer.

DIW—Dead in the water; a ship that is not moving through the water.

DOC—Diving Operations Compartment.

Dolphins—The insignia worn by qualified submariners, silver for enlisted, and gold for officers. It represents about a year of hard study to gain complete, detailed knowledge of the submarine.

Drift ice—A large field of floating sea ice consisting of many *ice floes*.

DRT—Dead Reckoning Trace. A mechanically generated ship's track based on input from the *SINS*.

DSRV—Deep Submergence Rescue Vehicle, a type of deep-submergence vehicle used for rescue of downed submarines and clandestine missions.

EB—Electric Boat Company, short for General Dynamics Electric Boat Company.

Emergency surface—Dumping high pressure into the main ballast tanks at a high rate, causing the submarine to surface very quickly.

Engineering Officer of the Watch—*EOOW*; the individual on watch who operates the powerplant.

EOOW—see *Engineering Officer of the Watch*.

Executive Officer (XO)—Second in command of a ship or sub. Responsible for ship's administration and personnel.

Fast-attack—See *Nuke fast-attack*.

Fast cruise—A one-to-two-day period alongside the pier where all sub's systems are checked out just prior to deployment.

Fish—An ROV with high resolution, sidescan sonar that produces detailed images of the seafloor.

Fish—A torpedo.

Floe—See *Ice floe*.

General Dynamics Electric Boat Company—A General Dynamics company that has designed, built, and maintained submarines for the U.S. Navy since 1899.

Gertrude—Underwater telephone. (See *Secure underwater telephone*.)

Hawser—Heavy line used to moor subs and other vessels.

Heaving line—Also *messenger line*. A light line, often with a *monkey fist*

at one end, used to haul or support a larger cable.

Helm—Ship's wheel and steering mechanisms. The person manning the helm.

Humboldt Squid—A large (5ft to 20+ft) squid found in the central pacific and along the Southwest coast of North America.

Ice floe—A floating piece of consolidated sea ice typically at least 20 yards across and often miles long. *Drift ice* consists of many ice floes.

JOOD—Junior Officer of the Deck; the individual (usually an OOD in training) who works directly for the OOD. The JOOD is responsible only to the OOD.

Keepers—One-piece rubber straps that wrap around the ankle and under the arch. Keep the feet of a Unisuit from filling with air and blowing off a diver's feet when he is inverted.

Kirby-Morgan helmet—A hard helmeted full facemask specifically designed to work with both umbilical and rebreather saturation diving systems from the 1970s and 1980s.

Long Range Patrol ration—Also called LRP ration. Lightweight ration packets developed in the 1960s and 70s for use by special forces commandoes. They were packed in a cardboard box of twenty-four meals in eight varieties: 1) Beef hash, 2) Beef and rice, 3) Beef stew, 4) Chicken and rice, 5) Chicken stew, 6) Chili con carne, 7) Pork and scalloped potatoes, and 8) Spaghetti with meat sauce. Each meal came in an aluminum foil packet covered with olive-drab cloth, with a brown-foil accessory packet. The accessory packet contained instant coffee (2 packets), cream substitute (1 4-gram packet), sugar (1 6-gram packet), salt (1 packet), Candy-Coated Gum (2 pieces), toilet paper, a book of cardboard matches, and either a compressed fruitcake bar or a tropical chocolate bar. The freeze-dried ration required 1 1⁄2 U.S. pints of water to reconstitute it—hot water if the user wished a hot meal.

LRP ration—See Long Range Patrol ration.

Main ballast tanks—Saddle-shaped tanks that fit around a submarine's hull near the bow and stern. They are open to the sea at the bottom and have large valves at the top. When the valves are opened, water quickly fills the ballast tanks causing the submarine to submerge. Air entering the tanks forces water out through the bottom openings, bringing the submarine to the surface. Dumping high pressure into the main ballast tanks at a high rate causes the submarine to *emergency surface*.

Man-in-the-Sea Program—A program put in place by the U.S. Navy to develop saturation diving.

Maneuvering Room—That part of a sub where the engines are directly controlled.

Maneuvering Watch—The special set of watch assignments for a sub or ship that is getting underway.

Messenger line—A light line, often with a monkey fist at one end, used to haul or support a larger cable.

Monkey fist—A type of knot, so named because it looks somewhat like a small, bunched fist/paw (also called *monkey paw*). It is tied at the end of a rope to serve as a weight, making it easier to throw, and also as an ornamental knot.

Nav—Depending on context, the ship's/sub's Navigator; or the navigation stand—typically near the *Conn*.

Nuke fast-attack—A nuclear fast-attack submarine; a hunter-killer submarine.

OCS—Officer Candidate School. Three months of specialized training for college graduates who choose to become commissioned officers in the U.S. Navy. (See *ROT-C*.)

Øer—Danish word for "islands" (Ø means "island").

OIC—Officer in Charge; the Officer in Charge of a unit or operation. A lesser command responsibility than a Commanding Officer

Okean—The automated tactical sonar system console on the Soviet *Alfa* submarine.

OOD—Officer of the Deck; the individual in charge of the ship or submarine at any given moment. The OOD is responsible only to the captain.

Operation Ivy Bells—A Top Secret Cold War plan to retrieve Soviet missile parts and tap into their underwater communication cables.

Ops—The Operations Officer.

Outboards—Maneuvering thrusters that were normally concealed in the sub, but could be lowered from the keel near the bow and stern. These could rotate to help steer the sub, or if pointed in the same direction, they could move the sub sideways.

PBX—Polymer Bonded Explosive. A type of explosive used in postWorld War-II torpedoes.

Peacoat—A heavy woolen double-breasted coat worn by sailors.

Polynya—A semipermanent area of open water in sea ice.

Port—Left.

PTC—Personnel Transfer Capsule; a spherical bell that mates to the shipboard DDC and can transfer a maximum of four divers to the underwater working site.

PUC—Presidential Unit Citation; a presidential award given to a ship or unit for exceptional performance (very rare).

R-C-H—Slang for a very small measurement.

Ringknocker— Slang term for a graduate of the U.S. Naval Academy.

Ritm—The machinery control console on the Soviet *Alfa* submarine.

ROTC— Reserve Officer Training Corps, a commissioning program offered by many U.S. universities. (See OCS.)

ROTC—Slang term for an officer who received his or her commission through the ROTC.

ROV—Remotely Operated Vehicle, an unmanned underwater vehicle that is remotely piloted either by wire or untethered, using sound

RTG—Radioisotope Thermoelectric Generator. An electricity-generating device that uses an array of thermocouples to convert the heat released by the decay of suitable radioactive material into electricity. This generator has no moving parts.

Sargan— The weapon control system console on the Soviet *Alfa* submarine.

Satnav—A satellite-based navigation system developed by the U.S. Navy for obtaining accurate positions for its Boomer and fastattack fleets.

Secure—Stop or finish a process, such as "Secure from Maneuvering Watch;" or when used as a verb, to make something safe, as in "secure the lines in the locker."

Secure depth-sounder—A device that uses *spread-spectrum* sound to determine the depth below the keel. It is undetectable without the proper equipment.

Secure the hover—Stop hover operations.

Secure the sidescan—Shut down the sidescan sonar.

Secure Gertrude—See *secure underwater telephone.*

Secure underwater telephone—A code division multiple access (*CDMA*) underwater telephone for secure underwater communications between submarines and between subs and surface ships. Without proper receiving equipment, it sounds like a faint, broad-spectrum hiss that blends completely into the background noise. Consequently, this type of underwater communication is undetectable. (See *Spread Spectrum.*)

Sidescan sonar—A towed-fish or *ROV* sonar that looks to both sides to produce a high-resolution image of the ocean bottom.

***Sierra-I* Submarine**— A Soviet nuclear submarine (Project-945) with the NATO reporting name *Sierra-I class.* The Sierra-I submarine was a larger version of the *Alfa*, but because of its size, it was slower. It could lock-out divers. The *Sierra-I* was noisier but faster than the *Victor*. It had an escape pod in the sail that could hold 110 people.

SINS—Submarine Inertial Navigation System, A system developed for nuclear submarines that sensed the actual motion of the sub to produce a fairly accurate position that it sent to the *DRT*. Over time, the SINS position deteriorated and needed to be updated by a satnav fix.

Sirena— A Soviet-made two-man underwater vehicle shaped like a torpedo. It carries a double warhead. Sirena has small homing readout—no range, just direction. Also a magnetic compass.

Sonar Shack—That part of a sub or surface ship that houses the sonar display equipment, where the Sonar Techs stand their watches. Usually close to the Bridge/Conn.

SOSUS—Sound Surveillance System; a chain of underwater listening posts located worldwide in places such as the Atlantic Ocean near Greenland, Iceland, and the United Kingdom—the GIUK gap, and at various locations in the Pacific Ocean. The system was designed to track Soviet submarines.

Sound-powered phone—A shipboard communication system powered only by the sound of the speaker's voice.

Sozh—The navigation system control console on the Soviet *Alfa* submarine.

SPP—SPP-1 Underwater double-action pistol. Darts load in a cartridge of four—lethal range 20 feet. The *SPP-1 underwater pistol* was made in the Soviet Union for use *underwater* by Soviet frogmen as an *underwater* firearm. It was developed in the late 1960s and accepted for use in 1975. Under water, ordinary-shaped bullets are inaccurate and very short-range.

Spread spectrum—A method for transmitting electronic or sonic signals that divides the signal into individual packets, each with lower intensity than the background, and spreading these packets across the entire electronic or sonic spectrum. This creates an information carrying transmission that cannot be detected without specific knowledge of the spread pattern used in the transmission. (See also *CDMA*.)

Starboard—Right.

Steerageway—The minimum speed a vessel requires for proper response to the helm.

Stern—Back of a ship or sub.

SUBDEVGRUONE—Submarine Development Group One; the Navy command in charge of Operation Ivy Bells, where Mac had trained as a saturation diver.

SubLant—Short form of COMSUBLANT.

SubPac—Short form of COMSUBPAC.

SUBRON—Submarine squadron.

Teuthis Squid—Also Colossal Squid, full name *Mesonychoteuthis hamiltoni*. It is part of the family *Cranchiidae*. The only member of the *Cranchiidae* family to display hooks on its arms and tentacles. Inhabits the circumantarctic Southern Ocean. Adults are 39 to 46 ft long. Uses bioluminescence to attract prey. It is an ambush predator and is a major prey of the sperm whale.

Thresher—*USS Thresher (SSN 593)*. On 10 April 1963, *Thresher* sank during deep-diving tests about 220 mi east of Boston, Massachusetts, killing all 129 crew and shipyard personnel. Her loss was a watershed for the U.S. Navy, leading to implementing a rigorous submarine safety program known as SUBSAFE.

TOG—Test Operations Group; a code name for the team that operated from *Halibut* and *Seawolf*.

Topside—The outside deck of a submarine. Can also refer to the watch station at the top of the sail when a sub is underway.

Transit bird—A satnav satellite.

TV-1—The television optical system console on the Soviet *Alfa* submarine.

Under-ice sonar—A high-frequency, upward-looking sonar for examining the undersurface and thickness of overhead ice.

Unisuit—The first commercial diving drysuit made by Poseidon.

Ushanka—Also known as a trapper hat, aviator hat, shapka, chapka. A traditional, yet stylish, Russian winter hat with ear flaps that is very warm. The flaps can be folded up and tied at the top of the hat, or tied at the chin. The word ushanka translates from Russian as "with ears." Ushi means ears in Russian.

Victor III **Submarine**—A Soviet nuclear submarine (Project 671RTM/ RTMK) with the NATO reporting name *Victor III class.* The *Victor III class* submarine featured a teardrop shape like the *Alfa*, but made of steel, allowing it to travel at high speed, but not so fast as the *Alfa*. It could launch diver vehicles through two bow torpedo tubes. It featured a towed sonar array pod on the top of the rudder and two small propellers next to the hull on the stern planes. It had an escape pod in the sail that could hold 110 people. The *Victor III* was the quietest sub that the Soviets built.

Watchbill—A list of a ship's company divided into watches.

WTD—Watertight door.

XO—Executive Officer (See Executive Officer).

www.ingramcontent.com/pod-product-compliance
Lightning Source LLC
Chambersburg PA
CBHW041748310726
48978CB00011BB/361